"Make room in your schedule to spend a litt~~~~~~~~~~~~~~.
Karen Doornebos provides #pureJaneAustenfun ~~~~ into the steamy corners of Jane Austen, *Undressing Mr. Darcy* takes the reader on a trip through
Austen adoration in all of its marvelous, and modern, forms. Doornebos's clever
wit and wry observations make this book a treat for Austen fans and newbies
alike." —Beth Pattillo, author of *Jane Austen Ruined My Life*

PRAISE FOR

Definitely Not Mr. Darcy

"Composed of equal measures of romance, captivating characters, and
clever writing, *Definitely Not Mr. Darcy* is a fun read."
—*Chicago Tribune*

"Doornebos gives the historical romance novel a hilarious update in this
delightful debut . . . The amusing secondary characters, sidesplitting faux
pas, and fiery romance will make Doornebos an instant hit with readers."
—*Publishers Weekly* (starred review)

"Doornebos's novel is witty and, most importantly, refreshing . . . A great
escape to the world of ball gowns and breeches, [and] Doornebos gives us
a fantasy/reality that will delight those who want a Jane Austen–inspired
excursion into Regency England, warts and all." —*Austenprose*

"Doornebos keeps up a sparkling pace in her debut novel . . . Everyone
needs an amusing confection to curl up on the couch with on a chilly
winter's afternoon—and this could well be it."
—Joceline Bury, *Jane Austen's Regency World* magazine

"[A] fun, funny, and perfectly satisfying dip into the world so many of us
would like to time travel back to—but with a thoroughly modern twist."
—Arielle Eckstut, coauthor of *Pride and Promiscuity*

"Chloe deals with Regency underwear, spiteful costars, and chamber pots
with determination and sass . . ."
—Margaret C. Sullivan, author of *The Jane Austen Handbook*

"A fun romp that combines Austenalia and a modern-day reality show.
You'll root for Chloe to win and laugh yourself silly!"
—Syrie James, bestselling author of *The Missing Manuscript of Jane Austen*

Berkley titles by Karen Doornebos

DEFINITELY NOT MR. DARCY

UNDRESSING MR. DARCY

Undressing Mr. Darcy

KAREN DOORNEBOS

BERKLEY BOOKS, NEW YORK

THE BERKLEY PUBLISHING GROUP
Published by the Penguin Group
Penguin Group (USA) LLC
375 Hudson Street, New York, New York 10014

USA • Canada • UK • Ireland • Australia • New Zealand • India • South Africa • China

penguin.com

A Penguin Random House Company

This book is an original publication of The Berkley Publishing Group.

Library of Congress Cataloging-in-Publication Data

Doornebos, Karen.
Undressing Mr. Darcy / Karen Doornebos.
pages cm.
ISBN 978-0-425-26139-2 (pbk.)
1. Austen, Jane, 1775-1817—Influence—Fiction. 2. Dating shows (Television programs)—Fiction.
3. Americans—England—Fiction. 4. Chick lit. I. Title.
PS3604.O67U56   2013
813'.6—dc23
2013031064

PUBLISHING HISTORY
Berkley trade paperback edition / December 2013

PRINTED IN THE UNITED STATES OF AMERICA

10 9 8 7 6 5 4 3 2 1

Cover photograph by Susan Fox/Arcangel.
Cover design by Lesley Worrell.
Interior text design by Laura K. Corless.

To Jacques

Acknowledgments

Many thanks to the History Wardrobe, a British website where, back in 2011, I stumbled across a presentation titled "Undressing Mr. Darcy" and couldn't resist . . . however, all characters and situations appearing in this work are fictitious.

A special thanks to my husband, my kids, and my mom for tolerating me in this endeavor. Boundless gratitude to my editor, Leis Pederson; the editorial staff at the Berkley Publishing Group; copy editor Sheila Moody; and my agent, Paige Wheeler of Folio Literary Management.

Please note that I have taken liberties with the timing of Jane Austen festivals and society meetings in this book.

I have so many people, bookstores, book club hosts, bloggers, and publications to thank that I can't possibly thank everyone here, and I know I will forget someone just like I did last time, so, Tiffany McManus, I'm thanking you first this time. I would also like to thank: Afterwords Bookstore, Alice Peck Editorial, Melissa Amster, Anderson's Bookstore, Jamie Anderson, Frances Archer, Austen Authors blog, Melanie Bates, Robin Benoy, Arnie Bernstein, Beverly Art Center (especially Penny Golden), Bingley's Teas, Blueprint Tours, the Book Stall, the Bookies Bookstore, Betty Braun, M. J. Bressler, Kelsey Buttimer, Lauren Cartelli, Chawton House Library (especially Lindsay Ashford and Steve Lawrence), *Chicago Tribune*, Chicago Writers Association, Donia Clark, Sheila Daily, Dyanne Davis, Lori Davis, Teresa Domek, Linda Dunbar, Nancy Dvorak, Stephanie Elliot, Meredith Esparza, Monica Fairview, Flavour Cooking School, Chris Foutris, Angela Gordon, Keir Graff, Sharin Greenleaf, Ann Harper, Bill and Susan Havel, Nancy Hutchings, Juliet Hwang, Jane Austen Books bookstore (especially Amy Patterson), Jane Austen Society of North America–Greater Chicago Region, *Jane Austen's Regency World* magazine (especially Tim Bullamore and Joceline Bury), JASNA–Greater Louisville Region, JASNA–Greater New York Region, JKS Communications (Julie Shorke), Rick Kogan, Jen Kovar, Jack Laney, Kordt Larson, Elisabeth Lenckos, *Library Journal*, Kathleen Longacre, Jean Lotus, Ann Macela, Nick Malone, Deb Miller, Meghan Miller, Jan Moretti, Laurel Ann Nattress, the *New York Review of Books*, Jean Newlin, Jeff Nigro, Kim Piotrowski, Jane Porter, Javier Ramirez, Elyce Rembos, Miriam Rheingold-Fuller, *Riverside Landmark*, Riverside Public Library (especially Janice Fisher and Dorothy Sikora), Cyndi Robinson, *RT Book Reviews*, Nara Shoenberg, Elaine Soloway, Kerri Spennicchia, "The Ballroom Blitz" by the Sweet, Anne Tabat, Liz Taylor, Cindy Vitek, Katie Walsh, Sherry Weddle, WGN radio, Windy City RWA, and Nili Wronski. There are so many more! Check my website for shout-outs.

This Side of the Pond

Chapter 1

Mr. Darcy's plane landed forty-five minutes late.

Vanessa, with coffee in hand and an earbud in one ear, steered her aunt in the airport wheelchair toward the throng of people gathered at the international arrivals area of Chicago's O'Hare.

She leaned over her aunt's shoulder. "How are we doing, Dowager Countess of the local Jane Austen Society?"

Aunt Ella turned and smiled. She eagerly awaited Mr. Darcy, a.k.a. Julian Chancellor, from England. He was her honored guest and a keynote speaker for the Jane Austen Society of North America's annual conference.

He'd written a book called *My Year as Mr. Darcy*, with a quill pen no less, detailing how he'd spent a year living as if he were a Regency gentleman, and accepted the invitation to speak and promote his book at the conference. He and her aunt had been corresponding via handwritten letters for months now and had become such good friends that she'd invited him to stay, as academics often do, in her condo.

But even a week with a Mr. Darcy clone couldn't change her aunt's status to healthy. Even he couldn't delete a dementia diagnosis.

Still, from the perspective of Aunt Ella's red-framed reading glasses, Julian's arrival couldn't be topped even if it were a visit from a royal. She'd had his September arrival date circled on her Austen calendar for months.

Vanessa's aunt, who had done so much for her and now faced dementia, considered this conference her final legacy to the literary society she had founded with a few other women and a teapot full of Earl Grey back in the 1970s. Now more than six hundred professors, scholars, and young, Web-savvy Austen enthusiasts the world over were coming to the conference—the last one to be held in Chicago for at least fifteen years.

Vanessa wanted this whole thing to be white-tablecloth perfect and as festive as the Queen's Jubilee. She needed all the *i*'s dotted and not a single *tea* crossed. That wasn't too much to ask, was it?

A magazine slid from Aunt Ella's houndstooth-skirted lap and Vanessa stopped to pick it up. The cover story title read: "Pottery Shards Prove Jane Austen Never Lived the Upper-Crust Life." A photo of blue and white china plates, broken apart, with pieces missing, topped the page. She could almost hear the clatter of the china as she handed the magazine back to her aunt, and the sharp, jagged edges of the shards gave her a chill. They reminded her of fragile hearts and fragmented . . . minds.

"Excuse me," she said with a wiggly smile, while people darted all around, and sometimes into, the two women. Her seventy-nine-year-old aunt didn't need the wheelchair, but it did make it easier for them both, if only people could successfully text while walking!

#*Grrr*, she thought, but didn't post. Posting would only bother her aunt.

When the Austen Society board had asked Vanessa to take on the public relations work for Julian, she'd said yes as a favor to her aunt and declined pay in order to help the cause. Since she ran her own boutique PR agency, she figured this would be a straightforward pro bono job. She'd already laid the groundwork—in fact, she'd planted an entire English garden—to ensure his success.

She'd treated him as one of her top-tier clients and plugged everything into her online calendars, complete with alerts and reminders. She'd established his online presence, since he had surprisingly little of that; generated thousands of followers across all the social networks for him; and lined up newspaper and radio interviews, book signings, and even another major appearance. Now all she had to do was escort him around Chicago, drive him to Kentucky for the Jane Austen Festival, do the real-time social networking, grab photos of him to post, film his events for uploading to various websites, hope something would go viral, and boom. He'd be back in England reaping the book sales benefits and Aunt Ella would be pleased with her niece's crowning achievements.

She nudged the wheelchair to the front of the cordoned-off crowd, right behind the rope, and pulled out the sign she'd printed. It did double duty as a PR stunt while letting Julian know where they were in the crowd, since he wasn't the texting type. The sign read:

LOOKING FOR OUR . . .

MR. DARCY

A young woman standing next to her read the sign. "Are you two—waiting for Mr. Darcy? *The* Mr. Darcy?"

Vanessa knew better than to wait for Mr. Darcy . . . or any man.

After her latest relationship #*fail* she had determined she wouldn't meet her next boyfriend in a bar or in a train car or in a house or with a mouse. She'd signed up for eBelieve, an online matchmaking service. Now she had many potentially perfect men's messages filling up her in-box, all of them sharing her interests and goals, all in her age range, and each geographically desirable—but she had yet to find the time to reply to any of them.

Statistically, one in five relationships began online. What better way, really, to get matched with someone these days? It made complete sense to her, especially after surviving this past summer, also known as yet-another-wedding-season, when, if she hadn't been invited in person, she'd endured the wedding photos and videos splashed all over her formerly single friends' social media. How many wedding gowns, bouquets, and kissing-at-the-altar images could a single girl take? And if they weren't wedding pix, they were baby photos.

Online. That was how it would happen for her.

Oh, she eBelieved.

She reached into her overstuffed but completely organized bag for a promotional postcard to give the young woman. "His name is Julian Chancellor and he's the author of the book *My Year as Mr. Darcy*. Proceeds from his book will help save his historic family estate from demolition."

It was all very *Downton Abbey* of him—she knew this because she had absorbed some of the BBC miniseries from behind her laptop as her aunt watched on Sunday nights. He wanted to save his family home and had written the book to raise awareness and garner donations to restore the place.

Aunt Ella nodded toward the young woman. "He is very much talked of in England for his foray into the life of a gentleman. His publisher paid for his flight over to the States, and we're all hoping his book is a raging success on this side of the pond. It's for a good cause, you see."

Vanessa handed the woman the postcard. "You can follow him on all the social networking sites. And to help promote his book and generate donations for his estate he'll be doing a show called *Undressing Mr. Darcy*—"

Vanessa now had the attention of several people in the crowd, and the woman's green eyes flickered.

Sex sells, even to smart, liberated women, and Mr. Darcy was the smart girl's pinup boy.

"Undressing?" she asked.

"Yes, he gives a little historical background on his Regency-era clothing as he proceeds to take it off—down to his drawers." Vanessa smiled.

"I'm in," the woman said as she looked at the postcard.

Nobody, it seemed, was above watching Mr. Darcy remove his cravat, breeches, and boots all in the name of history.

A few others in the crowd turned their heads and Vanessa handed them postcards, too. Jane Austen fans, she had learned from her target-market research, were everywhere, including online. They made Austen one of the most popular, if not *the* most popular, dead authors on social media, and they fueled a marketing bonanza for Austen-inspired merchandise. Just searching for "Jane Austen" plus "gifts" on the Internet yielded more than six million hits. These modern Janeites were well educated, often professors and lawyers; they preferred cats over dogs, tea over coffee; they enjoyed opera; and many played the piano.

Her aunt played the piano, too, only now she needed her sheet music.

"Vanessa, you and your electronics! Must you keep that wretched thing in your ear?"

She'd forgotten all about her earbud, and she lifted a hand to take it out, but a text beeped on her phone from a client just as her aunt spoke—

Aunt Ella continued, "Did I tell you I saw your old friend Lexi on the conference attendee list? She's getting her master's in history, specializing in sex during the Regency era."

Vanessa almost dropped her phone, although none of this surprised her. The name dredged up feelings almost as unwelcome as being left for yet another "sleepover" at her aunt's condo when she was thirteen, her parents separated and her mom heading out on a date. That little girl sported a backpack on her back, clutched her favorite blanket, and stared into Aunt Ella's glass curio cabinet at antique teacups and a framed silhouette of a woman she came to know as Jane Austen.

Lexi was no more her friend than she was the typical Austen fan.

Vanessa needed to switch up her mindset and turned to her phone, where she tapped on another one of her charity clients' social media pages: the Cat's Meow, an urban cat shelter. She flipped through this week's pictures of cats and kittens. She liked cats and kittens. That much she did have in common with Austen lovers. The cat shelter proved to be her favorite client and they didn't even pay her.

Still, she couldn't scratch out the name: Lexi. She turned her attention back to her aunt. But the young woman and Aunt Ella weren't looking at her. They were beaming at a tall, dangerously good-looking man on the other side of the rope wearing a form-fitting Regency tailcoat, cravat, buff breeches, and black riding boots. He had an antique, leather-bound book tucked under his arm and didn't carry suitcases but toted old leather trunks—leather trunks on a wheeled cart? A tumble of black hair spilled onto his forehead.

How could he look so much better in person than in his author photo? She made a mental note to update that shot—it would increase their crowds. Pleased with his looks (for marketing purposes, of course), Vanessa cleared her throat, as if to clear her mind.

He wore his Mr. Darcy garb on the plane? Then she found herself trying not to notice the slight tug of his breeches, the snug way they fit him—

Huh? He was a *client*, after all, regardless of whether he was paying her or not.

Even if he had been a prospect, she preferred a man in a well-tailored Italian suit or blue jeans and a button-down shirt, didn't she? What woman, at thirty-five years old, with a condo, her own business, family ties, and a thing for modern American amenities, would consider a man from another continent—not to mention the nineteenth century? She didn't understand it.

And, let's face it, Mr. Darcy's skill set—chiefly, diving into a pond in his shirtsleeves—would get him nowhere in today's job market.

"Miss Ella Morgan and Miss Vanessa Roberts, I presume?" he asked in a bass-range voice that needed no emoticons to get attention. Then he bowed.

He was none other than a very official-looking Mr. Darcy. On the big-screen TV above him, a bomb exploded on the news, and when Vanessa tucked her long brown hair behind her ear, her earbud popped right out.

Chapter 2

Two women materialized from the arrivals door and flanked him. They were dressed scantily for having just disembarked from an air-conditioned plane and looked extremely well made-up for having endured a seven-hour flight. They giggled and flirted and batted their fake eyelashes at him.

All the women and even a gay guy in the crowd proceeded to fall under his spell.

The young woman next to her squeezed Vanessa's arm. "He's so handsome and has such presence, just like Mr. Darcy."

No doubt about it, he carried himself well. Was it his posture?

His posture reminded her of his rare e-mails and more usual posted, handwritten letters: stiff, formal, and polite. His formality worked for her, though, especially since he would be staying at her aunt's condo, which happened to be right across the street from Vanessa's. This was a first for a client. Her aunt had already informed her she hoped her niece would spend meals and evenings with them.

"And that accent. I *love* British accents," the young woman said.

Was Vanessa the only American woman who didn't swoon over men with British accents?

She stepped out from behind the wheelchair to turn it around.

For a brief moment his dark eyes darted from her eyes to her breasts, then down to her peep-toed sandals revealing her black pedicure. He lingered on the tattoo above her ankle, a small heart wrapped in barbed wire, and then his gaze shot back up to her face— stopping himself from giving her the complete once-over.

Maybe he wasn't as proper as he'd like to be. Was his attitude toward women as evolved as his nineteenth-century clothing? His expression soon revealed his determination not to let his eyes wander below her neckline, though, giving her a sense of relief.

She nodded toward the back of the arrivals area. "We'll meet you over by the elevator, okay?"

"Absolutely. Thank you for taking the time to collect me." He turned his face, revealing dark square-cut sideburns on his clean-shaven skin.

"Of—of course," Vanessa said. "My aunt wouldn't think of your taking a cab."

"The English call an elevator a 'lift,' Vanessa dear," Aunt Ella said. "We'll see you at the lift," she said to him and then lowered her voice for Vanessa. "If only you'd agreed to travel with me to England, you would know these little things. But you never wanted to go. I still can't fathom it."

True. She'd been to France, Germany, and Italy . . . but never had the desire to go to England. She wasn't the type to watch the young royals on TV or buy tea towels that said *Keep Calm and Carry On*. And tea wasn't her cup of tea. She liked coffee.

One of the two women next to Julian piped up, handing Vanessa her phone over the rope. "Wait! Will you take a picture of us with him? He's so amazing! We had the *best* time sitting next to him on that flight!"

He smiled. "Everybody needs a little Mr. Darcy in their lives, don't they?"

The women laughed and agreed.

Vanessa wasn't sure why, but she didn't want to take a picture of them with him. She'd taken thousands of pictures of clients before; why not now?

"Smile," Vanessa said and took the picture, then she took another one with her phone to add to the social media sites. This phase of the PR job had begun in earnest, and to make sure everything would work out well for him, she had taken this week off from her other clients, but the e-mails and texts from them persisted. The twenty-four/seven of running her own business never really allowed her time off. "Here, take a postcard with all of his appearances on it. Hope you can make one of them!" She handed a postcard to the gay guy, too.

Vanessa hadn't read *My Year as Mr. Darcy* yet. It sat on her e-reader along with a litany of other books she meant to read. Getting all her other clients' work taken care of so she could take this time to focus on him had absorbed so many late nights and weekends. Thankfully, she didn't have a boyfriend at the moment—that, too, took time.

"Nice to meet you, Mr. Darcy." The blond woman who'd asked for the photo waved and winked.

Julian delivered a nod.

The other woman fluffed her red hair. "We'll see you at one of your signings! And, like, thanks for inspiring us to read Jane—Jane—"

Vanessa smiled. "That would be Jane Austen." She had to admit, though, it was cool that he mingled with the masses so easily, took his "Mr. Darcy" persona so seriously, and clearly made Austen converts out of a younger market than she'd been targeting. All this would make her job easier, at least.

The young woman who had asked for the picture signaled with her hand for Julian to call her and, just for emphasis, she mouthed the words with her shiny lip-glossy lips: "Call me."

"Call you what?" He bowed.

The women laughed at the joke.

He rolled his leather trunks along behind him.

No wonder it had taken him so long to get through customs! Vanessa made a mental note that getting from A to B might take a little longer with a man who attracted so much—attention. But that was good, right? What she wanted in a client, really.

She wheeled Aunt Ella around toward the elevators, thankful that she wouldn't have to struggle getting him to wear the Regency outfit for the cable TV interview. He seemed to be more than into his role.

Once at the elevators, she kneeled down alongside her aunt, asking the usual questions before any car trip. "Do you need to go to the washroom? Are you hungry? Thirsty?" But her aunt only wanted to get Julian settled in the guest room of her Gold Coast condo.

Vanessa took a moment on her phone to upload the photo of him with the two women and key in on all the social networking sites she'd set up for him:

Mr. Darcy has landed. #JASNAagm #UndressingMrDarcy

A male cleared his throat, and out of the corner of her eye a pair of black leather equestrian-like boots came into her sight. She deliberately looked right into his face and tried not to stare at his gorgeous dark eyes. He, meanwhile, looked away from her and downward, to the headline on Aunt Ella's magazine.

"Miss Morgan, I see you are reading about the archeological excavation recently completed at Austen's childhood home. It seems the Austens were not even as well off as the Bennet family."

Aunt Ella nodded in recognition of a kindred spirit and her gold earrings bobbed in agreement. "Amazing what can be gleaned from broken china plates and rusty nails."

He switched his leather-bound book to his other arm. "She was an author with great gifts, not the least of which were a rich imagination and spunk."

"Shall we head off to my chaise-and-four in the parking lot?" Vanessa asked. "Or would you like to check your phone first, Julian? There's free Wi-Fi here."

"Check my phone? No, no, thank you."

"Let's get Julian settled," Aunt Ella said.

The September heat created mirages in the distance on the blacktop, and surely he had to be hot in those boots and tailcoat.

Certainly he was one of the hottest clients she'd had in a while, literally and figuratively.

"I'm reminded of a Jane Austen quote," he said as he shielded his eyes with his book. "In a letter to her sister Cassandra, in September of 1796. Perhaps you're familiar? 'What dreadful Hot weather we have!'"

Aunt Ella nodded her head and chimed in on the second half of the quote with him: "'It keeps me in a continual state of Inelegance'!"

They both laughed, and Vanessa did, too, thrilled to see her aunt enjoying herself. Resigned to what was sure to be more than the usual dose of all things Austen, she navigated them toward the car.

Julian laughed. "Did I mention that Security asked me aside and gave me a thorough search?"

"No!" said Aunt Ella.

"Regency-era profiling?" joked Vanessa.

"Yes. I suspect they half assumed they'd find a sword in my luggage."

"That'll make a fabulous post," Vanessa said. "Hold on, it'll only take me a minute." She pulled out her phone.

"Oh, dear, Julian," Aunt Ella said. "I must apologize for my niece."

"No apologies necessary."

Vanessa keyed in:

Mr. Darcy gets a pat down at the airport. #JASNAagm #UndressingMrDarcy #shocking

"The poor dear is always on her electronic devices for work, Julian."

"Three replies already." Vanessa smiled as she pushed the wheelchair with one hand.

"It is most unfortunate," Julian said. "I cannot tell you how I valued my year without all of that as I wrote my book by candlelight. I'm extremely skeptical of modern technology. When it comes to reading, I like a real book. When it comes to conversation, I prefer it in person, preferably over a cup of tea."

"My sentiments exactly!" Aunt Ella said.

Louis Armstrong singing "You like tomato and I like tomahto" played in Vanessa's brain. But she couldn't call the whole thing off, could she?

Once at the car, while Julian and Aunt Ella played the politeness game over who should sit in front, Vanessa whisked the wheelchair back to the cart corral. By the time she got back, she found Aunt Ella sitting in the back and Julian waiting on the driver's side, where he opened her door for her and made a flourish with his hand.

The last time a man had held open a car door for her was . . . what? Senior prom?

"Thank you?" was all she could muster. He was attractive *and* polite.

"The pleasure's all mine," he said.

Once he'd opened his door, he leaned in.

"I'm sorry, would you mind if I removed my coat? It's a bit warm."

Sorry? And "a bit warm" for a woolen tailcoat? She had to smile at his British propensity for apologies and understatement.

"No, I don't mind," Vanessa said. "By all means, take it off." She laughed. "With your *Undressing* show I'm sure you're used to women encouraging you to take it off."

"Yes, quite." He smiled.

He proceeded to fold himself into her small car. His broad shoulders invaded some of her space. He was so tall his legs barely fit, even with the seat pushed back. She tried not to watch, out of the corner of her black sunglasses, as he maneuvered to get comfortable.

"Buckle up, Mr. Darcy." She smiled.

He finally noticed that she had mounted a plastic Jane Austen action figure, all of about five inches high and wielding a quill, on the dashboard where a hula girl might be.

"Whatever might this be? A plastic Jane Austen?" He smiled.

"I thought she might bring us good luck," Vanessa said.

With that she turned the key in the ignition and they were all blown away by the simultaneous blast of hot air-conditioning and super-loud, blaring rap music. She scrambled to turn off the music as Julian and Aunt Ella covered their ears.

"Sorry about that! Forgot I had cranked up the music after I dropped Aunt Ella at the door."

Julian looked at her askance while her aunt said, "My goodness! It's enough to scare our poor guest all the way back across the pond!"

"It's quite all right," he said.

"Do you prefer classical, Julian? I have that, too." She'd pegged him as a classical guy and handed him her phone as she ramped onto the highway. "Take your pick. I have lots of choices—operatic, jazz, or blues playlists."

He stuck the phone back in its mount under the dash.

It was so strange to witness a man *not* check his phone after an eight-hour flight and refuse a playlist.

She felt his eyes on her.

"Perhaps we might—converse?"

Talk? What man ever wanted to talk?

* * *

*I*n the condo, as they prepared for dinner, Aunt Ella headed toward the screen door to her rooftop garden terrace. "I like a young man who enjoys conversation," she said over her shoulder to Vanessa.

Julian opened the door for her with a smile.

"Now, where were we, Julian? Discussing how the Austens abandoned poor little seven-year-old Jane and Cassandra at a girls' school in Oxford, I believe."

In her aunt's kitchen, Vanessa opened the freezer for the tray of ice cubes. Her aunt preferred them, and not the ice-maker cubes, for the cut-crystal water goblets. She could hear everything through the screen door.

"Yes," Julian said. "And after nearly a year the poor dears contracted a vile infection whilst at school and came very close to dying. Yet, just a year later, the Austens sent the two of them off to another girls' school in Reading."

The ice tray froze Vanessa's fingertips. She didn't know much about Jane's younger years, nor that she had been in any way . . . left.

"Children are only too aware when they're being forsaken," Aunt Ella said to Julian. "It's no secret that I practically raised Vanessa once her parents separated. We're like mother and daughter, really."

"I can see you have a very special bond."

Vanessa nursed a lifelong prejudice against Austen's *Pride and Prejudice* after being assigned it in high school, during her parents' divorce. That was when she decided, at seventeen, after spending so much time with her aunt, that she might as well just live with her when her parents sold the family home. The judge granted her request, in part to keep her in her high school. Her mother moved into a more affordable apartment in the suburbs while her father moved out to California for a new job and, ultimately, a new wife and family. They all stayed in touch, but her aunt was her family.

Vanessa had, as a young teen, developed a sibling rivalry of sorts with Jane Austen, competing with her for her aunt's attention, even though her aunt doted on her. She never could get through *Pride and Prejudice* and, much to her aunt's chagrin, she'd only read the outlined study-guide version.

To this day she didn't quite believe in happy endings.

Condensation rose from the ice cube tray as Vanessa ran it under water and the ice crackled. Each time she opened a freezer, she thought of—even though she tried not to—her life plan and . . . her eggs.

Vanessa was a planner of things, a maker of timelines, but things hadn't gone exactly according to schedule. She had thought for sure she'd be married and a working mom by now, but the minor detail of finding Mr. Perfect had somehow eluded her. So to take the pressure off, she'd decided to freeze her eggs and take back the power. Five of her eggs had been harvested and frozen, but she aimed for an even dozen. She hadn't told her aunt about it, but often cracked jokes about her eggs to herself. Cracked. Jokes. The jokes weren't that funny, obviously.

Once she'd refilled the tray and put it back in the freezer, something sparkly caught her eye near the bag of frozen artichoke hearts.

Several of her aunt's golden chunky necklaces sat on the shelf collecting ice crystals. They gave her a searing sort of freezer burn as she pulled them out and set them on the granite counter in the sunshine, but she couldn't leave them there.

The trouble had begun weeks before with a petunia in the microwave. Stress increased these episodes, and Vanessa knew she had done the right thing by taking time away from her clients to help her aunt with this conference. The doctor had assured her that until the rest of her aunt's test results came in, the goal was to keep her aunt living as independently as possible.

Vanessa poured the water in the goblets and ran the necklaces back to her aunt's vanity in the bedroom.

"Vanessa? You're not on your phone again, are you?"

"You know me," Vanessa called out when she carried the water goblets on a tray, rather unsteadily, toward the screen door. She needed to tell Julian about her aunt's condition and let him know they were awaiting test results revealing whether it was Alzheimer's or not.

Julian stood, his head hitting the branches of a dwarf weeping willow, to open the door for her.

"So nice to have a gentleman around," Vanessa said.

"Pleased to hear it." He smiled.

Tuberoses, the traditional flower of a bridegroom, filled the air on the terrace with fragrance. Julian had loosened the cravat around his neck, removed his tailcoat and waistcoat, and rolled up his sleeves, lending a certain frisson to the gathering, considering that until now he had been all buttoned-up, in both clothing and actions.

Who was the man underneath the Darcy facade? Could he relax and be—himself?

"There you are, Vanessa. I was just telling Julian about our little secret."

"You were?"

"I told him how, sometimes, when you or I have a particularly bad day, we go for a nice cocktail or two somewhere."

"It's true." Vanessa stooped to smell the potted lavender before she plopped down at her dinner plate. "We do."

"It's our little secret, Julian." Aunt Ella smiled. "Our little secret."

"Don't breathe a word of it to any of my aunt's esteemed colleagues, Julian," Vanessa teased.

"Even Jane herself enjoyed a good glass of French wine," he said and smiled at Vanessa.

Would Julian figure out she wasn't a card-carrying member of the Austen and Anglophile club?

"Here's to Jane Austen," he said as he raised his wineglass.

"To Jane!" Aunt Ella clinked his glass.

"To Miss Austen." Vanessa raised her glass to the little girl left at the boarding school.

After Vanessa cleared and washed the dinner dishes, refusing Julian's help, and brought out the tea and coffee, Aunt Ella tapped a green leather photo album that sat on the table next to her antique tea set reserved for the terrace. Her hands looked less and less familiar, but instead, more like the hands of an old woman. "Vanessa, you simply must see the photos of Julian's estate he's just shown me."

All she could think was: Her aunt had put a petunia in the microwave and now her necklaces in the freezer. What next?

"She need not bother with it," Julian said.

Vanessa snapped to. "Oh, of course, Julian, I'd love to see the album." She settled into the wrought iron chair next to him, with ever-blooming green and blue hydrangeas surrounding them and the cityscape opened up to them against the evening sky.

Good thing she didn't go for Regency bucks, because it made it easy to remind herself this was work. It had been a long time since she'd socialized with a client, much less a male client just a few years her senior, who also was very good-looking. And polite. And doting on her aunt. In fact, that had never happened.

Aunt Ella took the flickering on of the Italian lights dotting the terrace as her cue to stand. "I will say good night, then. Tomorrow's another busy day and then the ball . . ."

Julian stood and bowed. "Yes, do rest. We have so many festivities to look forward to!"

He held the door open for her while Vanessa popped up and

gave her aunt a gargantuan hug, a kiss on her velvety cheek, and a playful twist of her necklace.

"Do you need any help with anything?"

"No, no, you two enjoy the evening."

A glimmer of hope washed over Aunt Ella's face, and Vanessa needed to nip that in the wedding boutonniere. She knew the machinations of her aunt's mind.

"We have *work* to discuss. But I won't keep him up past his bedtime. Especially with his acclimating to the six-hour time difference."

"Good night, Ella." Julian smiled.

Once her aunt had left, Vanessa lowered her voice to a whisper. "Julian, I have to tell you something."

"No need to bother. I already know," he said as he sipped his tea.

"You already know what?"

"You do not particularly like Jane Austen."

How did he know that? Unless Aunt Ella had told him . . .

"No, no, I need to tell you that my aunt has been recently diagnosed with dementia. Tomorrow the doctor is going to call me with the test results. We'll know whether it's Alzheimer's or not."

"Oh. I knew that, too. She told me."

"She did?"

"We're rather good friends. You must know we met at a Jane Austen gathering in England years ago. Your aunt is quite open about the dementia; in fact, she wrote me about it weeks ago, when you went in for the first appointment."

"I see. And the Jane Austen thing—?"

"It's obvious to me."

"I have nothing against her, you know—" She really didn't. It was just a bad association more than anything.

"No need to explain. It's quite all right."

"I hope you understand that just because I'm not a lifelong member of the Jane Austen Society, I've still done and will do everything

I know of to help you sell as many books and earn as many donations for your estate as possible."

"You have done a bang-up job and all without any remuneration—"

"I do like to donate to good causes when I can."

"Yes, your aunt told me about the cat shelter."

"She did? Now you're going to think I'm a crazy cat lady—"

"That's not what I think about you at all."

What *did* he think of her? Wait a minute. Why did she care what a client thought of her? She only cared about what he thought of her work.

"I'm most appreciative. I certainly never anticipated so many radio interviews and telly interviews."

"Cable television, but yes. But you never know, we could still end up on prime-time news if something goes our way! As for the dementia, I wanted you to know in case she does something odd. Just this evening I found her necklaces in the freezer."

"I am most, most sorry. Whilst I'm here I will surely look after her."

Vanessa sighed. "Thank you. So. Julian." She gave the photo album a quick tap. "Give me the grand tour of your humble abode."

As he pulled his chair closer to hers, church bells chimed down the street, and for an awkward moment their eyes met, but Vanessa looked away and at the album.

He'd carried this thick, heavy photo album overseas?

With ceremony, he opened it up.

The pages were the color of coffee cream and each black-and-white photo had been carefully mounted with black corners.

He began by showing her photos of the ornate front gate, lawns, a pond, and semicircular gravel drive. The front grounds alone looked bigger than the city block that her condo building was on.

"And this is the view from the road."

Her coffee spoon fell with a loud clank on her saucer. She pushed her coffee aside, wiped her fingers with her napkin, and took the album in both hands. Was dropping her spoon terribly obvious? She might as well say it. "Julian, it's gorgeous. Wow."

"Do you like the style?"

"Very much. What's not to like?"

"It was built just before Jane Austen's time, and she would've been very familiar with the architecture."

"When was it built?"

"Seventeen twenty-six. So it's not that ancient by many standards."

Vanessa laughed. "Not by English standards."

He smiled, too, and their eyes locked again.

"We think of Aunt Ella's place here as vintage, and it was built in 1920!" She laughed.

He smiled.

"But your place—" She focused on the photo.

"It does have a gorgeous Palladian ashlar facade, does it not?"

She wasn't even sure what that meant, but the six-columned, three-storied gray stone structure had twenty-something windows on the front alone and a tricorner pediment topped it off. It could be a museum. To say it was impressive would be an understatement, but there was something else about it, too; she just couldn't figure out what.

"You live here all alone?" Was that a question she would ask any other client? "I—I mean it's a huge place—"

"I am living alone in the drafty old place at the moment, aside from the skeleton staff it takes to keep such a place from crumbling entirely to bits. Most of it is cordoned off and the back grounds in particular need more tending than I can afford, I'm sorry to say."

Vanessa stared at photos of an interior marble staircase in crumbling disrepair, water damage in the basement kitchen, and another room with peeling wallpaper and furniture draped in white tarps. "I didn't know it was so beautiful and needed so much work."

Julian sat back and folded his arms. "I didn't think you'd read my book. I spend a large portion of the middle chapters addressing my challenges with inheriting an estate in such a—state."

Did Vanessa just feel herself blush? When was the last time she'd blushed?

"I'm sorry, no, I didn't. I just haven't had the time. But that hasn't affected the campaign I've created for you. And I will read it—I have some time now."

The rest of the photos documented the disrepair of this once-handsome home. She wanted to read his book, and suddenly she regretted not reading it. Instead she had put her energies into what she thought was a better use of her time, lining up media opportunities for him.

For the first time in a long while she had the urge to read, and she only hoped his book could hold her attention. These days she never seemed to get past any opening chapters in her recreational reading.

"Since you didn't read the book, you may not know that the home, in my extended family for generations, fell into neglect under my great-uncle's occupancy. He was an eccentric old bachelor who suffered an undiagnosed neurological disorder, and he lived there his entire life, until he went into a home, and then the house really took a turn for the worse as it remained vacant for four years, complete with roof leaks. I was the next in line to inherit, and I didn't want to leave off being a history professor, but—well, my younger brother laughs at me, considering the inheritance more of a curse than anything. It's a massive responsibility."

Still fascinated by the photos, Vanessa sipped her coffee and pointed to a photo of what appeared to be a tomb, built atop a hillside overlooking the estate.

"What's this?" she asked.

His hand brushed against hers and she moved her hand to her lap.

"Oh, that." Julian laughed. "That's my great-great-grandfather, looking down on me, making sure I don't catapult the family estate into ruination."

"No pressure, right?"

"Exactly."

The project took a grip on her in a way it hadn't before. Seeing these photos, meeting Julian, sensing his passion for the restoration made it personal, just like her work had been in the beginning, when people took the time for face-to-face meetings instead of Skype sessions, conference calls, and endless e-mail volleys.

"I'm doing everything I can to restore it to its former glory and open it to the public to see, but it's going to take millions. It's currently listed in the English Heritage at Risk Register and I have only two years to turn it around or it could be condemned and torn down. This is why I wrote *My Year as Mr. Darcy*. Maybe I'm daft, but I can picture it fully restored. Perhaps even turned into a hotel with public areas open for touring."

"I can see it, too. Yes, Julian, you're going to make it happen!"

He smiled. "You have a wonderful enthusiasm. Whilst many are encouraging, others are not so optimistic."

"Like . . . your significant other?"

Did she just say that? Really?

He looked right at her with his dark eyes. "It takes an extraordinary person to be keen on such a massive project."

She pushed her chair farther away from him. "I'm thrilled to have you as one of my clients, Julian, and I look forward to working on this with you while you're here."

He leaned back in his chair. "There is one lady in particular who wants me to restore it."

So, he had a girlfriend after all.

"Perhaps then she will leave me alone."

Wait. He didn't have a girlfriend? She wished she didn't care. "Who's that?"

"The female ghost in the drawing room."

"You're kidding. There isn't really a ghost, is there?"

"There is. She wears a very fragrant rosewater perfume and she delights in knocking over chairs."

Vanessa didn't know what to make of all this, with ghosts, roof leaks, untended gardens, and questions of a client's relationship status swirling through her mind.

Suddenly, something hit her like a fallen roof beam and she had to set her coffee down, she was so excited.

"Julian, do you have these photos on a chip? Are they digital? Do you have any digital video footage of your home?"

"No," he said. "I still use my old film camera from when I was a student. And I have my own darkroom, so—"

Vanessa had to laugh. Of course he didn't have a digital camera. "You own a huge estate but you don't have a digital camera."

He smiled. "Even though I'm what you Americans would call 'house poor,' I can afford a digital camera, but I've refused on principle. Everyone who owns a digital camera tells me they never print their photos. It's one of the curses of modern technology. This way one values the pictures and gets them developed."

"You have a point." She would have to scan these photos in, but it would be worth it. "Julian, we need to leverage this!"

"Whatever do you mean?" He stirred a lump of sugar into his tea.

Vanessa popped up. "Give me some time and I'll lay it out for you."

He smirked. "You will do what, precisely?"

Her response betrayed her with too much innuendo. "I simply meant I'll introduce you to some new ideas for our PR plan."

"Oh."

"I have to get to work on my laptop."

He looked at the watch dangling from a fob at his waist. "Yes, but it's half seven in the evening your time."

"And?"

"And you are planning to work now?"

"Why not?" She laughed.

She had gotten a glimpse of the man beneath the Darcy trappings, and, oddly enough, she liked what she saw.

Chapter 3

She woke the next morning with her e-reader on the pillow next to her, open to the last page of *My Year as Mr. Darcy*. She had breezed through it, but after working late on the new additions to the PR plan, she'd fallen asleep from sheer exhaustion.

She wanted to tell him about the new elements of the plan, but that would have to wait. This morning marked the opening of the conference and Julian was the second keynote speaker.

Aunt Ella had gone ahead with her friend Paul, while Vanessa escorted Julian to the conference hotel. He, in his full Regency attire, carried her video cam tripod for her—ever the gentleman.

"I must warn you, Julian, that our conference hotel has been double-booked with a comic-book sci-fi conference called Hero Con. At first I was upset, but then I realized we could spin this to our advantage, and I've been plugging your book and *Undressing* show to their conference attendees, too."

"I admire your ingenuity and glass-half-full perspective, but I can't imagine that extraterrestrials would have any interest in Jane Austen."

Vanessa laughed. "Their conference has three times the attendees, and yet a third of them have also signed up for our conference. Don't be surprised if you see a Batwoman or two in the audience."

A man dressed as Mr. Spock stood outside the hotel lobby doors.

Once they stepped into the lobby, they saw that Caped Crusaders, goth girls, and werefolk peppered the escalators and main floor. Julian, in his breeches, tailcoat, and hat, faded into the comic-book background.

Vanessa happened to be the one who stood out. She had to be the only one in a skirt and blazer. She'd seen these comic cons on the news but had never been to one. She'd never been to a Jane Austen conference, either, for that matter.

A fortune-teller with heavy makeup lasered in on Vanessa from across the lobby and came right up to her. "I see foreign travel in your future. It's what you need, darling."

Vanessa furrowed her brows. She dismissed the gypsy's prediction. She wouldn't go overseas—not with her aunt's health problems.

"Mark my words, you will be flying abroad very soon."

Vanessa watched her walk away, leaving a hint of jasmine.

"Perhaps you will be going to England," Julian said. "She seems convinced you are going abroad."

"She's also wearing gym shoes under her fringed skirt."

He laughed.

This had to be the most fun she'd had with a client in a while.

"If you do venture across the pond, I can offer you free all-access tickets to the Jane Austen Festival in Bath. I'll be doing my show there. Nine days of Jane Austen for you!"

She smirked. "I've practically grown up with Austen. Nine days wouldn't phase me. Look over there by the coffee bar. It's Obi-Wan Kenobi eating a cake pop."

He smiled. "As Austen would say, 'I am excessively diverted.'"

Thor sipped a frozen coffee topped with whipped cream from a straw.

Vanessa's intern, Kai, arrived exactly ten minutes late. He always showed up late—it was his m.o.—but then again, what can you expect from a kid who gets paid in college credit and the occasional coffee?

Kai really wanted to be a film director, not a PR man, and he dressed, always, in a T-shirt, black jeans, and black high-tops. He wore a silver ring on his thumb, and to her friends in the biz, Vanessa referred to him as her "bf"—short not for "boyfriend" but for "boy Friday."

She'd always joked about getting a boy Friday, as opposed to a girl Friday, to help her out with things, but this past year she'd made it happen, and it was worth dealing with his tardiness and hangovers. Kai did have a talent for shooting, and she often let him do the filming and editing for client sites. Today she'd asked him to come as a backup, just to be sure she got all the footage of Julian she needed.

"This is so cool," Kai said.

"Quite," said Julian.

Vanessa stifled a laugh. These two couldn't be more diametrically opposed. She made the necessary introductions.

"Lean on us, Julian; we've got your back," Vanessa said. "Whatever we can do to help you out, just let us know."

"Will do."

"We all have each other's cell phone numbers, so we're only a text or call away."

Julian cleared his throat. "I shall not be using my mobile, as I prefer to keep it off. It breaks character. People don't expect Darcy to be texting."

Kai looked at Vanessa.

"We'll do our best, then, to stick near you, Julian, won't we, Kai?

But I am expecting an important phone call from my aunt's doctor today, and I do have to keep in touch with my other clients and may need to step away. And Kai has homework to squeeze in. If you need us and can't find us in the crowd, please, consider stepping into the men's room to call."

What did he have against modern technology? He couldn't exactly send a messenger on horseback.

"Okay. Ready to roll?" Kai asked Vanessa, as he always did, as if she was the one holding him up, even though he always arrived late.

As the three of them made their way through the lobby, Vanessa felt as if she had fallen into a parallel universe. Even though she had been immersed in Darcy fandom for the past several months, clearly he wasn't everyone's cup of tea. From what she was seeing, apparently some women preferred vampires.

When they entered the West Tower and left Hero Con behind in the East Tower, a wash of familiarity and, yes, warmth came over her. The conference check-in area looked more elegant than she'd imagined, with white-tablecloth-covered check-in tables; lavish floral arrangements with pink cabbage roses; cellophane-wrapped raffle baskets filled with tea, quill pens, and books; and silver trays of frosted cookies in the shape of teapots and Austen's silhouette.

She peeked into the "Emporium," nothing more than a conference room but abuzz with vendors of all sorts selling everything from bonnets to tea to antique books. Everything seemed in order and going as planned, just the way she liked things to go.

A group of professors pulled Julian aside and Vanessa spotted a sprightly, petite woman who had fallen behind her flock of Janeites to read her conference program. She looked fantastic in her Regency gown and gloves. The nearly sheer white fabric begged to be touched, the low, square-cut neckline proved the opposite of matronly, and the tiny off-the-shoulder cap sleeves suggested a certain state of—undress. The blue ribbon drew attention to the woman's bust while tight gray leather gloves accentuated her arms and culminated in loose bunching at her biceps. The effect proved mesmerizing.

Vanessa had never associated anything Austen with anything—sexy. She couldn't help but stop and stare at this gown. What had gotten into her? She hadn't seen anything so fetching in a long time, it seemed.

Fetching? Since when did she use the word "fetching"?

She just had to ask. "Your gown is gorgeous. Where did you get it?"

The woman smiled. "I had it made by the mantua maker, who is right there in the Emporium. It's muslin."

"Muslin" didn't mean anything to Vanessa, and neither did "mantua maker."

The woman began to rifle through her little silk-tasseled bag.

"What's a mantua maker?" Vanessa asked.

"A dressmaker. This one is superb." The woman pulled something out of her little bag. "Here's her card. The secret is the corset. They were called 'stays' during the Regency era. One must wear stays. Do remember that."

"Okay. Thank you." She didn't think she'd need stays or a mantua maker, but she slipped the card into her wallet anyway. Everywhere Vanessa turned, attendees with their conference badges smiled and hugged one another, some costumed, some not, but they all seemed to be one big Regency family.

Julian inched his way through the conference-goers, so many of them stopping him, congratulating him on his book, wanting a picture with him.

"He's a rock star here, isn't he?" she said to Kai.

"I guess," Kai said.

Vanessa posted:

Mr. Darcy will reveal all very soon . . . #JASNAagm #UndressingMrDarcy

Finally she led him toward the stage and introduced him to Paul, Aunt Ella's friend, who had volunteered to act as valet during his *Undressing* act.

"Ella's in her element hosting you, Julian," Paul said. "We all wish you great success. I have heard that several regional societies have pooled funds to donate to your cause, and you can thank Vanessa for that."

Julian tipped his hat to her. "She is a most brilliant promoter. And she has done it all without compensation. Most kind. And she's lovely as well."

Vanessa took it in stride. Clients complimented her all the time, didn't they?

"Where's Aunt Ella?" she asked Paul.

"Here she comes with her entourage through the doors now." He nodded toward the opposite side of the huge room. "And after I'm done onstage, I'll be by her side for the duration."

"Thank you, Paul." She turned to Julian. "Break a—booted leg, then, gentlemen."

Julian went backstage while she and Paul helped Aunt Ella and her friends get settled.

Her aunt took a seat and quickly grasped Vanessa's hands. Aunt Ella's forehead was creased with worry. "Ladies"—she turned to her friends—"I'm sure you all know my Vanessa. What would I do without her?"

Vanessa knew all of them. "Welcome to the big day, everyone. I hope you enjoy the conference."

The ladies nodded and smiled.

"Darling, everyone agrees we must have Julian open the ball tomorrow night. But who shall be his opening dance partner? I can't believe I forgot this ever-so-important detail. It's so unlike me!"

Paul didn't skip a beat. "He should open with Vanessa. Who else? They'd make such a stunning couple." He cocked his head at Vanessa. "You even look a little Miss Elizabeth Bennet–ish, if I do say so myself. 'Fine eyes' and all that."

"Oh, it can't be her, unfortunately." Aunt Ella let Vanessa's hands drop and snapped open the antique fan she'd bought in England on her last visit. "I'm afraid Vanessa merely *tolerates* all this for my sake."

"Auntie E, I think this whole conference is just delightful, really. I'm actually enjoying it!"

"It hasn't even started, dear."

Vanessa smiled. "We've been working on it for months now and I'm so glad to see it come together so beautifully."

"I really think you and Julian would be perfect," Paul said.

"She doesn't even have a gown, Paul," Aunt Ella said as she fanned herself.

Vanessa pulled out her phone. "Not to worry. I'll send out a post and in no time we'll have enough takers to fill his dance card for the entire evening. It'll be sort of a . . . contest . . . and help generate more buzz for him and his book."

"Are you suggesting we leave his opening dance partner to chance?" Aunt Ella closed her fan and tapped it in her palm nervously.

"Who in this room wouldn't be worthy? A room full of Janeites is a room full of fascinating, quality women, is it not? Anyway, I'll screen the top three just to be sure." She winked.

Aunt Ella sighed with a bit of relief. "Once again you've won me over. Or worn me down. I'm not sure which!"

"Leave it to me, Aunt Ella; it's a win-win. Don't give it another thought. Now, please excuse me, everyone. I have to set up the cameras with Kai."

Once the cameras were set up, she sent out the post:

Mr. Darcy needs a dance partner to open the ball tomorrow night. Any takers? #JASNAagm #UndressingMrDarcy #onlyMissBennetsneedapply

Within seconds she had a handful of replies.

Almost seven hundred people had filled the room by this point, chatting around her as she volleyed back some e-mails and texts to her clients. The congeniality and camaraderie that surrounded her could practically be poured into a teapot, it was so palpable.

"Well, you know," she overheard a woman behind her say, "it's just like Jane Austen and Tom Lefroy."

"It is?" was the female reply.

"Yes. A handsome stranger comes into town, and the local girl falls in love."

Vanessa tried to concentrate on an e-mail from one of her clients, but instead she followed the entire conversation behind her.

"Do you believe Austen and Lefroy were in love?"

"I want to believe that Jane had, at least once in her life, experienced love, yes. But she was so young when they met, both of them twenty, it's hard to tell what it was."

"And it ended so quickly—prematurely—they knew each other only very briefly."

"They flirted quite famously, though. Quite a statement in those days. As she said in a letter to Cassandra, 'I am almost afraid to tell you how my Irish friend and I behaved. Imagine to yourself everything most profligate and shocking in the way of dancing and sitting down together.'"

"Yes, yes, good for her. I like to think of our Jane as 'shocking.'"

"I've always thought of her that way."

Jane Austen? Shocking? Vanessa was the one who was shocked. For some reason she'd always thought of Austen as prim and proper. A titan of literature, yes, but never "shocking."

She wanted to know how the Jane Austen–Tom Lefroy story played out, but the women had moved on to a discussion about a manuscript that Austen never tried to get published titled *Lady Susan*.

"When you talk about Lady Susan, her adulterous heroine—"

Austen wrote about an adulterous heroine?

"—it reminds me of a lecture Professor Gibbs gave about how Lady Susan fits all the modern-day criteria for a sociopath. It was fascinating."

Adultery? Sociopaths? Did Vanessa really know Jane Austen at all? She might have to download this *Lady Susan*.

She put her phone on vibrate while the current Chicago group president welcomed everyone and introduced the opening speaker, Dr. Cornel West.

Dr. West commanded the stage . . . and Vanessa's attention. Who knew that a man, a progressive, modern, activist, African American professor of philosophy at Princeton—and a Harvard grad—idolized Jane Austen?

With passion and fervor, he leaned over his podium in his hipster glasses. "Jane Austen didn't go to Oxford," he said to the crowd, who nodded and smiled. "But *two* Oxfords went through her."

The crowd clapped, and more than one woman in a gown gave a wolf whistle.

"Austen will teach you how to live," he said more than once.

"Jane Austen is on *fire*," he said to the crowd, who rose to a standing ovation.

Vanessa watched in amazement as he brought down the manor house, so to speak. She stood and clapped with everyone. Her aunt turned, spotted her, and smiled.

It felt as if some of his Austen quotes were speaking directly to her at times, and it occurred to her that it might be time that she gave the author another chance.

Perhaps her aunt had been on to something all these years. Was there something beyond the happily-ever-after stories and the demure portrait of a woman in a white ruffled cap that popped into Vanessa's head every time "Jane Austen" was mentioned?

Julian was up next. Time for another post:

Get your photo with Mr. Darcy in loosened cravat & unbuttoned waistcoat after the #UndressingMrDarcy show—stage left. #JASNAagm #smileforthecamera

This was just one of Vanessa's ideas for Julian that had taken some persuading via handwritten letter, but the donations already garnered from the photography session had proven sizable.

She turned on her video cam and panned the crowd. She zoomed in on a woman in a blue Regency gown, her hair up in a bun and her gloves pinned at her side with one elbow, texting. Another woman, also dressed in a gown, had a fake stuffed pug dog in her lap.

Men came to these conferences, too. Some in the crowd had dressed in Regency regimental red, while others wore coats and cravats. None, though, looked as convincing as Julian.

She did a final pan of the crowd with the camera, then swiveled it toward the stage, where Paul began to rally the room in anticipation of Mr. Darcy.

Someone, meanwhile, lifted Vanessa's video bag from the chair next to her and set it on the ground.

"I needed to get closer for this one," a voice said. The curvy woman, probably in her early thirties, with rosy cheeks and chewing bubble gum, wore gym shoes, white pants, and a white T-shirt. The *I* ♥ *Mr. Darcy* on her shirt in huge black letters with a gigantic red heart really popped. She didn't fit the usual Janeite profile.

She leaned in toward Vanessa and whispered as Paul spoke. "Mr. Darcy saved my life, you know." She nodded, raising her eyebrows high.

Vanessa couldn't help but notice her suspenders and conference badge, studded with flair. Buttons galore glared at Vanessa with Mr. Darcyisms such as *How ardently I admire and love you* and *Every savage can dance.* Then there were the buttons and stickers proclaiming things such as *Mrs. Darcy* and *Married to Darcy*. She even had Darcy earrings, and Vanessa could see why she must've pulled her thick black hair back into a ponytail. It was punctuated with a button: *Darcy's Baby Mama*.

Seven hundred intelligent people in the room, and Vanessa got saddled with the resident superfan. But maybe she could use a young insider's perspective.

"I was on the verge of suicide I was so depressed," she said. "But then, walking home from work one day, on the sidewalk, there it was: a beat-up, paperback version of *Pride and Prejudice*. I took it as a sign, picked it up, went home, read it, and fell in love with Mr. Darcy. He saved my life." She sighed and held out her hand. "I'm Sherry, a.k.a. Mrs. D."

Of course she was! Vanessa shook.

"Or do you like one of Austen's other heroes better?"

Vanessa smiled. "No, no. I like Darcy." She couldn't believe she just said that.

"What a smorgasbord of activities for us, huh?" Sherry asked as she leafed through the conference brochure. "I've been looking forward to this all year. It's like an all-you-can-eat buffet for people like us, isn't it?"

"Yes." Vanessa chuckled. She liked Sherry. She liked how she just assumed Vanessa was one of them.

Sherry was right, too, about the conference program. The program committee had painstakingly selected the lecture and workshop topics to appeal to a broad range of fans—from scholars to the moviegoers who had never even read Austen. Even a person as indifferent to Austen as Vanessa could find several of the workshop and lecture topics intriguing. Beyond the lectures about Austen and the novels, you could learn about everything from snuff to Regency dance to "fallen women" of the Regency—mistresses, courtesans, and prostitutes.

Vanessa checked to be sure the video cam was focused on Paul. He was such an adorable and entertaining man, just a little younger than Aunt Ella, but healthier. His antiques auction house kept him busy and traveling. Vanessa wanted to listen to what he was saying, but Sherry interrupted.

"So"—Sherry nodded toward the video cam—"you know this Mr. Darcy? You have—access?"

Vanessa laughed and whispered back. "Access to Mr. Darcy? Yes, I have access."

She figured she had a live one, so she handed Sherry a postcard with all Julian's upcoming appearances, even though she'd already made sure that all the conference attendees had the information in their tote bags. She'd designed and printed hundreds of these "invitations" from Mr. Darcy that looked very much like an invitation to a ball, but really just listed his appearances, and Aunt Ella and the hospitality committee found the invitations to be "very clever indeed."

Sherry gave a toothy grin and her cheeks turned redder as she read the card and then stuck it in her tote bag, which she had decorated with more Mr. Darcy buttons. Snapping her gum, she said, "I'm sticking with you, girl."

Vanessa heard Paul say, "Without further ado, I introduce to you the master of Pemberley, Mr. Fitzwilliam Darcy."

The crowd clapped enthusiastically as Julian sauntered out.

Sherry pointed her finger at Vanessa and mouthed, "Sticking with you, girl," again because by now the crowd was clapping even louder for Julian, who stood center stage.

"Wow, he is h-o-t," Sherry said as she fanned herself with her conference program. "You know what I mean? Smokin'. Best damn Darcy I've seen yet, don't you think?"

Vanessa nodded yes, even though she had never seen any Darcys other than the ones on film, inadvertently, at her aunt's.

As she made sure the video cam was focused on Julian and Paul, the "valet," Sherry kept fanning herself.

"Mmm-mmm," Sherry said until the bonneted woman in front of them turned around.

Vanessa looked at Sherry and, with a smile, put her fingers on her lips to shush her, and then pointed to the video cam. She got the message.

When Vanessa pulled out her camera to take still shots for posting later, Sherry started taking pictures with her phone, and Julian's deep voice dominated the room.

"Welcome. Welcome everyone," Julian said.

He wore a black top hat pulled low over his forehead, just above his black eyebrows, really accentuating his dark brown eyes. His shoulders looked even broader in an outer coat with a shoulder cape. His white cravat had been lavishly tied and jutted out just enough from his tailcoat to draw attention to his neck and face. He wore flesh-colored breeches, black boots, and leather gloves and sported a walking stick, flicking it back and forth as he crossed the stage.

Even Vanessa had to admit he pretty much rocked this look like nobody else could. He played the rooster in the henhouse very well.

He shot the audience a serious look, rubbed his jaw, paused, and then smiled as he said, "Welcome . . . to Mr. Darcy's dressing room."

The audience went aflutter. Sherry pumped her fist and mouthed, "Woot! Woot!" to Vanessa, who realized she needed to be tweeting during the performance, too. She picked up her phone and set it in her lap. She'd received several more replies to the opening dance contest.

"My valet, Nelson, is here to do the honors of assisting me today."

Julian pronounced "valet" with a hard *t* at the end. Even though Vanessa spoke French and knew the French word required a silent *t*, she suddenly took a liking to the English way of saying it. Va-let.

Julian made a flourish with his hand. "Nelson?"

Paul took a bow and everyone clapped.

Julian began to pace the floor in his sexy boots and Vanessa had to scramble just to keep the video camera on him.

"Now. No doubt many of you are concentrating on my—ahem—" He paused to great effect, giving his coat a swoosh and the audience a flash of his breeches. The audience laughed. "My—hat."

He tipped his hat to the assembly, and Nelson readied to take it from him, but Julian was bluffing, garnering yet another laugh from the audience.

He was a master at working the crowd!

"The beaver hat is a staple in the gentleman's wardrobe, and a gentleman certainly wouldn't be seen riding a steed without one."

Vanessa didn't want to visualize him riding a horse, but there it was, stuck in her head now, thanks to him.

"Hat production is integral to the British economy, and it employs many workers, from carders who comb the fibers to highly skilled journeymen and master milliners. Hats are made for all manner of occasion, from fashion to the front lines."

She had never thought of the legions of people who must've been employed to make something so simple as a hat, and she needed to post something but—

Julian took off the hat, sending some dark hair tumbling forward, and held it out for the audience to admire. A far cry from an Abraham Lincoln–style top hat, this "beaver hat" had a style all its own.

"The hats are crafted with the undercoat of a beaver and quite impervious to the—lovely English weather. Beaver pelts were imported from Russia and Scandinavia, but due to overtrapping, hatters have turned to a place we call the American Colonies. Perhaps you've heard of them?"

Once again, Julian scored a laugh.

"Beaver pelts were the first great commodity to come out of the Colonies, and upwards of thirty thousand pelts a year are exported.

"The beaver fur holds up well under successive dousings, and these high-quality hats can really take a beating and still retain their elegant and handsome shape."

Along with everyone else, she smiled at his undertones, but she appreciated the education—a perk seldom received from most of her clients.

"Nelson? If you please?" Julian handed Paul his walking stick and then the hat, which now held a history. Paul took them offstage.

Julian ran his fingers through his black hair. "A gentleman no longer wears a powdered wig as our fathers did. We keep our hair short on the sides, sideburns squared off, and combed forward, rather like a classic Roman statue. Indeed, the style is known as 'à la Brutus' or 'à la Titus.'"

Vanessa straightened in her chair as soon as she realized she was twirling her own hair around her finger.

Paul returned to the stage as Julian slid off his brown leather gloves, finger by finger.

"A gentleman's gloves," Julian said as he paced the stage with Paul following, "need to be prepared afresh every day. They get rather gritty with all the riding and traveling from Pemberley to London."

Poof. Her brain provided a snapshot. Him. On horseback again.

"These gloves for outdoor use are made of calfskin, and ideally a gentleman owns no less than six pairs of gloves, to be worn at certain times throughout the day. Each with distinctive material and cut for each unique use." He handed the gloves to Paul, who bowed and whisked them offstage.

Vanessa looked at Sherry, who nodded her head in approval and smirked. She whispered, "Uh-huh. That's what I'm talking about. He's taking it off!"

Vanessa sent out a post:

We have seen the pale flesh of Mr. Darcy. He has removed his riding gloves. #UndressingMrDarcy #JASNAagm

"My greatcoat," Julian continued, "is made of wool. It is caped to keep me warm and to repel the rain." He gestured toward the wool capes that bracketed his shoulders. "The caping has the added effect of broadening a gentleman's already broad shoulders."

A slight murmur rippled through the audience as Paul removed Julian's greatcoat.

Sherry leaned in to Vanessa and whispered, "Now we're getting somewhere."

Vanessa snapped a pic and leaned back. Maybe it was because she had to look up at him on the stage or maybe it was his most revealing breeches tucked into riding boots or perhaps it was the way he all but strutted onstage . . . but she suddenly felt starstruck. Every woman in the room had her eyes on him.

She scanned the crowd for Aunt Ella, who was, evidently, pleased. The entire room seemed transfixed. Even the knitters had set their knitting in their laps.

"A Regency gentleman's entire wardrobe is styled on riding wear and emphasizes the natural beauty of the male form," Julian said. "The tight-fitting, perfectly tailored tailcoat you see me wearing is cut away here." He motioned around his hip bones, then his rib cage. "To provide even more flexibility in the saddle, the coat is high waisted. And . . ." He turned his back to the audience. "Two long tails have been cut so as to lie well whilst on horse."

He put a hand on his hip, swooshed the tails, and slowly turned to face the audience. He had swagger in clothing that had been out of fashion for more than two hundred years, and Vanessa heard an audible sigh from the audience.

"As you can see, I chose the green tailcoat. Choice of clothing is very important. I believe I said to my valet, 'No, no, the green one.'"

This must've been some kind of inside joke, because everyone but Vanessa laughed.

Sherry leaned in. "That was the color coat he insisted on wearing when he proposed to Elizabeth—the second time. In the 1995 *Pride and Prejudice*."

Vanessa nodded.

He unbuttoned his tailcoat and Paul slid it off his shoulders, revealing his form-fitting breeches, waistcoat, and puffy shirt (as she liked to call it).

Julian turned sideways and paced the stage again. All the bonneted and feather-topped heads in the room followed his movements.

He stopped, folded his arms, and spoke. "Naked from a distance."

That got attention, all right. Sherry squeezed Vanessa's knee for a moment.

Julian put a hand on his hip. "The snugly tailored, flesh-colored breeches, the tan silk waistcoat, the white shirt—it's all meant to create the illusion of 'naked from a distance' just like a classic Greek or Roman marble statue."

He did look rather—statuesque . . . Vanessa snapped to and then snapped a pic to post.

Naked from a distance. #JASNAagm #UndressingMrDarcy #wishyouwerehere

"As you know, we emulate the classic Greek and Roman eras in our clothing, our architecture, and our art."

Vanessa didn't know that, and she'd always been intrigued by classical Greek and Roman culture.

"My waistcoat is cut a little lower at the front than my day coat, to show off my watch chain and key-fob attachment. This is where my signet—my wax seal for my letters—hangs."

Sherry nudged Vanessa with her elbow. "Are you thinking what I'm thinking?"

Unfortunately, yes, Vanessa thought.

Julian unbuttoned his waistcoat, and was it her imagination, or was he looking right at her? She looked away, toward the clock that didn't seem to be moving fast enough. By the time she looked back, Paul had removed Julian's waistcoat and taken it offstage.

"To be seen in my shirtsleeves, as you know, is absolutely indecent."

The crowd laughed.

Sherry nodded her head. "Uh-huh. Uh-huh!"

Vanessa took another picture and posted across the sites:

How very risqué of Mr. Darcy to appear in his shirtsleeves @TheHyatt. #JASNAagm #UndressingMrDarcy #hot

She began to believe her own hype, a very dangerous situation for her. She could easily crank out this kind of stuff when she didn't fall prey to it herself. He was not hot. He was a client.

"The white linen shirt is considered an undergarment, and I would not take off my waistcoat in front of a lady unless I knew her *very* well."

The audience went abuzz.

"The collar points of the shirt and the cravat are designed to outline the strength of a gentleman's jaw."

Now that he mentioned it, he did have a very strong jawline. Vanessa sighed, exasperated with herself, and, determined to focus on more significant issues, she scrolled through her e-mail in-box and double-checked her phone to be sure it was on vibrate for when the doctor called.

Now Julian had settled into a chair onstage and she had to adjust the video cam again.

Once she had focused on him with the camera, she found it difficult to take her eyes off him. He commanded the stage even while sitting.

"During the course of a day, I dress, and undress, some three or four times. I require, per week: twenty shirts, twenty-four pocket handkerchiefs, ten summer breeches, thirty cravats, a dozen waistcoats, stockings, and a chintz dressing gown and Turkish slippers for taking my breakfast and reading the day's paper."

Turkish slippers. His morning paper. This painted a picture she didn't want in her mind.

"My cravat, made of fine Irish muslin, is a triangle folded twice and wrapped carefully around the neck, and can be tied in various knots, depending on my mood." He smiled, slid his index finger into the front of the knot at the base of his throat, and pulled. With another yank, he successfully untied and slid off the cravat.

"Beau Brummell declared the starched cravat fashionable, and it is reported that washerwomen fainted upon the declaration. Not only do they have yet another thirty items to add to the washing and ironing, but each cravat has to be semistarched. Not full-starched with the rest of the wash, mind you, but semistarched."

With the cravat handed to Paul, Julian began unbuttoning his shirt.

"I'm undoing the small Dorset buttons at the neck of my shirt. Note that the buttons do not run the full length of the shirt."

He undid his cuff buttons, and, in a dramatic swoosh, he yanked his shirt from his breeches, lifted it over his head, and handed it over to Paul, and the audience clapped and smiled at Julian, his bare torso rippling with muscles, in only his breeches and boots.

Sherry cocked her head at Vanessa. "Are you all right? You look flushed. Sure you're okay?"

Vanessa wasn't sure. "Of course. I'm fine." The room sort of spun around her. It was Julian—that's what it was. She was attracted to him, and the thought hit her like a ton of starched cravats. Why a client? And why *this* client?

"I'm worried about you." Sherry turned and pointed to the stage. "Whoa! Check him out! He is ripped!"

Vanessa made sure the camera followed Julian as he strutted across the stage, his broad shoulders and muscular biceps evident.

"You can see I've been spending time fencing, riding, and boxing. Which is why I don't require a stomacher, or girdle, as some men are wont to rely on. Nor do I need padding for my calves." He motioned toward his boots. "We gentlemen of the Regency pride ourselves on our well-turned calves."

Sherry kept whispering, "Wow. Check out his abs. Those abs!"

Vanessa, still feeling dizzy, felt her phone vibrate with a call. It was the doctor. She had to take it, or she'd miss talking to him for another grueling twenty-four hours.

"Sherry, I have to go. Can you stay with my equipment? I'll be back. My assistant is right over there." She pointed to Kai.

She signaled to Kai that she was stepping out.

"Sure. But he's about to take off his breeches," Sherry whispered. "You're not leaving *now*, are you?"

Vanessa nodded and, as discreetly as possible, phone and briefcase in hand, she bolted.

*T*he test results are in," the nurse said as Vanessa leaned up against the wall in the hotel hallway. "The doctor would like you and your aunt to arrange an appointment as soon as possible to discuss everything."

Behind the closed doors in back of her, the room resounded with applause. She looked out the hall window onto a cloudless blue urban sky. For once she was speechless.

"I'm going to transfer you to reception, okay?"

Vanessa booked the appointment for the following day, knowing

Aunt Ella would not be pleased at having to miss some of the conference. But, with Vanessa's upcoming trip to Louisville with Julian, when else could she do it?

Her eyes landed on a tray with several Jane Austen silhouette cookies left on it. She picked one up and took a bite, inadvertently decapitating Jane, leaving only her silhouetted neck.

She headed toward the window, seeking the sunshine, running another Internet search of "dementia" on her phone when—smack.

She bumped right into—a leather-vested pirate?

"Sorry," she said and continued her search.

"I'm not," said the pirate.

His aftershave hinted of cocoa butter. Or was he wearing tanning oil?

She finally looked up. He resembled Johnny Depp's Captain Jack Sparrow from those—what—*Pirates of the Caribbean* movies?

"Wait a minute. Don't I know you from somewhere?" he asked and squinted at her, his brown eyes lined with kohl.

She was in no mood for a stale pickup line from a pirate.

He continued talking. "But *where* do I know you from? Are you an auctioneer?"

Why did he think she was an auctioneer like Paul?

He leaned against the opposite wall and crossed his buccaneer boots.

Another man in costume and boots? Major skull-and-crossbones red flag.

"Can I buy you a drink?"

"At ten thirty in the morning?"

"You look like you need a drink. Or coffee?"

He was right. But she didn't want to lead the pirate on. "I don't chug rum out of a bottle before noon, thank you very much for the kind offer. I need to get back to work."

Her phone vibrated with a call from the doctor's reception desk. "Hello?"

The pirate snapped his fingers and nodded.

"Yes," she said into the phone. "Of course I'll bring in a list of all her current meds. Thank you." She hung up. How could she break this to her aunt?

"Vanessa Roberts?" he asked. "Ella Morgan's niece?"

"Yes . . ."

She checked her watch.

"I'm Chase MacClane. We met briefly a few months ago? At a cocktail party? I wasn't dressed for Hero Con then. I work with your aunt's boyfriend, Paul."

She looked up from her phone. "They're close friends, and it's very sweet, but Paul's not her . . . *boyfriend*—"

"Don't tell him that! Anyway, you were pretty preoccupied at the party with some business crisis or another, so you may not remember me."

She met so many people in her line of work. No, she didn't remember him. And she needed to get back to Julian—er, work. "Nice to see you again, but I have to get back."

"Paul asked me to meet him here. This session should be letting out any minute, right? Give my best to your aunt." He stopped smiling. "If there's anything I can do, let me know."

Had Paul told him, an employee, about her aunt's diagnosis? "I'll let Paul know you're here."

"Would you like to join us for lunch? Your aunt will be there."

"I'm afraid not—I'm working through lunch today. But thank you."

Back inside the main conference room, a speaker was giving closing remarks while Julian sat waiting at the photo setup, his hair mussed, cravat loosened, and waistcoat slightly unbuttoned.

Another image she didn't need seared into her mind: the slightly disheveled, post-historical-striptease look.

Kai was adjusting his camera on the tripod, searching for the best angle on Julian, so all seemed fine on that front, and she needn't intervene.

"Welcome, once again, to Chicago," the speaker said as everyone started to clap. "And enjoy the conference!"

The entire room stood and Vanessa hurried to Sherry, asking her to join Kai if she could, and she seemed thrilled to do so. Vanessa then hustled over to her aunt.

"Aunt Ella!"

"Oh, Vanessa, thank goodness you've come to see me. I do wish, sometimes, that I could bring myself to use that cell phone you gave me. But it's such a bother."

"We have to talk," Vanessa said.

"Yes, we do. We have a problem, I'm afraid."

"Wait. What problem are you talking about?"

Paul came and put his arm around her aunt.

Vanessa noticed a gorgeous bouquet of flowers in her aunt's arms. "Where did the flowers come from?"

Aunt Ella looked at her quizzically. "Why, Julian, of course."

"Julian?"

"Vanessa, we have a delicate situation on our hands. Do you remember my friend Anne, the bonnet maker from Nebraska?"

"Yes."

"It seems that her young daughter Emily . . . remember her?"

"Of course. But I haven't seen her in a few years."

"It seems Emily has run off into the city—with a masked twenty-year-old man from Hero Con."

"What?" How did her aunt get word about this so quickly without so much as a cell phone?

"Surely if a girl's going to run off, I would hope it would be with a Regency rogue at worst, but this I cannot understand. The girl's hardly eighteen, and Anne's beside herself. Emily isn't responding to any of her calls or texts and Anne can't leave her vendor stall in the Emporium to look for her and—"

"You understand, Auntie E, that Emily is legally an adult."

"I do. But I've known her mother for almost as many years through this society, and I won't have a comic-book character bring down my conference with this kind of scandal. Any thoughts?" Beads of sweat formed on her forehead.

Vanessa had to take care of this for her aunt's peace of mind, that much was clear. She looked at Paul, and then it hit her. "Paul, what's your employee Chase MacClane's number?"

"Smart thinking, Vanessa. Chase is right here in the building and he will get to the bottom of this. He's very good in quests of all kinds." Paul pulled out his phone. "Here's his number."

Vanessa called.

"But he's not just my employee, no, he's much more than that. He stands to run the auction house very soon. He's my protégé."

"Chase? Hi. It's Vanessa. Vanessa Roberts? Didn't expect me to take you up on your offer so soon, did you?"

The distraught bonnet maker twisted fabric in her hands at her vendor stall while she spoke with Vanessa and Chase, showing them the latest texts from her daughter that morning, hoping for a clue of some kind. Bonnets hung around them like balloons, but the occasion wasn't happy.

Vanessa keyed Emily's name and number into her phone, even though Emily wasn't responding to texts. Vanessa immediately followed her on all the social network sites she could. "She hasn't made any recent posts, but let's see if she uses any location social media— if she's checked in anywhere."

"Good idea," said Chase.

"Excuse me?" the bonnet maker asked.

"You're in good hands," Chase reassured the woman.

"We can't alert police yet," Vanessa said. "Technically she's of age, and she's only been gone an hour. It also sounds as if she went willingly—"

"Oh, I'm sure she went willingly. She's just like Lydia Bennet and she'll be the death of me!"

That reference was lost on Vanessa. Her phone pinged. "It looks like she just checked in at the Millennium Park fountains."

"She's wearing an Empire-waist day gown," the bonnet maker said. "She should stand out in a crowd."

Aunt Ella and Paul broke into the tiny circle.

"So nice to see you, Chase," Aunt Ella said.

Chase beamed and hugged her. "And you. Only not under these circumstances."

Aunt Ella took the bonnet maker's hand in hers. "Not to worry, Anne. We'll have Emily back in no time."

"Could someone please find her for me? I don't even know my way around Chicago," Anne said.

Aunt Ella turned to Vanessa as she rubbed her pearls between her fingers. "We'll take care of it, Anne. She won't get into trouble like last year."

Vanessa e-mailed photos of Emily to Chase's phone. "Chase, do you have time to help out with this?"

"I'm happy to help. I'll start off at the fountains. I'll call as soon as I know something." He pivoted to leave.

"Wait." Aunt Ella raised her hand to stop him. "Vanessa, I want you to go with him. It's only proper when a teenage girl is involved."

"But—what about Julian?" Vanessa asked.

"Julian is fine. This takes precedence. We just passed by his photo session and there are enough women in line to last at least an hour.

Kai is in charge. And I see Sherry has stepped in to help you with him."

"You know Sherry?" Vanessa asked as she stepped backward, toward the Emporium's exit.

"I know all of the Chicago members. Sherry often does theatrical readings for us. She's very talented that way. She's a gem."

Vanessa continued walking backward, checking her phone for signs of Emily. "Oh!" She brushed against something and when she turned around, she saw it happened to be a little boy dressed in gold-buckled shoes, knickers, a waistcoat, and shirt. "I'm so sorry!" The boy ran back to his mother at the Jane Austen Books stall. "Is he okay?"

"He's fine." His mother picked him up.

Chase tipped his tricorn hat to the boy, who giggled.

"Oh, good!" She couldn't help but smile at this young Austen inductee, attending the national meeting *in costume*, no less.

"We'd better go," Vanessa said to Chase as she looked back at the Emporium, a world with one ballroom-slippered foot in the Regency and one here in the twenty-first century.

It wasn't until they got out of the cab in the searing sunshine of Millennium Park that she remembered she was with a costumed pirate.

They hustled to the Bean, a mirrorlike chrome sculpture, polished to a high shine, in the shape of a kidney bean, and nearly three stories high. Officially the sculpture was known as *Cloud Gate*.

As they passed it, she caught a glimpse of Chase behind her in the reflection, his honeyed skin as tanned as if he really were a pirate. People stopped to gape at him, but he didn't flinch.

Vanessa leaned over the thick concrete rail and scanned the crowd on the sidewalks and then the Crown Fountain.

"I think we need to split up," Chase said. "You start on the north side of the fountains and I'll hit the south."

The modern fountains, great blocks of streaming water with a wading pool between them, had attracted a throng of people who had taken their shoes off and walked barefoot in the water on this warm September day. Then she saw a blue gown with a gray bonnet hanging from the back of it, and a girl lifting her hemline as she stepped into the water.

"That's got to be her." Vanessa grabbed Chase's hand just as he began to step away.

Why did she do that? She let his hand go.

"Come on! I have a plan." Her plan included making sure this girl was Emily, because it had been a while since she'd seen her. She slid her sunglasses on and hurried to the wading pool.

Once there, she kicked off her shoes and headed right in toward the girl, who was chatting with a guy in a Batman costume, except for his bare feet.

Vanessa yanked her phone out of her bag. "Excuse me, are you two here for Hero Con and the Jane Austen Society conference?"

They looked at her askance.

"Can I take a couple of shots of you for the press? One of the Chicago papers will probably run the shot online."

Yes, it was Emily.

"Oh, no!" Emily said, not recognizing Vanessa. "No, thank you." She turned her back and dropped her gown and the hemline got wet. She yanked it out of the water.

Vanessa flagged Chase. Now to lure the teen in.

"Excuse me again?" she said to the young, unlikely-looking pair. "Would you take a picture of us, then? We're here for the conferences, too."

Emily rolled her eyes. "Okay."

Chase splashed in next to Vanessa.

"This nice couple is going to take a picture of us, honey," Vanessa said. She stood next to Chase and smiled, racking her brain as to how to lure the teenager back without offending her.

"Oh, good!" Chase said. "We never get enough pictures of us as a couple, do we?" Without hesitation he put his arm around her waist and pulled her close, so they stood hip to hip. Then he patted her ass!

"Dar-ling!" Vanessa said as she wriggled away from him.

"What?"

"You know what! We don't want to embarrass ourselves."

"Don't be silly, sweetheart," Chase said. "An old couple like us, embarrassed? Come on." And he kissed her on the lips! She swore she could taste coconut.

"Listen," he said to Emily and Batman, "why don't you let us spring for a cab back to the hotel? It'll save you seven bucks. The next session starts in fifteen minutes, and something tells me that Batman wouldn't want to miss the martial arts demos, would you?"

Vanessa stepped closer to Emily and took off her sunglasses. "I think we'd better come clean. It's me, Vanessa Roberts? My aunt is Ella Morgan?"

"Vanessa?" Emily asked. She raised her voice. "My mother sent you two after me, didn't she? She's always so overprotective and freaking out and stuff!"

"Well, of course she is," Chase said. "You're a beautiful young woman."

Emily's face softened. "Thank you."

"And you've run off with a Dark Knight." He smirked.

"We didn't run off . . ." Emily's voice trailed.

"I know, but you'd better explain that to her," he said. "She's worried sick about you. We'd better hustle. Let's go introduce your mother to the Caped Crusader." He walked toward the fountain's edge, dried his tanned feet, and pulled on his buccaneer boots. To Vanessa's surprise, Emily and Batman followed him. He was like the Pied Piper of renegade young adults.

Vanessa never thought she'd be in the backseat of a cab between Batman and a young Bennet sister, with a pirate riding shotgun in the front.

The three of them sat in awkward silence in the back until she complimented Emily on her ring, a familiar and beautiful, if simple, gold band with a turquoise-colored stone. Her aunt had a ring just like it.

"Thank you," Emily said. "It's a replica of the only Jane Austen ring that's ever been auctioned to the public. The original had been in the family for generations, passed down from Cassandra—you know, her sister? But someone from the family offered it up for auction at Sotheby's not too long ago. Maybe you heard about it?"

"No—what happened?"

"Kelly Clarkson won the auction and paid more than two hundred and thirty thousand dollars for the ring."

"Kelly Clarkson the singer—is a Jane Austen fan?"

Emily furrowed her blond brows. "Lots of people are Austen fans."

"Yes, yes, I know."

"The sad thing was she couldn't even take the ring out of the country, because once she bought it, Britain declared the ring a national treasure."

"Wow, that's too bad," Vanessa said. She wondered why the family would have auctioned it off instead of just passing it down. Hard economic times even for the descendants of Austen?

"Do you have a gown for the ball?" Emily asked, in a non sequitur only a teenager could pull off.

Chase slid open the plastic window between the front and back seats, as if waiting for her answer.

"Well . . ." Vanessa hadn't planned on going in costume to the ball.

"Is he going as a pirate?" She nodded toward Chase.

Chase turned around. "I *do* hope we're going. We are, aren't we? In our costumes? It'll be a blast."

Vanessa smiled and took up her phone to text Emily's mother, letting her know they were on their way. Several e-mails had piled up, reminding her she needed to get back to #*working* and posting for Julian.

"This whole thing reminds me of the story of how Vanessa and I first met," Chase said. "You'd never believe this, but we were just about your age."

"You were?" Emily asked.

Vanessa sat back and folded her arms, ready to take in the show. Who *was* this guy?

"She was a senior, I was a junior, and I voted for her for student council president."

Vanessa had to smile at his improvisation skills.

"How sweet," Emily said.

"Go on," Vanessa said. She wanted to see where he was going with this, although she did run for, and win, the election for student council president as a senior. "Tell her which high school we went to."

"Lincoln."

Her phone slid from her hands and into her lap. Then again, maybe he knew that through Paul. Or even her LinkedIn profile.

"I asked her out for a burger, but senior girls never date juniors, do they?"

Emily smiled.

That never *happened*, did it? Did they really go to high school together?

"Flash-forward a few decades later, and we meet at a party, but she's preoccupied with a client on the phone and doesn't even remember meeting me *or* the fact that we went to high school together."

"Really?" Emily asked.

Even Batman sighed. "Harsh."

She remembered the party now, and yes, she remembered him there. Handsome. Funny. But she didn't remember him from high school. "In my defense, it was code blue for one of my clients while I was at that party," Vanessa said.

"But, apparently, meeting for the third time was the charm. Here we are!"

"What do you mean 'here we are'?" Vanessa asked.

"I mean we're here, at the hotel." Chase smirked as he paid the cabbie. "Everybody out and straight to the Emporium!"

Who was this man-pirate? She knew the conference hotel well, but which portal had she fallen into with rebellious bonnet makers' daughters and pirates from her past? Had they really gone to high school together? When would be a good time to tell Aunt Ella about tomorrow's doctor's appointment? And what state of undress would Julian be in after being left improperly chaperoned with a roomful of Darcy fans?

Chapter 4

*M*other and daughter were reunited, Batman was brought into the fold of bonnet makers, and the scandal had been averted. Vanessa made Julian her next priority despite her compulsion to check up on her aunt. She explained to Chase that no, she wouldn't have time for lunch; she needed to find her client.

Her phone pinged with messages. "Thank you, Chase, for wrangling our wayward young Janeite back. It was very nice of you." He seemed about to say something, but she left him with that and hurried to the main conference hall, where all that was left on the chair where Julian had been sitting was an untied cravat and a note.

She sent out a post:

MIA: Mr. Darcy. Message me with any sightings. #JASNAagm #UndressingMrDarcy #heissointrouble

When she picked up the cravat, it looked out of place in her black-manicured fingers.

And a *note?*

The note, nothing more than a thick piece of paper folded in half, had hints of his cologne, that musky, citrusy mix. Or was it coming from his cravat? She held the cravat to her nose, and yes, it came from the fabric, and the cologne hit notes of fresh lime. She began to realize that Julian was the first man in a long time that had the power to make her slow down and smell the—cravats—

"Did you find your Mr. Darcy?"

It was Chase who approached from behind her, a corner of his lip upturned in a smile, amused at catching her with her nose in Julian's cravat! She whisked it away from her face and folded the starched thing as best she could, and the note fluttered to the floor.

Chase picked it up and handed it to her.

"No, I haven't found him, but he left this note."

"Seriously?"

"He doesn't like to break his Mr. Darcy character by using a phone."

"I see." Chase smiled.

She could see he thought something snarky, but he didn't say it.

"I thought you had to find Paul," Vanessa asked.

"I do, but he's not picking up. His phone's probably not getting great reception in here. I figured he's with your aunt and the Englishman. So. Where is this elusive client of yours?"

She unfolded the note.

Dearest Vanessa,

He had gorgeous penmanship. She'd never seen her name so beautifully written. Come to think of it, she hadn't seen her name handwritten in cursive by any man in a long time.

I have had the pleasure of meeting one of your friends, Lexi Stone, who has kindly invited Sherry, Kai, and me to lunch at the sushi

*restaurant in the building. She asked your aunt and Paul, but they
declined. Please join us at your earliest convenience.*

*Yours,
Julian*

"Is everything all right?" Chase asked.

"Yes," Vanessa lied. It hadn't taken Lexi long to find Julian. Then
again, maybe Lexi had changed. "But Paul and my aunt aren't with
them."

She didn't know what to do first—try to find her aunt or hunt
down Julian. She dialed Kai. "Kai? Where is everyone right now?"

"We're in the lobby having coffee at the coffee bar. Well, Julian's
having tea. Your friend Lexi bought us lunch. Why haven't I met her
before? She's really something."

"She's something, all right. Is Julian with you? And Sherry with
the equipment?"

"Yeah. Speaking of which, I have to show you the footage—"

"Yes, I want to edit it and get a teaser uploaded to the sites right
away. I'll be right down." She eyed her watch. "I'm going down to
the lobby first," she said to Chase as she took long strides toward the
elevators.

"I'll find your aunt and Paul and let you know where they are."

"Thank you, Chase." He was a quick thinker, and that was cool!

Once she stepped into the lobby full of creatures from Hero Con
and headed for the coffee bar, she had the sense that Lexi had already done some damage.

Sherry made her way toward her through the winged, caped, and
antennaed crowd, her ponytail bobbing.

"Guess what?" Sherry asked. Without waiting for an answer she
said, "We're all going to Bath! Bath, England! For the mother of all
Jane Austen events: the nine-day Jane Austen Festival! Julian invited

us and you're invited, too! Your friend Lexi was already planning on going, but Julian has given us free passes! Do you have any plans for the week of September fourteenth?"

"I don't think I'll be . . . going to Bath," Vanessa said as her eyes landed on Julian. Was it his height, or something more, that set him above the crowd? "I'll be working, for one thing. But how nice of him to give everyone free passes."

The costumed woman next to him turned around and it was none other than Lexi in the guise of Xena, Warrior Princess, complete with a black-haired wig to cover her usual severe red bob, an armored bustier, scrolled wrist guards, studded leather miniskirt, and black fringed boots.

Her costume alone could slay entire nations.

She air-kissed Vanessa.

"Vanessa. Great to see you again." She eyed Vanessa up and down. "You look fabulous, if a little—plainly dressed for the occasion. But you never did like playing dress-up." She lowered her voice to a whisper. "Listen, I'd really love for us to be friends again. Bury the hatchet? I've changed, thanks to you."

It didn't look like she had changed at all, not even her fashion sense.

Vanessa took a deep breath. "Hello, Lexi." She had run into her a few times since their fallout but had managed to avoid any real interaction since she'd dissolved their co-owned PR boutique.

They had honed their PR chops together, but Lexi had slept with a client who happened to be a friend of Aunt Ella's. It turned out he was not the first of their mutual clients she had slept with. Aunt Ella never found out. But all this had happened more than six years ago now, and the details had become fuzzy. Vanessa found it hard to remember exactly what happened, and the anger had long since subsided. They were, after all, just kids in their twenties, and people grow up, don't they?

Nevertheless, Vanessa had no desire even to befriend her on social media, but she didn't want to engage in female warrior combat, either. She just wanted to go on without Lexi in her life. A simple request, really. "I'm guessing you're here for Hero Con and not the Jane Austen Society?"

"Both. I'm here on business for Hero Con first and foremost, though."

Had Lex Luthor hired her to do damage control? Perhaps she had joined forces with Darth Vader. Or was she sleeping with the Joker *and* Mr. Freeze? Instead Vanessa asked, "Oh? For whom?"

"I'm doing the PR for a graphic novel publishing house promoting a series of books about Xena."

So, she was putting the "graphic" in "graphic novel."

"Hero Con has become so huge. Huge! But, you know, not even the young vampires of Hero Con can keep me away from Darcy." She cast her blue eyes at Julian, who held a ceramic mug of tea from the coffee bar in one hand and a pen in another.

He had attracted a sizable crowd. Fans encircled him, asking him to sign his book, and this meant the show had been a hit.

Vanessa took a shot of him with her phone and posted:

Found: Mr. Darcy. Join the fray in the lobby near the . . . tea bar. #JASNAagm #UndressingMrDarcy

She waited for a natural break in the impromptu signing before talking to him. "I see you've met Lexi."

Julian nodded. "Oh, Lexi, yes. Listen, I do hope you'll join us all in Bath. It seems to be all settled."

She smiled. "Thank you for the invitation. But I'm sure you understand I can't possibly go to Bath—but, more importantly, how did the photo session go?"

"Brilliant! Just brilliant." He turned from his posse and looked her in the eye. "You've done some fabulous work for me."

"When we have a chance I'll take you through those new ideas I had."

"Looking forward to some time alone with you, Vanessa."

She took a step backward. "Now, don't let Lexi distract you from interacting with your fans. I'm just going to step aside to post some of the footage of your show. Don't go anywhere without me, please."

"Absolutely not."

Lexi nudged in next to him. "Don't worry. I won't let him out of my sight."

That was exactly what worried her. She had her doubts about leaving Julian with either Lexi or Xena, Warrior Princess, much less a combination of the two. She pulled Sherry aside. "Sherry? Would you be willing to chaperone Mr. Darcy while I'm editing the footage?"

Sherry cracked her bubble gum with a smile. "I am Mrs. D, after all, aren't I?"

Aunt Ella had been right; Sherry was a gem. "I'll have to think of some way to compensate you for your work."

Sherry laughed. "Oh, I'm compensated! It's hardly *work*."

A text came in from Chase saying he was having lunch with her aunt and Paul, and all seemed fine with them. Vanessa considered herself lucky to be so suddenly surrounded by reliable, helpful people like Chase and Sherry. Certainly, when it came to men, reliability ranked right up there along with good communication skills, and Chase, so far, seemed to have both. With the whole bonnet maker's daughter–Batman debacle he had proven himself resourceful, flexible, on time, and on task. He'd make a great business partner, but clearly Paul had already recognized that.

She found Kai at a tall table behind his laptop with headphones on, but she knew him well. Instead of working he was staring at Catwoman sipping a Bloody Mary. Vanessa slid his headphones off. "I didn't think you liked cats."

"Now I do." He laughed.

"Did we get some decent footage?"

"Yeah. I also got the audience reaction, too. Pretty flippin' awesome."

"What do you mean the audience reaction?" Vanessa asked.

"Those women were hot for him."

"That's exactly what we want!"

"Lots of fans fluttering in that room. Your photo session idea really worked, too."

"I guess it gave his donations an uptick. Did he announce his book signing and the social media handles?"

"He had Paul do that for him."

"Okay. Good solution. At least he took my advice in some capacity."

"Um, I just have to tell you that you and Julian really did a cool thing for your aunt today."

"What are you talking about, Kai?"

"You weren't there, but after his show was over, the audience was really into it, I mean, as jazzed as people get at one of these things, but he got them all to calm down, and he said you and he wanted to take a moment to recognize the founder of the Chicago Jane Austen Society, and he had your aunt stand up and said all kinds of amazing stuff about your aunt, and then he asked everyone to give her a hand, and they did, and she started tearing up, and I got that on video— you have to see it—and then the audience stood up and gave her a standing ovation, and, well, since this is going to be the last meeting in Chicago for another ten years or so, I just thought you should know. The guy's a dude, really. A cool dude."

"Wow. I didn't know a thing about it. Is it cued up? I have to see it—I can't believe I missed it—I had to take a call from the doctor's office—" She steadied herself by setting down her phone and holding on to the table.

In the frozen frame on the laptop, Julian stood onstage with a bouquet of flowers in hand, the very same bouquet that ended up in her aunt's arms.

Vanessa's phone vibrated with a call and, without looking at the caller ID, she picked up.

"Vanessa? It's Chase."

Vanessa kept staring at Julian holding the bouquet of flowers. "Hi," she said. She liked this shot of him holding the bouquet of cabbage roses, snapdragons, foxgloves—

"If you're free, why don't you join me for a swordsmanship workshop tomorrow at eleven thirty?"

Kai signaled to her that he needed to rewind a bit.

"Yes, that's fine," Vanessa said to Kai and, inadvertently, Chase.

"Great!" Chase said. "I'll let you get back to work. I'll be in touch."

Wait. What had she just said yes to?

"Let me know if you need any help rescuing wayward bonnet makers' daughters."

"I—I will—"

And he hung up.

A few seconds later he sent a text:

Swords r provided btw . . .

Vanessa stared at her phone. "Oh, no."

"Another thing to do?" Kai asked.

"Another thing to undo. I think. It was very nice of him—never mind. Let's get rolling here."

"Okay." He put the headphones on her and pressed play.

On the screen, Julian put his hand over his eyes and looked out into the audience. "I will ask again, is Vanessa Roberts in the house?"

"She had to step out," Sherry called out from the audience.

"I see. I know she wanted very much to help, as we both agreed to honor her aunt, the illustrious Ella Morgan, at this point in our program."

Vanessa hadn't known anything about this! Why did he mention her name?

Julian continued. "Ella Morgan, might you please stand up?"

He made his way to her with the mike, stopping briefly to pick up a bouquet of flowers from the front row.

When, where, and how did he arrange for the gorgeous flowers?

"Oh, my," Aunt Ella said as she stood.

"Miss Morgan," Julian said in a sincere and reverent voice, "you are solely responsible for bringing me here to this side of the pond, and I thank you, but that is the least of your many accomplishments. You are a one-of-a-kind 'lady' in the truest sense, because, much like the lady to the lord, you care for, and help take care of, so many people in your sphere of living. You are a benefactor to many causes, including helping to start the Chicago chapter of the Jane Austen Society in 1979 for the simple purpose of promoting study of her work. Look around you and see what you started!"

Aunt Ella laughed and blushed and beamed.

People in the audience began standing and clapping.

"Let us all take a moment to honor and thank Ella Morgan." Julian bowed and handed her the flowers.

Soon the entire room stood to clap and shout.

Aunt Ella was tearing up, Vanessa could see that.

Vanessa dabbed the corners of her eyes. More than the overwhelming feeling of guilt over missing that moment came the undeniable feeling that she would never again meet a man like Julian.

But he was a client, he would be gone in just over a week, and worse, he was, at the moment, surrounded by a throng of women and Lexi, leather-clad warrior princess.

"Let's edit this and get it uploaded as quickly as we can, Kai," she said.

She pulled a business card out of her wallet. "I have a mantua maker to see."

"A what?"

"I'm going to have a gown made."

The mantua maker, it turned out, was no fairy godmother.

"I'm not a fairy godmother," she said when Vanessa asked about a gown for the following night. She didn't laugh so much as she actually cackled along with her assistant. Her green eyes turned into little half-moons and her cheeks grew red with laughter. "These gowns are not off-the-rack. They're custom-made, just as they would've been in the Regency era."

Vanessa looked around, hoping the crowd in the Emporium, and especially Julian, who stood across the room, mixing and mingling at the Jane Austen Books stall as she'd instructed, didn't hear the dressmaker laughing at her.

The room buzzed with people, and the vendors on either side of the mantua maker were busy. On the left stood a table dedicated to Jane Austen Christmas ornaments, and on the right a woman sold Regency "reticules," silk drawstring purses.

Vanessa found herself drawn to one of them—for Aunt Ella, of course.

"If you need the gown for tomorrow night, you're best off going to a costume shop and renting one," the mantua maker said.

Vanessa made a mental note to look up costume shops.

The mantua maker eyed Vanessa up and down. "Although, a rental will look like a gunnysack on you, you're such a thin thing. Although you are well endowed . . ."

Vanessa blushed. She hadn't been—sized up like this ever. She leaned in and whispered, "What if I paid you overtime?"

The mantua maker folded her arms. "What kind of a gown are we talking about?"

Vanessa pulled out a pen and began sketching on the conference program. Her graphic skills were marginal at best, but she narrated as she went along. "There's this woman. She gave me your card, and she's petite, with brown hair? She had on a white gown—muslin, she called it—and it had a low, square neckline like this and off-the-shoulder sleeves like this, see? And—"

The mantua maker ripped the mediocre drawing out from under Vanessa's pen. "You're describing Jane Austen's gown."

"What? No. It was someone here, someone at the conference—"

"Yes. That's our Jane Austen. She's a Jane Austen actress—she plays Jane Austen. Her name is Deb Miller."

She had spoken to—Jane Austen? And Jane Austen had advised her to get a corset?

The mantua maker raised her voice. "That's a custom creation. You can't have Jane Austen's gown!"

The customers at the surrounding booths looked sideways at Vanessa.

This time *she* was causing a ruckus at the Jane Austen conference.

Suddenly she felt a hand on her shoulder, and she feared it would be Julian, but then she recognized the rings. It was Aunt Ella.

"Vanessa, my child, whatever are you doing here with Martha?"

"She wants a gown," the mantua maker said. "Not just any gown, but our Jane Austen's gown. And she wants it ready by tomorrow night."

Vanessa hadn't realized a group of customers had formed behind her.

"Never mind. I'm sorry. Please. Let your other customers go first—"

Aunt Ella held fast to Vanessa. "Wait. You want a gown? For yourself?"

Vanessa stepped back.

Aunt Ella smiled. "Answer me. Do you want a gown?"

Vanessa looked down until, just like when she was a little girl, Aunt Ella's hand lifted her chin. "You want to go to the ball in costume?"

"Yes."

Aunt Ella turned to the mantua maker. "Martha, my niece Vanessa needs a gown for tomorrow night. I have some ideas on how we could make it work."

"She's your niece? Why didn't she say so to begin with? Of course we can make something work!"

The two women conferred while the Emporium swelled with people buying their Jane Austen paraphernalia. Julian could be heard talking to a gaggle of women, and Vanessa leaned against the dressmaker's table for sheer strength.

She had wanted to keep this gown thing on the down low and see if she still felt as strongly about dressing up for the ball tomorrow, but now with Aunt Ella in the know, there was no going back. Her going to the ball in costume, though, might soften the blow of the doctor's appointment . . .

A quick check on her phone confirmed she already had two hundred and eleven women hoping to open the ball with Julian. Two hundred and eleven!

"It's all 'sorted,' as the English would say." Aunt Ella smiled. "We shall have a fitting tonight at my place. By the way, thank you, Vanessa dear, for the lovely tribute from our Mr. Darcy at the opening of the conference. How very thoughtful of you."

If only she *had* thought of it. She had Julian to thank, that was for sure.

She looked over toward the bookstore stall, but he had vanished. If he was following the schedule she had drawn up for him, the schedule that maximized his exposure for the sake of his book, he should be on his way to the Cravat Tying 101 Workshop.

"Auntie E, would you and Paul like to join me for Cravat Tying 101?"

"I thought I'd never hear you ask such a thing," she said. "What's happening to you? Let's hurry before you change your mind!"

Vanessa linked her arm in her aunt's. "Although I think it would be much more useful to learn how to *untie* a cravat, wouldn't it?"

"You're really getting my hopes up, darling."

"I'm just kidding. Whatever you're thinking—don't."

She couldn't spoil this moment by telling her about the doctor's appointment. It would have to wait.

As she sat in Cravat Tying 101, the message she sent out to the Internet floated around the cell phones and tech devices of Janeites the world over:

Want to tie the knot with Mr. Darcy? He's in Cravat Tying 101 right now. #JASNAagm #UndressingMrDarcy #OrDressingMrDarcy?

"To best learn how to tie a cravat," Julian said to Vanessa, "one must put one's phone down and actually interact with the neck cloth."

He gently took the phone from her hands, their fingers brushing against each other, and set it facedown on the table.

Vanessa laughed. She had been struggling with the swath of white fabric and the wooden post in front of her while fielding messages from her clients *and* tweeting on his behalf! She sat squarely between him and Aunt Ella. Paul sat on the other side of Aunt Ella, while Lexi flanked Julian, and Sherry sat behind them all.

"I'm doing my best," Vanessa said as she once again pulled the fabric over the knot she'd made on her post. But something wasn't working. She figured the faster she went, the better.

"It's a dying art, but it's also an exercise in patience."

"What are you implying, Mr. Darcy?"

He smiled. "It's a skill best acquired slowly, through practice. After all . . . one never knows. You may one day find that the gentleman in your life needs a hand."

Was it getting hot in here or was it just her?

She whispered to Aunt Ella, "I've often found that men in my life have needed a hand, but not, alas, with their cravats."

"Vanessa!" Aunt Ella whispered with a giggle.

Really, her aunt was still as sharp as her hatpins, and she had tied her cravat impeccably. How could Vanessa reconcile it with the dementia diagnosis?

Paul laughed.

She hadn't thought Paul could hear her. She'd only wanted to amuse her aunt.

"Perhaps you haven't met a true gentleman yet," Julian said.

Hmmm. She could say a lot of things, but he was a client, so she chose silence.

"Allow me," he said.

He stood and, from behind her, reached over, his arms brushing against hers, and unwound the fabric she had just carefully wrapped around the pole in front of her.

"It looks like I've pushed your patience to the limit," she said as she watched his hands deftly wrap the cravat around the pole.

He laughed. "You have, I'm afraid. You must keep one end of the neck cloth longer than the other, you see. You'll need the extra length to create the 'waterfall' effect the instructor was referring to for this particular knot. There." He sat down and Vanessa felt a blast of air-conditioning on her back. "Now try tying it."

"I'm sure I'll have just as much trouble *tying the knot*," Vanessa whispered to Aunt Ella.

Her aunt laughed. "It's not as if nobody ever asked you, either. The trouble's all yours, dear."

These were the moments with her aunt she wanted to remember. This conference, time like this spent with her aunt, it might never happen again.

She brought the long end over to hide the knot and made a picture-perfect waterfall over it.

"There," she said as she shook off her wistfulness. "Does it pass muster, Mr. Darcy?"

"Well done. Well done." Julian smiled.

Lexi began whining from the other side of Julian, no doubt because Vanessa was getting too much of his attention. Her cravat, though, looked perfect.

"What do you think of mine, Mr. Darcy? I'm quite good at tying things up, aren't I?"

More than one bonneted head turned around in front of them and then turned back.

"Quite," Julian said.

Aunt Ella nudged Vanessa and whispered, "See what you've started. You've gone and provoked Caroline Bingley again."

Vanessa sighed. "What have I done?"

Lexi continued to chat with, or rather, chat up, Julian.

"You'd best let her have Julian's attention. There are friends of mine from all over the country in this room, and if Lexi causes a scene, I know it will be due to the fact that you took something she wants. It's always been this way with her, Vanessa. Now, just share your toys and play nicely."

"He's not mine to share, you know. He's a client."

Aunt Ella looked disappointed. "You always let work spill into your leisure time—why not mix business with pleasure in the man department?"

Vanessa laughed and reached for her phone, but her aunt's purple-veined hand gently stopped her.

The instructor, Jake Laney—a historian and an expert on cravats, snuff, and firearms—stepped back up to the front of the room after checking on his students' progress and continued his lecture.

"You may untie your waterfall knot and we'll do the mathematical knot," Jake said. "It's a simple but elegant knot and reveals much about the gentleman who chooses it. He is, of course, an upstanding gentleman, proud to express his individuality, but not overly fussy about his outward appearance, unlike dandies such as Beau Brummell.

"Beau Brummell, after all, came up with the idea of starching one's cravat, much to the chagrin of the laundresses, and he would often be found knee-deep in discarded cravats, trying to get it just right."

Vanessa methodically followed Jake's instructions as to how to tie the mathematical. First she spread the neck cloth on the front of the pole, or, as he liked to call it, the "neck." Then she made a crease coming down from under each "ear" toward where the knot would be. She made a horizontal crease above the ear creases, brought the ends to the back, crossed them, continued around to the front, and then tied them in a knot.

She did it. Her cravat looked as perfect as the one on Jake's PowerPoint presentation. She smoothed it down, and, for some reason, she felt as if it were the smartest, sexiest thing she had seen in a while. Why, then, did it look familiar?

Then it hit her. Julian wore his cravat in the mathematical style.

He was the elegant, upstanding gentleman Jake was talking about.

Upstanding?

Julian moved his chair slightly away from Lexi and closer to Vanessa.

Yes, upstanding.

"Time to untie your cravats," Jake said. "We're moving on to what our gentleman would wear to the ball: the ballroom knot."

Vanessa very slowly slid her fingers through the mathematical knot, pulling it apart, letting the cloth spill into her hands, keeping her thoughts from spilling into choppy waters.

Suddenly she wondered: wasn't the modern tie a bit of a letdown? It didn't take any skill or creativity whatsoever to put one on and didn't reveal as much about the individual as these knots did.

After the ballroom knot everyone stood to go to the next session, and Lexi needed to dart back over to Hero Con. Vanessa found herself face-to-face with Julian, and, for a moment, they seemed all alone in a sea of untied cravats.

"Julian, I have to thank you, belatedly, for honoring my aunt the way you did this morning. I saw it all on video and it was fabulous."

"My pleasure," he said. "It was rather an impromptu decision, and I shouldn't have assumed you'd be in the room."

"I'm so sorry I missed it."

"I am as well. Most sorry."

"The flowers were so gorgeous. How did you manage—?"

"Hotel concierges are quite obliging." He smiled. "By the by, I am very much looking forward to the plan tonight."

Images of them out to dinner at a candlelit restaurant and swimming in her condo's rooftop pool in the moonlight flashed through her mind. Holy cravat! She rubbed her forehead. "The plan? What plan?"

"The PR plan. I am quite anxious to see it."

Conference attendees closed in on him now, and she stepped backward.

"Oh! Yes, the plan. Yes."

He turned his attention to his fans and Aunt Ella arched a penciled-in eyebrow at Vanessa. "It looks as if he may be coming to the table with a plan of his own," she said.

Vanessa laughed. "Don't be ridiculous."

Chapter 5

*L*ater that afternoon she stood in Aunt Ella's creamy dressing room with the gold gilt crown molding, gold slipper chair, and gold vanity, wearing a shimmering yellow gown from her aunt's closet that left everything from her shoulders to midcleavage bare, it seemed.

"You'll catch more men with this than those blazers of yours," Aunt Ella said. "Women of the Regency knew a thing or two about that!"

"I have no desire to catch any men," Vanessa said.

She was aware of and thinking about one man, and that was Julian, who sat in the living room reading and resting while all this went on clandestinely, at her request.

Aunt Ella hadn't worn the gown in decades, but she and Martha agreed this one would work best. Vanessa hadn't paid full attention to everything the women were saying, as she had to deal with some e-mails and worked on her phone while they worked on her. They didn't want her to get in front of the mirror until they had put some time in, apparently.

"I'll have to modify a corset I have on hand, too, of course," Martha said.

"Of course." Aunt Ella nodded. "Oh, Vanessa!" Her gray eyes sparkled with a faraway look as she stared, and Vanessa knew her aunt was reminiscing about the gown.

She stepped over to her aunt and gave her a huge hug and a kiss. "Just wait till you dance with Paul tomorrow night! Kai will be filming all of it so we can watch it every Sunday night—instead of the BBC."

"Instead of the BBC? Never."

Martha swooped in with pins, tacking up the hem, then the sides. "I'll have to take it in."

"She's getting too thin," Aunt Ella said as she rifled through her drawers, pulling out various pairs of gloves and examining them. "And she's spread too thin." Aunt Ella continued to speak as if Vanessa weren't there. It was an old, endearing habit of hers. "She's so overworked with that crazy business of hers."

She held up a pair of long gloves. "Ahh. Here they are." She handed them to Vanessa. "Put your phone down, please, child, and put the gloves on to hide that garish black nail polish."

Vanessa knew better than to disobey.

"All right," Martha said. "Time to look in the mirror."

They trotted her to the mirror as she slid the gloves on. Just as she arrived at the mirror, Aunt Ella gathered Vanessa's hair in a ponytail, twisted it, held it up on her head, then stuck a long, gorgeous white ostrich feather in. Martha clasped a simple chain with an amber stone around her neck and it fell just at the bottom of her throat.

Vanessa couldn't believe what she saw.

"That gown is made for you," Martha said.

"That gown was made for *me*," Aunt Ella quipped. "But she looks a damn sight better in it than I would at this point!"

Vanessa had never seen herself in a Regency gown. Granted, it covered her best asset: her legs. But the gloves made her arms appear longer, and yes, more feminine without the black nail polish. The cinching just below her bustline, along with the low cut, proved, well, attention getting.

"See how, with your hair up, your cheekbones look even more prominent?" Aunt Ella asked. "And, being a relation of mine, your bone structure is of course impeccable."

"Just wait until you see it with the corset on. It'll be worth all those measurements I had to take. You'll look fabulous, darling."

Maybe, just maybe, she could pull this off. "You two really are like fairy godmothers."

Aunt Ella smiled. "You are opening the ball by dancing with Julian, aren't you, dear? Isn't that what we decided?" Aunt Ella said.

The little room seemed to close in on Vanessa. Her aunt had gotten confused again.

"There are hundreds of other more qualified women ready to take on that task. Remember we decided to run a contest to see who would open the ball with him?"

Aunt Ella sighed and dropped Vanessa's ponytail, sending the feather fluttering to the floorboards and Vanessa's hair falling around her in a cascade.

Martha unbuttoned the gown from the top of the neck on down.

Her aunt rubbed her temples. "I was sure you told me you wanted to open the ball with him."

Martha looked down and quickly gathered up her pins and measuring tape. "I'll get the garment bag for the gown." She went into the bedroom.

Vanessa put her hands on her aunt's shoulders. "I don't even know the minuet. I couldn't ask him to teach me."

"You don't have to ask him. I've already done that."

Vanessa's chest sunk. "What?"

"He's thrilled to teach you; he said so himself. Couldn't think of a better way to spend the evening, he told me."

"We were supposed to go over some new facets of his PR plan."

Aunt Ella tossed her head. "One can always work!"

Like a deck of cards, she had her evening all neatly stacked, but now everything had been reshuffled.

"We have an English gentleman to entertain and a ball to launch. I thought it the perfect solution! I—I forgot you said you'd have someone else open the ball with him. It slipped my mind."

Vanessa wriggled out of the dress and tried to figure out how she could wriggle out of not only this, but her commitment to Chase and the swordsmanship workshop tomorrow.

How did she get herself into these things—gowns and minuets and swordsmanship workshops? And how could she get out of them? There was one thing, though, she couldn't get out of.

"Auntie E, don't worry. The ball will go without a hitch. You don't even need to think about it. However, the doctor called, and he wants us in for a follow-up first thing in the morning."

She gave her aunt a hug right there in her leopard-print thong and lacy black bra. "It won't take long. I just didn't think it would be smart to wait. After all, I have to drive Julian to Louisville after this conference, and I'll be gone a couple of days."

Aunt Ella sat down in the slipper chair. "You're right. We have to go. If the doctor knows the results, I want to know the results."

Vanessa breathed a sigh of relief, and with that came the brainstorm that she should visit the costume shop up the street for something suitable to wear to a swordfight workshop. "I just have a quick errand to run right now; it'll take me half an hour tops. You and Julian should eat dinner, and as soon as I'm back, you can turn in for the night."

"That is how you get too thin, dear, and cause those fainting fits of yours, by skipping meals." Aunt Ella eyed her up and down, stopping at her bare butt cheeks. "And is this really what you wear under those suits and sheath dresses?"

She scored a rental Wonder Woman costume at the costume shop. The workshop tomorrow with Chase felt more like a date than anything else, and she couldn't disappoint him by showing up to Hero Con in anything from her closet.

Two costumes in one day?

Who knew life off the grid and untethered by clients could be so interesting? She had actually forgotten to check her eBelieve in-box.

She and Julian had left Aunt Ella safely tucked into bed, and, at Vanessa's suggestion, they took a walk in the sand along the beach, stopping and sitting on the embankment so she could show him the PR plan on her tablet.

He wore modern clothes, an indigo and white striped button-down shirt and jeans that made her forget, initially, this was all business.

Her strappy sandals and his loafers comingled in the sand in front of their bare feet.

He had nice feet. Nice feet? What did it matter if a client had nice feet?

She cleared her throat. "In order to gain maximum—exposure for you—"

Suddenly her business-speak took on innuendo?

"—we want to make sure you appear on as many websites and social media outlets as possible. Just last night, once I saw the plight of your property, I decided to contact all the English interest groups here in the States I could find, and not just the Jane Austen ones you and your publisher have been targeting."

"Such as?"

"Such as English heritage and genealogical societies, literary societies, historical preservation groups . . . Here, I have a list of them. There are millions of people here with English ancestry and sentiments that could be approached for donations to your property. It's just a matter of capturing them—and their attention. I've also put together the bones of a website dedicated to the property itself. Before it goes live it should have a video tour of your home on it, and an interview with you, too. You can even include some photos of your great-great-grandfather and stories of your ghost. Get people invested."

He moved closer to see the tablet.

"Impressive. I'd never thought of it."

"I've already managed to get your book added to more than a hundred online catalogs and websites. Here's the list right here. I'll keep contacting more as they come up."

"Thank you."

"And to further expand your reach—"

Innuendo, again?

"I have Kai putting together a book trailer using the footage from your show."

"A book trailer? Similar to a film trailer?"

"Exactly. I also have him brainstorming ideas for a free app. Our goal is to have your trailer, your app, your cause in general—spread all over the cyber world. If something—anything—were to go viral, that could bring you all the donations you'd need."

"Viral."

"Yes, something, let's say, on YouTube, that garners us millions of hits. It seems you and your publisher have just been focusing on selling the book—the steak—when in fact you should be selling the sizzle."

"What sizzle?"

"What sizzle?! Why, your *Undressing Mr. Darcy* show, of course! Why would you reserve that for just the seven hundred or so at this conference and then the three or four hundred in Louisville, when, via the Internet, you could literally expose yourself to the entire world and their wallets?"

"When you say it that way, it sounds as if I'm some cheap strip-tease act."

Vanessa laughed. "You're a classy, *expensive* striptease act. We want people to make significant donations to your property."

"What would my great-great-grandfather say?"

She smiled. "He'd be thrilled at your ingenuity. Is it any better or worse than marrying into money to save the property? Come to think of it, that would be another way to go. Have you thought of *that?*"

He tossed his head back as if the idea caused him pain. "Dear God, no! I couldn't marry just for money." He looked her in the eyes. "I could only marry for love, to someone I respect, someone that's a true partner."

Vanessa looked away from his face and back at her tablet. "Well, then. I've also come up with a QR code for you. It's one of those digital codes that people can scan with their smartphones and then watch some of your show. I'm still trying to figure out where we can place it—and I'm surfing around to see what other causes you could partner with. But all of this is a start."

"I should say it's a start," Julian said as he slipped the tablet from her hands, shut it down, and slid the hinged cover over it. "I'm profoundly grateful, Vanessa, but I must ask you, would you like to dance?"

He stood and took her hand.

"Right here? On the beach?"

"Why not."

It wasn't a question.

She stood facing him, just an arm's length away.

He smiled. "This particular minuet that I'm about to teach you does not start out with us facing each other—"

"Oh." She stepped back and the sand felt a little cooler on the balls of her feet.

"But this is lovely, I have to admit."

Lovely? Well, no American guy would be caught dead saying that word at a time like this, but it really was . . . lovely. Even the wispy clouds overhead oozed orange in the blue sky while the waves provided a rhythmic background.

Was it his modern clothes, the fact that he lorded over a large, albeit derelict, estate, or simply his personality that created his magnetism?

He took both of her hands, her cool hands, into his large, warm ones. He slowly pulled her closer to his body and—OMG—he was going to kiss her!

She could see his long dark lashes dropping, his lips parting ever so slightly, his neck turning to the side, and she wanted to reach out and touch his razor-stubbled cheek, but luckily she restrained herself just long enough to watch his eyes open and his jaw tighten as he stepped back.

He changed his mind?!

Never, in all her dating years, had a man come so close to kissing her only to clearly change his mind and deliberately, willfully, not kiss her! WTH? Was the setting not perfect? The moment not ideal? The girl not worth kissing after all?

Then again, they had a business relationship, and maybe he'd decided not to jeopardize it.

Her phone rang in her bag and she dropped his hands. Saved by the cell. It wasn't the first time. Thank God for modern technology.

"I'd better check that—it could be Aunt Ella."

It was a client, after hours, and she chose not to pick up. Instead she just tossed her phone back in her bag. "So where do I stand, then?" she asked. A good question.

He took her hand. "You're meant to be here, by my side."

For a moment, she stood, stuck in the sand, while that line struck her. *You're meant to be here, by my side.* How could she ever read into such an offhanded remark when the guy refused to even kiss her?

Determined to get this minuet thing over with, she moved to stand next to him, he dropped her hand, and she learned the minuet as the sun went down behind the skyscrapers and the streetlights flickered on.

All this time she'd lived downtown and she'd never danced with anyone on the beach. Although, admittedly, many a man had kissed her on the shores of Lake Michigan here, and some had managed significantly more than that, but now one man had *not* kissed her on the beach. *That* was a first.

Well, she didn't want him to kiss her anyway, as it would only complicate a very simple business relationship, and it would make things awkward, as they had to travel to Louisville and then, poof! He would be gone, off to New York and then back to his life of writing books and shoring up his country estate, and she would be bereft of nothing—nothing more than a client who didn't pay.

"Congratulations, you're ready to try this with music now," he said. "Wonderful work. You're a quick study. It's going to make your aunt so happy if you open the ball."

"Yes—about that. I'm not so sure I'll be the one opening with you."

"Oh?"

"It's a long story . . ."

He bent down to pick up her sandals, bag, and jacket.

Was this what it was like to be treated like a lady? He certainly did surprise her with the gesture, and, even though he hadn't kissed her, he did look adorable carrying her bag.

They walked right by the beach volleyball courts, with girls in their bikinis gleaming under the lights, and Julian didn't flinch. He didn't look. Was he really a gentleman? One thing was for sure, he wasn't a hookup, clubbing, player type of guy, Vanessa knew that. He had a crumbling estate, a legacy that was losing the race against time, and maybe that weighed heavily on him. Or it could simply be jet lag. It had been a long day.

"Let's get you back," she said.

On the way she checked the number of responses to opening the ball with Julian. Three hundred and fifty-one? She had initially thought twenty, maybe thirty women would respond.

She also no longer felt impartial enough to judge the contestants.

When she unlocked the door to Aunt Ella's condo, she heard a shrill noise and fear ran up her spine. She hurried in and found, there in the kitchen, the teakettle on the electric stove, boiling and whistling without water in it. She twisted the burner to off, tossed the kettle into the sink, where it made a sizzling sound, and barreled into her aunt's bedroom.

Her aunt lay sleeping soundly in her bed, her ample chest rising and falling regularly, thank God. Vanessa would have to tell the doctor about this tomorrow—what luck that they were going so soon.

When she closed the bedroom door, she backed right into Julian, who stood directly behind her. His strong, tall body took her at first by surprise. Then she felt only palpable relief. He put his hands on her shoulders and slowly turned her around.

"She's safe," he whispered. He led her to the living room and took her in his arms. "You mind her so well. But some things are out of your control."

She fought back the tears welling in her eyes. It felt so good, so right, to be comforted by him. Then again, she might have felt the same about any man there at that moment, right? It didn't have to be a Mr. Darcy from England, did it? She didn't want to become . . . attached . . . or had she already? Would he try to kiss her again? She didn't want a kiss. No, she didn't want the *possibility* of a kiss and the possibility of a changed mind. He was a client, after all.

She broke away from him with a smile. "Aunt Ella isn't the only one causing me problems at the moment."

"Who else is?"

"You."

"Me?"

If he only knew. "Yes, you." She pulled out her phone and got an updated tally. "There are three hundred and fifty-seven women—and two men—who would like to open the ball with you tomorrow night. One of the women is Lexi. Some of the people who responded aren't even at the conference!"

He watched as she scrolled through the litany of responses. "Vanessa. Whatever have you done out there in cyberspace? You are being cautious, aren't you?"

"Cautious? This is the kind of stir we want to create." She sighed. "Mostly. But now my aunt has her heart set on my opening the ball with you. Any suggestions, Mr. Darcy?"

*L*ater that night, propped up with her laptop in bed and her phone by her side, she replayed his response to her in her head.

He had brushed her cheek with his hand and said, "You need to tell them all, and that includes Lexi, that I've made my choice, and I've chosen you."

He had said it so quickly, and with such determination, that, under different circumstances, she might have thought he was flirting with her. But why would he flirt with her when he had chosen not to kiss her?

As she stared at her eBelieve in-box in the glow of her laptop screen, she convinced herself that he probably chose to open the dance with her simply to please Aunt Ella.

Vanessa told him she didn't quite feel comfortable communicating the news to everyone, and he said he would post the message himself tomorrow. Julian on social media? *That* she couldn't wait to see.

She clicked on her eBelieve in-box, but none of the men nor their messages appealed, and she soon found herself doing an Internet search on Julian. She had done this before she put together his Chicago PR plan, to get a feel for what kind of media coverage he'd received, but now she found herself digging for personal information about him.

His name garnered hits in the six-figure range, but absolutely everything related to his book, his show, or his property. Did he have a girlfriend? Pets? Silly pictures someone had taken of him drinking a pint at the pub? No. There didn't seem to be anything about his personal life at all, and nothing dated further back than three years. But then again, she was tired, it was late, and she'd only checked a handful of hits.

A few months before, she had, just as a precaution, run a background check on him to confirm he could stay with her aunt, and everything checked out. Many of Aunt Ella's colleagues vouched for his character and had known him for years, so she wasn't concerned about anything criminal, by any means, she had just become . . . curious. But his Internet reputation proved very clean and professional. And he didn't have any personal social media presence whatsoever. No blogs, nothing. Odd for an author.

She chided herself for wanting more dish on him, cursing the fact that this kind of digging was even possible, and admitting that yes, she liked him a bit more than as a client. She didn't run Internet searches on just anyone.

She shut down her laptop with a sigh. She felt much like Julian's estate—projecting a strong facade, but dealing with a crumbling interior in serious need of repair.

Chapter 6

She had landed Julian a morning radio interview and posted:

Wake up with Mr. Darcy! 9:00 a.m. @91.1FMChicago #JASNAagm #UndressingMrDarcy

Her posts were, disturbingly, now revealing her innermost thoughts.

But she had posted this before the early-morning doctor's appointment with her aunt. It would be hard to keep up the spunky posts after that appointment.

She and her aunt made their way into the Quilling Paper Workshop at the conference while Vanessa's head rattled with the doctor's news. It had taken weeks of blood tests, scans, and questioning, but yes, Aunt Ella had Alzheimer's, one of the most common and deadliest forms of dementia. At her age, the average life expectancy once diagnosed was only about seven years.

Medication could slow it, but the disease would progress. Her aunt would, in time, eventually lose all her independence and need to move into a home. Vanessa had frantically taken notes on her laptop, keying in that accommodations for the condition would have to be made, and finances, wills, and power of attorney needed to be reviewed. Did they have a caregiver in mind?

Aunt Ella had shaken her head no.

"If I wanted to live with someone," she'd said, "I would've remarried decades ago. And then I could've driven someone else completely mad without having to pay for it! No, no, I cannot have a stranger coming to live with me."

Vanessa had bought herself one coffee for each hand after the appointment and then determined to brave the quilling class despite being arts and crafts challenged. It made her aunt happy to have her in the workshop, by her side. Paul sat on the other side of her and Sherry in front of them in a *Dibs on Darcy* T-shirt.

Vanessa's hand shook as she tried to slip a yellow strip of paper into the quilling tool's slot. Sherry chatted and quilled as the ponytail that stuck out of her baseball hat swished from side to side. Her hat read *Mistress of Pemberley*. She was the Mistress of Pemberley while Vanessa seemed to be the Master of Nothing.

Julie, the instructor, a pert young Asian American dressed in a day gown with a bonnet hanging down her back, filed up and down between the rows of tables, checking on everyone's progress. They were supposed to decorate a small wooden picture frame with paper filigree designs, and she had demonstrated how to roll the thin strips of paper into curls and then glue them onto the frame to create hearts, flowers, and teardrops.

"In *Pride and Prejudice*," Julie announced, "Mr. Bingley refers to young women being accomplished, and he said, 'They all paint tables, cover screens, and net purses. I scarcely know anyone who cannot do all this, and I am sure I never heard a young lady spoken of for the first time, without being informed that she was very accomplished.' Quilling, or paper filigree, was one of the ways an accomplished lady spent her time."

Aunt Ella, Paul, and Sherry had all practically finished decorating a third of their frames, while Vanessa struggled to make lopsided hearts, wilting flowers, and misshapen teardrops. From across the room she eyed the finished wooden picture frame Julie had on display, and it looked gorgeous. Why couldn't Vanessa make it happen?

A strip of pink paper, at first seemingly coiled around her quill, completely unraveled and spilled into a swirling vortex of pink in front of her that looked nothing like a heart.

She looked up only to see that the woman across from Paul was actually crocheting a doily and quilling at the same time.

Distracted, Vanessa put too much glue on her attempt at a blue paper coil to make a flower petal, and the glue glopped everywhere.

"Do you need help?" Julie asked, eyeing Vanessa's rapidly uncoiling flower.

Yes, she needed help! Lots and lots of help, and maybe a fishbowl-sized martini, too.

"No, thank you. I'm fine," Vanessa said. "I'm just not as 'accomplished' as everyone else, clearly."

That got the whole room laughing, including her aunt, and that made it all worth it.

How could it be that she could field press conferences on live TV but couldn't roll a strip of paper around a quill to save her life?

Julie couldn't hold back. She bent over Vanessa's picture frame, and within minutes the glue had been forced into submission, and the sad little frame appeared more populated, and Vanessa could actually distinguish the hearts from the teardrops.

At least now she was on par with the eighty-year-olds and the one eleven-year-old in the crowd, but the women her age were nearly done.

"Thank you," Vanessa said to Julie. Maybe if she rolled her coils looser, she could cover more of the frame.

Julie caught on to Vanessa's hastily rolling her paper. "I'm here to help, you know. In Austen's *Sense and Sensibility*, Elinor Dashwood helps Lucy Steele by rolling papers for a basket Lucy's working on."

Aunt Ella looked up from her quilling. "Are you implying that my niece is a Lucy Steele?"

Everyone in the room laughed, except for Vanessa, who didn't get any of these insider Austen jokes. But she was glad to see that her aunt's wit was still as sharp as ever. Aunt Ella hadn't been able to remember which high school she went to, during her battery of tests, but she could make a roomful of intelligent Janeites laugh! And which, really, was more important?

"Lucy Steele," her aunt whispered, "was a villainess in *Sense and Sensibility*. She was secretly engaged to the hero, Edward. Elinor Dashwood couldn't account for his odd behavior. But all along it was the secret engagement!"

Secret engagements, happily, were a thing of the past, from a time when people didn't have "it's complicated" as a relationship status option.

There. She'd covered her entire frame and managed to be the first one done! She couldn't recognize anything except what Julie had glued down, but it was covered, and colorful, too. If she'd taken more time and had more patience, it could've been beautiful. Regardless, she gained something from this experience, and that was a few stolen moments of peace.

She had to admit she felt better. She hadn't made anything by hand in a while. She propped the frame up to admire it. Not bad.

"Next thing you know you'll be speaking French, sketching landscapes, and singing at the pianoforte," Aunt Ella said.

"I don't think I'd subject anyone to that," Vanessa said.

"It's lovely, dear, really," Aunt Ella said as she eyed Vanessa's frame. "Especially the flowers at the bottom."

Okay, so, did her aunt remember that the instructor had done the bottom of the frame for her? She didn't want to scrutinize everything her aunt said or did, but the "Alzheimer's" label changed everything, it seemed.

The door to the workshop stood ajar, and she noticed Julian pacing in front of it. Back from the radio station already? She hoped he'd remembered to ask them to e-mail her the audio files for posting. She stood and gently lifted her frame. "Aunt Ella, this was fun! Is Paul going to stay with you? Julian's back and I need to check on him."

"Go right ahead. Perhaps you and he can join us for lunch. We're hosting a small gathering, and Chase offered a picnic on his boat for our friends. He's going to pull his boat over to the riverwalk especially for us."

"That's nice of him," Vanessa said.

"He is a dear. Always has been. Ever since you two were in high school together."

Vanessa almost dropped her frame, with the glue still wet. So it was true. They had gone to high school together. Or was it? How could her aunt remember Chase and she couldn't? Could she trust her aunt's memories?

"Sherry will be there, won't you, Sherry?" Aunt Ella asked.

"I wouldn't miss it!" She beamed.

Chase had a boat? Everything from a dinghy to a yacht to a cigar boat flashed through her mind. She picked up her frame and smiled at Julie, the instructor. "Auntie E, Julian has lunch plans with a group of professors, and I need to work through my lunch. So I may not see you until the promenade at five. Is that okay?"

"Of course it's okay, dear. I'm fine, you know. Paul won't let me out of his sight."

She kissed her aunt on the head and swooped down to pick up her purse and gym bag.

"What's in the duffel bag?" Aunt Ella asked.

"A Wonder Woman costume," Vanessa said.

"A what?"

"Chase convinced me to join him at Hero Con for a swordsmanship workshop, but maybe I can bow out of it."

"You'll do nothing of the kind," her aunt said. She pointed her finger at Vanessa. "I insist that you be nice to him. He's Paul's right-hand man. I won't have you leave him hanging." She turned to Sherry. "I can't tell you how many poor men Vanessa has let fall by the wayside over the years. Half of them end up at my place, practically crying into my teacups. Someday you will meet your match. I'm hoping for sooner rather than later."

But by the time Vanessa extracted herself from the class, Julian had disappeared. She saw the door to another conference room close and she figured he must have gone in there.

All this chasing him around made her realize how dependent she'd become on texting. He ranked right up there with her aunt in not using the phone, and it was a wonder his publisher dealt with it.

She opened the door to the conference room, but the room was so full, and so quiet, other than the lively Professor Miranda Fuller, one of her aunt's friends, up at the podium lecturing, that she dared not draw attention to herself but instead found a seat as quickly as possible.

As she scanned the room for Julian, she heard Professor Fuller speaking of Lydia Bennet, explaining how a slit in her gown suggested her loss of virginity before she eloped. Loss of virginity? She scanned the entire left side of the room, but Julian wasn't there. Professor Fuller went on to discuss the sexual significance of Elizabeth Bennet's petticoat being stained with "six inches" of mud.

Okay, Vanessa had to look up the schedule and see exactly what lecture she had stumbled into here. It happened to be "Slits, Spikes, Steeds, and Scandals!: Coded Sexual Indiscretion in Jane Austen's Fiction," and it was enough to make even her blush!

She scanned the right side of the room for Julian, but got distracted when Professor Fuller spoke of Kitty and Lydia Bennet cross-dressing a soldier in a gown, of carriages and horses symbolizing male sexuality, and how a certain Mr. Rushworth from *Mansfield Park* didn't seem to have the "key" to a certain "gate."

Who knew? Maybe the time had come for Vanessa to read the full Austen canon. Even as she sat in the lecture, she decided to download all the novels to her phone. As much as she wanted to find Julian, she found herself fascinated by the lecture—and paralyzed by the rapt audience. She didn't dare leave now.

Once everyone clapped and stood to leave, she saw Lexi, once again in her Xena costume, approach the professor afterward.

Vanessa hurried out of the room, and there, in the hall, leaning against a pillar reading a book, stood Julian. He looked over at her with a smile.

"There you are. How did you find Professor Fuller's lecture?" he asked.

"Intriguing."

"The conversion has begun. It's in your blood. Resistance is futile." He looked into her eyes and took a step backward. "You're becoming an Austen fan."

She picked up on his cue. "I am. Check out the picture frame I made in the quilling workshop." She showed him her handiwork.

"Fantastic. I most especially admire the flowers and hearts on the bottom here."

Vanessa smiled and neglected to tell him Julie had done those.

"I'm quite glad I found you at last," he said with a pause.

She didn't want to read anything into that statement, but he did seem to drink her in as he looked at her.

"I would like to hear all about your aunt's appointment, and we need to let everyone know you are opening the ball with me tonight. I am very much looking forward to *that*. However, it seems I am always chasing after you and waiting for you at every turn," he said.

"Really?" She felt exactly the same way. "You realize that using your phone would actually solve all of these logistical issues, right?"

"I do, but you know my stance on technology."

"I know it, but I don't understand it."

"I shall explain when we have time. There are good reasons."

In the meantime, having to actually see him for their every communication wasn't that bad. Not being able to text, call, or IM him only added to his value and mystique.

She couldn't help but wonder if we moderns were doing ourselves a disservice by being so available—remotely, electronically. There was something to this archaic face-to-face time.

"Perhaps you will reconsider my invitation to the Jane Austen Festival in Bath."

Perhaps she would. But how could she with her aunt's Alzheimer's?

"Mr. Darcy, can we talk with you for a moment?" A woman and her friends broke into their bubble.

Vanessa had to remember this was just a job, and, hassle though it had been, she realized she didn't want it to end.

When she looked at the time she realized she'd better take this opportunity to change into her Wonder Woman costume.

"Please wait here, Julian," she said to him as a crowd gathered around him. "I'll be right back."

"I'm not going anywhere," he said.

Once she stepped out of the ladies' room stall and caught a glimpse of herself in the full-length mirror, she surprised herself. There, standing in the mirror, looking right back at her, was the sexiest Wonder Woman she had ever seen, complete with strapless red and gold bustier; tight blue satin panties covered in little white stars; a golden rope hanging at her side; a red, white, and blue cape; and red boots that wouldn't quit.

She hadn't worn a costume in years. She took a deep breath and opened the restroom door.

"Wow! You're certainly no plain Jane," Sherry said when she saw Vanessa coming toward Julian and his entourage. "Watch *out!* Wonder Woman's in the house!" She pumped her palms toward the ceiling.

"I promised Chase I'd join him in a swordsmanship workshop at Hero Con," Vanessa said.

"O-kay," Sherry said.

"Can you stick with Julian while I'm gone? It won't be long."

"You don't need to ask! But listen, before you go, could you take a picture of Julian and me? With all of your superpowers, you should be capable of busting through the crowd." She handed Vanessa her camera.

"Excuse us, Mr. Darcy?" Vanessa asked, and the group of women around Julian turned and gaped at her.

Julian nearly spit out the tea he had been sipping. "This is a far cry from quilling, Miss Roberts."

"She's a woman of many talents," Sherry said.

Every woman needed a friend like Sherry!

"I can see that," he said.

"I inadvertently signed up for a swordsmanship workshop with a pirate."

He linked his arm in Sherry's for the photo. "It makes opening a ball with a gentleman seem positively passé."

"*You're* opening the ball with him?" Sherry asked.

The women he had been speaking with turned and chatted among themselves.

"I wouldn't have it any other way," Julian said. "But now it seems we must announce it publicly, mustn't we?"

"Yes," Vanessa said. "We'll take care of that right after this shot." It took a few seconds to frame the picture, and then Sherry blinked, so a few shots later, they agreed on one, and Vanessa loved the picture so much she posted it right away on the social networks with the message:

The Mistress of Pemberley has Dibs on Darcy. #he'ssexyandheknowsit #JASNAagm #UndressingMrDarcy

Julian bowed to his fans. "If you will excuse me, ladies, I have some business to attend to with Miss Roberts and Miss—" He looked at Sherry.

Vanessa didn't even know Sherry's last name.

"Pajowski," Sherry said.

"Miss Pajowski."

The three of them stepped aside, toward some stuffed chairs near the elevators.

He waited until Vanessa and Sherry took a seat, then he smoothed his coattails and sat down. "I do believe we have a throng of women we need to thwart. How shall we handle it?"

Vanessa crossed her legs in the red boots and propped her laptop on her bare knee. "I'm not going to say a word. It needs to come from you, in your language."

"How does one tell a woman, or women, in this case, that one is spoken for?" He smiled. "I've got it. 'Dear Ladies, I have found my Miss Bennet.'"

Vanessa squirmed in her chair and keyed in the message, including the necessary hashtags. "And? You have seventy characters left."

Her phone pinged with a text from Chase:

En garde! Where can I find u? I'll walk you to the workshop . . .

She texted him back, letting him know where she was.

Julian stood and walked over toward Vanessa. "I'm afraid I'm going to need to see it." He leaned over and tilted the laptop toward him. "Right. How about . . ."

He typed on the laptop as it sat on Vanessa's legs.

"No, not quite." He reached from behind her, locking her in with his arms. Did he need to do that? No. He deleted a few words.

The elevator opened and Chase, once again in his pirate costume, stepped out of the elevator and smirked as he saw Julian practically draped over Vanessa.

"There," Julian said as he wrapped up his typing.

Vanessa read the post:

Ladies, I have a Miss Bennet for the minuet, but my dance card isn't yet full. Shall we? Sincerely, Mr. Darcy. #JASNAagm #Undressing MrDarcy

"Perfect!" she said.

The elevator doors closed with a ding. "So I have been told," Chase quipped.

Sherry giggled.

Julian crossed his arms.

"I'm sending it off right now," Vanessa said to Julian. Once she'd sent the post, she stood. "Julian, I'd like you to meet Chase. Chase—Julian."

Chase reached out and shook Julian's hand. "Hey, great to meet you. I've heard lots of good things. I hope you'll join us for lunch today on my boat."

"Your boat?" Lexi had materialized from a crowd of women in gowns. "I thought you'd never ask, Captain Jack. I'm Lexi, a friend of Vanessa's."

Vanessa couldn't believe the nerve of her!

"Any friend of Vanessa's is welcome," Chase said. "We'll meet out by the riverwalk at twelve thirty. Sherry, I know you're on the list."

He put his arm around the small of Vanessa's back.

Julian pursed his lips. "Much obliged, but I am booked for luncheon today."

Chase smiled at Vanessa. "Love the costume. Makes me proud

to be an American." He elbowed Julian. "What do you think, Mr. Darcy?"

Julian smiled. "It suits."

Vanessa grappled with what she could possibly say to divert the attention from her costume, but her phone pinged with a text message from a client.

Chase tipped his tricorn hat at her. "Did you know that Wonder Woman's lasso was formed from the golden girdle of Aphrodite? And, as the daughter of Queen Hippolyta, you're a paragon of feminist Amazon power. Strong, intelligent, and beautiful. Your choice of costume speaks volumes about you, Vanessa."

She laughed. "Don't read too much into it. It was the last one left. It was either this or a female gorilla suit with a pink hair ribbon."

"Well, I'd like you in a monkey suit, too. I'm just thrilled that you wore a costume! Off we go. I want to hear all about your aunt's appointment. Paul told me you'd be going this morning. I want to know what I can do to help."

"How nice of you," Vanessa said.

They were actually in the elevator when Julian stepped between the elevator doors to stop them from closing. "Excuse me, Vanessa?" He glanced at his watch on its fob. "Work question."

She stepped out of the elevator while the doors closed on Chase, who simply raised an eyebrow.

Julian waited until the elevator had gone down. "What would you recommend I do while you're playing swords with a man who steals for a living?"

Vanessa smiled. "He's an auctioneer, Julian, at a well-respected auction house. Why don't you make an appearance at Jane Austen Books in the Emporium and then join in on one of the lectures?"

"Right."

"You knew that."

"I did."

Lexi cat-walked over. "I'll keep him busy—I mean—working the crowd."

That was what Vanessa was afraid of. She didn't want to leave but couldn't disappoint her aunt by reneging on Chase. "Lexi, Sherry's really the one helping us out, so she's in charge. I'll see you all in forty-five minutes."

Her mind turned to Julian as she pressed the down button. She was going down, all right—down for the count with her increasing thoughts about him.

*J*ulian likes you," Chase said after they did a few stretching exercises surrounded by the likes of Captain America, Elvira, and Dr. Who in a ballroom fitted out for sword fighting.

The instructor, a tall, bald African American man dressed in black, handed out blunt wooden swords to everyone.

"Of course he likes me—most of my clients like me and my work. And I like them."

"I think he likes you more than just as his PR manager."

She hadn't allowed herself to articulate it, but coming from Chase, it sounded official and took her off guard. She didn't know quite what to say. "He's British. They're overly polite."

"Call it what you will. Would you like to be offensive or defensive?" Chase asked.

"Which do you think I'd prefer?"

"Offensive."

"You're figuring me out pretty quickly."

"You think so?"

"Either that or I'm totally transparent."

"I wouldn't call you transparent."

"What would you call me?"

"Call you? I'll call you tomorrow. To thank you for the fabulous date we're going to have tonight."

Vanessa laughed and swung her wooden sword back and forth like a golf club. He took her mind off Aunt Ella and he even managed to derail her increasing thoughts of Julian. "We're not going out on a date tonight, Chase."

"Why not? I have it all planned out."

She was curious to know what he'd envisioned, and she liked nothing more than a man with a plan. His cocky, assertive attitude scored points, too, but she had to make it clear that not only couldn't she do tonight but she couldn't do any night in the foreseeable future.

"Tonight I'm going to the ball. You should join us. Paul will be there."

"Oh, yes, your aunt and Paul invited me. They gave me a ticket weeks ago."

"Really? Well, then, you have plans."

"I'll go if you're going to be there. That changes everything."

He was a charmer . . .

"How about tomorrow night?"

And persistent.

"Tomorrow afternoon I'm driving Julian to Louisville for another Jane Austen appearance."

"Louisville?"

The ninja who stood next to Chase turned his head. "If you're going to Louisville, you'll have to eat at Bootleg Bar-B-Q. The restaurant used to be a gas station."

She smiled as she pictured Julian eating in an old gas station and getting barbecue sauce on his starched cravat.

"What's in Louisville?" Chase asked. "And why isn't he flying there?"

"It's a Jane Austen festival. Six months ago this all sounded like a good idea, but now that it's here . . . Originally my aunt was coming with us, but that's not happening anymore . . ."

"I can have my assistant get him a flight out of Midway. Then we can go out tomorrow night."

The glare of the daytime ballroom lighting made her squint, and she steadied herself by leaning on her wooden sword. She was actually looking forward to the road trip with Julian and didn't want it taken away from her!

She rubbed her temples with her free hand. Just how long had she been looking forward to the trip? When did this sneak up on her? Then the glare went away. She'd been excited about this trip before she'd even met him. She hadn't been on a vacation in a while, and even though she'd be working, it would still be a vacation of sorts.

"It's okay, Chase, really. Anyway, I lined up an author signing for him in a very cool indie bookstore in Indianapolis, and the local paper just ran a story on it—so we have to drive in order to stop there on the way."

"I'm sure he can drive himself. He's a big boy. You must really like that stuffed puffy shirt because you're going way above and beyond the call of duty. You're a PR person, not a chauffeur."

"I'm interested in his cause. He has a historical property he's trying to save—and I'm doing it for my aunt, too. She invited him here and she feels personally responsible for showing him a good time in our country."

He smiled. "And a good time I'm sure he'll have with *you* as his personal ambassador."

Vanessa pretended to lunge at him with her sword, but the instructor took hold of the shaft. "Your form is completely off," he said in a deep voice. "And just what were you aiming for?" He gave a slight smile.

In trouble already and the class hadn't even begun.

The instructor stood right beside her. "Everyone, stand opposite your opponent. Now, to begin our choreography—"

"Choreography?" Vanessa interrupted.

He tilted his head toward her. "Wonder Woman. You've already preempted my class with a sloppy strike. Are you interrupting me now, too? Disturbing my flow? Upsetting the chi of the class?"

Vanessa shifted her weight in her fire-engine red boots. "I didn't realize we would be learning choreography."

The instructor sighed. "You expected mortal combat in the Hyatt Chicago? We won't be spilling blood in the ballroom, I can tell you that."

Someone across the room laughed. It was an overgrown Yosemite Sam with a false mustache gone askew.

"Now," the instructor continued as he paced the carpeting, pointing his sword toward the ground like a walking stick, and, much to her chagrin, it reminded her of Julian. "The art of staged combat requires practice, confidence, and a sense of fun. But most of all, you must trust your partner. After all, they will be coming down on your head with a wooden sword. People have been known to get hurt."

Trust? For a choreographed swordfight? But yes, she supposed she trusted Chase.

"The point of staged combat is to put on a show for your audience, and, as such, it's much more flamboyant and drawn out than actual fighting, which, with any luck, would be swift and deadly. For showmanship, you must work with your partner, anticipating your partner's moves and meeting those moves."

The instructor stood right next to Vanessa and practically shouted. "Offense! Stand with your feet apart and your sword held overhead like this." He stood with his sword overhead, ready to slice his opponent vertically in half. It was anything but subtle.

Vanessa had to wonder if her boobs would stay in her bustier with this stance.

Chase seemed to be picking up on this vibe. "I'm not so sure I want to resist your attack." He smiled. "Maybe I'll just wave the white flag and you can do with me what you will."

She laughed. He was a flirt, a big flirt, and she found it refreshing only because he wasn't a client and she didn't have to . . . watch her every move with him. "I'm not sure what I'd do with you, quite frankly."

"Now," the instructor continued. "Defense. Stand with your feet apart, your sword held horizontally, like this, ready to parry the blow from your opponent. This will be our first, most basic move. Okay, everyone relax while I point out the six basic attack zones. Captain Jack Sparrow, I'll need your assistance."

Chase stepped forward.

With his sword, the instructor pointed to the top of Chase's head. "This is the number one attack zone. You want to come down on your opponent's head like this." He brought his sword down slowly on top of Chase's head, but Chase parried it with his sword.

"In fact, I'll have Jack Sparrow here demonstrate with me all six of the attack zones. He looks as if he could do this in his sleep. Ready, Jack?"

Chase nodded. "Always."

Vanessa hoisted her bustier a bit. The costume wasn't really made to save the world in, evidently.

"First I come down on his head—attack zone number one. Defense must block the strike by raising the sword above his head, horizontally. Parallel to the ground. Excellent parry, Jack!

"Then I move my sword horizontally as I aim for his right shoulder for a horizontal cut. He moves his sword as vertically as possible to the right of his body and confidently parries the strike. That's attack zone number two. Number three is the left shoulder, where we repeat. Yes!

"Now I take a downward swinging cut to the opponent's left leg.

Defense, swing your sword down, making sure your blade is pointing at the ground, and parry the attack away from your lower body. And now, the same on the right. See?"

Vanessa had to smile at how confidently and fluidly Chase moved through the attacks. He really made it look like fun. She could see him up on a stage, or even before a camera, performing. Who would know he was really an antiques dealer? What a quirky and cool career and hobby he had going for himself.

"Here's the most risky maneuver—the thrust to your opponent's torso. Step forward and lunge, aiming your sword outward, right at his chest. Defense uses a perfectly timed downward swing to knock the attack to one side. Defense, keep your sword vertical and strike your attacker's sword to whichever side you like."

With this the instructor stopped and looked at Vanessa. "Got it? What are the six attack zones, Wonder Woman?"

Yes, he was picking on her.

Vanessa counted off the zones on her fingers. "Head. Left shoulder. Right shoulder. Left leg. Right leg. Torso."

"Very good, Wonder Woman. Now let's see you put it into action. From the top, everyone! Take it slowly!"

Within no time Vanessa was laughing and having a blast as she and Chase got into a groove right away, their moves perfectly in sync, and he hammed it up with some very Jack Sparrow–inspired facial expressions.

The instructor nodded his approval in Vanessa's direction. "Keep repeating this sequence. In a few minutes you'll be comfortable enough with it to switch up the offense and defense."

Vanessa lunged in for her third torso attack on Chase. "How did you ever get into this?"

"Do you really want to know?" Chase asked as he held his sword horizontally above his head to parry her attack.

"Yes!" She went in for his left shoulder. "This is some crazy shit for a stodgy antiques dealer!"

"I got a call from one of my good friends on a Saturday. It was his son's fifth birthday party. They'd hired a Jack Sparrow impersonator, but the guy canceled just a few hours before the party. He thought of me—said I looked just like Johnny Depp. So I went to the costume shop and bam—the party was a hit. The kids loved me!"

"I'm sure they did," Vanessa said as she aimed for his right leg. She could see him, hamming it up with a yard full of kindergartners. It made her smile.

"The rest is history," he said.

She aimed at his head. "What do you mean?"

He blocked her strike. "I do a couple of birthday parties a month just for the fun of it."

Vanessa was laughing so hard she had to stop, and she leaned on her sword. "You are kidding me!" She was really having fun. She never guessed she'd be in a hotel ballroom dressed as Wonder Woman sparring with a pirate who moonlighted as a kids' party entertainer.

"No." He smiled. "And I need an Elizabeth Swann. What say ye, my beauty? You seem like a natural with a sword."

He had to be the quirkiest, most interesting guy she'd met in a long time.

"Well, wielding a sword isn't exactly on my LinkedIn profile—"

"It can be after this class. The cake and ice cream is a real perk. And I drive to some very interesting Chicagoland neighborhoods. I know where to get the city's best food now, that's for sure, because, generally speaking, I avoid the meals at the kids' parties. Plus I've been checking out all the local landmarks and buildings. This isn't my only hobby, though." He winked.

"I'm sure it's not." She had to admit, he had more than piqued her interest.

The instructor clapped to get everyone's attention. "Not bad. Not bad, people. Now we're switching it up. Offense will take the defensive stance and vice versa. Take it slow, now."

"Finally," Chase said as he raised his sword. "I get to attack you. Are you ready?"

"Of course I'm ready." She parried his attack. "I've been fending off men like you my entire life."

He aimed for her left shoulder. "I'm not like the other men."

Their swords resounded with a click as she parried his thrust again. "Guilty until proven innocent."

"I see. Just like in eighteenth-century France. Harsh. But I would expect no less from an Amazon princess." He aimed at her right shoulder, but she missed a beat and didn't block in time. He stopped just short of her neck but held his sword there for a second. "Maybe you're just afraid to let your guard down. Even a Wonder Woman like you can be afraid of getting hurt."

He was right. How had he managed, so quickly, to find her weakness?

He pulled the sword away from her and leaned on it.

They did another round with him on the offense, and then the last one with her on the offense. It was choreography so it felt like a kind of dance, more of a dance, even, than the minuet with Julian.

After the workshop ended and they were in the hallway, making their way through the werewolves, manga characters, and even a few other Wonder Women, Vanessa stopped, recognizing a Jane Austen Society conference program that had fallen on the floor. A guy dressed as Iron Man called out to Chase and they chatted for a minute.

She picked up the mangled program and noticed the back of it had a giant footprint on it and a Jane Austen quote:

I consider a country-dance as an emblem of marriage. Fidelity and complaisance are the principal duties of both.—Henry Tilney, Northanger Abbey, *by Jane Austen*

Dancing analogous to marriage? She may have to quibble with Austen on that one, or at least read this quote in context.

Once Iron Man had walked away with Jessica Rabbit, Vanessa and Chase made their way through a crowd of Trekkies waiting in line for a photo op with William Shatner. "So how about lunch? My boat is waiting and lobster and champagne will be served."

"I'm afraid it's going to be my laptop and a box lunch for me, followed by an afternoon lineup of Jane Austen lectures and a book signing for Julian. But I will be attending the Jane Austen happy hour before the promenade."

"I have to put in a few hours of work myself, and I'll be a little late, but I'll make it to the ball. How about a spin around the ballroom?"

"I hate to keep turning you down, Chase, but I won't be dancing. The only Regency dance I—barely—know is the minuet, and Julian and I will be opening the ball with it. Dancing is not really my thing. Wish me luck!"

"I'll do better than that. I'll buy you a drink afterward."

He made her smile. A lot. "I'll take you up on that. I'll probably need it to drown my mortification. The things I do!"

"Are you doing it for Julian or for your aunt?"

"For my aunt, of course."

And that was partially true.

Chapter 7

Had she consumed too much port at the Jane Austen happy hour before the ball or did Julian look more handsome and appear more congenial than ever? He stood at the hotel lobby doors, greeting everyone right alongside Aunt Ella, and Vanessa grew wistful at the sight of it.

She stood far enough away—he hadn't seen her yet tonight dressed in her gown—and she thought for a moment about keeping it that way.

The conference attendees were gathering near the doors, hundreds of them, for what was sure to be one of the most embarrassing moments of Vanessa's life. Aunt Ella had strongly suggested that Vanessa, as Julian's leading partner, head up the "promenade" with him. All the attendees of the ball were to walk in a procession to Michigan Avenue, cross over, walk down to Adams Street, cross back, loop up Michigan Avenue, and then walk back up Wacker Drive to the hotel.

Vanessa had never imagined she'd be in a gown, putting herself on parade through the city, but what was a modern girl swooning for a Mr. Darcy to do? And she did have a really fabulous time with her aunt getting ready for the ball. Nothing could take that away from either of them. No, not even the Alzheimer's. Vanessa had set up the video tripod and recorded the whole thing and even turned her phone off.

She lingered in the background, taking in the oddity of the moment. Everyone wore full ball regalia: the women, from their ballroom slippers to their elaborate headdresses, and the men, in their tailcoats and, with some exceptions, badly made and incorrectly tied cravats. Yet they all wore their plastic conference badges on lanyards. It wasn't nineteenth-century England, after all, but modern-day Chicago, and conference workers had to verify entry to the ball with the distinctly twenty-first-century American conference badge.

The costumed crowd looked completely at odds with the sleek hotel lobby. Some of them were texting, or perhaps even posting on social networks, while others took pictures with their phones. All of them were being admired or stared at, depending on how you looked at it, by the other people in the hotel, many of them in costume for Hero Con.

Julian smiled and chatted with a swirling mass of people about to squeeze through a few lobby doors to the street. She felt the urge to post something, to reach for her phone, but for the first time in a long while, she had no idea what to say.

She didn't feel like herself in ballroom flats, curls cascading from her forehead where her blunt-cut bangs would be, and a foot-long feather that bounced with every movement of her head. Her gown stretched to her ankles, covered her tattoo, and softened her. Her black polish had been hidden by white gloves that extended beyond her elbows and spoke of a certain innocence she did not possess. Did she ever possess it?

She was some sort of imposter in silk. Everyone else looked more natural in their gowns and seemed at ease in their costumes. "All ease and friendliness," as she had heard Julian quote from *Pride and Prejudice.*

Women stood in circles, laughing, fanning themselves, taking pictures. Couples stood together, smiling, chatting. The whole thing made her uncomfortable. She wasn't used to such milling around, that was it. Yeah, she needed a task, or multitasks. Multitasking was her friend. Maybe even her best friend. Speaking of friends, where was Sherry?

Vanessa had thousands of friends on her social media sites. Why couldn't she make a few friends at this Jane Austen thing?

She needed, perhaps, another shot of that port or the Madeira she'd sampled at the happy hour lecture to steel her nerves for this evening, even though she now knew that these were men's drinks and off-limits to women of the Regency era. Sweet punches such as ratafia, negus, or claret cup would be served to a lady such as herself at a ball.

Interesting to think of a world so divided into male and female, right down to the drinks, the hobbies, and even the clothing. Today a woman could wear breeches and cravats if she wanted. She could sword fight if she preferred that to quilling.

But didn't such clearly defined roles make life infinitely less complicated? Imagine if you woke up and merely had to choose a gown color instead of: skirt? dress? jeans? dressy slacks? casual slacks? shorts? Granted, this was a first-world problem, but a problem nonetheless.

Lately, Vanessa had been stupefied in the breakfast cereal aisle or the bread aisle of the grocery store, completely baffled by the sheer number of choices. Certainly, looking for "fiber" narrowed it down, but more than once she'd walked away from the store with nothing, overwhelmed and confused by what should have been a simple decision. She had solved the problem by ordering from an online grocery delivery service so she could order the same things every week, with the added bonus that she no longer needed to deal with the people who worked at the cash register.

Against her aunt's wishes, she pulled her phone out of her little silk purse that Aunt Ella called a reticule. The thing was so small she had to sacrifice all kinds of necessities like lipstick and her emergency tampon in order to get her phone in there, despite promising she wouldn't touch it except strictly for work tonight.

Surely her aunt couldn't object to her capturing the moment, so she took her phone camera and zoomed in on Julian, watching and clicking photos. Zooming in on his cravat, she saw that yes, he had tied it in a perfect ballroom knot. Panning back, she had to admire his black cutaway coat, his crisp white shirt, and his strong calves in white stockings. Stockings? Since when did she find stockings on a man attractive?

A glint of silver caught her attention out of the corner of her eye.

It was Chase's sword catching the light as he leaned up against a column, dressed in a showy black velvet pirate coat, a white shirt, and dark pants tucked into boots. He stared at her with his arms folded, an uncharacteristic slight frown on his face.

He had been watching her watch—and photograph—Julian.

Despite the awkwardness of it, she walked over to him, relieved to see him.

Her throat went dry and she could hardly speak. "I'm looking forward to a drink with you."

His phone beeped with a text message. "Yes, yes. Likewise. Excuse me, though," he said. "I have to respond to this."

He keyed something in while she stood there, and it hit her how often she had done this to other people but rarely had been on the receiving end of it.

"That was Lexi." Chase pocketed his phone. "She's asked me to dance and she's waiting for me right now by the escalators. But let's grab a drink when we can, my lady." He tipped his hat and sauntered off.

Two young Janeites, probably thirteen-year-olds, in their gowns, stood watching. They weren't too young to understand Vanessa had just been completely blown off by a . . . pirate! They gave her a pained, then sympathetic, look.

"No need to feel sorry for me," Vanessa said to them. "I'm opening the ball with Mr. Darcy tonight."

They giggled. "You are?" one of them said.

"That pirate was totally cute, though," said the other.

Vanessa smiled and began to skirt the mass of people to make her way to the front where she belonged. This was a business gig, first and foremost, and she'd best start treating it that way and less like a high school dance.

"Vanessa! Vanessa!" It was Sherry, dressed in a baby blue gown and sparkling tiara, waving a white fan. When Sherry leaned in to hug her, Vanessa could smell the bubble gum.

"Wow," Sherry said as she stepped back to look at Vanessa. "That gown looks smokin' on you. Me-ow."

Of course, this was Sherry talking. "Come join me up front, Sherry," Vanessa said.

Sherry linked her arm in Vanessa's, something this crowd seemed to be fond of.

"Should we ask my Ask Mr. Darcy app just how gorgeous you look?"

Vanessa knew better than to deny Sherry a chance to shake her Mr. Darcy Magic 8 Ball on her phone.

"Mr. Darcy says, 'You must allow me to tell you how ardently I admire and love you.'"

The word "ardently" struck her like an arrow. Mr. Darcy's words were really getting to her. How soon could she read *Pride and Prejudice*?

"Are you going to be walking in the promenade with—him?" Sherry asked.

"With Julian, you mean?" Vanessa laughed. "Yes. Want to join us?"

"Oh, no, no, I couldn't do that."

"Of course you could, Sherry."

"Oh, no! You two are the lead couple of the evening! But have you checked your Twitter feed? You set something off out there and now something's brewing."

Vanessa stopped in her ballroom-flat tracks and her gown brushed up against an ATM. "What's going on?" She whipped her phone out.

It took her all of about a minute to realize that she had whipped up more than a frenzy with her competition to open the ball with Julian. It seemed that someone in the group was upset about not being chosen and they'd incited the wrath of the local Brontë Society. The Brontë fans were rallying to gate-crash the ball?

"Vanessa!" Aunt Ella's tone of voice said it all.

Vanessa squirreled her phone away in her reticule.

"It's time to lead the promenade, my *dear*." She flashed her laser eyes on Vanessa's reticule, making it more than clear that the phone was off-limits.

Paul stood by Aunt Ella's side and linked his arm in hers.

Julian was scanning the lobby for someone, looking past the semicircle of women surrounding him, and when he found Vanessa he locked eyes with her.

Had she been holding up the promenade? She hoped not.

"Excuse me, ladies," he said as he broke through them and gave Vanessa a deep bow. "You look—exquisite."

How much of this was for show? Vanessa couldn't say.

"The lady might simply accept the compliment," Julian said.

It took a moment, but Vanessa mumbled, "Thank you."

He did seem to have a hard time taking his eyes off her, and she noticed his eyebrows rise up in a quick flash.

She remembered reading something about body language years ago, when she was having trouble decoding the mixed signals her serious boyfriend at the time kept sending her. When a man raised his eyebrows at you quickly, almost unnoticeably, it was entirely sub-conscious on his part, but if you saw this flicker of a move, it meant he was extremely interested. In. You.

Or he could just have something irritating his eye.

She fumbled a curtsy.

In her head she rattled off the short list of body language clues that indicated a man's attraction to a woman:

His feet pointed toward you in a crowd. Check.

His body acted like a shield, blocking other people. Check.

He touched you frequently. Check. Check. Check.

He adjusted his tie—or (ahem) cravat—to preen. Check.

This only meant physical attraction, and maybe he just enjoyed seeing her in this gown. As soon as they were on the road tomorrow things would be back to normal because she'd be in her jeans and T-shirt.

This was business, not a dance. He was a client, not a prospect. And she had a job to do here.

She linked her arm in his and hardly said a word as they sallied forth into the city, where, like in a silent film, people pointed and smiled, but Vanessa was too absorbed in her own thoughts to notice. She had to rack her brain on how to thwart this impending Brontë mob, until, right there on Michigan Avenue, she had a better idea:

Embrace it. This gate-crashing could be the best thing that hap-pened to Julian and his book. In fact, why the hell hadn't she thought of alerting the Brontë Society herself? She really was losing her edge. Still, she would make sure it got on the news—if only she could tip off the media soon enough!

"Miss Roberts." Julian broke into her rapid-fire thoughts as they walked toward the hotel. "You're not being your usual self. Could it be that you're actually enjoying the Jane Austen festivities and you've become a convert? That you're a changed woman in a floor-length gown?"

She needed to sneak off somewhere to use her phone, but where and when? Respond to Julian, she told herself. Respond.

"I think it would take more than a gown to change me," she said. "Don't you?"

"Well, frankly, yes, I believe it would take infinitely more."

She glared at him. He didn't have to go that far!

"But silence is so unlike you."

Vanessa laughed and looked at him, trying to find something to take a jab at. "I like your tights. Where did you get them? I'm in the market for some white ones like that myself."

"Excellent. You're still in there, somewhere. They're not tights. They're men's stockings made out of the finest silk, and you would know this if only you'd have bothered to watch my entire presentation."

Ah, but she *had* watched his entire presentation. Little did he know, she had watched the entire thing on video. Twice.

How soon could she bolt to the ladies' room to use her phone? She looked behind her to gauge how long the procession was and how long it might take all these people to settle into the ballroom, because she had to be back in the ballroom before the last straggler was in or Aunt Ella would have her head faster than Henry VIII.

When she looked back, though, something like happiness spilled over her. It was a gorgeous September eve, the sun was setting, turning the buildings aglow in warmth, and behind her was a long, long procession of people in finery and feathers that really got everyone on the street to stop, pay attention, and smile. The Janeites were laughing and chatting, and it was a beautiful sight, really, and a beautiful moment, but she had missed most of the walk obsessing over the flash mob. At least she could watch the video of the promenade she had Kai shooting. They rounded the corner to the hotel.

"Miss Roberts, something must be amiss. Is there something wrong? Something I might help with, perhaps?"

Help. She hadn't thought about asking anyone for help with this. Well, what could anyone really do, anyway? Especially Julian, who barely knew how to use his cell phone.

"Well, you're right. There is something . . . But, if you'll excuse me for a moment? I'll meet you in the ballroom. I need to visit the ladies'."

"Just let me know if I can be of assistance," he said. "Not—not in the ladies', of course, well—"

"Of course I don't need your help in that department! Look, I'll keep you posted," she said as she walked backward.

He gave a slight bow. "Yes, do. Keep me—posted."

She turned, hiked up her gown, and vaulted toward the escalators. Once in the bathroom, she yanked out her phone to start calling all the local TV news stations first.

But her phone was out of juice.

It took a lot to make her swear out loud, in public, but there, in the marble-floored bathroom with glittering mirrors and ladies lined up in their gowns, was Vanessa, fanning herself with her fan, pacing the floor, staring at her phone, shaking it, and yelling.

"You have got to be fucking kidding me!"

The ladies in line went silent while she stopped to look at herself in the mirror, a strange amalgam of lady and modern smut-mouth.

There was a girl in line, probably no more than twelve years old, in a gown and bonnet, and Vanessa felt the sting of her f-bomb rant.

"I'm sorry. My phone is out of battery," she explained. "A lady should never use that word, you know. It's very uncool."

The women in line looked at her in horror, but the twelve-year-old smiled. These women, some of them armed with PhDs, knew a lot, but they didn't know that a Brontë flash mob would be descending upon the Janeites at any moment, and the media needed to be here! If she didn't get at least one news channel here, she'd have failed Julian, her aunt, and Janeites everywhere, and most of all, she'd have failed herself in the face of a once-in-a-lifetime chance of something going viral.

Quickly, under the glare of the fluorescent bathroom lights, she considered her options, checking them off in her head, eliminating each and every one. No, she couldn't ask anyone else for their phones because she didn't have the media reps' phone numbers memorized. All her contacts were in her phone—and her laptop—but she'd left that at home because of the damn reticule that was the size of a kid's toy purse.

Kai? No, she'd thought of copying all her contacts into Kai's phone, but then she'd thought better of it because he was only an intern and he would leave her, and she didn't want him to leave with the coveted list of contacts she'd spent years cultivating. After all, the real contacts at the stations and papers weren't always the obvious ones. In many cases, the people who'd jump the quickest were personal assistants, interns, and rookie reporters.

Several toilets flushed in succession as Vanessa realized something quite shitty: only Lexi would have the numbers she needed.

Without so much as adjusting her drooping ostrich feather, Vanessa, to the sound of Dyson hand dryers, propelled herself into the hall and toward the ballroom, where, after a quick scan of the room, she discovered Lexi was nowhere to be found.

Her eyes landed on a nearby couple dressed in exquisite Regency garb and hovered over a smartphone laughing, presumably looking at pictures. It took everything in Vanessa's power not to just yank the phone from their hands, but something about them hit her hard. She could feel it. They were in love—nauseatingly in love—and Vanessa, even in her rush, felt the power of it.

"Henry!" The woman laughed. "Really?" She looked to be about Vanessa's age and so happy with this Henry.

Vanessa slid up to them and smiled, bursting their little love bubble. "Excuse me. Can I borrow your phone to make a quick local call? It's an emergency and my phone's out of batteries."

Henry dug into his pocket and handed her his phone right away. "An emergency? Of course." He had an English accent. Why did that surprise her?

"Thank you, umm . . . ?"

"Henry. Henry Wrightman. And this is Chloe Parker."

"Hi." Chloe waved with a smile. She was from Chicago; Vanessa could nail the accent anywhere.

Well. International couples are everywhere, really.

"I do hope everything's quite all right. Let us know if we can be of any assistance," Henry said.

She keyed in Lexi's cell number—a number she hadn't forgotten even after all these years.

"Hello?" Lexi answered.

"Lexi. It's Vanessa. Where are you? I need to talk to you right away. It's an emergency."

Henry had his arm around Chloe now, and Vanessa turned away.

Lexi sighed. "Of course I'm preoccupied, Vanessa. What kind of emergency?"

"Just tell me where you are." Vanessa's eyes continued to scan the room.

"I'm by the potted palms, palming your Mr. Darcy. He's a bit stiff, in every sense of the word. I quite like that about him—"

She was with Julian? What happened to Chase? Vanessa ended the call, tossed the phone back into Henry's free hand, said a brisk thank-you, and beelined for the potted palms across the ballroom until someone hooked into her arm, jolting her backward.

"Vanessa!" It was Paul, Aunt Ella's friend. "You look absolutely ravishing."

"Paul, something's come up and—"

He nodded and took her hand in his. "I need to ask you something very important. It's about your aunt."

"Is everything okay? Where is she?"

"Everything's fine. Better than fine. She's in the restroom right now with Helena, powdering her nose, which is better than powdering her wig—of course that would be a Georgian ball and not Regency."

"Paul. I'm really sorry, but I have to dash. Can we talk later?" Vanessa sidestepped away.

"Yes. Yes, later, but not too much later. After the first dance. Come and find me. It's important—"

Vanessa left the poor man rambling while she darted toward Lexi, who stood near the potted palms, a palm leaf suggestively covering her pelvic area as if she were Eve herself, and sure enough, she was feeding Julian a strawberry.

Julian's eyes did widen a bit when he saw Vanessa approaching, but his mouth was full of strawberry, and he couldn't say a word.

Lexi turned and rolled her eyes. "Whatever *do* you want? I was just showing our guest how hospitable some of us Chicago women can be."

"I need to use your phone."

"Nobody uses my phone. Ever. Ask somebody else."

"I need your phone, Lexi. I need to call the TV stations. Please. For old times' sake. Mine's out of batteries."

Lexi smiled and put her hand on the small of Julian's back. "I see. You want to call *my* contacts. I've been holding out the olive branch to you for two days now, you don't even so much as talk to me, but now you want my contacts?"

Julian leaned in to Lexi. "Miss Stone, perhaps you would acquiesce on my account? It seems Miss Roberts is in dire need of your phone. Perhaps there is something I might do for you in return?"

Lexi batted her fake eyelashes at him. "Well, I can think of any number of things you can do for me, or with me, or to me, and the thought of it makes me quiver, but I'd rather have Vanessa be beholden to me. If I give you my phone, Vanessa dear, you must agree to do my bidding."

Vanessa held out her hand for the phone. "Name it. I'll do it."

"Excuse us, darling," Lexi said to Julian as she took Vanessa aside. "If you hand him over to me as a client, you can use my phone the entire week."

"'Him' who? Julian?"

"Yes."

"No."

"He means that much to you, does he? Now I really want in. Surely it can't be for the money."

"There's no money in it," Vanessa said.

"I began to gather that. You must really like him."

"I'm doing it for my aunt. Please, I just need your phone for a few minutes."

Lexi looked away, feigning boredom.

The quartet began to warm up and the cacophony of instruments underscored the rush of conflicting thoughts in Vanessa's brain. If she didn't make the calls now, she'd lose her chance. She had to strike a deal now.

Lexi spoke first. "I'll tell you what. We'll share him as a client. Like we used to back in the day. It'll show you I've changed—especially since I think he's kind of hot." She sucked in her cheeks, emphasizing her already chiseled features and her pallid skin.

"But there's no money to split. It's pro bono."

"That's a deal, but with two conditions. One, that I open the dance with him tonight. And two, that I go with you two to Louisville. Even though I hate Louisville. The *South*. The *countryside*."

Damn. Julian must've told her about Louisville. She should've warned him about Lexi, but it was already too late. Vanessa couldn't disappoint Aunt Ella by letting Lexi open the dance with him. And, much as she dreaded the thought of driving to and from Louisville with her, she didn't have the luxury of time to bargain.

"I will open the dance with him," Vanessa said. "But fine, you can come with us to Louisville." She sighed. Even as she said it, she regretted it. "He rides in the front with me, though."

"You've gotten better at negotiating," Lexi said.

"I learned from the master, didn't I?"

"Yes, you did, Padawan." Lexi held out her gloved hand to shake, and Vanessa shook, thinking she should've gotten all this in writing, then quickly made a flurry of calls while Lexi fed a somewhat reluctant Julian an oversized purple grape. Was Julian smart enough to see Lexi for who she really was? Regardless, Vanessa wouldn't be the one to intervene—she'd made that mistake before. Let him find out for himself. After all, he was a big boy, and men never wanted to hear the truth, did they?

She had bigger things to worry about, and she sincerely hoped this was a slow news day out there. She hadn't had time to check her local news apps, but the TV cams would only show if nothing else was going on. Her last call was to Kai, reminding him to film the entire evening, but he just sighed, saying of course he knew that, duh.

The dance caller brought the room to attention and the quartet struck up the chord that was the cue for Julian and Vanessa. With a bow from him and a curtsy from her, they began the minuet they'd practiced so diligently on Oak Street Beach the previous night, and as Vanessa counted her steps and figures, she could see Aunt Ella beaming at them from her perch at the head table.

That alone made all this—the wearing of a Regency gown, the recurring thoughts of a man who would be gone in a few days, and now Lexi in tow—worth it.

Although even Vanessa had to admit that the quartet added a new, brighter dimension to their dancing, and she couldn't help but smile. The music seemed to play her, and were she a more sentimental girl, she might have read something into the fact that she and Julian were thrown together at this point in time and meant to meet, and dance, and . . . and what? Nothing had happened, and he'd be back in England before his tea got cold.

Were she not so preoccupied with the fact that she needed to be posting witty remarks about the ball on social media via Lexi's phone and that, at any moment, a flash mob would appear and she could only hope the TV cameras could get here in time . . . she might have taken more notice of Julian. She realized he was looking at her rather intently and that he danced very well. Even though she tried to look like she knew what the hell she was doing, they had made a few glaring missteps.

When she could, she allowed her eyes to dart to all corners of the room, wondering when the Brontë flash mob would strike and what they would look like. Would they be a throng of wide-eyed women, without makeup, in black Victorian dresses, their hair in buns, brandishing *Jane Eyre*, *Wuthering Heights*, and *The Professor*? Or would they be more like Sherry, wearing T-shirts that said things like *I'd go to my grave for Heathcliff*? Would they have baseball hats on saying *Blinded by love for Mr. Rochester*? Vanessa didn't remember much about *Wuthering Heights*, but it did, in her opinion, revolve around some seriously screwed-up people isolated in the English moors, and as she recalled, the sociopathic Heathcliff made Darcy look like a real catch.

She began to dance with a little more Elizabeth Bennet in her step once she spotted a news camera crew enter the room.

As she spun around, she noticed Chase standing near the punch bowl, his arms crossed as Lexi spoke to him.

One of the last things Lexi had said to Vanessa in a rage all those years ago was that Vanessa would end up a crazy cat lady, and maybe that was true.

She began to worry, though—not about her destiny with cats, but that the Brontë Society flash mob might not appear at all or they might not somehow make it past security with their potentially passionate ways, and the media would never listen to her summons again.

There: another TV crew appeared. When she looked toward Aunt Ella for approval, she saw that her aunt's chair stood empty, and that rocked Vanessa to the core. Where did she go? Did she miss Vanessa's performance? She would never leave the ball, surely!

Finally Vanessa saw her aunt and Paul standing on the side of the ballroom floor, arm in arm, smiling, very near to that sappy Chloe and Henry couple.

The dance ended, Julian bowed, she curtsied, and the room resounded with clapping.

"You were amazing," Sherry said as she stepped right up to Vanessa.

She wanted to believe Sherry but was only too aware of the flaws in her minuet.

Sherry nudged Vanessa with her elbow. "You and Julian, eh? Looking good together!"

Vanessa shook her head. "No, no, Sherry, don't go there."

"What? He's into you. Everyone around me was talking about how obvious it is."

"He's a client, Sherry. He lives in England. How could I possibly be into *him*?" Vanessa asked just as Sherry began making the "cut" sign with her hand.

Julian appeared as if out of nowhere. Had he overheard her?

He leaned in toward Vanessa and Sherry. "Do you know what Jane Austen said about dancing?"

He looked directly at Vanessa, who smiled. She said, "How do I have this feeling I'm going to hear it whether I want to or not?"

Sherry just gaped at Julian with awe. For her, this man was too good to be true.

"It was in *Northanger Abbey* that she had her hero Henry Tilney say, 'I consider a country-dance as an emblem of marriage. Fidelity and complaisance are the principal duties of both.'"

That quote again! Vanessa dismissed it, but Sherry was practically orgasmic with joy over it.

"I love that scene with Henry and Catherine! Love, love *Northanger Abbey*!"

"Then you, Miss Sherry, will love Bath as well. You must climb Beechen Cliff, visit the Pump Room, and see the Assembly Rooms where Henry and Catherine danced."

Sherry clasped her gloved hands together. "I can't wait!"

But Vanessa's attention was on the dance floor. She had the feeling something newsworthy was going down, and sure enough, Henry was going down on one knee in front of Chloe, on the dance floor.

"Sherry, quick. Give me your phone!"

"Miss Parker," Henry said as he looked up at Chloe and presented a ring, "I thought it only fitting that I propose to you here. I have already asked your daughter for the permission of your hand—"

Vanessa couldn't believe someone would propose . . . here? She began snapping pictures with Sherry's phone.

An adorable girl dressed in a Regency gown and spit curls emerged from the crowd, smiling, and hurried to Henry's side.

"And that permission has been granted. Thank you, Abigail. Miss Parker, will you marry me?"

The crowd collectively said, "Awww . . ."

Vanessa whispered to Sherry as she continued to get more shots. "Who are these two?"

"Henry Wrightman and Chloe Parker. She's a Chicago Jane Austen Society life member and spent a couple weeks last year on a reality show set in England. She had to give up her phone, computer—everything—and live as if it were 1812."

"Who would be crazy enough to do that?" Vanessa asked.

"Only just about everyone in this room," Sherry said. "And that's where she met Henry."

Chloe seemed about ready to cry with joy. "Yes, Mr. Wrightman, I do believe I will marry you."

The crowd clapped and cheered and flashbulbs flashed while Abigail grinned from ear to ear.

Just as Henry rose to kiss Chloe and Abigail hugged them both, Paul escorted Aunt Ella to the center of the dance floor.

Vanessa took a picture. What sort of announcement was Paul going to make? Would he honor her aunt just as Julian had? But then, right before her eyes, Paul bent to one knee, and he, too, held out a ring.

What the hell?! What was Paul doing? He looked over at Vanessa.

"Vanessa, I meant to ask your permission, but, well, this shouldn't be a big surprise to you." Vanessa couldn't breathe. Something sliced into her chest. Sherry's phone shook in her hands until she dropped it.

Julian picked up the phone, handed it to Vanessa, and hooked his arm in hers to steady her. "Are you quite all right?"

She couldn't speak.

"That answers my question."

"I'll get her a glass of water." Sherry turned and spun off.

Chloe, Henry, and Abigail took hands and skipped to the sidelines. Paul turned to Aunt Ella.

"For so many years," Paul said, "I have ardently admired and loved you, Ella. Will you, could you, marry me and make me the happiest man in all the—shire?"

The crowd cheered and clapped.

Vanessa put Sherry's phone in Julian's hands. He knew what to do, and that was to take the pictures Vanessa couldn't. Much to her amazement, Mr. Darcy knew his way around a cell phone camera, and he clicked away. Vanessa steadied herself against him.

"Yes!" Aunt Ella smiled. "I thought you'd never ask! I haven't gotten any younger waiting for you!"

Everyone except Vanessa laughed.

"I was waiting for just the right moment, and this is it." As Paul slid the ring on Aunt Ella's finger, Vanessa felt as if she were swirling in a sink and then getting sucked down the drain.

She couldn't lose her aunt! What would Aunt Ella do? Move in with Paul in his mansion on the north shore? What about Vanessa? Why hadn't anyone consulted her? What the hell was she supposed to do? She hated herself for thinking it, she didn't want to think it, but: her seventy-nine-year-old aunt would be walking down the aisle before her, too? Her mind flashed to her frozen eggs in that vault—

Suddenly the room tilted and the ballroom floor came up right under her face.

Sherry held a glass of water to Vanessa's lips and, once she'd sipped and looked up, she found herself surrounded by Julian, Chase, the newly engaged Henry and Chloe, and the newly engaged Aunt Ella and Paul.

Chase spoke first, and she realized he was cradling her head. "Are you all right?"

Chloe smiled down on her. "You fainted. Do you faint easily?"

"I do," Vanessa said. She'd had the odd stress-related fainting fit ever since her parents' divorce.

Julian waved a little open tin of something under her nose. It reeked of rotten eggs and vinegar. "What the hell, Julian!" Her eyes started watering.

"They're smelling salts. Feeling less faint now?"

"Yes, and more nauseous, too!" She tried to scramble to her feet.

"Works every time," Julian said.

"But—thank you," she said. She picked up Sherry's phone.

"Of course."

Chase and Henry helped her up to her feet. Henry had to be the nicest guy she'd ever met. He hardly knew her, after all! Whoever this Chloe was, she certainly deserved a Henry more than Vanessa did. No doubt Chloe was a golden girl herself. Vanessa could tell the real deal when she saw it.

Aunt Ella had worry all over her face, and her wrinkles and worry lines looked more visible than ever. She knew stress could only exacerbate her aunt's dementia. She was supposed to be keeping her from stress and not causing it!

She went to hug her. "Aunt Ella, I'm so happy for you and Paul! Congrats! This is such great news. I can't believe I fainted from happiness! So that's what you wanted to talk to me about, right, Paul? Sorry I didn't take the time—"

She didn't take the time for a lot of things, she realized. She was throttling through life full speed ahead, with all systems go and all channels on, listening to nobody and stopping for nothing. If she'd just taken a moment to listen to Paul she would've been warned and she wouldn't have fainted and destroyed his proposal and worried her aunt into another probable episode. Aunt Ella, more than anyone, after a lifetime of sacrifice taking care of Vanessa and righting her own baby sister's wrongs, deserved to be happy. How could Vanessa dash all of that?

"I have to get a picture of this! Smile . . ."

Aunt Ella and Paul smiled, then they both hugged Vanessa, and just as they were all finally able to say something, the dance caller shrieked.

"Security! Security!"

A posse of women in black, with *Heathcliff* printed in white on their black T-shirts and bright red lipstick on their lips, took over the dance floor, and with their long hair loose and flowing, they turned on a boom box, blasted "Wuthering Heights" by Kate Bush, and began some wild dancing, all in sync. The Janeites stood back and watched, confused and aghast.

Vanessa spun around, making sure the TV cams were on this, and they were. Kai, too, scuttled around the room, filming the crowd from various angles. She couldn't believe it. Something was going her way! She had to find a reporter and tell them Julian would be available for interviews afterward! She had to post that this was going down!

Just then the ballroom doors burst open and a tall, tanned, and muscular man with wavy, shoulder-length, dark brown hair and dressed in a nineteenth-century caped coat and riding boots stormed straight up to Julian. He stripped off his coat, revealing his billowing shirt, unbuttoned to the chest and not secured with any cravat. His chest looked too broad and strong to be contained by the shirt, much less a cravat. He brandished a sword. It was a stage sword, but a sword nonetheless. "This is a challenge, Mr. Darcy!" he said in a fake, but pretty accurate English accent. "One that's long overdue. A duel! A duel to the death!"

This was better than if she'd scripted it herself. A duel? "Brilliant!" as the Brits would say!

Julian stepped back. He didn't have a sword.

"Security!" the dance caller yelled into the microphone.

But Vanessa had already alerted security, before the ball, to say that all this was anticipated and staged. She'd had the authority and she'd used it.

Julian stripped off his frock coat, untied and removed his cravat, and rolled up his sleeves, and while he did that, Chase handed him his stage sword even as he borrowed another one from a nearby redcoat.

Vanessa couldn't believe her luck.

By now the Brontë mob was chanting, "Heath-cliff, Heath-cliff," and the Janeites followed suit, clapping and chanting, "Dar-cy, Dar-cy!" The Janeites outnumbered the Brontë fans, and they seemed to take it in stride that this was part of tonight's show.

Chase positioned the men in front of the quartet and readied them for the duel. The musicians backed off.

Heathcliff made the first move, and Vanessa could tell, now that she'd taken her swording class, that he was taking the offense, and all Julian could do at this point was defend himself.

Her blood pumped. Never in her professional life had anything so spontaneous played out so well; nor had she ever, on a personal level, seen anything so sexy as these two gorgeous men in their shirtsleeves, their swords flashing, their hair tumbling, and their bodies so taut, so skilled and strong as they lunged and struck.

She took as many photos as she could and posted:

Literary heroes face-off in a duel—R u on Team Darcy or Team Heathcliff? #JASNAagm #UndressingMrDarcy

To the clink of swords and the sight of Julian's strained muscles as he proceeded to defend . . . and win the duel in Mr. Darcy's honor, Vanessa allowed herself to think that the nineteenth century in general might've been a great era and Julian in particular was a man worth getting to know better.

While the Janeites, including Aunt Ella, clapped and smiled, and Heathcliff slunk away, and the flash mob disappeared as quickly as they'd arrived, and Paul took Julian's arm and held it up in victory, Vanessa got that familiar feeling deep in her abdomen. It was a feeling she'd only had about three times in her life, a gripping, all-encompassing yearning, an ache, really, for proximity.

Julian was hot, there was no doubt about that, but it had taken this duel to bring it to Vanessa's attention that he was more than just another sexy client. He happened to be a stand-up man, the kind of man who fought (or at least fake fought) for his principles and who valued and honored older women like her aunt, and it made her want to get to know him better.

She watched, as if it were a movie she'd written herself, as the TV cameras panned over Julian and the reporters vied for his attention, but all he could do was look across the ballroom, past the fawning women in their glittering gowns, low-cut bodices, and baubles in their updo hairstyles, and gaze at Vanessa, who smiled.

She posted:

To Mr. Darcy go the spoils. #JASNAagm #UndressingMrDarcy

The quartet struck up a lively English country dance, as if on cue to Vanessa's heart.

"There's no denying it." Lexi jabbed Vanessa with her elbow. "He's Mr. Hot-for-You. Please tell me you're going to take advantage of this—of him."

She didn't say a word to Lexi because she couldn't take her eyes off him as he nodded and answered the reporters' questions while cameras flashed around him.

"It's just what the doctor ordered," Lexi said. "A minifling. He's the perfect candidate."

"No, he's not. He's a client and my aunt's friend."

"How about *after* the job's over? He's irresistible, and with this kind of tight deadline, with him leaving the country so soon, you need to act fast. If you don't make a move, he might start going after me. Because if you can't get the girl you want, you might as well sleep with her best friend."

Vanessa laughed. Lexi was the crazy one—with or without cats. Why hadn't she seen this in her twenties? "You're hardly my best friend, Lexi."

"Oh, but I am," Lexi said. She pretended to look around. "You've invested too much time with your virtual friends. I don't see anyone else filling the position."

"Vanessa!" Sherry bounded up to them, her boobs jostling in her low-cut gown. "Julian's asking for you. He says you've got the first dance on his dance card."

But she had told Chase she couldn't dance, she wouldn't dance, and hadn't she agreed to a drink with him after the minuet? "Sherry, you need to take that first dance. Just tell him I'm not up to it after fainting."

Sherry smiled. "If you say so."

"And, Sherry, I'd love it if you could join all of us for a jaunt to Louisville tomorrow night for their Jane Austen Festival. We'll be back by Tuesday."

"Louisville? I've always wanted to go to that festival! I'll have to see if I can get off of work." With that she headed back to the dance floor.

A crowd had been gathering around Vanessa, a costumed, friendly, female crowd that had only good things to say.

"Are you Ella Morgan's niece? You did a wonderful job opening the ball. Can I buy you a glass of wine?"

And then the head of the Chicago society approached and said, "We'd like to bestow an honorary Chicago membership to you, for all of your work on the conference. It's been a resounding success."

"Thank you," Vanessa said. Her aunt and Paul nodded and smiled at her from across the room. A sense of belonging came over her unlike anything she had known in a long time.

Lexi, in her gown, sashayed away.

"Come on, everyone," Chase said. "Let's raise a glass to Ella and Paul."

After the group made a toast, Vanessa spoke to Chase. "Did you know Paul was going to propose tonight?"

"I knew he had bought the ring, but I had no idea he'd do it tonight. I guess now I know why he bought me the ticket to the ball tonight."

"Yes, all along he's been hounding me to come, too."

"I'm a little surprised he didn't tell me he was going to propose tonight."

"Why do you say that?"

"I'm the best man." He clinked his glass with hers.

She laughed. "If Paul says so, then you are—the best man."

"I'm glad you agree. You've finally come to your senses. I wonder if you'll be maid of honor."

"Always a bridesmaid! I have a closet full of hideous dresses to prove it."

She took a sip of champagne and glanced out on the dance floor at Julian and Sherry, laughing together as they made their way down the line of English country dancers.

As Julian joined the end of the line, he shot a glance at Vanessa, who raised her glass to him. He nodded with a smile.

Vanessa drank her champagne, watching Julian, knowing she had won all across the board tonight. But there was one thing she was losing: the battle against her attraction to Julian.

Chapter 8

The next day Vanessa felt something like regret, or maybe it was the chicken salad she'd had for lunch with her aunt. But she hadn't protested when Lexi offered to take Julian to Hero Con, and maybe she should have. He had actually wanted to go—or was he simply being polite?

Either way it gave her an opportunity to catch up on work and be sure her aunt was all squared away before tonight's road trip. A text from Julian couldn't mean anything good had gone down, though.

A text . . . from Julian? She didn't even know he could text. It read:

V pls help me! 4th floor mens toilet in the Hyatt! Hurry!

She texted back:

4 real, Julian?

Please, I'm begging you. Hurry! I'm rather tied up in the mens toilet in head 2 toe leathers and I can't get out!

Tied up? In head-to-toe "leathers"? Leather? They had been gone for all of three hours!

Within twenty minutes Vanessa burst through the men's room door. "All right, Mr. Darcy. Where the hell are you?" He wasn't at the urinals and neither was anyone else, thank goodness. The last thing she needed to see would be Jabba the Hutt's or Mr. Spock's genitalia.

A guy dressed as a zombie was washing his hands and he didn't seem at all surprised to see a woman come in.

"Trying to get the blood off your hands?" Vanessa joked to him.

The zombie smiled. "Too long of a line in the women's bathroom?"

"Actually, I'm looking for my Mr. Darcy," Vanessa said as she looked under the doors of the stalls.

"In here? Does Mr. Darcy actually take a shit?" the zombie asked.

Vanessa laughed. Who knew zombies would have a sense of humor? "If he does, it would no doubt smell of roses."

The zombie laughed. "Let me know if you're ever in the market for a zombie."

A zombie, yes, that would be the perfect match for her. Right.

He checked his matted, fake-blood-spattered hair in the mirror and left.

"I'm over here." A British accent floated out of the last stall door.

Vanessa slowly edged the stall door open, and there, standing on top of the toilet with the lid down, was Julian, in the tightest brown leather pants and leather shirt she'd ever seen on anyone.

She couldn't help but laugh. Tears came to her eyes. "I never say this, Julian, but LOL."

"Go ahead, laugh," he said.

"I'm sorry." She giggled. "This is entirely different from seeing you at a formal ball, on your best Mr. Darcy behavior."

"I agree. I cannot account for what I may do in a leather outfit."

She took a picture with her phone. "Actually, it's a good look for you. Very hot. I'm trying to think of how I can spin this one."

"I am most glad you are excessively diverted."

"But—you're not tied up."

"Not literally, no."

"You said you were tied up."

"Is Lexi out there?" He was changing the subject.

"I didn't see her."

"She came in here looking for me."

"Of course she did. You're not the first man to hide from her in a men's room."

He looked at her knowingly.

"And at least one that I know of tried to ditch her by hiding in a women's restroom."

"I wish you wouldn't say 'restroom.' Might you perhaps call it a 'toilet'?"

"Here I am rescuing your leather-clad ass"—she laughed—"and you're playing Britspeak with me? Julian. How did you ever get yourself into this mess? And speaking of toilet, why not just get down from there?"

He frowned. "I can't. The trousers are too tight. And then not only would I be in leather trousers, but worse, I'd be wearing *torn* leather trousers."

"You really are out of your comfort zone, aren't you?" He looked good in those tight leather pants, though, and Vanessa couldn't help but appreciate that fact. "Need I ask how Lexi got you into them, anyway? And why?"

He frowned. "She wanted me to be Gary Mitchell for her."

"Gary Mitchell?"

"A nemesis of Captain Kirk, evidently. She's in a *Star Trek* outfit with three breasts today."

"Three? As if two of hers aren't enough? Now, that I'd like to see. How did she pull that off?"

"Prosthetics."

"How do you know?" Vanessa smirked.

"Well, after doing a treble take, I asked. She wanted me to join her in some role-playing and photo ops at the Star Trek Pavilion."

"So she helped undress Mr. Darcy? And get him into the leather pants, then?"

"If you please, the word 'pants' means 'underpants' in England. Might you consider saying 'trousers'?"

"You're changing the subject again. Did Lexi get you into those leather—trousers?"

"Essentially, yes."

Vanessa spun on her heel and waved a hand in the air. "Then she and her three breasts can help you out of them." She headed toward the door.

"Vanessa! Nothing happened! She just helped me zip up. Who knew you would care, regardless?"

"Of course I care—you're my client. You're my aunt's friend."

"And yet you are more than that to me."

Vanessa couldn't say a word. But she could think it: OMG.

"I'm merely a polite Englishman trying to appease various American women who are nothing like the English girls, I can assure you."

This brought a smile to her face, so she stopped just before the door and said nothing. She and Lexi were hardly the typical American girl next door. Julian had really been tossed into the fire with the two of them. And she was sure they were a far cry from the nice English girls.

He continued. "How could you agree to let me go off with Lexi? Now she tells me she and Sherry are accompanying us to Louisville, when I was hoping beyond hope it would just be you and I."

She turned back, leaned on the stall door, and put her hand on her hip. He wanted to be alone with her? She couldn't let herself go there, so this time she changed the subject. "If you can't move, how did you get up there, then?"

"Sheer survival. I had to get away from her. I had to jump, and quick."

She laughed again, knowing that if Lexi really wanted Julian, she would've landed him by now. Vanessa offered him her hand. "You're going to really owe me for this one."

He looked at her hand with genuine gratitude and perhaps even a little smugness at winning her over.

"I plan on thanking you profusely." He took her hand, leaned on her shoulder with his other hand, and, with a wince, stepped off the toilet and onto the floor, which brought him face-to-face with her. He kept a hand on her shoulder, and with the other he interlocked his fingers with hers, pressed her up against the cold tile bathroom wall, whispered "thank you," and shocked her with a kiss, better than any man in leather had ever kissed her, or ever could kiss her, for that matter.

She put her free hand on his leather butt and pulled him in closer. She could feel everything, and he grew harder as he pressed into her with a slow rhythmic movement that matched his expert kissing.

This had to be the hottest encounter she'd ever had in a men's room—in fact, it was the only encounter she'd ever had in a men's room. She opened her eyes, only to see his were intently closed. She worried about someone walking in on them and could hardly breathe.

He pulled his lips away for a moment, just far enough so she could feel them move when he spoke.

"I've been waiting a long time to do that," he said.

He had been? Waiting? To kiss her? Why *had* he waited so long? "We really shouldn't be—"

His lips brushed against hers. "I know. In some aspects you are extremely, exasperatingly old-fashioned."

"Nobody has ever called me old-fashioned."

"But you do have some very traditional values."

Could he stop the talking about values and get back to the kissing? Before she changed her mind about this digression?

She looked at him askance, at his lips, and gave her lips a quick flick with her tongue. "This really shouldn't be happening."

"No, it most certainly should not. But I find myself very much attracted to you, Vanessa. And in such a short time, too." With that he took her wrists and held them up over her head, against the wall, as he proceeded to slowly grind into her and kiss her neck, her collarbone, her cleavage—

But the door opened and Northstar, the first openly gay superhero, stepped in, wearing his signature black and silver suit. Someone in a *Planet of the Apes* costume filed in right behind him.

The toilet in the stall Julian had been in automatically flushed, causing them both to jump.

Northstar and the ape didn't even look at Vanessa but headed straight for the urinals, and, just like that, the moment was gone and too much time had been wasted talking. Once she heard zippers unzipping she knew she had to get out, and fast—

Julian took her hand and led her toward the door, giving her a generous glance at the leather butt she'd just squeezed.

"Where are your clothes anyway?" Although she knew the answer.

"Lexi has them."

Vanessa sent the three-breasted Lexi a text message.

"It would be most appreciated if you could get us the hell out of here," Julian said. "Thank you."

That was Julian. Always polite.

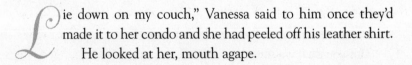

ie down on my couch," Vanessa said to him once they'd made it to her condo and she had peeled off his leather shirt. He looked at her, mouth agape.

"Really, Julian. I'm only going to try and get you out of these things. We need to get you to your book signing in Indianapolis by seven P.M."

He sprawled out on her zebra-striped couch, dwarfing it in an instant as he flattened himself and attempted to squirm out of the leather pants.

"Zipper's broken," he said through tightened lips. "Too much of a bulge, I assume."

"Too much of an ego is more like it." Vanessa put her hands on her hips and sighed. "It looks like we're going to have to cut you out."

"One more try. Just indulge me one more time."

She leaned over him, propped one knee on the couch, and gripped the waistband of his pants along with him. He lifted his hips and sucked in his already well-carved abs, and, as the pants budged slightly, they both let out a growl.

That was when Aunt Ella and Paul walked in.

"Oh, dear Lord!" Aunt Ella squealed as she dropped her handbag.

The thud prompted Vanessa to spring up.

Paul scooped up the purse.

When Aunt Ella saw that the half-clad body belonged to Julian, she regained her composure.

"Oh, Julian. It's you. I *do* hope we're interrupting something."

Vanessa sighed. "You're not interrupting anything, Aunt Ella. I'm just trying to help him out of these leather—trousers Lexi somehow got him into."

"I love it when you say 'trousers.'" Julian smiled.

Vanessa returned the smile.

Aunt Ella came closer to survey the situation. "Lexi got him into these things? I told you not to leave him with her! Well, dear, you'll have to cut him out. It's the only solution. You told me he has a seven o'clock signing in Indianapolis. Shouldn't you already be on your way?"

Vanessa dashed into the kitchen to get her shears. "Yes, we

should." She rifled through her knife drawer, pulling out three pairs of scissors.

She bolted back into the living room and slid one blade of the kitchen shears into the waistband along the side seam.

"Take it slowly, now," Julian said. "Of course, I would trust nobody but you with this kind of an operation."

"That might well be your downfall," Vanessa said as she cut very carefully down the seam.

"I don't think so," Julian said. "You're a lot sweeter than you let on. And there is something simmering just below the surface of your consummate professionalism."

She almost nicked his pale skin with the scissors.

Aunt Ella and Paul sat down as if to enjoy the show. Just another event in the life of Vanessa and her men.

"What brings you two here, anyway? Is everything okay?" Vanessa asked as she concentrated on the seam.

"I was so worried, Vanessa." Aunt Ella piped up. "You haven't answered your phone for about an hour now, and I even had Paul type to you and tweet to you and God knows what other hocus-pocus he pulled, but you didn't respond. And that's not like you. So I wanted to come over here and make sure you weren't collapsed on your laptop or something of the sort."

Vanessa was at his thigh now, and she did her best not to look at anything but the seam. His thigh felt warm and muscular against her hand.

She must have inadvertently shut her phone off, and she couldn't ever do that—not with Aunt Ella's Alzheimer's.

"Collapsed at my laptop?"

"Really, Vanessa, I do worry about you."

"Worrying must run in the family, because I worry about you, too, Aunt Ella." Although now she had Paul to help out with her aunt, right?

"I'm sorry to say all this in front of you, Julian, but my Vanessa means so much to me. And sometimes she just pushes me to my limit."

"I can see why," Julian said.

Vanessa shot him a look. "Who's holding the scissors here? You'd better watch what you say. And, Auntie, you have an entire wedding to plan! Please don't waste any time worrying about me."

Just as Vanessa reached his knee, the doorman buzzed at the intercom.

Julian stood, clasping his pants together and sidestepping toward Vanessa's bathroom. "I think I've got it from here. Thank you, Vanessa, for releasing me. Now, I'll get into my breeches and cravat, and pack not just the books I'm selling but also the books I'm reading for leisure. Then I'll be all ready for Indianapolis." He looked at his watch. "Although it is nearly teatime. I would fancy a tea."

Him and his books—his tea—his—him! She buried her head in her hands. The sad thing was that tea sounded good to her, too. Tea!

"Miss Roberts? Are you in?" asked the doorman.

"Yes, I'm here, Chris."

"You have two ladies down here to see you. They say they're all ready to go with you to Louisville? A Sherry Pajowski and a Lexi Stone?"

Vanessa shot a glance at Aunt Ella. "Are you sure you'll be okay while I'm gone?"

"Vanessa, if you don't escort our Mr. Darcy to Louisville, I will."

"Oh, no, you won't," Paul said.

"You see. This is what happens when you get a good, strong man in your life." She looked at Paul and smiled. "And I wouldn't have it any other way."

Vanessa laughed. "Well, then. Look out, Louisville, here comes Mr. Darcy and entourage."

Chapter 9

Outside of Indianapolis, after a hugely successful book signing, both Lexi and Sherry had fallen asleep in the backseat.

Moths, drawn to the headlights, splattered on the windshield as Vanessa and Julian endured flatlands, cornfields, and an increasing awareness of their proximity to each other in the dark.

Julian tried to read his book, but there wasn't enough light anymore. Only their path on the GPS system offered the faintest glimmer.

"You know there are these things called e-readers and tablets and phones, and they light up so you can read in the dark?" Vanessa smiled.

"It's not the same. I prefer the heft of a book." He lifted the book and set it down on his lap. "It's the smell of it." He opened the book and breathed it in with a satisfied sigh. "The turn of the pages." He turned a few pages, running his fingers gently down the length of each page.

Out of the corner of her eye Vanessa watched him. Only he could make turning the pages of a book *sexy*.

"I like to know exactly where I'm at in a book. Am I halfway? Three-quarters? To me it's not just the reading, but the tactile, sensory experience." He rested the palms of his hands on the leather book cover.

Vanessa's mind turned to other tactile, sensory experiences, and she wished she could shut those thoughts down as easily as turning off a reading gadget.

"There's something on the horizon," Julian said, breaking the silence.

It was the Midwest at night, and there was nothing on the horizon—ever. "Even I have to admit there's nothing on the horizon, Julian. You're hallucinating. Why don't you take a nap?"

"No, look. Perhaps you see them? Colored lights?"

"Must be another alien abduction. Or maybe they're making crop circles."

It turned out to be a Ferris wheel all lit up and turning, signaling a county fair. She'd been to a county fair once, with her parents, before the divorce. "Hey, you're right. There is something there. It's a Ferris wheel."

"Might we go for a ride?"

"Julian. We're here on business. You have a big day tomorrow."

He folded his arms, clenched his jaw, and stared straight ahead.

She laughed. "Are you brooding? I don't go for brooding. Unlike all the women we're about to meet at the Jane Austen Festival in Louisville, I'm not into the brooding-hero thing."

"Mr. Darcy doesn't brood."

"Really," she said.

The Ferris wheel came into clear sight now, along with pink, yellow, blue, and green lights highlighting the other carnival rides, and Vanessa could almost smell the cotton candy and kettle corn.

Julian sighed.

"Okay. Okay. We'll go for a ride. And maybe eat a funnel cake. Have you ever been to a county fair?"

"Not since I was a child."

She knew so little about his life, and it all seemed so vague to her. Did he have any siblings? What were his parents like? Did he grow up in London or a village? What did he study in college? Had he ever been engaged or—married?

Still, she didn't dare say a word because now Sherry began to move around, and she didn't want either one of them to wake up. So when she saw the sign and the turnoff for the fair, she just turned toward it and wasn't even sure why. It would set them back at least an hour, and that would mean they'd pull into the hotel past midnight.

Without saying a word, she and Julian left Lexi and Sherry asleep in the backseat, she locked the car doors, and off they went past the sign that read MONSTER TRUCK RALLY 9:00 P.M.—try explaining that one to a foreigner—toward the admission booth, where more than one person stopped to look at Julian's Regency coat, breeches, and boots.

"Deep-fried Pepsi? We're trying it!" Vanessa said after she took a picture of him in front of the Butter Cow, a cow sculpted out of five hundred pounds of unsalted butter in the dairy barn. She posted the picture and:

500 pounds of butter and Mr. Darcy . . . Does it get any better? Soon to be #UndressingMrDarcy @ #JaneAustenFestivalLouisville

"Would you like deep-fried Pepsi or would you prefer a deep-fried candy bar, Oreo cookie, or Twinkie?" Vanessa asked him in front of the deep-fry stand.

"What's a Twinkie?"

Well, since he didn't know what a Twinkie was, there wasn't much point in eating a deep-fried one, so she bought him a deep-fried candy bar and the deep-fried Pepsi for herself. "We'll share."

"Much obliged," he said, not very convincingly.

"Come on, Julian, it's America—on a stick."

Children's laughter surrounded them, as did twinkling fairground lights and fiddle music, and even with the distant sound of chain saws buzzing for the giant-pumpkin-carving contest, Vanessa thought this one moment was perhaps more romantic than anything she'd experienced in the past year, at least.

Julian fed her a bite of the candy bar and she fed him a piece of the deep-fried Pepsi.

He tried not to wince. "It must be . . . an acquired taste. And my boots seem to be stuck to the ground in some sort of—"

"Cotton candy," Vanessa said. "Or is it pink kettle corn? Hard to tell in this light."

She had to laugh at him checking out the bottoms of his boots, the poor guy!

She tossed the rest of their deep-fried candy bar and Pepsi in the trash can.

"It's a shame," Julian said.

"The food or throwing it away?" Vanessa smiled.

"Both, to be brutally honest."

"You'd better watch out or I'll sign you up for the cherry-pie-eating contest. There's no better time to go on a ride, though, than after eating something deep-fried." Vanessa led him toward the salt-and-pepper shaker.

"Must we?"

"Unless you're afraid, of course."

"I'm not afraid. 'Bring it on,' as you would say."

Vanessa walked right past the giant-pumpkin-carving contest (with chain saws) until she realized Julian had stopped to watch. She tugged on his sleeve and led him toward the salt-and-pepper shaker.

He continued to look back at the pumpkin carving. Once they were out of earshot of the chain saws, Vanessa figured he'd never seen anything like it, so she filled him in. "Chain saw carvings are really an art form here in the States," Vanessa said. "And the medium isn't just limited to overgrown pumpkins. We Americans also carve ice blocks, wood, and huge chunks of cheese."

"Such talent. Such—resourcefulness." Julian smiled as he put his arm around her.

She stopped before getting in line for the ride. Her stomach really did feel a little fluttery—it was either the deep-fried stuff or . . . butterflies?

"On second thought, let's do the Ferris wheel."

"Let's," Julian said. "After I win your heart at the shooting range over there. I'm quite a good shot."

"So am I."

Her phone had been vibrating with calls from Lexi for a while now, but she ignored it.

After three rounds of shooting at rubber duckies, Vanessa won an oversized stuffed pink puppy dog, and Julian lost miserably. Like a true gentleman, though, he offered to carry the thing for her.

At first he set the dog in between them on the Ferris wheel but then he moved it to the side and took her hand.

"It really is beautiful here," he said as he looked up at the sprinkling of stars in the night sky. He looked into her eyes and stroked her cheek. "You're beautiful. And you make it all—beautiful."

She felt so much, there was so much she wanted to tell him, but he began kissing her, and he tasted so good, like salt and something delicious and new that must've been his Englishness, and by the time they got to the top of the Ferris wheel they were kissing and groping with a fierce hunger and curiosity that the seat could hardly contain. First the men's room, now the top of the Ferris wheel? Why did he choose such inconvenient places? Their seat rocked with a rhythmic motion and she ached to be on top of him or under him or—she'd never wanted any man so much before. She couldn't believe that the breeches, when pressed against her, felt even more revealing than the leather pants. They proved much more of a turn-on. And that cravat! How she wanted to untie it!

She had to admit: she wanted nothing more than to undress Mr. Darcy.

His hands, strong and confident, moved all over her while his boots rubbed against her bare legs. The barrage of sensations, from her tongue to her calves, overwhelmed her.

She slid her hand under his vest while the other ran up the length of his thigh—

"Vanessa! Vanessa!" someone down on the ground was yelling. Once she opened her eyes and unlocked from Julian's lips, she saw Lexi with her hands on her hips.

Sherry stood next to her, and with two red, white, and blue glow-in-the-dark light sticks, she repeatedly made signals with them as if she were landing a plane. "Come in for the landing," she joked.

Sherry cracked Vanessa up.

Lexi, however, was something else. "Vanessa! What the hell? Is it middle school date night or what? Get yourself and that boy-in-breeches down here! I need a drink!"

Chapter 10

anessa only wanted to get through this Louisville Jane Austen Festival without getting any closer to Julian. Could she just deliver him safely back to the airport without her ever having removed a stitch of his clothing? Then her job would be done and she could move on with her life.

Or would it serve her better to sleep with him and get him out of her system? The crazy thought crossed her mind as they pulled into the Louisville hotel parking lot just around midnight. She had never really tried sleeping with a man to get over him, but she was willing to consider it. She certainly didn't want to risk breaking her heart over some man who lived almost five thousand miles away.

Once they checked in, she noticed clusters of people who must have been part of the festival dotting the bar, the common areas, and the elevators. Their bonnets, Jane Austen Festival tote bags, and T-shirts gave them away.

The Jane Austen crowd really did know how to party, and late into the night, too.

They turned and looked at Julian. A few of them recognized him and stepped over to chat. Soon Vanessa, Sherry, and Lexi had been introduced to a smattering of the festival-goers, and many of them, it turned out, knew Aunt Ella.

Up on their floor, another group of festival attendees played whist, a Regency card game, in a seating area close to Vanessa's room. Sherry and Lexi settled into their shared room, and Vanessa stripped herself down to a tank top and her leopard-print thong. She all but collapsed into bed.

Just as she drifted off to sleep with images of Julian and her on the Ferris wheel dancing in her head, there was a knock on her door.

"What the—" She padded over to the door and looked out the peephole. It was Julian, *in a nineteenth-century-style white nightshirt.*

"Good God." She grabbed her little silk robe and wrapped it around her.

"Vanessa? Are you awake?"

She cracked open the door. "Shh, be quiet, Julian!" He reeked of whiskey. Had Mr. Darcy discovered the minibar? Or had Lexi bought him one too many drinks?

"I must talk to you," he said.

She looked up and down the hall. Nobody had seen them. And nobody *could* see them like this, in a hotel together, past midnight, him in his flippin' nightshirt. She wanted fame and book sales for him, not notoriety. "We'll talk tomorrow morning, Julian." She tried to close the door, but he stopped her.

"No, it cannot wait. I shall stand here until you let me in."

Vanessa sighed and opened the door. "Quick, then. Get in here!" She shut the door right behind him and flipped on the lights, only to be blinded by the glare. Once she had rubbed her eyes and adjusted to the light she realized he stood there smiling and gaping at her.

"You look lovely," he said. "You *are* lovely."

"And you, my friend, are drunk. And in a nightshirt! I know you have modern clothes—I've seen them. Why the nightshirt?"

"It happens to be very comfortable."

Vanessa put her hands on her hips, but her robe fell open, and she yanked it shut and tied it with resolve. "If you would just use a phone like everyone else on the planet you could text me or call or IM or e-mail—"

"And miss this?" He eyed her up and down as he sunk into the armchair near her bed, staring at her. He crossed his bare legs and she didn't want to imagine what he did, or didn't, have on under there.

"Why don't you use a phone, Julian? *Why?*"

"Must you know?"

"Yes. I must!"

"Have a seat."

"No, thank you. I'm going to stand."

"It all started about five years ago, when I was on my way to becoming a professor, and I was like you, Vanessa. All plugged in. Do you know how useful electronic media is to a history professor up to his neck in research?"

"Yes, I can imagine."

"I had a vast array of social media accounts. Colleagues from all over the world whom I shared information with. And my followings helped build my platform, making me a more appealing candidate for publishers."

"Go on."

"Someone else wanted my position, and he got it."

"How?"

"He hacked all of my accounts, created a false persona, and put together an electronic trail of 'evidence' indicating that I'd had indiscretions with several of my female students."

"What?"

"You're very vulnerable online. Anybody can bring you to ruination with just a few clicks. You know, I cringe when you post on those locational social media sites exactly where you are and when. At the very least, your apartment could get burgled. After all, you're announcing to the world you aren't home."

Vanessa tried to process all this. "Back to the indiscretion. Was there one?"

"No. But no one gives any regard to the facts. It's the perception. My reputation was blackened within a fortnight. The university's choice was clear. Him or me? They chose him."

"Which university?"

"Oxford."

"Ouch."

"Precisely."

"Why didn't you fight it?"

"Money, for one thing. Futility, for another. I did the only thing I could. I took down all of my accounts, and with what money I had I hired an online reputation firm to clean up the mess. There is no erasing it—they can only bury the information. There. Now you know."

"I'm sorry, Julian. I had no idea."

"I don't like computers and mobile phones anymore."

"Of course not."

"I've taken some issue with you splashing me all over cyberspace, but the accounts are all in your name, not mine."

Vanessa sat down in the desk chair.

"Now I know why I couldn't find anything on you dating further back than three years."

"As I said, it's there. It will never go away. You just have to know how to find it."

"Do you . . . want me to modify my promotional approach?"

"Oh, no. No. I thought that all through long ago. I really didn't want to discuss this. That's not why I'm here."

"Why are you here, then?"

"I'm here because I want to be here. With you."

"That's the whiskey talking."

"No, it's me talking. Julian. Not the whiskey, and not Mr. Darcy. I want—you."

She stepped back. "Kentucky whiskey hits you hard if you've never had it before."

"This has taken me by surprise as much as it may be a surprise for you to hear it."

Vanessa leaned up against the closet. "Julian, it's late."

"There's more. I need to tell you something else."

Vanessa put her hand up. "I think you've revealed enough for one night. You're drunk, and you may regret what you've said already."

"No regrets. I try to live my life with no regrets. What about you?" He approached, and never in her life had she thought a nightshirt could be hot on a guy. It took all of her willpower to step back, yank open the closet door, and pull out a large gown she planned on using as a prop for his book signing. "You need to get into this gown and bonnet, Julian."

The look on his face: priceless.

They both burst out laughing.

She held out the gown to him. "Under no circumstances will I let the festival women in the hall see you coming out of my room. You, of all people, don't want a scandal. It wouldn't look professional, and it might ruin your book sales tomorrow night."

"You may be right about that," he agreed.

"They will see a woman, in a gown and a bonnet, reeking of whiskey. And they won't see the very hairy legs underneath her gown, either."

Julian frowned as she marched him into her bathroom to change. When he came out in it, she laughed. He looked absolutely adorable, although the gown didn't quite button up the back nor reach his ankles. "Light blue is your color." She tossed a shawl around his shoulders.

"Enjoy. Because you'll never see me in this again." With that he took her face in his hands and kissed her, his tongue tasting of whiskey, his body masculine even in the gown.

"Have you ever kissed someone in a gown before?" he asked.

"No." She smiled. "This is a first."

"Remember what I said to you, because it's true."

"Sleep off the whiskey, Julian."

She put the bonnet on him and tied it tight, so that nobody could see his razor-stubbled face. She made him step into her fuzzy pink slippers. "There. Now off you go."

She shut the door and through the peephole watched him go to his hotel room with his nightshirt in his hand.

How could a man in a gown possibly have swagger?

She locked every conceivable lock on her door and then propped the desk chair under the doorknob. Would it be enough to keep her from revealing her feelings to him? Could it keep this attraction contained? Her eyes fell on the DO NOT DISTURB door hanger she'd forgotten to hang. He'd better not disturb her. She found him charming, but she had to resist or he just might break her heart when he went back to England.

After slipping off her robe she pulled out her tablet, sprawled out on her bed, and did a quick search on how much it would cost to fly to London for the Jane Austen Festival during the week of September fourteenth—if for no other reason than that she would never look at a gown the same way again.

She wasn't going to buy a ticket. Was she?

N o, she didn't buy a plane ticket.

The next morning, Julian slept off his hangover while she woke to her priorities: Aunt Ella and work, in that order. When she called her aunt to check in, everything was fine.

She then posted a few plugs about Julian's upcoming appearance, prepped for the show that would be capping off the festival that night, and fielded a few things for her other clients from her laptop. In the afternoon she joined Sherry and Lexi at the bare-knuckle boxing event on the green near the festival manor house.

The boxers faced each other, shirtless, in white breeches, one with a red sash tied around his waist, the other with a black sash, both without boxing gloves, bare-knuckled in the Louisville sun.

And she had thought the Regency was all ballroom and no brawl!

Yet, even this spectacle had a genteel air to it on this warm afternoon in the country, on the grounds of a lavish estate. Would her aunt love it here? Yes.

The ringmaster called out various facts while the two fighters prepared to slug it out. "During the Regency," he said, "a boxing match, called a 'fancy,' was much more violent than it is today. Men would often wear spiked shoes. Throwing and kicking were allowed. Just imagine the injuries resulting from such fights. But if a man won, he could acquire a vast sum of money."

Lexi wore a hunter green archer's gown complete with quiver and bow while Sherry wore shorts and a pink T-shirt that simply said *Darcylicious* in sumptuous cursive. They were among a large crowd of mostly costumed women (and men, quite a lot of impeccably dressed gentlemen!) gathered at the ring.

Vanessa wore the gown she'd worn to the ball, but Lexi didn't approve. "That's a ball gown, Vanessa, not a day gown. And who wears the same gown twice? Only the Jane Fairfaxes of the crowd."

Vanessa didn't get it.

"You haven't read *Emma*, have you?" Sherry asked in a whisper.

"No."

"Jane Fairfax is the poor girl. The good girl."

"I see."

"Nobody cares if you wear a gown twice, though."

"Thanks, Sherry."

The dark-haired boxer delivered a resounding punch to the stomach of his lighter-haired rival, and even though it was just a demonstration, Vanessa cringed at the blow while some of the crowd cheered and others booed. She couldn't help but watch the two men punch and wrestle each other, both sweating and grunting while members of the crowd fanned themselves. It seemed rather brutal, though, without boxing gloves and headgear, and she had to remind herself that, surely, this had to be choreographed. Right?

"Where is our Mr. Darcy?" Lexi asked, unfazed by the fight.

Vanessa took off her gloves and checked the time on her phone. "He should be showering and dressing now. He had to sleep off the hangover you gave him last night by having him pound Kentucky whiskey."

"He's a big boy. He could have said no. Do you want my advice about him?" Lexi asked. "As in, him and you?"

"No, thanks," Vanessa said. She had done quite well until now at not allowing herself to think about it. "He's a client, he's my aunt's friend, and he'll be back in England in a few days."

"Excuses. I know you better. You actually want a guy who is a friend to your aunt, and I can tell that's partially what you like about him."

Vanessa checked her e-mails.

"He should be here with you right now. A man who has feelings for you, with only a few days left, would chase a girl as amazing as you even with a hangover, a gaping chest wound, and two wooden legs."

She took the compliment with a large grain of salt. "Thanks, Lexi. It's cool, okay?"

"Do you know his middle name? If he has any pets?"

"No." Although now that Lexi mentioned it, what was his middle name? She could find out easily online.

"Good. You don't want to know too much about him. You don't want to know his favorite food or his favorite color. And trust me, you don't want to picture him with a puppy, a tabby cat, or—God forbid—a baby."

Vanessa smiled. "Okay, Lexi. You can get off your soapbox now." She knew her well enough to know that this was her way of apologizing, of making up. It was Lexi, offering advice, showing she cared. But was Vanessa ready to forgive her? She wasn't sure.

"I'm not finished yet. You don't want to think of him as a boyfriend or husband or the father of your child—in fact, don't think of him as a person at all."

Vanessa laughed. "Let me make sure I heard you right: he is not a person. I can see all of this advice has worked out well for you."

"It has! Listen, it takes less than one-fifth of a second to fall in love."

"You mean to fall in—lust."

"Never underestimate lust! Without lust there isn't love. The medial prefrontal cortex makes a snap judgment whether a person is attractive to you, while the rostromedial prefrontal cortex decides whether the person is compatible with you."

"Chemistry," Vanessa said. Had she just said that out loud? She and Julian had chemistry, all right—PhD-level chemistry.

"Once the decision's made," Lexi said, "the floodgates open and the sudden rush of stimulation to twelve centers of the brain works like cocaine."

"It's a turn-on. I get it."

"Exactly. And you want more."

Vanessa didn't say a word.

"You can become an addict."

"I'm not addicted to anything," Vanessa said as she updated her personal statuses. "I don't have an addictive personality."

"Right!" Lexi pulled the phone out of Vanessa's hands. "Here's my theory—"

"Here we go," said Vanessa as she took her phone back.

"Men look for sex and accidently find love. Women look for love and find sex. You want to objectify him. Picture him naked. Think the way a man would."

"Uh-huh." Vanessa refreshed her e-mail in-box.

"Okay, if you can't picture him naked—"

"I didn't say I *can't* picture him naked."

"Well, if you *won't* picture him naked, then picture him in very sexy underwear. I have just the thing." She slid off her archery gloves, pulled out her phone, and, after a couple of clicks, showed her phone to Vanessa. "Picture him in these."

Vanessa had to laugh. There on Lexi's phone was a photo of two male acrobats, shirtless, in English bowler hats and tight, tiny, Speedo-style pants with the British flag printed on them.

Sherry leaned in to look and cracked her bubble gum very loudly once she got a peek. "Wow. I need to get me some of *that!*"

Vanessa looked away from the phone and toward the boxing ring. She found herself rooting for the boxer pinned to the ground, struggling to flip his competitor.

"These two British guys at the burlesque show did the most amazing acrobatic act to 'God Save the Queen' in nothing but their patriotic skivvies." Lexi sighed. "It was enough to make a girl relinquish her United States passport, I'm telling you. Anyway, Vanessa, can you picture him in these? Because I sure can. I can see him—in and out of them. Your turn."

Vanessa could picture him in the British flag barely-there pants, yes, she could.

"See?" Lexi asked. "See how good it feels to let go of all those complicated, emotional snares and just live in the world of the physical? It's liberating."

Sherry now had her back turned to the boxing green. "Next time you go to a show like that, call me, okay?"

"Will do. Just remember, my friends, there are three stages of love: lust, romantic love, and attachment. You want to stay in the lust stage. You don't want romantic love and you certainly don't want attachment."

Vanessa laughed. "Who would want attachment, right?"

"Attachment is a very dangerous thing when you're attached to the wrong man."

The dark-haired boxer, the one Vanessa had been rooting for, stood, took a serious hit, and fell to the ground while the referee started the count. Evidently, in Regency boxing matches, a man had thirty seconds to get up. "Thirty. Twenty-nine. Twenty-eight. Twenty-seven. Twenty-six . . ."

Lexi clapped and cheered. "Hurrah! My man's going to win!"

Lexi happened to be, of course, rooting for the winner.

The ref raised Lexi's champion's hand in victory while the crowd clapped, cheered, and began to disperse.

"And another thing—" Lexi wanted to continue her lecture.

"Lexi, my number-one priority right now is my aunt. I have my hands full. I'm not even checking the messages in my eBelieve in-box. I don't have the time."

Lexi looked confused.

Vanessa could only feel sorry for her. Lexi had never known such love, never known the ultimate joy of putting someone else first once in a while, never known the satisfaction that came with mature adult compromise and with having to, for once, accommodate someone else's needs. She might never know the happiness of give-and-take.

But this kind of relationship that Vanessa had with her aunt, it primed a person for a real partnership, and she had been practicing for decades. Now that her aunt had chosen to marry, and once she was married to Paul, maybe Vanessa could put herself first again. But only after she had this Alzheimer's thing covered.

"Shall we visit the Shoppes at Meryton and sashay by the Naval Encampment?" asked Lexi.

"Let's see what my Ask Mr. Darcy app has to say," Sherry said as she shook her phone and read it aloud: "'Indeed I do not dare.'"

They laughed, and the Meryton "shoppes," under their white canvas tents, like peaks of meringue, beckoned from across the lawn. Here, smiling, costumed people sold everything from tea to Regency shoes to antique books. The breeze rippled through the trees, and children, many in Regency garb, ran past them from the shadow puppet show to the children's tea. Surely this was part of the appeal of the cult of Jane Austen: a netherworld that us moderns could step back into, if only for a day or two. Vanessa got it now.

Her phone pinged with a text. It was from Chase, and somehow she just knew it would be about Aunt Ella.

Like the boxer in the ring, she'd been sucker-punched.

All is fine—but wanted u 2 know Paul let ur aunt go for all of an hour . . . but she locked her keys in the car @ the grocery store. She was confused. She & Paul chose not to alarm u, but I thought u should know. I'll stay w them as much as I can <3 Chase

She thanked Chase and sent an e-mail off to Aunt Ella's doctor informing him of the situation and asking if there were anything she could be doing for her aunt . . . from Louisville.

Lexi and Sherry laughed with some of the naval officers at the encampment. Vanessa's fingertips hovered over the call button. Should she call her aunt? Or would that only exacerbate the situation?

She noticed a new e-mail had come in, and it could be from the doctor, but no, it was from Aunt Ella.

Dearest Vanessa,

(Because of course Aunt Ella wrote an e-mail as if it were a letter.)

I have tried to call you, but you are no doubt in the countryside and aren't getting reception as my calls went to voice mail. Or perhaps you are becoming less dependent on your electronic devices and have shut your ringer off? I will have to thank Jane myself if this is the case.

Regardless, darling, I have been in touch with the doctor today after an incident involving my locking myself out of my own car. Imagine! I wanted you to be the first to know that as a result Paul and I have decided to be married by the end of the month. Save the 30th of September for the wedding! It will be a small affair, very small, but I will need you there, my dear.

Carry on!

Much love,
Auntie Ella & Paul

A quartet began to play Regency-era music as Vanessa wrestled with this bittersweet news. She checked her e-calendar for September 30, and of course it was stacked with obligations, most of them client related. One of her retail clients would be celebrating a fiftieth birthday that day.

When she thought of "birthday," it hit her that the surprise party she had so meticulously planned for Aunt Ella's eightieth at the Drake Hotel might be—too late. She leaned against a tree.

She needed to move up the surprise eightieth birthday party and take the surprise out of it. Or could she combine the party with the upcoming wedding? Her aunt's birthday wasn't until the end of December, and she'd made elaborate plans for it, but she had to move it up. Would her aunt approve of a birthday-wedding combo? Vanessa knew the answer to that. An emphatic no.

Aunt Ella never combined birthdays and holidays, much less a birthday and a wedding. Besides, Vanessa knew her aunt wanted a small, quiet wedding. Meanwhile, Vanessa wanted a big, elegant blowout of an eightieth birthday party for her aunt.

She'd have to move up the big party—and fast. To avoid putting the emphasis on birthdays and her aunt's illness, she wouldn't call it a birthday party anymore. She'd turn it into . . . an impromptu engagement party. It would still be the blowout she wanted, but with a better spin.

She'd have to pull some serious strings to get this off the ground. She cranked out a few e-mails, one of them to the special events coordinator at the Drake, and a text to a party-planner friend. And she had to figure out something really special for entertainment. But what?

Just beyond her phone screen, two black leather boots with a brown flap folded down on each came into view. She had seen a lot of gentlemen's boots in the past few days, but none compared to the authenticity of—Julian's.

Her phone flipped from vertical to horizontal texting mode.

Her eyes trailed up from the boots to the muscular legs in tight breeches to the tailored coat, the cravat, the strong jawline, the smiling mouth, the squared-off sideburns, and the dark eyes, sparkling despite the hangover.

"Feeling better?" she asked.

"Now I am."

She got another e-mail; this time it happened to be a message from an eBelieve prospect. "Do you remember what you said last night, or is it rather fuzzy?"

"I meant everything I said, Vanessa."

He did? People began to recognize him. They stopped and looked at him. Others pointed at him from across the green and walked over.

She snapped her fingers. "Wait a minute. You're exactly what I need . . ."

"I thought you'd never realize it, my dear. You've finally agreed you need a bit of Mr. Darcy in your life?"

"No, really, Julian. What time is your flight to New York again this Thursday?"

Her party-planner friend texted her back. The Drake had had a last-minute cancellation, and a smaller room had become available Thursday, from six to eight thirty. *I'll take it!* Vanessa texted back.

"My flight departs at noon."

"Oh."

"Why?"

"No matter. I'm bumping up a party to celebrate Aunt Ella's engagement to Thursday evening, and I thought if you were in town, you might make an appearance—"

"I will simply change my flight."

"You would do that for her?"

"I would do that for *you*."

Vanessa tried not to read anything into this.

"Consider it done. I don't have to be in New York until teatime on Friday for an *Undressing* show and book signing . . ."

"Could you dance with her—and her friends? I will pay you, naturally."

"Of course. I'd be honored. No remuneration necessary. It's the least I can do for you after all you have done for me."

She wanted to jump into his arms, wrap her legs around him, and hug him—and that wasn't all. Instead she simply smiled and said, "Thank you, Julian."

He bowed. He bowed?

But then she remembered he was on Mr. Darcy autopilot. Soon, fans engulfed him, and that was what she wanted, right? For women to swoon over him at every turn? She handed out postcards touting his appearance that night to everyone around. He had made her day by deciding to change his flight.

"Vanessa." Lexi motioned her over to the shoppes under the white canvas tents. "You have to see this. What an opportunity missed."

Lexi and Sherry led Vanessa past a shoppe that never, until a few days ago, would have tempted her. But she had to stop at Bingley's Teas. There, amid the aroma of tea, stood a tower of boxes of tea, cleverly crafted to look like books, and there on the cover of one, in a font Vanessa now knew to be a replica of Austen's handwriting, she read:

Jane Austen Tea Series

Mr. Darcy

A Mr. Darcy tea? She flipped over the back of the box: *Like the man himself, this elegant, dark tea, grown in rich soil, with a bold beginning, yet a smooth finish, has a complexity of character that will leave you wishing to know more . . .*

Lexi nudged her. "Let's go."

Vanessa laughed. "Look at this. Coffee? Tea? Or Mr. Darcy? How about two of the three?"

Lexi nodded. "It's all part of the marketing machine that is the Jane Austen brand. But look over here." Lexi dragged her toward the next tent. "It's Lizzie's Lingerie. Only they haven't taken full—advantage."

This shoppe sold Regency-inspired corsets and modern lingerie. Vanessa looked at the camis, boy shorts, and nighties.

"Are you thinking what I'm thinking?" Lexi asked.

This was what Vanessa had missed. She and Lexi had an eye for marketing, and just for fun, they would bandy about product ideas. This was what made them a great team back when they had their own business.

"Yes. They need someone to come up with slogans for these— thongs." Lexi held up a pink silk thong.

Vanessa lowered her voice to a whisper. "How about: *Mr. Darcy was here* printed on the crotch panel?"

Sherry laughed.

"Yes!" Lexi agreed.

Lexi pointed to a baby blue cami with a built-in bra. "The cami should say, *We Support Team Darcy* across the boobs." She actually bought the cami she loved her idea so much.

Vanessa smiled and picked up some white cotton boy shorts and held them up to her waist. "How about, *Mr. Darcy Likes Dirty Petticoats.*"

"I'm surprised you know about the muddied petticoats," Lexi said.

"I know all about the significance of six inches of mud on a lady's petticoat," said Vanessa.

Lexi pulled a sheer white nightie tank top from a clothes rack. "This nightie needs to say, *The Lake Scene Made Me Wet.*"

Vanessa laughed so hard she doubled over. A few women around them giggled, too.

She took a canvas tote bag from a hook. "We'll no doubt need a tote bag to put it all in. I can see it now: *I Bagged Mr. Darcy* in big, bold type. Or how about a door hanger? It could say *Do Not Disturb . . . Sleeping with Mr. Darcy.* Oh, my gosh. Poor Jane Austen."

Lexi smiled. "But she brought us together again, didn't she?"

Vanessa nodded. "Yes, she did."

When Vanessa and Lexi turned around, they could see they had attracted a lot of attention with their goofing around, and Vanessa took advantage of the moment by announcing Julian's *Undressing Mr. Darcy* show. She even left some postcards on the table next to a stack of lacy white garters.

But as she was announcing this, she spotted Julian standing nearby, leaning against a tree. He smiled.

Had he seen—or heard—all that?!

Lexi held up her new cami to her chest and turned, model-like, to the left and then the right, but Julian was looking at Vanessa.

"I thought you were immune to Mr. Darcy's charms, Vanessa, but it appears you've put some serious thought into the merchandising of Darcy-themed undergarments."

Vanessa felt herself blush—and it took a lot to make her blush. "It's all part and parcel of having a client and thinking out-of-the-box for him."

"Is it? Fascinating."

"It's what we do to unwind," Lexi said.

Sherry laughed. "I really liked your idea of *I Bagged Mr. Darcy*, Vanessa."

Vanessa looked at Julian, who raised an eyebrow.

An older woman and her friends approached Julian. "You look familiar to me. Did I see you at the last conference?"

Just as Julian was about to explain himself, the woman interrupted. "No, it was last night. I saw you on the fifth floor of the hotel dressed in a bonnet and gown."

*R*umor has it Mr. Darcy has been seen in a gown and bonnet . . . See him reveal all @ #UndressingMrDarcy 5:00 p.m. #JaneAustenFestivalLouisville

It was all in the spin. Crisis averted. Or, at least, that one was.

Julian, shirtless, and now up on stage in Louisville, had unbuttoned the side buttons on his soft leather breeches and the front panel fell open.

Just like some other women under the big tent, Vanessa wanted to untie his cravat, tear his waistcoat off, strip off his shirt, and unbutton the front panel of his breeches and peel them off—herself.

Yes, she pictured his cravat, his waistcoat, and his breeches in a crumple on her bedroom floor.

But with every stripping off of a garment, she was the one who felt that much more exposed. He had revealed for her, onstage, her hunger, her pain, and her loneliness. And soon he would be gone.

If only he were on a social networking site or even occasionally checked his e-mail. It occurred to her she'd never seduced a guy, and no guy had ever seduced her, without at least some e-tronic foreplay! Texts, e-mails, IMs, they were all weapons in the modern-day arsenal of dating and mating. What the hell was she supposed to do? Write a love letter? Swoon with a fan in her gown and gloves?

Maybe.

How the hell would you let a guy know you were hot for him in the early nineteenth century? Tell him about it face-to-face? She shuddered at the thought.

"To break in chamois breeches, and to be sure they conform to one's body," Julian said, "one must dampen them with water, as I have done. The point is to get them to fit like a second skin."

Men dampened their breeches with water? Maybe she really did belong back in Regency England. She uncrossed her legs in her seat, then crossed them on the other side, and hoped it didn't translate into a bump in the filming she was doing. She accidently nudged the tripod with her calf.

He leaned over to undo the buttons beneath his knee, and was it just her imagination, or did he have incredibly defined and expressive shoulders and biceps? As he stood up, his rippled abs, white though they were, seemed to glisten.

"Breeches were cut wider on one side, here at the top of the thigh, and higher on the other side, to accommodate the male physique in a custom known as 'dressing to one side.'"

Sherry elbowed Vanessa, who could only reach for her phone, her lozenge-shaped panacea, and send out a message:

Breeches were cut to accommodate . . . curves . . . #Swooning @ #UndressingMrDarcy #JaneAustenFestivalLouisville

Talk about fanning the flame—she really could use a fan. And this time she really was broadcasting her feelings.

Julian beamed a smile at the audience, and he seemed to look directly at her. Or did he make everyone feel that way? Anyway, he wriggled his hips once or twice, and the women in the audience went aflutter. Then he turned to the side, strutted, and tugged at the waist-line of his breeches, flashing a bit of his drawers underneath, and the audience went wild.

It certainly wasn't Vegas. But for the nineteenth century, Vanessa felt pretty sure it was smokin' hot. He really knew exactly how to walk the line with this intelligent but able-to-laugh crowd.

He turned around so everyone could see his taut ass as his valet unlaced his breeches in the back, and, for a split second, Vanessa could see him in tiny, tight British-flag briefs.

Had a preoccupation with him become her new, life-affirming obsession in the light of fear about her aunt?

Forget why. She wanted him.

The breeches were tight, but he pulled them off, literally, with cool British finesse and stood tall in thin, tight drawers that left little to the imagination.

The audience began to clap, but he spoke over them.

"In the summer, I would typically not wear any drawers under my breeches. These breeches in particular have a thin lining in them. But, it being early fall, I have chosen to wear drawers—also rather snug fitting."

Vanessa took a few still shots, for PR purposes, of course.

The crowd clapped louder, cheered, and stood, and he didn't even need to finish out his talk. He bowed and thanked the crowd, which now spilled beyond the confines of the tent.

Vanessa stood and made her way to the stage. "Thank you, Mr. Darcy, for, ahem, *exposing* us to such fascinating historical material. Rather seductive material, too, I might add," Vanessa said as she picked up his breeches from a chair and handed them to him.

She turned to the crowd. "Please allow our Mr. Darcy to get dressed, and he will be at the table in the back signing copies of his book. Some of the proceeds from the book go directly to helping restore his Regency-era mansion. You can get in line right now if you'd like a signed copy. Make sure you follow him on all the social media sites. Thank you!"

The line soon snaked all the way around the tent, and Vanessa guessed that at least two hundred people were lined up for the book. Meanwhile, behind the dressing screen, she caught a glimpse of him yanking his breeches back on.

For a moment she felt as if she were in his bedroom and he was getting ready in the morning. Exactly what did his bedroom in his crumbling mansion look like? she wondered.

She squeezed her eyes shut and pictured him in a white room, sprawled on a bed atop a white "duvet," as he would say, in nothing but his British flag briefs.

A ping signaled a new e-mail from Aunt Ella's doctor. He said locking the keys in the car combined with her aunt getting lost while driving a few weeks earlier meant it was time for Vanessa to have the talk with her aunt. The talk about taking away the car keys.

She steadied herself against the chair on the stage. How long could she possibly put that talk off?

As Julian made his way to the signing table, one of the Louisville conference coordinators came up to Vanessa.

"Great job. Thank you for everything," she said. "Your event was by far the best attended of the whole festival. I brought you and Julian a pitcher of ice water."

The ice clinked and cracked in the glass pitcher as she handed it over along with two glasses. It sent a chill right through Vanessa.

"Thank you," Vanessa said. "I'll bring it to the signing table for him."

The coordinator sighed. "Well. Last event of the festival! Hard to believe it's almost all over."

"Yeah, it is, isn't it?"

Chapter 11

The only thing better than picturing Julian in British-flag briefs was actually being with him on Oak Street Beach in Chicago, lying on the sand. They were steps away from the Drake Hotel, where everything had been arranged for the party, thanks to the combined efforts of Vanessa's and Lexi's connections. Chase, too, had helped out, and he would be there tonight.

They were also just hours away from the party and a day away from Julian's departure. Tomorrow he would be flying on to New York for the last leg of his tour and then back to England.

She didn't want to think of him in the hands—literally or figuratively—of another PR girl.

He had already complimented the beauty of the beach against the skyscrapers, and she'd treated him to Chicago-style pizza and a tour of the city, and they'd had conversations about art, literature, politics, and the campaign to raise more money for his estate. She'd done a very good job of sticking to her work and successfully avoiding being alone with him these last few days. She had also avoided having the car keys discussion with her aunt and, instead, asked Paul if he could take the lead in driving until she had a chance to broach the subject.

To avoid getting too close to Julian, she'd made sure not to learn his middle name or his favorite color, and she'd cut him off as soon as he started talking about his horses. She didn't want to hear about his pets.

But the truth was, even as he sat beside her, she missed him, as if he were already gone. He had packed his leather trunks.

His hot, if rather pale, body glowed in the glare of the midday sun as he read his stack of newspapers. He wore a British blue Speedo swimsuit, gold-rimmed steampunk sunglasses with round green lenses, and—nothing else.

She wore the sexiest bikini she owned.

"Still taking care of work on your tablet?" he asked.

"No, I'm finished now, until tomorrow," she said.

He folded his newspaper and peered onto her screen. "Hm, eBelieve? Whatever is that?"

"If you must know, it's an online matchmaking service. They've provided me with quite a few interesting matches."

"Are any of these suitors worthy?"

"They're not really suitors—I haven't even met them."

"You haven't met any of these men, yet you 'eBelieve' they might be interesting matches for you?"

"Yes. We share common interests, the same hobbies and life goals."

"I see."

She knew more about these online men than she did about Julian. "I can meet them if I want. Anytime! One in five relationships starts online, I'll have you know."

"Charming," he said with a half smile.

"It's smart," Vanessa said. "Saves time."

"Have you ever considered that you live a virtual half life by sifting through men on your computer? I believe in serendipity. That's what I believe in. A chance encounter, a smile across a crowded room. I believe in chemistry that is palpable. I believe—"

"I believe we should consider putting some sunblock on," she interrupted. He was leaving tomorrow and she didn't want to start anything with him now. "And let's finish up our discussion about how you can build on the momentum you've stirred up here with your show and your book."

"I suppose we should finalize our business together," he said.

"Finalize" sounded so—final.

Buff, tanned, and nearly naked beach bodies were piled up like beautiful, shimmering carnage all around them on this hot and gorgeous September afternoon. People had ditched work because it was fall and this could be the last summerlike day until May.

She pulled a tube of SPF 30 out of her bag. She handed it to him, but he refused to take it.

"No need."

"It's going to be awfully hard to wriggle out of those breeches in New York if your legs are sunburned."

He watched, unabashedly, while she smoothed the lotion on her legs, including over the tattoo near her ankle, the heart wrapped in barbed wire.

He sat up. "You're right. You do care for me, don't you?"

He'd called her on it. What could she say? What should she say at the eleventh hour?

"Of course I care. I wouldn't be here with you, making sure you aren't getting sunburned, if I didn't. I worked hard to be able to take time off to be with you right now."

"Thank you." He slid his sunglasses down the bridge of his nose and looked her in the eyes. "I'd like to kiss you right now."

"To what end?"

"Must everything have an end goal? Are there results that need measuring? Does every feeling have to be backed by a mission statement?"

What could she possibly do with this man-client?

Letting it go, he picked up the tube and handed it to her. "Perhaps you would oblige?"

She stood up and then knelt behind him, her knees touching his ass, as she rubbed the sunblock on his shoulders, neck, and back. Skin-on-skin contact. It felt good; it felt right. Her mind wandered as the lotion glistened on his back and a coconut aroma filled the beach air. Maybe he was right—not everything needed to be backed by a mission statement. Maybe she could give in to her attraction to him and not expect or want a relationship.

He leaned into her hands as she slathered his rock-solid biceps then moved seductively from his prominent shoulder blades down, slowly, to the small of his back and the line of his swimsuit. She snapped his swimsuit waistband playfully, and it was as if it were the first time all summer she'd relaxed enough to want, to crave, to hunger for someone, to hunger for . . . him.

Undeniably, she was tempted to kiss him, too, or maybe even devour him, there, starting with the back of his neck, and she very nearly did so, because he tilted his head back, with his thick black hair, and turned just enough for her to see his square-cut sideburns, which she had wanted to touch ever since she'd first seen him at the airport. He even let out a slight groan and readjusted himself on his towel.

But, as her luck would have it, just at that moment, a throng of loud little boys ran up, with a spray of sand, and plopped down beside them. They were all dressed as pirates, in plastic tricorn hats and wielding plastic swords. A very tanned pirate mom with a bandanna tied around her head and wearing a slinky bustier pirate blouse and shredded black miniskirt hauled a cooler decorated to look like a pirate chest.

Pirate chest. She sure had one!

"Guys, I have some treasure here," she shouted.

Okay, that ruined the moment. Although Vanessa stayed behind Julian, her knees had now sort of locked on his sides, and, for some reason, she couldn't wrench her hands from his shoulders.

"Anybody want a juice box?" asked the pirate mom. "Oh, look! There's Captain Jack Sparrow now!"

She pointed to the frothy waves, and there, as if rising out of the surf itself, like a male form of Aphrodite, Chase appeared, in his Jack Sparrow costume, doing a funny Jack Sparrow walk right toward the kids, who all squealed and ran toward him.

"Captain Jack! Jack Sparrow! Cool! Super cool!"

Chase sauntered up, with boys hanging all over him, and caught a glimpse of Vanessa with her hands on Julian.

"Why, fancy meeting you here, Elizabeth Swann," he said to Vanessa.

One of the boys piped up. "She's not Elizabeth Swann!"

"Perhaps not." He raised an eyebrow at her hands on Julian's shoulders.

She took her hands off Julian and stood. "Hello, Jack." She couldn't hold back a smile. Chase had to be slightly nuts.

He tipped his hat at Julian. "But her friend sure looks like Davy Jones, doesn't he, mateys?"

"Yeah!" The boys all jumped up and down, swinging their plastic swords, as if they were readying to do some damage.

But Chase diverted the pint-sized mob. "And who's this swash-buckling beauty?" He bowed to the pirate mom.

"That's my mom!" one of the boys said.

"Then you, my first mate, must be the birthday boy. How old are you now? Sixteen? What are you drinking here? Rum?"

The boys laughed. The pirate mom laughed, too, and got her camera out and started taking pictures of Chase with her son.

He had a way, a way with everyone.

"He's not sixteen!" one of the boys said.

"He's six, Captain Jack!" said another.

"And that's a juice box!" said another boy.

Vanessa bent down and picked up Julian's wrist to check the time on his watch. Vanessa felt comfortable around Julian—perhaps even more comfortable since in less than twenty-four hours he'd be gone. It gave him a certain cachet.

"Three o'clock?" she asked out loud and looked over toward Chase with her hands on her bikini hips. "Captain Jack, shouldn't you be at work?" She smiled at the kids, then at Chase. "I—I mean at work pillaging and looking for treasure—and, you know, all those things pirates do during working hours?"

Chase laughed and initiated swordplay with the boys. "I might ask you the same. What brings you to the beach during working hours?"

"It's Julian's last day. He's flying out tomorrow."

"I see," said Chase. He fended off the boys for a moment and leaned in toward Vanessa to whisper, "And this little birthday boy has leukemia, so that's why I'm here." And then in a louder voice he asked, "Savvy?"

Vanessa skipped a breath. "Yes—savvy." Her hand fluttered up to her chest. "I had no idea. Wow." She stepped back in the warm sand. "How cool of you."

Now that she felt like a complete idiot, she moved her towel and sat on the opposite side of Julian.

Chase lifted the birthday boy and ran around with him, pretending to hoist him into the lake. The boy's hat fell off, revealing a bald head with a red bandanna wrapped around it.

Julian leaned back and closed his eyes, but Vanessa couldn't stop watching Chase, thinking how easily he added meaning, deep meaning, to his life and his work.

After a few minutes he made his way back, with kids trailing behind him. "Since it's Mr. Darcy's last night, why don't you both join me for a boat ride after your aunt's party? I have a few friends coming. Around nine o'clock? DuSable Harbor?"

"Thank you, Chase, but I don't think—" Vanessa said just as Julian, without so much as sitting up, said, "Absolutely."

"Good," Chase said to Julian. "It'll be fun." With that he led the boys along the beach, pretending to fumble with and unfold a big treasure map.

"What did you do that for?" Vanessa asked.

"I did it for you. You're smitten with him."

"Really? How do you figure that?"

"It's obvious."

"Well, you're way off base." And just in case he didn't get that baseball reference since they played cricket in England, she clarified. "You're wrong."

How could he not see—anything?

"Regardless, I fancy a boat ride to see the city lights."

So that was what he wanted to see.

He sat up. "Oh, I almost forgot to tell you something. It's something important."

She sat up and propped herself on her locked arms, showing herself in her bikini to her best advantage—just in case.

But he looked her in the eye. "I've written down the perfect Jane Austen quote for you to incorporate into your speech tonight for your aunt. Remind me to give it to you at the dinner."

"Oh. Oh, thank you." She leaned back on her elbows.

He opened his newspaper with a distinct ruffle. "Being at the beach like this reminds me of a quote from *Pride and Prejudice*," he continued. "It was Mrs. Bennet who said, 'A little sea-bathing would set me up for ever.'"

Was he a method actor or something? Because he'd just switched back into his Mr. Darcy mode. It was all Vanessa could do to keep from screaming. And not in a good way, either.

That evening, when Julian entered the room in his Regency best, all the ladies turned their heads, and Aunt Ella beamed when he took her by the hand and led her to the dance floor.

Vanessa had told her aunt of the party, so she wouldn't be too surprised, and informed her just enough so she'd enjoy it and wear what she wanted to be seen in most.

Her aunt and Julian danced two slow waltzes together, even though the waltz, according to Julian, had just been introduced during the Regency and was considered very risqué due to hand-on-shoulder and hand-on-waist contact, but this only added to his appeal in the crowd.

The middle of the second waltz was Paul's cue to cut in, which he did, and then Julian acted as if he were truly affronted. That wasn't part of Vanessa's direction, but it sure got a laugh from the crowd. And he really started improvising when he asked her to dance while Aunt Ella and Paul were dancing. They were supposed to have the floor all to themselves.

"No, thank you, Julian," she said.

But he didn't give up and, instead, kept standing at her chair, holding out his gloved hand. Her eyes darted across the room, where Chase held court with an entire table of older women, all of them laughing and smiling. He did clean up well. He had swapped his usual pirate look for a white button-down and an off-white linen suit that really showcased his tan.

"Is your dance card full?" Julian asked.

She smiled. "Hardly."

"Go on," said one of Aunt Ella's friends at Vanessa's table. The entire room was ninety percent female. She nudged Vanessa with her elbow.

"I know," Vanessa said. "Men are a hot commodity around here, but—"

"It'll make your aunt happy to see you dancing with 'Mr. Darcy.'"

Vanessa took Julian's hand and stood. "Well, okay, but I must warn you, Mr. Darcy, I don't know how to waltz."

"I will gladly be your teacher," Julian said. "I think you're smart enough to catch on."

With that, Vanessa acquiesced.

She and Aunt Ella smiled at each other across the dance floor, and even though the party had been a resounding success so far, Vanessa couldn't help but dwell on the fact that by the end of the month her aunt would be married and moving to the northern suburbs to live with Paul—without her car keys.

When Julian clasped his hand in hers and settled his other hand on her shoulder blade as she rested her hand on his shoulder, it took the edge off, almost as if she'd guzzled a strong cocktail.

Yet she didn't want to call him intoxicating and she didn't let herself get drawn in by a false sense of—anything—just because he had an arm around her.

It was a dance. With a boy. A boy who would be gone and out of her life tomorrow. Yes, they had chemistry; yes, they had a thing for each other; but no, she couldn't risk it; it wouldn't be smart.

She realized, as she followed his lead, counting to three, doing the box step with him, that just having to talk herself out of him meant that she was a little more vulnerable than she'd originally thought.

She'd danced with a lot of guys in her lifetime. Why was this so different?

He was looking at her and smiling.

The room twinkled with chandelier lights, and, as more couples joined them on the floor, Julian drew her closer in until their cheeks nearly touched. She felt him against her, the warmth of him, his hard body moving so slowly and smoothly to the music.

This drove her "mad," as he would say. She tried to push herself away as the dance ended, but he resisted. Nonetheless, she knew it was best for the success of the party that he mingle, entertain, and dance with Aunt Ella's friends. Chase, too, asked as many older women as he could to dance.

As the evening progressed and Julian floated around the room, talking and dancing and falling in and out of her line of sight while she took video and pictures, she felt as if she *were* watching him in a movie dance with other women. Other white-haired women, but still.

The last thing she felt like doing was sharing him tonight. The only "sharing" she liked to do was on social media!

Which reminded her. She reached for her phone and scrolled through her texts, e-mails, and posts, looking for "urgent" or "emergency." How did she ever get through all this crap on a daily basis and still do her job? The sheer volume of it astounded her.

And then there was another message from an eBelieve prospect.

Could Julian be right? Maybe, maybe she didn't eBelieve anymore.

As far as she could tell, in Jane Austen's time you'd be limited to meeting the local eligible bachelors at the village dance, and maybe there was some merit to that.

"Coffee or tea?" asked the waiter.

"Tea, please."

Did she just say that?

It occurred to her she needed more tea parties in her life. More dancing. More gowns. Less cell phones and computers. More Mr. Darcy.

In fact, Julian had called it on the very first day he'd met her.

Everybody needs a little Mr. Darcy in their lives.

While the quintet took a break, she caught a glimpse of him again, across the room, entertaining a semicircle of women and men, too. Their eyes met and she smiled, then she raised her teacup to him. He beamed and bowed, reached for a cup of tea himself, and toasted her from across the dance floor. Then he started clinking his cup of tea with a spoon. Others chimed in.

It reminded her of the clinking of car keys.

Oh, shit—she'd almost forgotten to give her little speech!

Soon the whole roomful of people were clinking their glasses.

Vanessa stood up and smiled and pulled two index cards from her bag. The first one had her speech outlined on it, and the second had the quote Julian had recommended she use.

"I had a little something I wrote a while ago here, but"—she tucked the first index card back in her bag— "things have changed since then. For the better."

She looked out into the room, scanning for Aunt Ella, until she found her with Paul. "First of all, I wanted to thank everyone for coming on such short notice."

Chase began taking pictures of her from across the room, and she hadn't even thought of asking him to do it. For once, she wasn't the one behind the camera.

Julian pulled up a chair for Aunt Ella, who sat down.

Vanessa smiled.

"Once in a lifetime, you meet someone—someone like my aunt Ella—who not only loves you for who you are, but"—she began tearing up—"but also loves you for who you become when the two of you are together. Someone who recognizes, even when you don't, that together you're infinitely better than either one of you could be on your own." Vanessa dabbed a tear in the corner of her eye.

She laughed. "I'm going off my script here. Does that make any sense?"

"Yes, yes!" quite a few shouted out. Others clapped and nodded.

"Yes, dear," one of Aunt Ella's lifelong friends called out.

"As it turns out, I'm not very good at improvising," Vanessa said as she looked down. "But it makes you feel grateful to know that person, and even if you've only been together a short time, you know you've become a different, better person because of it.

"Aunt Ella is one of those people. That's why this room is full of her friends, her family, and everyone here loves her, am I right?"

The room resounded with clapping and heads nodding. Vanessa raised her teacup. "So here's to Aunt Ella, who took me in as a cranky, surly teenager, full of attitude and with more than a chip on my shoulder, and showed me that life could once again be elegant and good and full of hope. Thank goodness for people who can deal with sarcastic, wisecracking troublemakers! And thank you for showing me beauty and kindness and intelligence. After a lifetime of trying to resist it, I think I've finally come around."

She shot a glance at Julian, who half smiled.

"Well! Happy engagement, dear aunt, and here's to the exciting new chapter in your life with the most incredible gentleman in the room: Paul Nelson. Here's to the happy couple!" She raised her cup, everyone in the room followed her lead, and they all took a sip.

"I'm not done—you're not rid of me yet!"

Everyone laughed.

She held the second index card in front of her and her hand shook. She'd been on TV, radio, podcasts, video, Web streaming— still nothing had prepared her for this. The culmination of emotion, from her aunt's illness to her impending wedding and move, to Julian's arrival and his imminent departure, was almost too much to bear.

"I have a quote here, from one of Aunt Ella's favorites. None other than Jane Austen herself."

The guests nodded and smiled, knowing Austen was a favorite of Aunt Ella's.

"In October of 1815, Jane Austen's ten-year-old niece Caroline became an aunt herself. Jane Austen wrote in a letter to Caroline:

" 'Now that you are become an Aunt, you are a person of some consequence and must excite great interest whatever you do. I have always maintained the importance of Aunts as much as possible, and I am sure of your doing the same now.'

"Here's to my aunt—and Paul!" Vanessa raised her cup again, and everybody cheered and toasted.

In a blur, not only from her teary eyes but in the rush of adrenaline, she invited anyone else to speak, and they did, and, as she made her way toward Aunt Ella to hug both her and Paul, she felt the warm presence of Julian beside Paul as her aunt whispered in her ear.

"Vanessa, darling, you are everything to me. You are my niece, my daughter, my sister—my best friend." She hugged Vanessa, and Vanessa breathed in her Dior perfume. "Great, great things are in store for you, dear. I just know it! Thank you for this wonderful evening—thank you for everything."

After the embrace, Vanessa stood back and held hands with her aunt, and Chase took another picture.

Aunt Ella turned to Vanessa and Julian. "I certainly hope you two have plans after this, don't you?"

Vanessa looked at Julian.

"Yes, we do," he said. "We're going on a boat ride."

"Good! I'm glad to hear it! Keep her out late. I have Paul to look out for me now. I don't want to hear from anyone until the morning. I insist that you skip out the minute this is over."

"Well, then, it's settled," Julian said as he bowed to the Dowager Countess.

*   *   *

*C*hase's "boat" turned out to be a sailing yacht that comfortably fit about forty people, including two women who, Vanessa was convinced, were stalking Julian as he walked home with her under the midnight moon and city lights.

Julian looked back at the women dressed in their crisp, nautical blue and white outfits.

"Perhaps they just live in the same general direction as you and your aunt," Julian said. "I fail to believe they'd *stalk* me, as you say."

"Oh, they're stalking you, all right. Must be those tight breeches of yours. You had to wear them, didn't you?"

"I thought you liked that I stayed in costume. For PR purposes? I'm sure we sold at least forty books tonight, and it wasn't even an official event."

He was right. He'd made her job easy by staying in costume. Vanessa playfully nudged his elbow. "Let's turn this way and see if they follow us."

He locked his arm in hers and looked back.

"They turned."

"I told you."

"Hmmm. Let's cross the street," he said, clearly beginning to believe her.

Once they crossed, Vanessa pretended to stop and look in a shop window for a minute so she could look back. "They're behind us. They're stalking."

Julian smiled. "Ahh, the celebrity life. I must say I'm going to miss all this."

"I'm sure you will miss gorgeous American women swooning over you and stalking you at all hours!"

"No, I'm going to miss—everything. I'll miss the food, the city on the beach, even the American tea. I'll miss your valuable input on long-term fund-raising and your work on a sustainable PR plan for my estate. But most of all I'm going to miss—you."

She slowed her pace from the sheer shock of the comment. Then she eyed his ass, picturing the British flag briefs. She didn't want to think of missing him. She didn't want to think of Ferris wheel rides and coffee and tea in the mornings and road trips with his suddenly endearing leather-bound books.

British. Flag. Briefs.

She knew it would be easy to get into them. But would she be able to get out?

"You'll have another minder in New York," she said. "And before you know it you'll be back to things in England."

"Yes." He sighed.

Well, the sigh could be interpreted a hundred different ways, but she chose not to venture a guess and not to question it, either.

She looked back, remembering they weren't alone. "Uh-oh, they're gaining on us now," she said. "I have an idea—we'll lose 'em ninety-five stories up. Follow me."

She hustled ahead of him into one of her favorite haunts, the John Hancock. Touristy and crowded enough to lose two unwanted women? Yes. Sexiest damn building in Chicago? Yes. Romantic as hell with drinks and views to melt over? Hell yes.

She pressed the up button, trying not to think beyond how dashing he looked in his cravat and coat as he dashed through the marble lobby. How many hours did they really have left together? She couldn't stop her mind from clicking along.

The sight of him in his gorgeous Regency attire struck her as it did the people who filed in line behind him for the elevator, but the polite, upscale crowd only looked and didn't ask a thing about the handsome gentleman.

She and Julian went into the elevator first, and a mass of people crammed in after them, crushing the two of them against each other, waistcoat to V-neck dress.

While the two women from the party walked right past the elevator, he took her hand and squeezed it in acknowledgment. At first she pulled away, but then he interlaced his fingers in hers, and she acquiesced, because it really had been a fabulous night, and, well, essentially, the PR job was over.

The boat ride itself would've been fantastic, with the lake breeze and the skyline all lit up, were it not for, once again, a posse of women flocking around him. This meant she'd ended up inadvertently saddled with Chase as he manned the boat—no minor feat to raise a sail and guide a small crew on a one-hundred-and-forty-five-foot boat.

Once he'd put her to work steering, she found she couldn't beg out of it and could only catch glimpses of Julian as he flitted about while Chase pointed out various buildings in the cityscape and laid out his itinerary for the next two months.

Not only would he be traveling to London for auctions, but he would be representing the auction house at the Jane Austen Festival in Bath as a major sponsor, while Lexi, Sherry, and Julian were all there, too.

Why her brain went down a path about Chase when Julian was leaning in and angling his strong jaw and his inviting, falling-open lips her way, she didn't understand, except this was typically how her bait-and-switch mind worked to protect her from falling—falling for someone when things got dangerous.

But the elevator doors opened with a whoosh and a breeze on the ninety-fifth-floor lounge, and every girl looked better with a breeze blowing through her hair, didn't she? He dropped her hand as soon as they stepped into the glittering world of clinking cocktails high above the sparkling city, sending her mind reeling with conjecture. Yet the buildings, the beaches, and even the Navy Pier Ferris wheel below seemed to glisten just for them. She showed him around all the windows just as low-hanging clouds began to roll in. The crowd thinned, a window-view table opened up, and they each had a drink while the clouds moved below them, offering peeks at the city lights.

He may have let go of her hand earlier, but now his leg brushed up against hers under the table and, despite the attractive women in their cocktail dresses at the table right next to them, he seemed to just have eyes for her. He leaned in, too, when she spoke, and, just as Lexi had taught her years ago, she looked for more body language clues to determine his interest, and she found them. He reached for his cravat and straightened it. He ran his fingers through his hair. Preening again. A clear sign of a male being attracted to a female—no matter what the species or country of origin.

Just as she raised her glass to take another sip, she saw the two women from the boat party across the room. She set down money for the drinks and tip. "Julian. Those two women are here."

"They are?"

He almost turned around.

"Don't turn around!"

"Absolutely right. Especially as I'm enjoying my time alone with you, and I don't want to be interrupted. How can we escape them? How can I get you all to myself?"

Vanessa eyed them as they walked around toward the east side of the lounge.

"Come with me." She grabbed his hand. Her plan was to take the elevator down, but when she looked back, she saw them coming toward them through the crowd, and there was nowhere to go—except the ladies' room, which she knew had the best view in the entire lounge.

She led him into the ladies' room, and there, as if it were meant to be, under a sink stood the neon yellow DO NOT ENTER—RESTROOM CLOSED FOR CLEANING floor sign. Without overthinking it, she took a page from Lexi's book and set the sign right out front by the door, took a rather surprised Julian by the hand, and together they hurried, laughing, toward the stalls. As fate would have it, only one woman was at the sinks and, after raising her eyebrows at Julian, she dried her hands and left.

Vanessa laughed and leaned against the floor-to-ceiling windows in front of the stalls.

He moved closer to her, put his palms on the window above her, and, with a gaze into her eyes, asked, "What is it with you and . . . the water closet?"

She wanted him to kiss her. It seemed like he planned to kiss her, but she didn't want to feel the sting of the letdown, so a deflection surfaced in her mind. She turned her head to look out the window. "Look, this view is better than the ones in the lounge."

He was unimpressed by the knockout view of Michigan Avenue as a cloud broke open, revealing lights and liveliness below. Instead, he looked at her, his head cocked. She could see his face staring at her in the reflection of the window and the intensity of it made her quiver for a second.

She watched him, in the reflection, with his arms caging her, the flickering lights of the entire city below her, as he went in for her neck, the flesh just above her collarbone, her weak spot, the place only men who had known her for months would discover. He had figured it out in just a week.

He didn't look as if he were kissing so much as confirming something, and the sensation of his lips, tongue, and even, for a moment, his teeth on her neck compelled her to lean her cheek on the window, inviting him to have more and coaxing him to let his hungry kisses move along her neck, shoulders, and back. He pressed against her in his breeches and she pressed against the window until finally she turned around and they kissed, long and hard, their reflection in the mirrors above the sinks across the room.

Though she didn't want to break the kiss, urgency razored through her and she went for his cravat, untied it with the expertise of a Regency woman of pleasure, gave it a final snap, and cast it to the marble floor.

He lifted her entire dress over her head in one fluid movement and it slid out of his hands.

Now she stood in nothing but her lacy bra, her skimpy thong, heels, and her necklace dangling into her cleavage on the ninety-fifth-floor public restroom of a skyscraper, with her butt cheeks pressed against the window for the entire city below to see. Anyone could walk in the restroom at any time, too, really, so she had to be quick.

She couldn't believe she was doing this, but she didn't want to let her brain talk herself out of it. She had to work fast, racing against her own thoughts, tossing aside anything that smacked of reason or doubt.

Deftly, she stripped him of his coat, waistcoat, and billowing shirt, confident that the growing bulge in his breeches meant that yes, he wanted her as much as, or more than, she wanted him. He took pleasure in watching her strip him and he angled his body to help her remove each piece of clothing.

Julian was new, he was from far away, and exploring him felt like exploring a new continent. His Floris cologne, which he had told her had been first blended in the 1700s, spoke of musk and limes, and in her mind's eye she saw cobblestone streets and gothic arches and centuries-old bridges over glistening water, and yes, she wanted to go there, and yes, he was the one to take her. There.

She yanked on the watch fob dangling from his waistline and looked up at him with a coy smile.

He kissed her fervently, his hands expertly moving all over her body, caressing and teasing and sliding her bra off.

He slid off his boots then cocked his hip as he brought her breasts to a new state of arousal with mere brushes of his fingertips.

"Do keep going, my lady," he said as he kissed her more, and harder.

She unbuttoned the buttons on the sides of his breeches. When she unfurled the front flap, she realized he had no drawers on, and it both surprised and excited her; and once she'd peeled off the breeches, she went down on him with a hunger and aggressiveness she'd never known, and, pressing him between her breasts, she took him in as he rubbed his hands in her hair, tilted back his head in surrender, and breathed in and out deeply.

Then, on an exhale, he brought her up and slid off her thong in an instant. She reached for her bag and rolled a condom on him, and he took her there, pressed up against the window, because he couldn't wait anymore. Her legs wrapped around him, the strength of his arms supporting her, and with an urgent wildness he brought her to new heights. He lifted her up and down on him—she could see it all in the mirrors, her riding him, him angling into her, both of them gasping and breathless.

She shot a glance toward the doorway, willing that nobody would interrupt. There would be no way now that she would stop; she couldn't stop. She wanted him and only him, all of him, and he let go of his famous control as they came together, and he spoke, finally, in that accent, the accent that now hit notes she never knew needed reaching, and he said, with every breath, just what she wanted to hear.

"I do believe we have something here" were among the words, and a smart comeback didn't even cross her mind.

Afterward he held her as their bodies jolted and smarted with the thrill of it all, and the slickness of their skin warmed each other, and she leaned into his chest, still heaving with little aftershocks.

With a smile she thought to herself, she had not merely *undressed*, but *done* Mr. Darcy.

Or had he undone her?

"Would you like to spend the night at my place?" she asked.

"I thought you'd never ask," he said.

The image of him and his chiseled physique in her bed seared into her brain, and she wouldn't soon forget it.

And then the restroom door opened, and as they scrambled for their clothes and locked themselves into the wheelchair-accessible stall to dress, Vanessa realized just how vulnerable, exposed, and naked she'd allowed herself to get with this man she'd only known for a short time and who'd be leaving for good tomorrow.

She tied his cravat for him in the mathematical style, and she worried about ties. Ties to a man she might never see again.

Chapter 12

An eventful week later, at Vanessa's condo, the doorman buzzed. "Your friend Sherry's here," he said.

"Send her up," said Vanessa.

She unlocked her door and plopped back down in front of the flickering TV.

Sherry stepped in with Lexi right behind her.

"Lexi? How did *you* get past my doorman?" Vanessa teased.

"You know doormen are my specialty. Remember how I got up to that penthouse suite to meet George Clooney?"

Sherry's mouth fell open so wide they could both see her pink bubble gum. "You met George Clooney?"

"I did more than just meet him—"

Vanessa held up her hand. "Stop. We don't need to hear it, do we? Now, Sherry, why did you bring Lexi up here?"

Today Sherry had on a T-shirt that read, *What do you mean Mr. Darcy isn't real?* She looked at her phone. "Well, my Ask Mr. Darcy app wasn't helping us determine whether you really should go to Bath or not, remember? So I thought I'd bring Lexi over to help us think it through."

Vanessa laughed. "There's nothing to think through. I'm going. I just bought the plane tickets. Nine-day Jane Austen Festival, here I come!"

Sherry gave Lexi a worried look.

Lexi shot a glance at the flat-screen TV. "What the hell, Vanessa? You're watching the 1995 version of *Pride and Prejudice* with Colin Firth?"

"What's wrong with that?" Vanessa asked.

Lexi sat down and crossed her long legs. "Nothing—except you can't stand *P&P* in any of its incarnations."

"People change. Right, Lexi? Would you like a cup of tea?"

Lexi gaped. "Tell me about the car accident. When does that neck brace come off?"

Vanessa adjusted the padded brace around her neck. "Tomorrow, thank goodness. I've been too embarrassed to go out much with this thing on. Grab a seat, Sherry."

Sherry sat.

"Okay, girls, let's watch this—it's my favorite scene! Where Elizabeth plays the piano at Rosings and Darcy gazes across the room at her, realizing that he loves her . . . This wasn't exactly in the book, but . . ." She lifted her hand to her heart. "And Colin Firth is so hot!"

Lexi stood and paced. "Wait a minute. You read the book?"

Vanessa paused the video, freezing Colin Firth. "There's *the Look*! Isn't it fabulous?"

"When exactly did you read *P&P*? You swore you'd never read Jane Austen—you told me yourself it only served to remind you of your parents' divorce and how you were suddenly transplanted into your aunt's life. How it was nothing but drawing-room drivel."

"Come on, Lexi, I said that years ago. Anyway, right after the accident, the doctor advised me not to use my electronic devices and not to watch TV for seventy-two hours because it would strain my eyes. He even gave me an eye patch, can you believe it? I looked like a pirate. So Aunt Ella gave me her audio collection of Austen novels. I listened to them all—a novel a day. Then I borrowed all of her Austen DVDs. It's been a great week with Jane Austen. I haven't slowed down like this—ever." She pressed play and it continued.

"Can you pause that and spill it, Vanessa? I'm here to help."

Vanessa furrowed her brow. "I don't need any help. I'm almost over the whiplash. Sherry, go ahead and tell her about the car accident. I don't want to miss this scene."

"O-kay. So. Vanessa and I were driving from here to the north shore hauling some stuff for her aunt. Her aunt's moving in with her seventy-eight-year-old fiancé—"

"She is?"

"Yes."

"Well, that's got to be tough for Vanessa."

"She's been really cool about it actually."

"A little too cool, maybe? As in: she's not dealing with it?"

"You know I'm right here, don't you?" Vanessa asked.

"It's all stuff you should be thinking about yourself anyway," Lexi said. "No secrets here. Go ahead, Sherry."

"That happened to be the day after she had to take the car keys away from her aunt, too."

"Ugh. Taking away her car keys," Vanessa said. "That was the worst. After all she's given me over the years, I have to start taking things away from her. Like her independence."

"They had gotten into a bit of a tiff over it," Sherry said. "Anyway, so everywhere we go, Vanessa's pointing out things—saying how everything in the whole damn city reminds her of Julian. She said all kinds of things, like, 'Oh, there's Oak Street Beach, where we danced the minuet; there's the John Hancock, where we had sex in the ladies' room on the ninety-fifth—"

"What? In the ladies' room on the ninety-fifth floor?! How did they pull that off? What was it, during the daytime?"

"No, it was a Thursday night."

"Well! I taught her everything she knows." Lexi smiled. "But there is no escaping the one-hundred-story Hancock; you can see it from all over the city. Have sex up there and you'll be reminded every damn day, for better or worse. Mental note taken."

"So she's driving along, talking to herself, saying she just needs a sign. Some kind of sign that she belongs with Julian."

"Oh, no, that doesn't sound like her at all. She doesn't believe in signs or horoscopes or palm readings or any of that shit."

"Really? Well, *that* I did not know."

"I've been her friend a *lot* longer than you have."

Sherry raised an eyebrow. "Anyway, she actually takes her hands off the steering wheel for a minute, saying 'All I need is a sign!' and boom." Sherry clapped her hands together.

"Boom—what?"

"We rear-ended a semi on LaSalle Street."

"Oh, my God."

"Luckily nobody was behind us, but Vanessa kept thinking she had dropped a tray of her aunt's teacups and favorite teapot. She kept talking about shattered china. It was very strange. But that only lasted a few minutes."

"Oh, wow," Lexi said. "Poor Vanessa. Once her parents finalized their divorce when she was a kid, she did drop her aunt's china tea service, and it traumatized her. Into her twenties she would freak if so much as a wineglass broke and shattered. The crash must've dredged all of this up for her."

"I don't like broken things," Vanessa said.

"The safety glass on the car's windshield was decimated," Sherry said. "We were very lucky, because I was fine and she was just diagnosed with whiplash and advised to stay away from screens for seventy-two hours to avoid eyestrain."

"Huh. I can't imagine her without her screen time."

"Here's the freaky thing," Sherry said. "The truck had one of those big, huge logos on it. You've seen these trucks before. On all sides of the truck was ENGLAND in huge red letters. C. R. England trucking. As soon as we hit the truck, the Clash's 'London Calling' came on the radio. Wild, huh? I told her after we got out of the ER, I said, 'That was your sign.'"

Lexi laughed. "It's called coincidence, Sherry; it wasn't a sign."

"Yes, it was. That was when she decided to go to the Jane Austen Festival in Bath. She said life is short . . . he may be the One . . . how will I know if I don't give it a shot . . . But after that letter from him I'm not so sure."

"Letter?" Lexi did a face palm. "Why didn't you tell me about this letter sooner? Where is it?"

Vanessa pointed to her fake fireplace mantel, and there, propped up against a teacup, was a gorgeous thick envelope with *Vanessa* written on it in very ornate handwriting.

Lexi snapped it up and read it out loud.

Dearest Vanessa,

First and foremost, I would like to thank you for a wonderful time in Chicago. You are a lovely girl and we had a fantastic time.

I also would like to thank you for all the hard work you put into promoting my book, which raised more funds than I could have imagined.

I find it difficult to leave you this way, but, due to circumstances,
I must. For that I am sorry, because you are a love . . .

All the best,
Julian

Lexi tossed the envelope and letter into Vanessa's fake fireplace.
Vanessa leapt up off the couch and whisked the envelope and
letter out, as if they would really catch on fire. "Don't do that!"

"So. You had sex with him."

"It wasn't *sex*. We made love."

"Uh-huh."

"It was the most thrilling lovemaking *ever*."

"The thrill was the excitement of maybe getting caught in a public restroom. And the fact that he had to leave. There's nothing more
thrilling than a man with an expiration date. It makes you want
more."

"You're such a buzz kill."

"It's the truth. Half the LDRs I know wouldn't last a week in the
real world."

"LDRs?"

"Long-distance relationships. They're total bullshit and they're
only possible because of modern technology. Why be together when
you can be apart and create a perpetual state of fake honeymoon?
LDRs are for amateurs. A relationship means you're *together*. What
good is having a man when you have to wait six weeks to sleep with
him again?"

"What's wrong with a perpetual fake honeymoon?"

"Did you see him the morning after?"

Vanessa slid the letter back in the envelope and set it back on the
fireplace. "No, but he left that letter. You know, nobody's ever left me
a letter the day after."

Lexi sighed. "That's because nobody's ever left you! No guy in his right mind would ever leave you!"

"Wow, thank you. That's very nice of you to say."

"Well, it's true. I've actually spoken to some of your exes and they still ask about you. I miss you, too. I wish you would forgive me already. And you're a great catch."

"Thank you. And I'm warming up to forgiving you—" Maybe she and Lexi could patch things up and be friends again. She could be a pain, but . . .

"My point is you've dumped every single guy you've ever dated. And how many proposals have you refused?"

"Two. One of which I accepted. I changed my mind the next morning, but still. Oooooh! Look! I skipped to the wet shirt scene!"

"Vanessa, you did not keep this Julian thing in the 'lust' stage, did you? Sounds like you went right from lust to romantic love to attachment in one night. Did you orgasm with him?"

Sherry buried her head in her hands.

Vanessa sighed. "Somehow I knew that was where this conversation was heading. And yes, I did. Four times. How's that for TMI? I'll never look at a pair of breeches the same way again."

Lexi flopped down in a chair. "Oh, no. This means you got extra hits of oxytocin."

"Whatever that is, I sure did!" Vanessa laughed.

"What's—oxytocin?" Sherry asked.

"It's a hormone that's released during orgasm. It acts as a neurotransmitter in the brain and it helps us to bond, trust, love, and attach. Basically, a few orgasms with one person, and you're hooked. It's like a drug. It's not love."

"But it could be the *start* of something. I can't help but think what might have been and what could still be. For once in my life I need to put myself out there. I need to go there and give it a shot. He and I had a thing going—"

"You and he had a one-night stand."

"You're wrong about that—I think. If I don't see what this is, I'll be thirty-six and wondering *what if.* You know what? Jane Austen *died* at forty-one. No time like the present."

Lexi sighed. "Darcy himself said something very poignant." She sucked in her cheeks, raised her chin, and lowered her voice for effect: "'A lady's imagination is very rapid; it jumps from admiration to love, from love to matrimony, in a moment.'"

Vanessa glared at her. "I'm not thinking of marriage—yet. But what if he *is* the One? My last chance? How will I ever know if I don't explore it?"

"Once you see him for what he is, you won't want him anymore. I can tell he's an ass. You were *his* last chance. He'll never land a better woman than you. Forget your age. Forget your timeline. Look at his actions. He slept with you and left you a Dear Jane letter—"

"He had to fly off to New York."

"And now he's home. It's been a week. Have you heard anything from him?"

"He doesn't use his phone, you know that."

"I've seen him use his phone. He *can* use it. It's very convenient that he chooses not to. This isn't really the 1800s."

"Fate threw him my way. What's the likelihood of my having any more Mr. Perfects thrown my way in the next five, ten years?"

"I'll throw one your way tonight, and he won't leave you in the morning! Trust me."

Vanessa shook her head. "It never happens when you're looking, Lexi. It happens when you're *not* looking. With the most unlikely guy ever. I don't want a hookup—especially now that I might have something meaningful on the line."

The doorman buzzed again. "Miss Roberts? Floral delivery."

She jumped up from the couch. "Send them up!" She shot a told-you-so look at Lexi.

Flowers! From Julian! She couldn't wait to read what the note on the bouquet would say. She flung open the door and, with ceremony, accepted and carried the vase full of gorgeous cabbage roses, rose hips, foxgloves, and snapdragons and set it on her glass coffee table. For a moment she just drank in the feeling of getting such a clearly lavish and expensive bouquet from him. The pinks, purples, reds, and yellows heralded sunshine and promise.

Lexi and Sherry watched as she removed the plastic and pulled the tiny card out of the card holder.

Nothing, nothing could have prepared her for the sheer drop from the top of the roller coaster she didn't even know she was on. The flowers were from Chase.

Just checking in on you . . .
I'll be calling you soon!

Love, Chase

"Oh," was all she could say as she dropped the card and it fluttered to the floor. Logically, how could Julian even know about her accident? And did she really think he'd send flowers? Well, she hadn't until she'd heard "floral delivery," and then it seemed to be a perfectly rational thing to assume.

Lexi picked up the card, read it, and showed it to Sherry, who instantly said, "How nice of him."

Lexi trotted the flowers out to the kitchen and came back.

"How did he know about your accident?" she asked.

"He works with Paul. And he came over with chicken noodle soup he'd made."

"He cooks?" Lexi asked.

"Evidently. It was pretty good, too, wasn't it, Sherry?"

"Yeah. Really good."

"He saw you—like this?"

"Uh-huh."

"And he sent you flowers today? Honey, when a man sees you at your worst and comes back for more, you have to sit up and pay attention."

"I'm not at my worst!"

Lexi laughed. "Well, *I've* never seen you worse off than this. It's not so much the neck brace as it is the hung-up-on-Julian thing."

"Chase is just being nice. That's how he is."

"Exactly. He's a great guy and he obviously has feelings for you, Vanessa." Lexi tapped the side of her cheekbone with her finger. "Didn't he say he'd be in London while the Jane Austen Festival was going on?"

Vanessa nodded. "Yes, the auction house is one of the festival sponsors, and he has some auctions to attend at Sotheby's. But strike my hooking up with him from your to-do list."

Lexi threw her arms in the air. "Got it. For better or worse, you're going to the festival for Julian."

"Yes. And you know what? He got through to me without texting and without a single emoticon."

"I know. At least you won't have to unfriend him on all your social media once you see who he really is."

Optimism never really was a tool in Lexi's toolbox.

Two days later, with Lexi's help, Vanessa had cleared enough of her work to leave for a week. She drove up north to tell Aunt Ella and Paul she'd be going to Bath for the Jane Austen Festival.

Not only did she drive the speed limit, but she didn't check her phone at every stoplight—just once in a while.

Paul's house was, appropriately, a well-landscaped redbrick Georgian with a circular drive just a few blocks from the lake. The simple wedding they had planned at the end of the month would be held in his backyard under white tents with a small crowd of immediate family. The doorbell had a regal ring to it, and truly, Vanessa couldn't imagine a more idyllic setting for her aunt than this, complete with the man she loved.

"Vanessa, darling!" Aunt Ella opened the forest green door into the vaulted-ceilinged foyer and kissed and hugged her. "Come in. What a gorgeous floral skirt you have on! And a pink silk tank? I don't believe I've ever seen you in pink. You look fantastic."

"The skirt is floral, yes, but it's still a miniskirt, isn't it?"

"A pink manicure, too?"

"*Hot* pink."

Paul came to hug and kiss her, too, and they all sat down in the dining room for a glass of wine before dinner. With the wine and the appetizers they spoke of the surprise engagement party; at dinner they discussed the wedding; and, with the apple pie dessert, Vanessa announced she'd be going to Bath for the Jane Austen Festival, unless they really needed her, in which case she'd exchange her plane fare for some other time.

They were both equally shocked and thrilled, but the thrill outweighed the shock. Of course they wanted her to go!

After they ran down the list of everything she had to see and do, and Paul tried to work out how often she could see Chase while in Bath, he went to take care of some paperwork. Aunt Ella sat with Vanessa in the living room just like they used to do when they lived across the street from each other.

Her aunt spoke first. "You're wearing pink, you've switched from coffee to tea, and you're going to Bath. I realize anyone can fall in love with Jane Austen after reading even just a few pages of one of her novels—that is the gift of any good author—but why do I get the feeling there's a man involved here? Specifically Julian?"

Vanessa smiled. "You may be right. But maybe I just want to take in the waters at the Pump Room."

"Vanessa, listen. You're getting a bit long in the tooth to be playing these games. You're going to go there, you're going to get him, and you're going to bring him back. For your sake *and* mine. I'd very much like to be cognizant of what man finally does win your heart!"

"Not this discussion again—not now, okay? You *will* see who I end up with, I promise you!"

"I certainly hope so, because nothing would make me happier than to see you settled. Here are some English pounds I have leftover from my last trip. Drink the healing waters at the Pump Room for you and me both. Daily, if you can stomach it."

"Do you think I'm unwell?" Vanessa asked with a smirk.

"You keep me young, Vanessa, that's for sure, with all of your antics. Be warned. The Jane Austen Festival attracts the real fanatics, you know."

"Pun intended? I've packed my fan."

"Let's be serious for a moment, Vanessa dear. Are you sure about this? Have you fully recovered from the shock of the accident? And have you really developed feelings for Julian?"

"Yes, yes. And yes."

"You can change your style of clothing for the sake of a man, but you shouldn't change yourself. Just remember that. That being said, I do think you must go on this journey. You're on a journey already, darling, just like me. I'm on a path with Paul and my health, and it's not as pleasurable as trouncing off to Bath. That is simply the reality. But you! You'll have a wonderful time and you shall do it all for me—I won't make it back to England ever again."

"Don't say that . . ."

"It's all right, Vanessa. I've come to terms with it. And you? Well, as Jane Austen herself said in *Northanger Abbey*, 'If adventures will not befall a young lady in her own village, she must seek them abroad.' "

After the hugs and kisses, Vanessa lingered outside in the dark, on the circular drive, looking at the house and the windows lit but shaded by draperies, and thought how safe and cozy it all looked. Her aunt had found happiness and security when she needed them most.

Still, Vanessa ached with guilt for leaving her at this juncture, even though it was only for a week.

Aunt Ella's nurse stepped out the front door—catching Vanessa by surprise.

"Oh, hi, Vanessa."

"Is everything all right, Kathleen? You don't usually stay so late! I didn't even know you were here."

"I see to it that your aunt gets into bed nowadays."

"Oh. She seemed fine tonight."

"I know, she *seems* fine. I'll let you know when she needs an overnight nurse."

"You have my cell phone number, right? I'm going to England for the week, so you'll need to use the country code. Here's my card. You can e-mail me, text, phone, whatever. Are you on any of the social networking sites? You can message me there or instant-message me—"

"Don't worry. I'll get in touch if I need to. One week isn't long. It's best that you go now, actually . . . Enjoy yourself!"

She would . . . do her best.

The Other Side of the Pond

Chapter 13

As soon as the plane landed, Lexi offered a quote from Austen about London: "'Here I am once more in this Scene of Dissipation & vice, and I begin already to find my Morals corrupted.' Could a girl ask for more? All sorts of sordid things happen in London."

Vanessa smiled, appreciating not only Austen's exaggeration and humor, but Lexi's humor, too. She and Lexi had officially made up during the flight at forty thousand feet in the air and it felt right to let the grudge go. Lexi was high maintenance, but her persistence had won Vanessa over, and she decided to give their friendship a second chance.

Sherry, who laughed at the quote, wore a T-shirt to commemorate the trip. This one read:

☐ *Single*
☐ *Taken*
☑ *Waiting for Mr. Darcy*

The two glass doors from customs to the international arrivals section of London's Heathrow Airport in Terminal 3 each had a palace guard painted on it, with fuzzy black hat and red coat. *Welcome to Great Britain*, it said under the guards. Welcome, indeed. She was on Julian's home turf now.

She wasn't prepared for the throng of people cordoned off at international arrivals, with their heart-shaped balloons and their welcome signs and the hugging and kissing and groping, and that, too, just brought her back to the first time she'd met Julian. Against all reason, she actually looked for him in the crowd. As if he would be there! She knew he could very well be at home in Chawton, a ways from both London and Bath, because his *Undressing* show wasn't scheduled until the end of the festival week.

Suddenly, it seemed, British accents rang out all around her, most of them nothing like Julian's. As she, Lexi, and Sherry whisked along the hallway, they passed a blur of shops sporting a barrage of images from Union Jack flags to red double-decker buses to the Tower Bridge, black cabs, and the royal family.

Yes, just in case she didn't know it: she had arrived in England. The airport versions of the Globe Pub, Harrods, Glorious Britain, and WHSmith confirmed it.

She stopped with her rolling suitcase at a dizzying array of shirts, ties, and cuff links on display in Thomas Pink. A placard in the shop window caught her eye:

Mr. Pink was an eighteenth-century London tailor who designed the iconic hunting coat worn by Masters of Foxhounds, whippers-in, huntsmen, and other hunt staff. The coat was made of scarlet cloth but was always referred to as PINK, in honour of its originator. Meticulous attention to detail, exclusive fabric, and exquisite craftsmanship were the hallmarks of a PINK coat . . .

Lexi moved her along. "We're not even out of the airport yet. How will we ever get you around England?"

"That story was just so—interesting. And spelling 'honor' with a *u* really lends it a certain elegance, doesn't it? Why don't we spell it with a *u*?"

Lexi sighed. "The English have *u* in all kinds of words, like 'colour' and 'favourite.' We Americans just streamlined it—that's what we do, right? The American way?"

Vanessa stopped at the Starbucks counter, where a sign on a pedestal read, QUEUE STARTS HERE.

"Julian says 'queue.'" Vanessa smiled.

Lexi sighed. "They all say 'queue.'"

"No Starbucks for you, girlie," Sherry said. "We're going local, okay?"

"I'm here to go native," Vanessa agreed.

Navigating through the crowd on her way to the Heathrow Express train, Vanessa found herself practically bumping into people, people who said "sorry" to her in their varied British accents until finally, when she settled on the escalator with her unwieldy suitcase, Sherry tapped her on the shoulder.

"You need to be standing on the other side. Even foot traffic goes the opposite direction here."

As soon as Vanessa moved to the other side of the escalator, a line of frustrated but very patient and polite Brits in suits and business skirts filed by in a huff.

"There should be an app for this," Vanessa said.

How had Sherry instinctively picked up on the foot-traffic flow and escalator etiquette and she hadn't? Sherry had never been to England before, either.

Everything struck Vanessa as familiar and foreign at the same time; even the train station's convenience store food and drinks looked similar but completely different as they loaded up for the train ride. She stared at the refrigerated section for some time before she decided to get an egg-and-cress sandwich, the cheapest one available, because she'd spent a mint on her last-minute flight to London. Although the pear cider she picked up seemed overpriced.

"Not very well globally traveled, are you?" Lexi asked. "It helps to get out from behind your electronic devices every now and then."

Her train ticket, too, when she read it, made her laugh. The English called a train car a "carriage" and their seats were in carriage C. How quaint, how cute—how English. Cuter still was the fact that they were heading to Paddington Station. Paddington? As in the adorable little bear with the yellow hat and toggle-buttoned coat?

"Here's to Jane Austen," Lexi said once they'd settled in and she raised her bottle of Pimm's.

"To the Jane Austen *Festival*." Sherry raised her can of Fanta.

"Yes, to both of the above, and Mr. Darcy, too," Vanessa said, realizing the pear juice she'd picked up had alcohol in it. Pear "cider." Note taken.

When at last they stepped from the train that took them from Paddington through gorgeous green countryside to the Bath Spa station, it hit her that she would be spending a week in a spa city. Would she come out of the spa experience feeling any better? She sure hoped so.

The late-afternoon sun shone, and they decided to hoof it from the station to the hotel rather than taking a cab.

They crossed east out of the station when they should've stayed on the west side of Manvers Street, where Vanessa stopped so instantly with her suitcase that Sherry crashed into her.

GEO. BAYNTUN, read the letters on the massive white stone-colored building. BOOKBINDER and BOOKSELLER wrapped around the arched windows, and Vanessa held on to the wrought iron fence in front of the building. OLD PRINTS, it said in painted letters on an outdoor gas lamp just near a window. Julian shopped here. She'd seen the bookplates in his books.

Lexi put her hand on her hip. "Really, Vanessa? A bookshop?

We've traveled a total of eleven hours to see the hundreds of men dressed in tight breeches and dashing red coats who are a mere ten minutes from here, and you stop at a bookstore. You have an e-reader anyway. Remember? You were the first to get one because they'd hired you to test-market it."

Vanessa left her suitcase on the sidewalk as she hopped up the stairs and peered in the glass-paneled doorway. The shop was closed, but she didn't think she'd ever seen anything as beautiful as the sun streaming in on the dark wooden floors and glass cases that rose to the ceiling full of leather-bound books with gilded lettering on the spines. A sign on the door read, BY APPOINTMENT ONLY. How quaint.

She could buy Aunt Ella a gorgeous edition of *Pride and Prejudice* here and maybe, just maybe, an elegantly bound book for herself.

"We're going now. It's pub time," Lexi said as she looked at her watch.

"After we check in with the festival, right?" Sherry asked.

"Right," Lexi confirmed as she crossed the street.

Vanessa trailed behind them, her suitcase bumping along and sometimes spinning out on the cobblestones, making her aware she'd left the United States and was officially across the pond.

Julian was right about the stone Georgian architecture being both stunning and elegant. Feeling as if she'd fallen into Jane Austen's *Persuasion* or *Northanger Abbey*, Vanessa floated by the abbey and the Roman Baths, craning her neck to see them, but stopped at the Pump Room.

"Lexi! Sherry!" she called out to them among the crush of tourists. She pointed to the gorgeous sign that read, THE PUMP ROOM. "We're going in."

"Not *now*," Lexi whined, cocking her hip.

"I'm thirsty and I'm getting a mineral water. Look—the sign says it's fifty pence a glass. My treat. Let the healing begin!"

"I'm in," Sherry said.

"Hurry up," Lexi mumbled. "I'll watch the bags. I didn't come all this way for a glass of water."

"You came all this way for a *tall* glass of water." Vanessa smiled.

"Or two. Preferably in breeches." Lexi laughed. "Go." Lexi waved them off as she smiled at a good-looking guy standing outside a shop across the way. He beamed back at her.

Vanessa, in her snug-fitting thin leather jacket and flirty skirt, flounced into the formal room to the strains of a classical trio playing piano, harp, and violin. It could've been worse—she could've been wearing her black nail polish, her earbuds, and scanning her phone. That was the old Vanessa.

Still, maybe her aunt was right. Maybe she did need healing.

The only sounds other than the music were the clinking of silverware and the hushed din of conversation under tiered tea plate servers. Floor-to-ceiling windows flanked the minty-green-colored room, punctuated by white columns, eighteenth-century oil paintings, and shimmering chandeliers.

As if she'd been here before, she felt that off to her right, in a light-filled, domed-glass alcove, would be the fountain. Of course, the short line of people waiting while others drank clear glasses of water might've been a clue. She laughed at her own folly. Folly? Had she ever used that word before? Why did she palpably feel Jane Austen's presence across the room, near the trio, with folded arms and laughing at her?

Vanessa had never seen a spa fountain before and had never been to an ancient spa town, so she had nothing to compare it to, but the sacredness of the font did not escape her, jaded as she was. Behind the fountain itself stood sand-colored Georgian buildings that left the entire alcove in a wash of honeyed light.

Beyond a waxed wooden counter stood the stone base of the fountain with THE KING'S SPRING etched in it.

"Wow. Cool," Sherry said as she took a picture with her phone.

Atop the rougher base, an urn-shaped vessel had been carved out of smooth stone and four spigots, each decorated with a bronze shell, poured a perfect stream of water into one of four bronze fishes' mouths below.

The server took Vanessa's pound coin and brought two glasses of water from the pump.

"Here's to our health. Especially our mental health." Vanessa laughed as she clinked with Sherry.

Sherry immediately made a sour face, but then drank half her glass.

Vanessa drank her entire glass even though it tasted like liquid metal. Panacea or not, she felt better already and toasted her empty glass to the smirking ghost of Jane Austen across the room.

"Let's swing by here every day for a glass," she said to Sherry as they stepped back out onto the cobblestones, where Lexi had already lured the man from across the street to her side. Evidently she'd procured his phone number, seeing as he gave her the universal gesture for "call me" before he took off.

"I'm pumped about the Pump Room!" Sherry said. "Anytime you want to go, Vanessa."

Three to an English-sized flat proved a bit snug even with the cot and foldout sofa, but the flat had its own washing machine. Besides, it meant more to Vanessa than she'd anticipated that their flat stood a mere block from Trim Street and just a few blocks from Queen Square and Gay Street—all three places that Jane Austen had lived. She couldn't wait to explore and see the actual houses she'd stayed in!

At the same time, she couldn't believe her excitement about that.

Once they'd freshened up and changed, they stood in line at the Bath Box Office to collect their preordered tickets for various events during the week.

The very polite ticket girl, wearing a bonnet garnished with fake fruit, handed Vanessa her lecture tickets and then an envelope. In her adorable English accent, she said, "Your vouchers are in here along with your punch card for the Dash for Darcy scavenger hunt."

Dash for Darcy scavenger hunt? Vanessa had given Julian that idea—he must've used it! He'd listened. But how had she gotten on the list?

"There must be some mistake," Vanessa said. "I didn't sign up for a scavenger hunt."

The girl smiled. "Vanessa Roberts, correct?"

She nodded.

"Right. There you are. Perhaps someone signed you up and paid for you as their special guest?"

Had Julian signed her up? Her heart literally leapt. "I suppose it's possible. What's it all about?"

"It's a brand-new event, introduced at the last minute, really, but it has sold out and people are clamoring to get into it."

Wow. Just wow.

"It takes place over a couple of days and has you crisscrossing Bath and even some out-of-town sights."

"Oh." That didn't sell Vanessa. She didn't want to go out of town.

"Our very own Mr. Darcy organized the event and offered the prize: a dinner with him at his historical home and recognition of winning the scavenger hunt at the ball."

But she had to be sure this was Julian. "Who is your 'Mr. Darcy'?"

"Why, Julian Chancellor, of course, the esteemed author and Jane Austen scholar. This is all to help benefit the restoration of his historical home. Excuse me, miss, but there is quite a queue behind you."

Flustered and flummoxed, Vanessa stepped out of line while Sherry and Lexi got their tickets.

"Julian must've signed me up for the Dash for Darcy thing," Vanessa said once Lexi and Sherry had ventured over.

"How do you figure that?" Lexi asked.

"Who else would've done it? It's one of the most expensive things on here. The ticket price is hefty—a fund-raising fee."

"That was nice of him, then, wasn't it?" Sherry asked.

"I—I guess so," Vanessa said.

"If he signed you up for it, he obviously knows you're here, then. Have you heard anything from him?"

"No."

"Clearly he wants you to chase him—the old-fashioned way."

"Did you two sign up for it?"

"I didn't sign up, but I have a voucher and packet for it," Lexi said. "How about you, Sherry?"

"I got one, too! He signed us all up!" She'd been rifling through the packet. "It looks like we'll be taking the train to London—and Chawton, too."

"Hurrah! We're trotting off to London town," Lexi said as she looked at each day's clues.

"But we just arrived in Bath! I don't know about this," Vanessa said.

"What?" Lexi said. "You came all this way and you're going to let someone else win and have dinner with Julian at his—place? After he paid for you to partake? I don't get it. Does this approach-avoidance method of snaring men work well for you?"

Vanessa sighed. "I need a drink. A Bath bitter."

Lexi put her arm around Vanessa. "Me, too."

"Not too many drinks," Sherry said. "Tomorrow morning's the promenade in our costumes."

Lexi opened her itinerary. "Look. We can start with a glass of wine at the prefestival gathering at the—wait for it—Bath and County Club in the Queen's Parade." She said the last bit in a fake English accent and laughed. "Are we in England now, or what, girls?"

"You mean 'ladies,'" said Vanessa.

She had, after all, come to Bath in order to, in as ladylike a way as possible, hunt down Julian in the costumed crowd, knock him over the head with her parasol, and drag him into her slightly screwed-up modern life. Had she not?

She saw a lot of fantastic things during her first few hours in Bath on Friday night, but she didn't see the one thing she was looking for—Julian.

Chapter 14

On Saturday morning, once she had her corset, gown, and white stockings on, she only had a few seconds to curl her stick-straight hair into a Regency updo, but when she went to use the mini curling iron she'd heated up, it was cold.

"Time to go, Vanessa; the promenade starts in ten minutes." Lexi stood by the door that led into the hall, tapping her fan in her hand.

Sherry looked at the watch in her reticule.

"For some reason my curling iron isn't working," Vanessa said. "Even with your adapter, Sherry."

Sherry came to investigate. "You're supposed to turn on this switch next to the outlet." She pressed a little switch and the curling iron light went on.

"You've got to be kidding me!" Vanessa cursed the fact that not only did the British have a completely different voltage system, rendering all her plug-ins useless without borrowing Sherry's adapter, but evidently each individual outlet had its own on-off switch.

"Leaving now," Lexi said as she opened the door. "Otherwise we'll miss the start of the promenade."

Vanessa unplugged her curling iron, switched off the outlet, and headed toward the door.

"Bonnetless? With straight hair?" Lexi looked disapprovingly at Vanessa.

"I don't want Julian to see me in a *bonnet*. I wanted to do my hair up with a tiara or something with curls. If I had something like what you have on, I'd wear that."

Lexi tossed her head. "This is a bandeau. And not only is it the only one I have, but it took me twenty minutes to do this—while you were sleeping."

"I can't help it if I'm a little jet-lagged. What is that you're wearing, Sherry?"

"A Regency turban. Maybe you can buy one at the Festival Fayre. But that won't be until after the promenade."

Sherry held the door open while Lexi and then Vanessa stepped into the hall.

"It's not cool, Vanessa, not cool to go with a modern hairstyle," Lexi said as the door closed behind her. "It screams 'American.'"

Bonnetless or not, they were off to Queen Square, and Vanessa thought *that* was pretty cool. She just liked the sound of it.

They'd passed by Queen Square the night before on their way to the Bath and County Club, with its black-iron fence, its grassy center punctuated with a *jeu de boules* patch or two, and a stone obelisk in the center.

As she trailed behind Lexi and Sherry among women and men in costume all streaming toward the square, she saw Julian everywhere— and nowhere. More than once she quickened at thinking she'd spotted him, but a turn of a head or a tip of a hat would prove her wrong. She almost wished she weren't surrounded by hundreds of men in breeches and beaver hats, as it proved to be a sort of tortur-ous game.

And yes, all the women she could see, even the ones pushing strollers with their babies in costume, had made some sort of an at-tempt at a Regency hairstyle or appropriate headgear.

Lexi was right. Her long straight hair exposed Vanessa for the American that she was. She would have to step it up for the ball.

She overheard a woman in a gown, a cropped jacket Vanessa now knew to be a "spencer" jacket, and Regency accessories to the hilt talking to a group of younger costumed girls who walked alongside of her.

"Look, girls," she said in her English accent as she pointed with a gloved finger. "On the far south side of the square is Number 13. Jane Austen stayed in that house for just over a month in 1799 when she was twenty-three years old. Just a bit older than all of you."

Vanessa squinted her eyes and craned her neck to see the last stone town house on the corner that looked just like, and just as el-egant as, the other town houses abutting one another and surround-ing the square.

Jane Austen stayed there? So close to her flat? She couldn't wait to tell Aunt Ella she'd not only seen Number 13 Queen Square but was staying very near it.

People in costume were politely standing on the stoop of the town house, taking pictures beside its wrought iron fence and in front of its glossy blue wooden door.

She needed to learn more about Jane's time in Bath, and then, when she finally did see Julian again, she could talk to him intelli-gently about it. She shook her head just remembering when she'd driven him from the airport into the city and tuned out an entire discussion about Jane Austen and Bath between him and her aunt. How snobby of her!

People in costume ebbed and flowed all around her, and she realized she'd lost Lexi and Sherry. She pulled her phone out of her reticule only to discover the battery was out and hadn't charged during the night because she hadn't flipped the outlet switch on. The soonest she'd be able to stop back at the flat and charge it would be after buying a much-needed turban at the Guildhall's Festival Fayre.

Hundreds of people in their Regency best swarmed the square, all of them in couples or groups. Well, Vanessa would be promenading alone. Still, as pathetic as that might be, she wouldn't think of skipping it.

Trying to locate an American accent, and maybe a group she could glom onto, she spotted a bunch who looked like they were Americans but turned out to be speaking German.

Jane Austen had attracted all kinds of people of all races from all over the world to Bath—no minor feat for a female author who had been dead for almost two hundred years. For the first time, Vanessa stood in awe of the sheer staying power of Austen. All these years, her aunt had been on to something, and all these years, Vanessa had done her best to avoid it.

Military drums sounded and about twenty or so "redcoats," uniformed army men dressed in their smart red coats with gold and navy trim, white breeches, and black hats, and bearing muskets, gathered at the top of the square while the "Town Crier" welcomed and rallied the crowd, which clapped politely.

More than once, groups of happy, smiling women asked her to take their photos. Maybe this was Jane Austen's way of getting even with her.

Maybe she *had* spent too much time behind her various screens and not enough of it with friends. She stood on her tippy-toes in her flats, the only appropriate shoe for Austen's time, and hoped that

Julian would be leading the promenade with the redcoats, but she didn't see him.

She followed the promenade uphill, past the enticing Jane Austen Centre on Gay Street with its museum, tearoom, and gift shop with windows jammed full of Austen paraphernalia. An Elizabeth Bennet statue stood out front, and she wore a blue gown that only served to remind Vanessa of the night Julian wore that blue gown. Austen had lived up the street at Number 25 with her mother for several months in 1805. The stone buildings arching along the cobblestone roads were achingly beautiful in their aged patina and a far cry from the modern steel and glass of Chicago.

From the Circus—tall, elegant stone houses complete with columns and elaborate friezes built around a circular park—to the stunning Royal Crescent topping a curved hill like a shining crown, Vanessa took in the beauty of it all.

It felt like a restorative just walking around Bath.

The bright blue sky provided a contrasting backdrop to the golden buildings and the clouds piled up in the sky like so much whipped cream.

At Number 43 Milsom Street, the famed street that, as she overheard, Jane Austen herself used to shop on, she noticed quite a few people stopping to take pictures of worn, painted lettering on the Bath stone above one of the shop fronts. CIRCULATING LIBRARY AND READING ROOM, it read in cracked black type.

No doubt Jane Austen used to frequent the library. Vanessa used to like libraries, too, but since she'd gotten her e-reader, she'd stopped going. Maybe she needed more library time in her life. More hushed time among rows of books waiting to be accidently discovered, rather than deliberately seeking one title or another, clicking to order, and moving on. Serendipity.

"There's Number 2," a woman with a white ostrich feather said to her friends who walked alongside of Vanessa. "That used to be the old sweetshop Molland's."

"Where Anne Elliot and Captain Wentworth saw each other again."

"Yes, yes," they all agreed and smiled in recognition.

Fact and fiction intermingled freely in this group, and Vanessa had grown to like it. If only Jane Austen could know that two hundred years after *Persuasion*'s publication, people in Regency costume were pointing out where her characters had supposedly visited! It boggled the mind.

At the end of Milsom Street, when the promise of Parade Gardens and the River Avon comingled, a dinged-up black car slowed down alongside her. The driver broke all the rules by turning onto the street—they had closed it off to traffic for the promenade. Why was this guy singling her out?

"Hey! Hey, you without a bonnet there!" the guy shouted from his car in an English accent that seemed to be the polar opposite of Julian's smooth Oxbridge one.

What the hell? At first Vanessa pretended she didn't know he was talking to her. As if it weren't embarrassing enough to be bonnetless in this crowd, walking alone, and now to have some guy shouting out at her from a car that shouldn't even be on this street? Now some people in the nice costumed crowd were glaring at her, as if he were her fault.

He wasn't in any sort of nineteenth-century costume and he drove his old sports car with black racing gloves. Really? Racing gloves?

She always attracted the idiots. More than five hundred people in this parade and he chose her. Her blood boiled. She was like a magnet for jerks, or as Jane Austen would say, for rakes, for lotharios.

She looked the other way, toward a gorgeous shop that sold

hats. A haberdashery. How nice it would be to shop in that haberdashery . . . He revved his car alongside her and it broke into her reverie. How could she ditch him and fast?

She couldn't believe her luck, or lack of. She'd flown more than four thousand miles to track down a gentleman, and she ended up doing nothing but attracting the attention of the English version of a hundred guys she'd already encountered in her lifetime in the States.

"I know you can hear me, luv," he shouted at her. "I'm parking my car now."

She cut into the crowd, trying to mix in with the people in the middle of the promenade rather than on the fringe. Why couldn't a nice gentleman-type in a coat, cravat, and breeches try to talk to her?

But sure enough, just as she turned toward the lush greenery of Parade Gardens where the promenade was to end, someone grabbed her shawled shoulder—with a black racing glove.

"Listen, luv, I need you for an interview. Let's have a sit-down."

She peeled the hand off her shoulder and found herself looking up at a tall, muscular guy who seemed to be at least five or maybe even ten years older than she was, wearing a wrinkled khaki trench coat, a tie that didn't match his shirt, and a sneer on his otherwise attractive face, which at the moment was looking the other way, scanning, presumably, for a place they could "have a sit-down." He squinted in the sunlight.

"There," he said as his eyes landed on a bench.

She considered enlisting the help of a nearby redcoat.

"Excuse me, but I won't be 'having a sit-down' with you. Thank you."

Just beyond him, though, the gardens stretched out toward the River Avon glistening in the sun.

He flashed a press badge, but she knew those could be created on anyone's printer—it wasn't exactly a credential.

"I'm a journalist. David Mills. I can see you're American and I need to interview you about the festival."

It could be the real deal, or it could be the oldest pickup line in the book.

"No, thank you."

She spun around to follow the crowd toward the curved frontage of the Guildhall, which she'd read had been built in 1775. In the same year in Chicago, Jean-Baptist-Point Du Sable hadn't even created the first wooden settlement yet. That would happen almost a decade later.

The three tiers of windows in the Guildhall reminded her, for some reason, of a tiered wedding cake. David stood in front of her, blocking her way to the Festival Fayre.

The Fayre in the Guildhall only went until four thirty in the afternoon, and she didn't want to miss it. Not only could Julian be there, but she needed that Regency turban, plus something to eat, and hopefully she'd find Lexi and Sherry.

She smiled, stepped around him, and picked up her pace.

"You are *exactly* the right girl for this piece. You're not really an Austen fanatic, I can tell."

Just because she wasn't wearing a bonnet?

"The economy's killing hacks like me. You could make this piece sing, I'm sure of that, I am."

She stopped for a moment.

"Come on now and help out a down-on-his-luck reporter. I need a fresh perspective. You think I just want to be interviewing the toffs with frilly bonnets, fancy pants, and walking sticks up their arses?"

She laughed. "Okay, David. You have ten minutes. Go."

* * *

*H*is interview questions really didn't elicit the kinds of snarky answers Vanessa knew he was looking for, either. He'd pegged her as some sort of a fan gone rogue, due to her lack of a bonnet, perhaps a modern prisoner held against her will here during Regency week with her fanatic friends, but he was disappointed to learn she'd come here intentionally, and worse, she'd paid an exorbitant plane fare at the last minute and was rooming with two other women to partake.

A few weeks before and her replies might have gotten her name in the paper.

He did answer the few questions she had for him, however. He was a freelancer originally from Lancashire, northern England, now relocated to Bath, and his article would be running in the *Bath Chronicle*, both the print and online versions. And yes, he would try to put in a plug in the article for her friend Julian Chancellor about Friday's *Undressing Mr. Darcy* event.

She was still pumping for Julian.

After the interview, David followed her into the Guildhall, trying to get her attention by calling several men "spooners," something derogatory, no doubt, and wondering out loud where he could get a pint. He called her a "cracker" as she ascended the wide staircase in front of him, and she interpreted that to mean something positive, but why did *he* follow her around? Why not—Julian?

At the top of the staircase, despite David's ramblings and the buzz of hundreds of people all around her, the strains of a Regency trio plucked at her heartstrings, reminding her of dancing with Julian. Off to her right, a room with an elevated ceiling, sparkling chandeliers, and afternoon sunshine gleaming in on walls the color of pastel green pastilles prompted her to stand in awe gaping at the oil paintings and floral molding until some woman, with a very sweet English accent, said, "Excuse me, dear."

As if she really had gone back in time, everyone in her immediate view (as long as she didn't look to her left at David) wore Regency clothes. It felt like time travel.

Her mind flitted to Aunt Ella as she gravitated toward the shop "stalls," as the English called them, surrounding the perimeter of the room, where she subscribed to the print version of a glossy little magazine produced there in Bath called *Jane Austen's Regency World*. It was the first nonelectronic magazine she'd ordered in years, and she sent one to herself and one to Aunt Ella's new address.

It would be nice, she thought, to get some real mail once in a while.

Across the room, beyond the haberdasher's stall loaded with decorated hats, straw bonnets, masquerade masks, a smattering of multicolored ribbons, and exactly the turban she had been seeking, sat Julian, in a shaft of sunlight, signing books.

He wore his Regency-era reading glasses and his head was bent toward the page. He sported the very coat she had stripped off him and a cravat tied in the same mathematical knot she had untied on their last night together.

Stacks of his books surrounded him on the table, and a line of mostly female fans stood in a—queue obscuring the walking stick stall next to him and snaking around into the middle of the hall.

She froze for a minute. She'd never been rendered so shy by any man.

She pretended to be engrossed in one of the vendors' loose tea offerings next to a silhouette artist who cut miniature silhouettes in a matter of minutes for his customers in their bonnets and feathers.

How she could stare at jars of tea, and even physically read their names and descriptions, but comprehend none of it was beyond her. Her face flushed, and she took off her shawl in the sudden heat.

Here she'd been hunting him down this entire time, but now that she saw him, she had no idea what to say or do. She picked up sealed bags of loose tea as she racked her brain.

Hi, Julian. Fancy seeing you here.

Or . . .

Come here often?

She shot a glance at him, because with the horde of people around, he'd never see her from here. For the first time in her life, she considered buying a bonnet, if for no other reason than that it would conceal most of her face and she could spy on him without being detected.

He looked so good, so peaceful, so smart, so . . . sexy. Damn. Why did he have to look so good? And why did he have to be doing some good—good for the historical money pit he'd inherited? It really made him endearing. She knew he really hated all this public show-manship. But there he sat, signing and chatting and smiling . . .

"Would you like to purchase that tea, miss?" one of the women at the stall asked with a nice inflection at the end of the question.

Translation: Put. The. Tea. Down. Or buy it. The English were so polite.

"Oh," Vanessa said as she set the tea down and stepped away. "Your tea sounds great. I have to think about it. Thank you."

She had to think about a tiny packet of tea that cost the equivalent of a dollar fifty?

She made up her mind—about the turban anyway. She would buy it *and* a spy bonnet.

At the haberdashery she tried on the straw bonnet with a rim longer than a dryer vent tube.

"That," said one of the bonnet makers, "is a poke bonnet. Lovely, isn't it?"

Lovely? Not really. Designed to make you appear invisible in a sea of nineteenth-century reenactors? Yes. Made to cast a dark shadow over your entire face? Absolutely.

"I'll take it," Vanessa said. "And that turban." She pointed to the turban she'd been eyeing.

"Oooooh, that bonnet is sooooo not a good look for you." It was Lexi—and Sherry. "It hides your gorgeous hair, your face, everything. You look like a stovepipe popping out of a smashing gown." A handsome redcoat trailed Lexi.

Someone tapped Vanessa on the shoulder. Was it . . . Julian? But when she peered from out of the tunnel vision of her bonnet, she saw David's ruddy face.

"Here, luv, I've bought you a pint."

He handed the glass to Vanessa and, even though it would've been more appropriate to be drinking ratafia or Constantia wine, she promptly took a gulp, though it proved difficult to navigate the glass to her lips without hitting the rim of her bonnet. She could use more than just a pint, too. How the hell should she approach Julian?

"Drink up and let's get the hell out of here," David said.

"You're such a charmer," Vanessa replied. "And I'm not going anywhere with you."

"If you want charm you'd best stick with the ponces around here, luv. I don't do charm."

Not all English guys were gentlemen. It struck Vanessa that she now preferred the "ponces," whatever that meant, to guys of his ilk. There happened to be one ponce in particular she had set her bonnet on, and David's no-frills tactics reminded her she needed to be as feminine as possible with Julian.

Lexi could smell the testosterone emanating from this Lancashire he-man. She took the other pint of beer from him, the one he'd bought for himself, and sipped.

The redcoat who had been following her gave up and walked away.

"Thank you for thinking of me, sweetheart, but you forgot to get Sherry a beer."

A smile broke over David's face. He had never run into the likes of Lexi before. The two of them would make a great couple!

"Let me make a formal introduction," Vanessa said. "David Mills, freelance journalist, this is Lexi Stone and Sherry Pajowski."

Lexi plucked David's smartphone from his shirt pocket and keyed something in. "Here's my number. Text us once you've gotten two more pints. We'll be around here—somewhere."

With that she slid the phone back in his pocket and turned her back on him, but he took his pint of beer back from her.

"Thanks for your number. I'll be dialing it tonight, around half past ten."

The bonnet makers were busy helping other customers, but they were also listening in on all this, looking up with their wide eyes as they relinquished their bonnets neatly trimmed with flowers and fruit.

"Hmmm, we shall see," Lexi said, eyeing him up and down.

David's mouth fell agape.

For a moment Vanessa forgot all about Julian sitting across the room, signing his books. It had been a while since she'd seen Lexi in action like this.

The women surrounding them fiddled with their topaz cross necklaces, tightened their bonnet strings, and moved on toward the silhouette-cutting stall.

Determined to take a more ladylike approach with Julian, Vanessa turned toward his signing table, confident her bonnet obscured her face, but the queue had disappeared.

And so had he. Damn.

Was this a good PR move? Creating scarcity? Generating a little mystery? Yes, it could work.

He'd left a note, scripted in quill and propped atop a stack of his books.

Dear Ladies (and Gentlemen),

Look for me tomorrow at the London leg of the Dash for Darcy scavenger hunt . . .

Yours,
Mr. Darcy

Chapter 15

*V*anessa woke to the sound of seagulls and pigeons squawking outside the flat's sash windows.

Who knew that Bath, the most exquisite Georgian city in England, had the same problem as the typical inland American parking lot with an influx of displaced seagulls?

Even this, however, wouldn't ruin her glittering first impressions of the city, and she was reluctant to leave for a day trip to London until, once again, her first thoughts of the day turned to Julian. He would be in London.

By midmorning—their scavenger hunt strategy mapped out, their Pump Room water downed, their breakfast-sausage "takeaway" sandwiches and nonalcoholic juices and coffee for three consumed—Vanessa sat with Sherry, plus a zonked-out Lexi, on the train, and the nearly two-hour trek from Bath to London was almost under her skinny faux-alligator belt.

Today she had dressed for London, her phone was charged, her e-mails and messages "sorted," as Julian would say, and she, Lexi, and

Sherry had shaken hands on conquering the Dash for Darcy together, pooling their knowledge, and letting Vanessa have the dinner with Julian, should they win.

"What do you mean 'should' we win?" Lexi asked. "I'm on Team Vanessa and we're going to win."

The first mission in the hunt was:

You will find Mr. Darcy at a certain madame's London residence. You must pay him a visit and have your photograph taken as proof. You need not leave your calling card as it is unlikely he will be returning your call. It is there you will receive your next clue.

"That's ridiculously easy," Vanessa said. "Even I knew this one as soon as I read it last night."

"You did?" Sherry had asked, while Lexi slept in the seat across the aisle from them. Was that drool glistening on the corner of Lexi's mouth?

She didn't get back until two in the morning, although her evening with David had started much earlier than ten thirty. She'd missed all the theatricals in the Guildhall that night and, unlike every other time she'd hooked up with a guy, she didn't wake up bragging about the hot sex she'd just had.

Vanessa leaned in to Sherry. "I'm going to whisper because you never know—our competition might be sitting right behind us. My self-quarantine after the accident paid off, because, in all my googling of Colin Firth, I stumbled across his wax figure at—"

"Madame Tussauds," they both whispered together.

"Once we hit Paddington Station, we each have to get an Oyster card and take the Hammersmith & City or Circle Line on the tube to Baker Street."

"You've got it all figured out," Sherry said.

"I do. Stick with me."

"I am."

She had a friend in Sherry, after all, she thought, a good friend.

"I figured it out last night and ordered three advance tickets thanks to the beauty of the Internet. Gotta love modern technology. Couldn't do that with a quill pen and paper."

Sherry smiled and cracked her gum. Her red T-shirt had a gold imprint of the crown and in gold block letters it said:

KEEP CALM

HE IS SINGLE

OF GOOD FORTUNE

AND IN NEED OF A WIFE

"I like that T-shirt," Vanessa said.

"Most Janeites do." Sherry nodded. "I get lots of compliments on it. You're one of us now."

As the train barreled toward Paddington, Vanessa actually looked forward to seeing Colin Firth's figure, wax or otherwise. She knew she'd officially crossed over to the Jane side. Still, she had to wonder at the nonpurist, nonscholarly choice to launch the hunt at Madame Tussauds. Could it be that Julian had actually listened to her and decided to branch out from his usual scholarly stronghold and include a pop-culture spin in his marketing mix?

Her phone vibrated with a text, and as usual, she had a glimmer of hope it might be from Julian. But no, it was—Chase.

"He heard from Aunt Ella that we're heading into London today and he wants to meet us," Vanessa said.

"And?"

"I don't want anything—or anyone—to slow us down."

"He might be able to help. He travels to London all the time, doesn't he?"

"Yep."

"Tell him what we're up to, where we're going. If he's game, he can join us. He knows London even better than Lexi."

"True." Still, she hesitated to type anything.

"And you know it makes your aunt happy that you two get along. You can't just go to London and blow him off."

"You're right." Vanessa started keying the message in.

"Soon you guys are gonna be like—brother and sister."

Vanessa cocked her head at Sherry. "Ewww . . ." Why did that thought repulse her?

"Or something. Cousins?"

"No," Vanessa said.

They transferred to the tube, where, after they stepped out of the tube car, the overhead announcement said "Mind the gap" repeatedly, meaning the gap between the tube car and the platform.

How could a country with the same language, plus or minus a few words, be so different from and so much more interesting than hers? Was it the centuries of history that made a difference?

The tube seemed very otherworldly to her, and the Baker Street stop featured profiles of Sherlock Holmes smoking a pipe imprinted on the white wall tiles. This proved appropriate for their day, since it would include a certain level of mystery and intrigue as they tried to kick ass in the capital city and score as many scavenger hunt items as possible.

When she emerged from the underground onto Marylebone Road NW1, as the street sign read—a very different street sign from the ones in Chicago—the verve of the city swirled around her. Red double-decker buses and black cabs really did speed along on the wrong side of the road and English coppers really did wear hats with chin straps.

Lexi wanted to hit a pub.

But Vanessa steered them right toward the massive green dome of Madame Tussauds and, finally, into the line for visitors with advance tickets.

"I need a drink," Lexi said. "Because I can't believe what I did with David last night."

"Let me guess. You slept with him."

"No. I *didn't* sleep with him! We—talked. For six hours. I'm exhausted and didn't get my eight hours of sleep. What the hell?"

"Sounds serious. Or maybe you just like him as a friend?"

"Honey, I have lots of men in my life, but none of them are *just friends*. What would be the point?"

They both laughed. Vanessa knew she was kidding.

"So you want to sleep with him."

"Of course!"

"But you didn't. Instead you had a meaningful first date. Congratulations."

"I have got to get my mojo back. This guy is turning me upside down. He invited me to a movie tonight."

"That's sweet."

"Exactly. And I said yes because it actually sounds—sweet."

"Good for you, Lexi. Consider it a change of pace. Do you see a map of the museum anywhere?" Vanessa had scoured the Internet for a map of the interior, and none was to be found. Now, in the admission line, she noticed the brochure didn't have any map, either. She grilled one of the ticket takers on the whereabouts of Colin Firth only to learn that he was somewhere in the "A-List Party Room" and no, there was no quick exit, they'd have to make their way through the entire museum and exit at the gift shop.

Vanessa was only too familiar with the old ploy of getting people to buy more by funneling them through the gift shop.

"Marketing!" she and Lexi said simultaneously with a laugh.

Vanessa led them away from the mob at the elevators to the stairs, and, as luck would have it, as soon as they reached the top of the stairs, the very first room happened to be a very cheesy-looking Academy Awards red-carpet room labeled THE A-LIST PARTY.

"Now, where is he?" Vanessa asked.

"How about right there?" Sherry pointed her finger, with Darcy rubber wristbands up her arm, and yes, there he stood, in a tux, commanding the room on a distant platform with an array of other stars, right in between Kate Winslet and Justin Bieber in front of a pinkish curtain.

Lexi bolted across the room, scissoring through the crowd and almost knocking over a woman taking a photo, which turned out to be a wax figure itself.

"What's up with her?" Sherry asked as they headed toward Colin Firth.

"She's very competitive and I don't think she got very much sleep last night. She gets crabby when she doesn't get her eight hours."

"What took you two so long?" Lexi asked as she handed Sherry her phone from her perch right next to Colin Firth. "Sherry, can you take a picture of me—of us?"

Lexi corrected herself as Vanessa stepped up on the platform and hooked her arm in Colin's left arm.

Vanessa smiled for the shot because even though he was made of wax, and this entire place was nothing but a shrine to celebrity worship, it felt pretty cool to be on Colin Firth's arm.

"Wait. Vanessa, I want that side," Lexi said. "Let's switch."

Vanessa glared at her. Not only had Lexi cut in front of people who were there before them, but more people had gathered, not so patiently waiting their turn.

Lexi came over to Vanessa's side and gave her a little shove with her hip.

"Fine," Vanessa grumbled. "Take this side. He's looking toward his right anyway."

Once they'd made the switch, Sherry announced she was taking the picture. "Hold still, Lexi."

Lexi looked at Vanessa. "I want that side again."

"No. Now smile, damn it!"

Lexi stomped over and pulled Vanessa's arm, but Vanessa stood fast and smiled for the camera until something . . . snapped. It was Colin's finger—in her hand!

"Lex-iii!"

Vanessa looked at the finger in the palm of her hand with horror. Did anyone notice? Were there security cameras? Of course there were!

Shock rumbled through her. It was the tip of his middle finger, and he seemed to be flipping her off! Her first reaction was to shove the finger in her purse and step off the platform.

Her second was to complete this mission.

"Sherry, get up there."

Sherry didn't move. Her mouth had fallen open, exposing her pink bubble gum, and the golden letters on her shirt shone in mockery.

Vanessa guided Sherry up onto the platform before anyone else could squeeze in. "Smile."

Sherry couldn't smile, but Vanessa snapped a few pictures of her bug-eyed face. "Got it." Vanessa took deep breaths. "Now. Where's the clue to the next checkpoint?"

As her face flushed at the thought of the finger in her purse, and while several people stared at her as others stepped up to pose with Colin, she looked all around for some sign of the next clue.

Could she have been wrong about this being a checkpoint? She was, after all, a neophyte Austen fan.

Her eyes darted around the room, which seemed to be getting more and more crowded, hoping to catch a glimpse of Julian, until a woman dressed in a Regency gown and carrying a wicker basket in her hand dipped into view from across the room, near Russell Brand. "Follow me," Vanessa said.

Lexi checked out Russell Brand in his tight pinstripe suit.

"Very hot, isn't he?" Lexi smiled.

"Any hotter and he'd melt," said Sherry.

Vanessa stammered to the woman in Regency garb, "H-hi . . . we're part of the Dash for Darcy—"

She didn't have to say anything more, thank goodness, because the thought of Colin Firth's finger in her purse had really taken her breath away.

The woman smiled and, without saying a word, handed off a calling card with elaborate script printed on it.

But before Vanessa could read it, three security men dressed in blue escorted her and her friends to the periphery of the room.

"How exciting!" Lexi said. "We're finally getting escorted by British men in uniform!"

The security guard with Vanessa spoke up. "Please hand over the finger."

"We don't know what you're talking about," Lexi said. "We need to call a lawyer."

"There will be no charges," the security guard said, "if you hand over the finger."

"Don't give him the finger," Lexi whispered in her ear with a giggle.

Vanessa thought about it.

"It's all on the security camera," the guard said. "Please hand it over and you will merely be escorted out. If you resist, we will have to take this to a higher authority."

Vanessa opened her purse, slid the clue card in, and pulled out the wax finger.

"Thank you for cooperating," he said as he took the finger.

"Now we will escort you to the gift shop and you will not be allowed reentry."

"Of course," Vanessa said. "We're very sorry."

The guards marched them through the museum, past the royal family, past the literary greats, beyond the Hulk, but Vanessa stopped in her tracks when she almost bumped right into Johnny Depp as Jack Sparrow.

Not only did he look completely lifelike—much, much more so than Colin Firth did, but it made her think of Chase. Chase! Would he have responded to her text message by now? Would he meet up with them? She might need his help after all.

"Let's keep moving," the guard said to her.

She looked back over her shoulder at Jack Sparrow, whose eyes, outlined in kohl, seemed to follow her.

Once in the gift shop, Vanessa's guard spoke. "Do you intend to make any purchases?"

"No," Vanessa replied, just as Lexi said, "Yes."

Vanessa shot her a look.

"I want," Lexi said. She nodded toward a life-sized replica of Colin Firth's wax figure propped up next to all kinds of Rolling Stones and Beatles memorabilia.

If there were two words that summed up Lexi, they were "I want."

"How much is he?"

Her guard escorted her over to the figure and looked at the price tag. "It's a one-of-a-kind item. It appears to be a hundred and fifty pounds."

"I've invested more than that in a man before," Lexi said.

Vanessa sighed. "And just how will we get around London with him? Not to mention the train back to Bath—the airplane back to Chicago? Forget about it, Lexi." She turned to her guard. "Please escort us outside. I think we've caused enough trouble for one day."

"Thanks for giving us the finger." The guard smiled.

Sherry burst out laughing.

Lexi was too busy getting a last look at the Colin Firth replica.

As soon as the security guard took Vanessa outside and gave her a final warning to "best stay out of trouble," she spotted a familiar figure standing on the sidewalk in sunglasses with gorgeous brown hair parted in the middle and cut to the length right around his Adam's apple, checking his phone with a skull and crossbones skin on it, leaning on his black umbrella.

It was Chase. He cocked an eyebrow at the three of them being escorted out by security guards.

"Why does this not surprise me?" he asked with a smirk as he walked over.

He leaned right in and kissed Vanessa, full on the lips. He tasted of coffee.

"Chase!" Vanessa said.

"What? We're practically family." Then he gave her a quick but determined pat on her butt.

"Right."

And he was wearing a nicely tailored gray suit. Most likely Italian.

*T*urned out that Chase couldn't resist a treasure hunt, as he called it, and he seemed to be good at it, too. Go figure. He was the one who solved the second clue:

Cassandra Austen drew her own conclusions about her sister. Where can one of these conclusions be found? You may find me there. Regardless, you will need to write up a description of the item in less than 100 words to get your next clue.

"Really?" he had teased while they were out in front of Madame Tussauds. "None of you have any idea?" He paused. "I think I've been spending too much time with Paul. We're going to the National Portrait Gallery, where you'll find Cassandra Austen's drawing of her sister, Jane. The only officially confirmed portrait of Jane Austen. Although that is being contested with the latest research on the Rice portrait."

Vanessa followed him as the back of his suit jacket flapped against him while he hustled up the stairs from the twisting tunnels of the Charing Cross tube stop. He moved pretty quickly for having nothing to gain by winning this scavenger hunt—Vanessa was impressed by his selflessness.

At the top of the stairs an entirely new vista of London opened up before her and the sound of whirring traffic surrounded them.

"There's the gallery," Lexi said as she took big strides across the square.

Chase walked briskly alongside Vanessa. "This is Trafalgar Square, and the far corner there, where the statue of Charles the First stands, marks the center of London. Distances in and out of the city are measured from that point. And if you look up, you'll see Nelson's Column."

Vanessa glanced briefly up, but was much more interested in making her way to the gallery.

Chase suddenly stopped and hung back.

"Chase?"

He looked at his watch. "Listen, you girls are busy. I'll get everyone some fish and chips to go."

"Wow, thank you," Vanessa said. "I pegged you for a fish-and-chips guy. Get it? 'Pegged'? Arrgh!"

The joke was lame and he cracked a small smile. Not his usual. He signaled a wave with his umbrella. "After you get the next clue, meet me at the top of the National Gallery stairs."

Without a word further he spun off in the opposite direction. In that split second she felt what it would be like to lose him—his friendship, his connection to Paul and her aunt. It was weird.

"Hello. Where is your portrait of Jane Austen?" Sherry asked once they got to the information desk.

"That's a popular portrait today." The woman behind the desk smiled.

Lexi shot Vanessa a concerned look. "We better get our act together."

"We?" Vanessa asked as they scurried up the stairs.

Lexi stood at the top of the stairs and glared at Vanessa.

"You're the one who got us kicked out of Madame Tussauds."

"I've been kicked out of worse places," Lexi said.

"Come on, people," Sherry said. She led the way to the portrait, in a very hushed room with creaky wooden floors and an arched skylight for a ceiling that let in the light despite the gathering clouds outside. The wooden trim had been lacquered black and the walls painted ocean green. Massive oil portraits, in gold-leaf frames, of John Constable, William Blake, John Keats, and Lord Byron dominated the room.

A small glass display box stood at about chest height, and if they hadn't been looking for it, they might have walked right by.

A throng of women encircled the box. Vanessa, Lexi, and Sherry looked at each other. They weren't leading the way on this scavenger hunt.

"We need to divide and conquer. Vanessa, you write up the description," Lexi said. "Sherry and I will look around for the next clue. We've got to get ahead of that crowd!"

Vanessa had already been scanning the room for Julian, or someone who might give them their next clue, even as she inched toward the display box.

Yes, she wanted to get a look at Jane Austen!

Finally the women around the display box moved on, and Sherry followed them for the next clue while Lexi got distracted ogling the portrait of Lord Byron.

Vanessa had Jane Austen all to herself.

Her first thought went something like: Thank you for the fabulous novels. Her second thought came just as quickly: Damn you, Jane Austen!

Austen had, after all, gotten her into this. Without her, a certain "Mr. Darcy" would never have Regency-danced into her life, wreaking havoc on her priorities and her heartstrings.

The light in the display box went off as if in response to her silent rant. She had to press the button to light up the display again.

It wasn't so much a portrait as it was a small drawing, about the size of a wallet photo, and unfinished, too—an underwhelming representation of such a powerful author.

Vanessa folded her arms just like Austen had her arms folded in the drawing. Austen looked a little smug in the drawing, and her head was turned to the side, looking away.

Vanessa unfolded her arms, pulled pen and paper from her bag, and began writing a description of the woman in the drawing, who didn't look anything like how she had pictured Jane Austen.

Unlike the other luminaries in the room, Austen was at a distinct disadvantage, though, and this actually made Vanessa feel sorry for her. The portraits of the men in the room gleamed in oil paint, and some had been painted larger than life. Austen's portrait was a mere drawing, done not by a professional artist but by her sister, an amateur.

Unlike Lord Byron, who had dressed in an Albanian costume for his commissioned portrait, Jane Austen sat in a simple day dress and cap. It occurred to Vanessa that neither Cassandra nor Jane ever intended this unfinished drawing to be displayed in London's National Portrait Gallery, and it might have really embarrassed them both to see it here!

Cassandra had, with watercolors, painted in brown tendrils curling out of her sister's cap, brown eyebrows, and big brown eyes as well as rosy cheeks. But she hadn't painted any further and left everything else in pencil, including a rather pointed nose and a small, pinched mouth.

As the notation on the display read: *This frank sketch by her sister and closest confidante Cassandra is the only reasonably certain portrait from life. Even so, Jane's relatives were not entirely convinced by it:* "There is a look which I recognize as hers," *her niece wrote,* "though the general resemblance is not strong, yet as it represents a pleasing countenance it is so far a truth."

After Vanessa finished writing up her own description of the work, she stared at the portrait with a sisterly feeling, as if the two of them got each other. Vanessa smiled at her.

"If you give me your write-up, I've found who will give us the next clue," Sherry broke in.

"Here it is." Vanessa said as she handed it to Sherry, who hurried off.

Vanessa gave a wink to the portrait, stepped back, and the light in the display went off, as if Jane Austen herself were winking back.

With that, another group of women and a few men encircled the display box while Sherry and Lexi caught up with her.

"Too bad we don't have time to see the Brontë sisters' portrait before we leave," Lexi said.

"Brontë? Isn't that blasphemy to Jane Austen? Do you want to curse our entire scavenger hunt? Besides, Chase is waiting out in front for us with food!"

"That's so nice of him," Sherry said.

"Yes, yes, it is," said Vanessa as they scrambled down the stairs.

"There's also a portrait of Charles Dickens here when he was young," Lexi said. "He was a sexy young Victorian dude, you know, before he grew all that facial hair."

"Forget Dickens, Lexi. Aren't you hungry?"

"I'm starved," Sherry said.

Lexi nodded in agreement. "I'm always hungry. But let's eat on the run. We're going to win this thing if it kills me!"

Once they were outside, Vanessa took two stairs at a time to the top of the National Gallery steps, but she didn't see Chase anywhere.

"We can't wait for him," Lexi said as she looked at her watch. "Here's the next clue: 'Something Jane Austen called all her "worldly wealth" almost went by carriage to Gravesend and then the West Indies, but it now resides in a library. Visit it, procure proof of your visit, and describe the item in twenty-five words or less, including what lies atop it. Perhaps you will meet me there . . .'"

Sherry and Vanessa gave each other blank looks.

"Wait a minute." Vanessa snapped her fingers. "I remember Julian saying something about this to Aunt Ella. But what was it?"

"I'm pretty sure whatever it is, it's at the British Library. Or it could be the London Library," Lexi said. "It's time to call your aunt. Give me your phone."

Vanessa handed Lexi her phone and looked out across Trafalgar Square for Chase. Beyond the fountains in the square, beyond various eighteenth- and nineteenth-century buildings, and above a few spires towered Big Ben, and a British flag flapped in the wind across the way under a clouded sky. Her heart thudded with the recognition that yes, she was in London, and it was gorgeous and exciting and new, well, new to her anyway. Just then, Chase came into view, carrying a large brown bag in each hand, his umbrella tucked under his arm and his sunglasses up on his dark brown hair.

"There's Chase!" Sherry said.

"Mmmm," said Lexi as she waited for Aunt Ella to pick up. "There's only one thing better than a gorgeous guy coming your way. It's a gorgeous guy coming your way *with food.*"

*　　*　　*

*C*hase. Thank you," Vanessa said as she squeezed his arm.

He no doubt made a great business partner for Paul, but she could see he'd make some lucky woman a great life partner, too. She was happy to have him as a friend.

"Aunt Ella didn't pick up her phone," she said. "Should I be worried?"

Chase shook his head no. "She's with Paul. Why don't you call him?"

"I hate to bother them."

Lexi scrolled through her contacts, trying to get hold of another Jane Austen Society member who might know. Meanwhile, on her phone, Vanessa searched for "British Library" and "Jane Austen," and it yielded a link to *Jane Austen for Dummies* by Dr. Joan Ray. Under the heading "The British Library at St. Pancras, London," she read:

The British Library in London is the official library of the United Kingdom, and they have Jane Austen's writing desk—

"St. Pancras! That's the Piccadilly Line, isn't it, Chase?" Lexi spoke a mile a minute.

"Yeah. Let's cut over to the Leicester Square station."

Off they dashed, crossing the city again underground, this time on the Piccadilly Line. Piccadilly. How English was that? They went right underneath Covent Garden of *My Fair Lady* fame, and Vanessa would've liked to have stopped! She also wished the Internet worked on the tube because she would've read more about the writing desk.

Had Julian inadvertently or purposely given her *all* the answers to the hunt during his time with her? Why hadn't she paid attention to his Austen spoutings? What a great loss, to have an expert on a subject in her midst and to have been completely oblivious to it.

Why did she find all things Austen so interesting now? Was it because of Julian? Because she'd read the novels and loved them? Or some strange brew of both?

Once out in front of St. Pancras Station, waiting impatiently for the light to turn in the drizzle, Chase opened his umbrella and offered it to her to share with Lexi and Sherry.

"Look, ladies." He pointed behind them as the drizzle gave his hair a sexy gloss and he pushed it back. "Check out St. Pancras Station behind us."

Vanessa looked back over her shoulder.

"It opened in 1868, and it's a glorious example of Victorian Gothic architecture."

Certainly the massive dark-red brick building, with its clock tower that seemed Big Ben–ish, its three tiers of arched windows atop a ground level of arched doorways, and its series of chimneys and spires sprouting up, impressed her, but then the light turned.

"They say the five-star St. Pancras London Renaissance Hotel is London's most romantic building."

Vanessa smiled at Chase. He was easy to travel with—a font of knowledge and a man who found joy anywhere, it seemed. This hunt just had her a little sidelined, that was all.

"Chase, once we get home, I'd like to take you out for drinks, get to know you a little better," she said. "Since we're going to be like family and all." She winked.

"A very *close* family," he joked. He put his arm around her until they stepped into the British Library.

Once she stood in the darkened, hushed Sir John Ritblat Gallery of the ultramodern library, in front of a glass case displaying Austen's portable wooden desk, her mind did not even flit to Julian.

On this day alone, between the National Portrait Gallery and the British Library, she had endured more silence than she'd allowed herself in an entire year, it seemed. Her phone sat silenced, too, in her bag, as per the library instructions, and she hadn't posted or used her earbuds all day.

On the gorgeous mahogany writing box, sloped for handwriting and hinged to store paper and ink, sat a pair of spectacles so small and fragile that Vanessa couldn't help but think, for some reason, of Jane Austen's heart.

Austen was, no doubt, a strong and resilient woman, able to wield barbs, irony, and satire the way a fencer wields a sword, but what of her heart? Vanessa suspected it might have been as delicate as these spectacles, made of two delicate glass lenses with the thinnest of wires to hold them together.

Austen's was, Vanessa decided, a vulnerable but all-seeing heart.

Meanwhile, her own heart, though equally vulnerable, lacked the all-seeing quality.

Could she, just a few years away from forty-one, Austen's age at death, acquire the vision the author had at half her age? She was in her twenties when she wrote her major novels. How could such a young girl, born more than two hundred years ago, have known so much about life and the nature of true love? How could she, without a computer, cell phone, TV, movies, or Internet, have been infinitely wiser?

Maybe it was just too late for Vanessa. Too late for her true life to take shape. Too late for love.

She thought she'd been smart, protecting her heart with barbed wire wrapped around it, just like the tattoo on her ankle, but instead, she'd ensnared herself and her ability to love and locked herself into nothing but loneliness. She'd trapped herself and stunted her own emotional growth, and she'd been doing this for years, for decades—deliberately.

It had taken the likes of Julian, a by-product of *Pride and Prejudice*, to crack her open and make her bleed.

Why she had to realize this in a library in England was beyond her, but sometimes you have to travel great distances to discover your own interior landscape.

"Well, there's her writing box," Sherry whispered with a sigh. "Isn't it gorgeous? That's where Darcy was conceived."

Vanessa flinched at the word "conceived."

Lexi squinted. "Yes," she whispered. Even she seemed in awe. "It was the original laptop. I'll dash off the description," she said as she scribbled in a notepad die cut in the shape of a woman's lips. "Vanessa, you look for the next clue."

But Vanessa couldn't tear herself away from staring at the spectacles.

Lexi nudged her. "Are you okay?"

No, she was not okay.

A warm hand touched her shoulder—Chase. "I have to pay homage to the Magna Carta. Come and get me before you leave."

The Magna Carta, the Gutenberg Bible, Shakespeare's first folio, they were all here, surrounding her, mocking her, it seemed, and her little missives on social media sites, her press releases, endless e-mails, and frivolous social media posts.

A step in any direction in this room led to greatness and genius, to the highest of human achievement. Austen sat in the company of the intelligentsia, where she belonged.

Within Vanessa's immediate sight stood Oscar Wilde's "Ballad of Reading Gaol" in his flamboyant cursive, and, further along, Handel's *Messiah* rang out to her with its bold score and crossings out. The page of the *Messiah* on display showed the score for the Hallelujah Chorus, and it resounded in her head—maybe it wasn't too late for her. Maybe she was just in time—for Julian.

Hallelujah! Hallelujah! Hallelujah!

Why had she kept herself so guarded for so long?

An older couple, probably in their early seventies, and looking American in their white matching gym shoes, approached the display. They exuded happiness and coupledom and emanated a vanilla scent as they stood arm in arm in front of the glass case.

Vanessa stepped back to allow the couple, both shorter than she was, a better view. She yanked Lexi out of their way, too.

"Look, sweetheart," the woman whispered to her companion, "it's Jane Austen's writing box. The one that, when she was twenty-three years old, was accidently put in a chaise with her dressing boxes, headed for the West Indies. She had all of her manuscripts, letters, and money in the box at the time. Can you believe it?"

He shook his head no and, when he smiled, his crows' feet crinkled around his blue eyes.

"All of her novels, in their nascent form, almost vanished."

He shook his head.

In the time before computers and backups, Vanessa could imagine a young Jane Austen, horrified at the thought of her work on a trajectory toward the West Indies, yet still rational and, no doubt, taking control of the situation.

Now Vanessa remembered half listening to this story while scrolling through her e-mails as Julian had told it to Aunt Ella over tea.

"What did she do again?" Vanessa asked the woman.

"She had a man on a horse sent to go after the chaise, and within half an hour, she had the box back. But as Austen herself said, she had lost 'all of her worldly possessions.'"

"That's right." Vanessa smiled.

"It would be like you losing your phone," Sherry whispered.

Vanessa managed a smile, realizing how pathetic it made her sound. Was that the most valuable thing she had to lose? If so, had she really lived?

"We'd all be lost without her work." The woman saved her by changing the subject. "The entire episode is written in a letter to Cassandra." She looked endearingly at Vanessa. "You must be an Austen fan."

Vanessa nodded. "Yes, yes, I am."

Her aunt would've been pleased. And admitting her fandom didn't even make her feel like she should sign up for a twelve-step program: *My name is Vanessa Roberts and I'm an Austenaholic.* She felt cool about the whole thing.

Lexi moved right between her and the older couple. She flung up her arms, and in a loud whisper she said, "We need to find the next clue—*okay?*"

"I'm talking to this nice couple," Vanessa whispered firmly while nudging Lexi aside.

Lexi tossed her head at them. "Where's Chase?"

"Calm down, Lexi. He's looking at the Magna Carta."

The security guard at the door had his eye on them, and other visitors in the library turned their heads toward them.

"Calm down? How can I calm down when you're chatting, Chase is MIA, and Sherry's in the gift shop?"

Vanessa craned her neck to speak to the older couple. "I apologize for my friend here—"

Lexi stomped her foot on the carpeting. "I'm only trying to keep us on task for *your* sake." She didn't whisper that time.

The security guard started coming their way.

"Thank you for telling me the story of the writing box," Vanessa said to the couple. "Great to meet you, but I have to go."

Lexi stormed off, brushing against the security guard, who then followed her.

"Before you go, perhaps you would like this?"

The woman held out a familiar card—a clue!

"What?" Vanessa couldn't believe it. "Thank you. Thank you very much," she whispered as she squeezed the woman's hand.

"I know your friend has the description of the desk in her notebook. You can just hand that in at the end. I hope *you* win, dear," the woman said. "Only one person can win, not an entire team. You'll have to break up your group. You're very near the end of the hunt for today."

Vanessa thanked her again, hurried off after Lexi, and left the library without seeing any of the treasures of the collection, including the Magna Carta and the Gutenberg Bible. A couple of weeks earlier, she might not have cared, but now—

Lexi paced in front of the café just outside the library with Sherry and Chase. The café was called, appropriately, the Last Word.

"What the hell, Vanessa?" Lexi stopped and put a hand on her hip. "We didn't get the clue."

One thing that clearly hadn't changed with Lexi was her fiery temper. Maybe the woman with the clue had a point.

"Lexi, I'm not sure if this is going to work out with us together," Vanessa said.

"Uh-oh." Sherry headed for the steps of the café. "I'm going to get some beverages for everyone . . ."

Lexi glared at Vanessa.

Chase cracked open a book. It had stopped drizzling so he leaned on his umbrella and began to read. "Let me know when you ladies are ready. I have to entertain clients soon at the Ritz, so I'm only free for another hour."

Lexi went right up to Chase, put her hand over the page he was reading, and asked, "Chase, why have you been so helpful? I only ask because Sherry and I want the recognition for winning this thing, and we all know why Vanessa wants to win this hunt. But what about you? Has her aunt put you up to this?"

"Ella may have mentioned she hoped I could check in on Vanessa, yes."

Vanessa dropped her phone on the concrete and the screen cracked. She picked it up and stared at the fissure.

"What?" Vanessa asked. "You're here because my aunt wanted you to *babysit* me?"

"No, it's not like that. She's been worried about you ever since they announced their engagement, and your car accident—"

"I don't need that kind of help. I'm not a charity case!"

"I never said you were," Chase said.

"And I don't need you, Lexi. I thought you changed, but you haven't."

Lexi flipped her blunt-cut hair. "You do need us, Vanessa." She put both hands, stacked with rings and finished off with a bloodred manicure, on Vanessa's shoulders. "Who helped you out after you slept with Julian?"

"Lexi—stop!" She soooo did not want Chase to hear that. Lexi knew damn well she wouldn't want Chase to hear it—for so many reasons! Did she have no boundaries? No sense of decency?

Vanessa eyed Chase, who raised an eyebrow.

"Who's done everything possible to help you win a goddamn dinner with a guy who doesn't even deserve to be in the same room with you?"

Vanessa pulled away from Lexi, who just moved in closer, getting all up in her face.

Chase closed his book. "So that's what this is all about." He raised and then hit the tip of his umbrella on the pavement. "You slept with him. And now you just want to get back into his breeches?"

"It's not like that at all! We have a thing, a connection."

"A connection? Where is he, then? Nowhere to be seen! I thought this was about Jane Austen!"

"It *is* about Jane Austen," Vanessa said.

"No, it's not," said Lexi. "Vanessa could care less about Jane Austen," she said to Chase.

She ignored Lexi and pleaded with Chase. "It wasn't originally about her, no, but I've come to know her and now I'm in it for her, too—to learn more about her and help raise money and awareness for preservation of her cottage and her brother's estate now functioning as Chawton House Library. And—"

"Am I really supposed to believe this?" Chase asked. "Because it sounds like PR-speak to me."

"If she wins she gets to have dinner with Julian at his estate," Lexi said. "That's the deal. Ticket fees for this event go toward preservation, but we didn't pay for the tickets—Julian did."

"I didn't know you slept with him," Chase said.

"I didn't know you cared! Or does this just fall under your babysitting duties?"

How could he be acting like her boyfriend? Or worse, a spy? She had no clue he really cared that way. He had no claim on her, either!

"I can sleep with whomever I want!" she shouted right there, in front of the British Library.

"I need to go," Chase said, all dignity and coolness.

"You must've known she had feelings for Julian," Lexi said to him.

"I did. But I didn't know she'd slept with him. That changes things—for me anyway."

"I'm right here, you know!" Vanessa said to them. "What right do you have to punish me for my actions that have nothing to do with you?"

"Is my leaving punishment to you?"

Yes, yes, it was. The cloud cover seemed to darken overhead and she struggled for words. Words usually came easily to her, but she couldn't say a thing.

"I see," Chase said. "Take care. I'll give you this. You might need it." He tossed her his umbrella—a gentleman to the end.

He turned and walked away, ripping something inside her, something she didn't even know was there.

Why? Why did she always mess things up with people she actually cared about? Yes, she cared about Chase. He'd taken time out of his day to help her out, and she'd managed to piss him off somehow! She thought about sending him a text, but what should she say?

How could she be so good at public relations and so shitty at personal ones?

*L*exi sighed. "There goes the guy you belong with. But you've really effed that up now, haven't you?"

When had Lexi ever been right about love? Never!

Vanessa ran after him, but he was walking pretty briskly toward the zooming traffic on Euston Road. "Chase!" she shouted after him.

Ignoring her, he took long, fast strides now toward a black London cab on the far side of the street.

It was too late. He'd gotten into the cab and it drove off. She steadied herself under the shadow of the British Library portico and nearly felt the weight of the massive brick and concrete slab above her.

She would have to fix this gaffe with him, but not now. It would have to wait. She hurried under the iron gate that read BRITISH LIBRARY BRITISH LIBRARY BRITISH LIBRARY over and over in black iron.

Lexi stood waiting in the courtyard, tapping her foot and checking her phone. "Once again, Vanessa, you're truly unable to see what everyone else does. I told you he's into you."

"You told him I slept with Julian, and you had no right to say that to him—or anyone! For once and for all, I'm done with you, Lexi!"

"Look, that line about you sleeping with him just sort of spilled out. And I do apologize about that, although I think it's better to let Chase know where you stand with Julian. He deserves to know the truth of the situation."

Lexi may have been right about that.

"And you're not done with me. I have the description of the writing desk and the ticket stubs to the library and Madame Tussauds, proving we were there." She patted her red leather purse. "You'll need them to win."

"And I have the description of the drawing and receipt of our donation to the National Portrait Gallery, proving we were there. So we're at an impasse."

"The thing is, I'm not in it to win the dinner with Julian. I was just trying to get my old friend back by helping her out. So much for trying to be good." She checked her watch. "But right now I need to dash over to the British Museum to see a Regency-era condom and some Italian wax phalli in the Secretum for my research project."

Vanessa did a face palm. "What?"

"You mean you didn't know that every major European museum had a secret room of saucy artifacts for leering Victorian gentlemen 'scholars'? Haven't you heard of the books *The Sinner's Grand Tour* and *Napoleon's Privates: 2,500 Years of History Unzipped?*"

"Um—no." Why was it that, no matter what, even if it involved going to museums, Lexi had more fun? "But don't you realize that it was *you* who screwed up everything with Chase by announcing that I slept with Julian?"

Lexi ignored her. "The British Museum had the Secretum, founded in 1865. It included the wax phalli collected by Sir William Hamilton. His wife, Lady Hamilton, had a scandalous affair with Lord Nelson—you know, the Lord Nelson on top of the column in Trafalgar Square?"

Vanessa's head was swirling. She needed to get back on task! What did she care about Lord Nelson other than that he reminded her of Chase trying to draw her attention to the column?

"Now most of the objects are on display in the Department of Medieval and Later Antiquities, like the famous Warren Cup, an ancient Roman silver cup depicting gay sex, and a replica of a statue of the god Pan copulating with a she-goat."

"Pan with a she-goat?"

"Now you're with me." Lexi smiled. "And you thought the British were all stuffy and repressed. The rest of the collection is only available to view by appointment. It's stored in cupboard number 55. How cool is that? I have an appointment at four."

Vanessa got her mind back on track. "I would say even though you've ruined mine, you haven't lost your mojo, Lexi."

"That's good because after the museum I'm heading back to Bath to meet David for the movie. Don't wait up for me."

"Have I ever?"

"But if you want the tickets and description you can have them. You'll just have to bring me back a little souvenir."

Vanessa didn't need to ask—Lexi would tell her. It would start with "I want."

"I want that life-sized replica of the Colin Firth wax figure in the Madame Tussauds gift shop. Buy it and bring it to me in Bath and I'll reimburse you, hand over the ticket stubs, and everything."

"Oh, right! How am I supposed to believe any of this?"

"Fine. Don't believe me. But you didn't want to believe me when I warned you Chase had feelings for you, either." She stepped back. "See you in Bath with the replica."

"You won't."

"I will. I'll see you with my life-sized Colin Firth under your arm."

"Nope. I don't care about Julian *that* much."

"I'm afraid you do. God knows why. He's not worth it. But that man who just abandoned you here in front of the British Library? Now *he's* worth it."

With that Lexi headed out of the courtyard, turning a few male heads as she strutted along.

"Lexi!" Vanessa shouted out toward Lexi's miniskirt. "I will *not* be bringing Colin Firth to you!"

Quite a few people, many looking up from their books and phones, turned around and gaped.

Vanessa grabbed her phone, only to see through the cracked screen that it was already three o'clock just as Sherry headed out of the Last Word with a bag full of seltzer waters and snacks.

"Thank you for buying the drinks. How much do I owe you?" Vanessa asked as she opened the next clue.

"Where is everyone?" asked Sherry as she looked around.

Vanessa read the clue as she spoke. "You don't want to know. Basically, they left. It seems that, after years of me leaving everyone, people are now leaving me. Do you want to leave, too?" She made a flourish with her hand toward Euston Road even as she mapped out where Twinings tea shop was on her phone, which, despite the crack, still worked, thank God.

"Now would be a good time because I have to hustle down to Twinings at the Temple tube stop."

"Hell no! I'm with you!"

Vanessa reached out and hugged her.

"Twinings? Where Jane Austen bought her tea!" Sherry beamed.

"How do you know that?"

"Oh, I read it on the Austen Authors blog."

Vanessa pulled out her phone. "What's the Web address?"

"AustenAuthors.net. It's a group of Austen-inspired authors and a couple of them have posted pictures of themselves visiting Twinings—where Jane Austen bought her tea when she visited her brother Henry in London."

"So that's why we're headed there. Here's the clue." Vanessa read it out loud.

"*I am sorry to hear that there has been a rise in tea. I do not mean to pay Twining till later in the day, when we may order a fresh supply.*"
—*Jane Austen to Cassandra, March 5, 1814*

Congratulations! You have been very successful on your hunt in London. You only have a few items on your shopping list to acquire before your return journey to Bath. One of them is a small purchase of the 1706 tea blend with receipt proving you were there. Hurry along now . . .

"We don't have much time left. I might need to hit Madame Tussauds gift shop before they close at six. I haven't decided yet."

"Huh?"

"I'll explain everything." She started walking, and quickly, leaving the Last Word behind.

Chapter 16

Okay, where the hell was Julian? She'd been in England for more than two full days, first in Bath, now crisscrossing all over London. What grown woman would chase all over the globe for a man like this? There was that word: chase. What was she chasing and why? She was too damn old for this schoolgirl behavior! Or was she? Do we ever really grow up?

They were at Twinings tea shop on the Strand, a narrow place crammed with colorful packages of tea and large copper bins promising every possible blend of loose tea while the entire place emanated—what else?—a tea-leaf aroma.

Vanessa, after standing in a line much like Austen herself might have done, bought the requisite 1706 Blend, which the cashier told her had been named for the year Thomas Twining opened his tea shop. She never knew that Twinings was more than three hundred years old, and she didn't think she'd ever look at Twinings the same again when she'd see it on the shelves at the grocery store back home.

Sherry, meanwhile, had been sucked in by the Loose Tea Bar in the back of the shop near the little Twinings "museum," complete with Twinings ephemera of all sorts. Among the displays were official instructions on how to make a proper cup of tea that resulted in Vanessa steeping her mind in—Julian.

"We don't have time to sample tea." Vanessa took the warm cup of tea right out of Sherry's hands and set it on the counter. "We need to figure out who's going to hand us the next clue."

Vanessa thought, it being so late in the London part of the hunt, that Julian must be making an appearance, but no, she didn't see him anywhere in the shop. Nor did she spot any likely person to hand off the next clue. For a moment she stood outside Twinings, looking up at the architectural detail above the white-columned doorway, wasting time admiring the artistry of it; having no new clue, she had no place else to go.

Above the very familiar TWININGS typeface in black letters on a gold bar above the doorway stood a golden family crest flanked by sculptures of two Chinese tea men and topped by a statue of a golden lion. The English truly knew how to build, decorate, and embellish. Almost everywhere she looked, both in Bath and London, her eye fell upon a gargoyle, a fan-shaped window, a pub sign so gorgeous it could be museum worthy.

Her mind turned to Aunt Ella and then, for some reason, to Chase. When she used one of her networks to pinpoint his location, she discovered he had done a check-in at the Ritz already. And he hadn't blocked her on any of their shared social networking sites yet, either. So that, she interpreted, was a good thing.

It was three forty-five already, and she paced in front of the tantalizing doorway until Sherry came out and took her bag of tea from her.

"How does it smell?" She opened up the tin of 1706. "Mm-mm."

"Really, Sherry? Can't you just help me figure out where to get the next clue? We're running out of time—"

"Hey, look, here it is!" Sherry pulled a slip of paper from the tin of loose tea leaves. "The clue!"

Vanessa read it out loud:

"'If you need to buy a small vial of lavender water fit for a queen, a genuine badger shaving brush, and a book, all from places Jane would've known, there's only one place to go: St. James's—where you will find yourself transported to Regency London. Fetch the lavender water from Floris, the shaving brush from Dr. Harris, Chemists and Perfumers, and a book from Hatchard's.'"

"It's a shopping list," Sherry said.

Vanessa did a quick search for Floris. "We're off to Green Park tube station."

She and Sherry emerged from the station and hurried up Piccadilly for a bit until Vanessa stopped suddenly.

"What is it?" Sherry asked.

Vanessa stood staring at the stone archway above her with the carved face of a bearded man in it, and, underneath, within black wrought iron scrollwork under the arch, were golden letters studded with lights: THE RITZ.

In an instant, she gathered herself. She was all about prioritizing and always had been. With a tap of Chase's umbrella on the pavement and a rustle of her Twinings bag she said, "It's nothing. Let's go."

"You're beginning to scare me," Sherry said.

"I am?"

"You really are obsessed about winning this thing, aren't you?"

"I'm just competitive, Sherry, and I always have been."

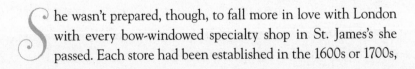

She wasn't prepared, though, to fall more in love with London with every bow-windowed specialty shop in St. James's she passed. Each store had been established in the 1600s or 1700s, and each exuded more British charm, more polished mahogany, and more mirrored glass cases than the last. The uncanny combination of quirk and elegance struck her like no American shop ever had.

The whirl of hatters, gentlemen's shirt makers, wine merchants, and antiques shops would have made her really feel as if she were Jane Austen, had it not been for the cars in the streets and the people on the sidewalks in their modern clothes checking their phones and walking, quickly, as the rush hour approached, with their earbuds in, toward a cocktail bar, restaurant, or home. Vanessa thought for a moment, she could live here, in London, quite happily, with history and modern times brushing shoulders.

The only thing missing was—Julian. An emptiness came over her, like a spoon with nothing on it.

The apothecary jars and rows of wooden apothecary drawers the size of old library card catalogs at Dr. Harris, Chemists and Perfumers, hadn't changed in two hundred years, and neither had the fact that they still made and packed by hand many of their perfumes, colognes, and soaps on the premises.

In the bastion of gentlemanly shops along Jermyn Street, including the clothier Thomas Pink she'd seen at Heathrow, they found the lavender water at Floris, perfumer to HRH (Her Royal Highness) *and* Julian.

"Jane Austen couldn't have afforded to shop here," Vanessa said to Sherry.

"No, but she might've been sent here to buy something for her rich brother Edward."

Sherry shook her head while they waited for change from a very handsome, suited cashier. "I can't believe we're just a few blocks away from Almack's, Beau Brummell's club White's—"

The cashier looked at Sherry while he ever-so-politely slid a velvet pad across the wooden counter toward Vanessa with her change on it.

That just about made her fall over. She couldn't take it anymore! She'd fallen for England, and she probably would buy an *I Love London* mug at the airport—if she even decided to go back home!

She was ready to sign on the Anglophile dotted line.

The hot Englishman behind the mahogany counter explained that the velvet salver had been in use for centuries because it had always been more genteel to put your purchases on account and not pay with cash, but once cash had become de rigueur, Floris would polish the coins and iron the bills flat, and present your change to you, the lady, in your clean white gloves, coins gleaming and bills pressed and perfumed, on a velvet salver.

Once Vanessa had gingerly taken the change and her navy blue and gold Floris gift bag, and smiled at whatever the gorgeous English guy had been saying to her in his silky accent as she put her wallet away, she hurried out the door amid a flurry of "thank you's" and "do come back's" from the other salespeople and leaned against a lamp-post outside the door for sheer support.

She looked up, wondering how much more of this English charm she could take without tossing her American passport into the Thames. But, as she looked up, she saw pink and white flowers blooming in the window boxes about the brass FLORIS nameplate topped with a royal coat of arms.

"Okay, I surrender!" she said to nobody in particular. "Aunt Ella was right. How can you *not* love England?"

"Wait till you get a whiff of this lavender water," Sherry said, suddenly beside her.

"No! I mean, no, thank you. That would do me in."

Sherry opened the bottle anyway and sniffed. "Oh. My. God. I could drink this stuff. By the gallon. It's lavender. On steroids. I feel like I'm in a tampon commercial, skipping through the lavender fields—"

Vanessa laughed so hard she began to cramp up. "Sherry, I think you deserve to have dinner. And a drink. A big, tall drink."

"And a tall drink of water, too," Sherry joked. "But what about you?"

"I'm going to have to part ways with you for the evening because I have to take care of two men: Colin Firth and Chase. In that order."

She couldn't deal with having Chase disenchanted with her.

"Colin Firth?!"

"The fake Colin Firth and the real Chase. I'll explain everything when I see you back in Bath tonight."

*V*anessa bought the life-sized Colin Firth replica just before closing time.

Now she stood in line at the London Eye ticket pavilion with him under one arm and Chase's umbrella under the other because, according to his location social networking site, he was here at the Eye. But now she couldn't get a signal on her phone anymore. Could the cracked screen have finally affected the phone itself?

"One ticket, please," Vanessa said.

"Is he going with you?" the humorless ticket woman asked at a fast clip, glaring at Colin.

"Let me ask him," Vanessa said as she stood him up and pretended to converse with the plastic replica. "Would you like to join me for a date on the London Eye, Mr. Firth?"

But the ticket woman was not amused; nor were the people in line behind her. "I'm afraid you'll have to pay for him."

Vanessa didn't have the time or the energy to argue, especially with a woman who had no sense of humor and spoke too fast, and especially when she needed to get out of this line and into the one for the Eye itself. She'd looked and hadn't seen Chase inside the ticket pavilion at all.

Of course Colin needed a ticket! He was, after all, six feet two. She'd have to set him down while on the Eye, so she bought the two tickets without a fight.

By the time she stood in line to get on, the sky had turned to twilight, one of the best times to see London from above, the Australian family behind her said.

But she hadn't come here to see an aerial view of London.

She scanned the snaking line for Chase, didn't see him anywhere, and feared he might already be in one of the futuristic Ferris wheel capsules.

But then, as she reached the top of the line, a crowd of Asian women and a few Asian men parted, and there, in the center of them, like the spoke on a wheel, stood Chase.

"Chase!" Vanessa called out as she hurried forward. He didn't hear her and she almost shouted again.

But one of the ticket takers grabbed her by the elbow. "You—and Colin Firth—must get back in the queue, I'm afraid, luv."

Queue.

"But—"

"Sorry." He firmly guided her back to her spot. She'd just missed the cutoff point for getting into Chase's capsule by about ten people, so she ended up getting on the one behind his. Using Colin as a shield she shoved her way to the window and stood him up next to her. The people in her capsule looked at her funny, but she didn't care.

She could see Chase from here! For a moment she put her hands on the rounded glass as she watched him laughing and chatting with the well-dressed and well-coiffed Asian women.

Vanessa looked down at herself, at what that morning had been a cute little outfit but now, after a day of literally running around

London both above and underground, not to mention carting a six-foot-two plastic man across town, looked bedraggled at best.

A woman next to her stared at Colin Firth while Vanessa pulled out her phone to text Chase. She still wasn't getting a signal.

She watched as his capsule floated up, above hers. She had to fix this rift with him. Still, she hadn't taken the time to take care of it until she'd accomplished what she needed to for the hunt, and he was smart enough to know this.

She thought she might gain points by smoothing everything over in person instead of her usual approach, which would've been via text or e-mail.

People around her began taking pictures not just of London, but of themselves with Colin. She became, by default, the most popular person on the ride, even though she didn't want the attention or the distraction.

She moved to every possible corner on the capsule to get her phone to kick in, but maybe the height had something to do with it. They were high above the city now, and she finally had to look away from her lifeless phone and marvel at Big Ben, the Houses of Parliament, and even the Tower Bridge far off in the distance.

She left Colin Firth with a group of American women so she could get a better look at Buckingham Palace lit up in the night. What a gorgeous, glittering, endless city London looked from above. She couldn't believe she'd be leaving tonight without having seen any of the sights up close. Who goes to London without seeing Buckingham Palace, St. Paul's, Westminster Abbey, or the Tate Modern, or touring the Tower of London?

As she looked at Buckingham Palace she had to laugh to herself at the thought of Lexi's stories from junior year abroad as she tried to get the palace guards to crack a smile.

Lexi had tried it all, from raising her skirt to flashing her thigh to sucking very suggestively on a Popsicle, but nothing worked. It made a great rollicking story and Lexi always added the punch line that this was why she needed to go back to London: to get a guard to smile.

Lexi. The female Peter Pan. Yet despite Lexi's emotional immaturity and the trouble she caused, Vanessa was glad to have her back in her life again. No matter what, Lexi brought life to everything, a liveliness Vanessa had been missing.

The lights of London and the grandeur of it only distracted her for a few moments, though, and taking Colin away from the American women, who laughed and made all kinds of "I get him Firth" jokes, she moved to the other side of the capsule, hoping to spot Chase again.

It had grown so dark she couldn't distinguish the shadows of people in the capsule ahead of her anymore.

Below her the River Thames flowed dark and she realized this would be her first and last glimpse of the famed river. Rain began to fall. Great. She had no raincoat and nothing but a white T-shirt and skimpy skirt on. She did, though, have Chase's umbrella.

As the capsule went down, she sacrificed the last glimpses of London in favor of tracking Chase and stood right by the door with Colin at her side. It rained harder now, pelting almost.

Once the doors slid open, she bolted out and without taking the time to put up the umbrella, she ran, with Colin under her arm, after the crowd that had emerged from the capsule in front of hers.

She didn't see Chase, but once she started calling his name, people turned back at her, giving her strange looks—she was getting used to attracting unwanted attention by now. She'd spent more time running and calling after Chase today than she had spent pursuing anyone, ever. But she'd come here first and foremost to chase Julian, hadn't she?

When she thought of the men she'd left and how she'd left them, it made her more than a little embarrassed. Her twenties were nothing more than a blur of men and public relations jobs.

In sharp contrast, Jane Austen, by the time she was twenty-four, had the better part of four novels written and high standards set for any man she would accept as a suitor or husband.

Meanwhile, Vanessa, in her early thirties, had climbed down a lattice from the second story of a house on the north side and hopped a fence just to escape a super-intense guy who seemed as if he would consume her body and soul. She couldn't see any way out—other than the second-story bathroom window.

Would a frank conversation and a walk out the front door have done the trick? Probably. But hell, she was thirty-one.

Now, instead of escaping men, she was chasing them. The tables had turned—they had flipped over, even, with a crash of silverware, broken wineglasses, and shattered china plates never registered for.

The rain came down harder now, and it made her cold and shivery with goose bumps, but she felt convinced that the group she saw ahead in the blurry distance at the corner of Westminster Bridge and the river was Chase's crowd, trying to hail a cab. She could see his familiar figure, even in the dark and the rain.

"Chase!"

The light turned and she ran across the street, yelling out to him, with Colin slipping and sliding in her hands as she kept her eye on the guy she was convinced was Chase. But she splashed in a puddle and tripped on the curb and, together with Colin, catapulted into a souvenir stand crammed with red, white, and blue British—everything.

The souvenir stand guy started belting out swearwords in his English accent, and never in her life had she heard such an impolite Englishman. But her elbow was stuck in a pile of toy red double-decker buses, a bunch of small British flags had toppled onto her boobs, and a rack full of Union Jack T-shirts covered her legs, while Colin lay at her feet on the wet pavement.

If a passerby didn't know better, it looked like she had "done" London, all right.

"Vanessa? Is that you?"

It was Chase, looking down on her in more ways than one.

"It looks like you've reached a new low."

"Oh, no, I've managed worse than this in my lifetime."

He lifted the Union Jack T-shirts from her bare wet legs while she struggled to get up, and the souvenir stand guy reassembled the double-decker buses and flags, cursing throughout.

Chase gave her a hand and lifted both her and Colin from the ground at the same time.

He smiled so brightly it made her want to kiss him. Where that impulse came from she wasn't sure, but she couldn't deny it.

"I'm going to buy you a shirt. You look like you've been in a wet T-shirt contest."

He pulled out his wallet while she looked down at her shirt, which had gone translucent, and the rain and cold revealed her lacy bra and hardened nipples. She instantly crunched her shoulders together.

He held up a small gray *I Love London* hoodie to her, sizing it up. "Much as I like the wet T-shirt look on you, I'm not willing to share it with the men of England." He lifted and turned Colin Firth toward the street. "Divert your eyes, Colin."

Vanessa laughed so hard her eyes started tearing up at this reverse wet-shirt scene from the 1995 *P&P.* She was tired and hungry and slaphappy and cold, and Chase was funny and warm and—sexy? And not upset anymore about her sleeping with Julian?

He pushed his wet hair back, paid for the hoodie, took off his trench coat, wrapped it around her, and popped his umbrella over the two of them and Colin, too.

Vanessa noticed his clients had gone ahead—they weren't standing in the rain. He must've sent them on.

"What are you doing here?" Chase looked at his watch and then at her with a twinkle in his brown eyes.

She had to state the obvious. "What do you think I'm doing here? I'm stalking you! To apologize to you. To beg you to be—friends with me again. I can't stand having you upset with me."

"I like the sound of that. Yes, I do. You begging me? But it's much more like you to send a text, though, isn't it?"

Vanessa didn't know what to say because he put his arm around her and it felt so good, so warm, so—right.

"I was a little out of line myself. *Capisce?*"

"*Capisce.*"

He tucked Colin under his arm. "I see you've bought a little souvenir. You have a thing for English guys, don't you?"

He wasn't going to confront her directly on the whole sleeping-with-Julian thing, and she liked that about him. It made him really cool in her eyes.

"Colin's not for me. He's Lexi's."

She could tell he didn't quite believe her, and for a split second it occurred to her how she must've appeared to the outside world: insane. And insane for one British man in particular.

"Don't you need to get back to Bath tonight?"

"Yes?" she said, not so sure of it herself. Not so sure of anything.

"Here's what we'll do. I'll take you and Colin to Paddington Station and buy you a cup of tea and something to eat while you change into your new sweatshirt. Then I'll get you both settled on the train and you'll be back in Bath in no time, okay?"

"Okay," Vanessa said, as if she were a little girl.

For once in her life she didn't have to think. She could put herself in his care and he would do right by her, and she liked that. She really liked that, if only in this one instance. Was this what it felt like to be taken care of?

Had no other man ever cared for her like this before? Or had she just not been ready for it? She fumbled for her phone, and it not only had a signal, but still worked. She sighed with relief.

As she sat on the train with her new hoodie on, Chase's trench coat still wrapped around her, his umbrella propped against her leg, the tea, sandwich, and soup he'd bought her on the tray in front of her, and strict instructions to text him upon her safe return, she wondered. Two men in her life at once. Three, counting the plastic Colin propped up against the seat next to her. What did it all mean? And could Lexi, despite her warped vision, be right about Chase being the guy for her?

Vanessa had never believed in the soul-mate thing; she'd always thought there were many different matches out there for everyone. But she also knew she'd only be lucky enough to bump into a couple of those right-for-her men during her lifetime in her wide, but limited, social circles. And increasingly, as time went on, her social circles were online and not . . . real.

Moreover, love, like anything else, was not just a matter of the right two people finding each other through some random twist of fate or another. The elements of timing, availability, emotional frame of mind, and chemistry had to be in place.

Perhaps most important of all there had to be that intangible, unmistakable, and hard-to-come-by quality best defined as chemistry. It was also known as attraction, sparks flying, *je ne sais quoi*, or as Lexi would aptly put it, simply wanting to tear the man's clothes off and have your way with him and *only* him—far into the foreseeable future.

If you didn't want to have on-the-floor, on-the-kitchen-counter, on-the-table sex with him twenty-four/seven, especially in the beginning of the relationship, Lexi would say walk away without looking back. It would never get any better. If you so much as thought of another man physically, it was time to walk. But that, of course, was Lexi.

Vanessa had gone to high school with Chase some sixteen or seventeen years ago. The timing, availability, and emotional and chemical matrix, evidently, weren't right back then.

But could Lexi be onto something about him being the right one for her now? Or did he belong squarely in the friend category? Wouldn't she be better off with a certain Englishman?

She had achieved her goals for the day—acquiring all the items for the Dash for Darcy scavenger hunt and setting things right with Chase.

Why, then, did she not feel like a winner? She was behind, worse off, and more invested in these guys than ever.

And why couldn't she get kitchen counters and these two men off her mind?

Chapter 17

The next morning in Bath, where life did move at a more leisurely, resort-town pace compared to London, Vanessa laid out her freshly washed underwear on the tiny kitchen counter of the flat. She had to hang some of her leopard- and zebra-print thongs plus a couple of lacy black bras from the kitchenette cabinet pulls since Lexi had already usurped the bathroom shower curtain rod and towel bars with her patterned stockings and camis. Vanessa didn't realize the flat didn't have a dryer until she'd washed her stuff.

Plastic Colin lay in Lexi's bed, alone, where Vanessa had jokingly tucked him in. And he looked good under the covers—quite convincing, especially with one of Lexi's red bras draped near his face. But Lexi never did come back the previous night, though via text she insisted she still hadn't slept with David.

Before Sherry had left that morning, she commented that Vanessa looked rather hellish, and when Vanessa looked in the mirror, she discovered her eyes had gone all puffy and watery, and her nose had turned red. Perfect timing for her end-of-summer cold.

Sherry went off with a festival crowd on an early-morning hike up to the top of Beechen Cliff, tempting to Vanessa on this fabulous blue-sky day, as Henry Tilney himself had escorted Catherine Morland up the hill for a picturesque view of Bath as well as his endearing lecture on "the picturesque."

But Vanessa, especially in light of the cold she'd acquired, slid a pack of travel-sized tissues in her bag and chose instead to take her daily dose of healing water from the Pump Room and a text from Chase surprised her.

He'd wrapped up his morning meetings and was on the train into Bath now. He told her to check in with her locational network and he'd find her. She rather liked how he assumed she'd be thrilled with this prospect, and she did find herself looking forward to it, but what confidence! What if she didn't want him around? Unnerving!

She did, though, want him. Around.

Why he said he'd be bringing his swimsuit and hoped she'd packed hers, she didn't bother to figure out. Certainly her flat didn't have a pool.

She stood on the narrow sidewalk very near the cobblestone street outside the Georgian town house where she'd had breakfast and texted Chase back as the morning sun bathed the streetscape. Was that a teahouse tucked into that Georgian town house across the street? Vanessa smiled and made her way through a group of women and men dressed in Regency attire filtering past as she walked into the café to buy the biggest English breakfast tea to go possible.

Chase. What other man had ever gone so out of his way for her? Who else had ever made plans—the swimming—without asking her first? She found it sweet and sexy all rolled into one.

But the Bath leg of Dash for Darcy came first and foremost. She had all of ten minutes to hoof it to the Bath Abbey, where she'd get her first clue of the day, and once she arrived, the abbey tenor bell struck eleven, making her arrival in the abbey churchyard undeniably dramatic—fitting, even—for a Regency heroine. A portent, perhaps, of good fortune?

Vanessa put an immediate stop to the dangerous flow of these thoughts. Who was she turning into? The hopeless romantic Marianne Dashwood or the naïve Catherine Morland? It wasn't the smart Elizabeth Bennet!

The grandeur of the abbey and the centuries-old churchyard humbled her, despite her modernity. She took a picture of the abbey and e-mailed it to Paul as well as posting it on all her personal social networking sites. This seemed to be Vanessa's, if not everyone's, way of processing intangibles and things much bigger than themselves.

Nothing gave a better sense of control than to capture it, caption it, and "share" it. Doing so meant you'd done it. Or, it would have, just a couple of weeks past. Posting just didn't give her the same jolt it once did, and both her work and her social media popularity had suffered as a result.

She realized she wanted to share—in person—with someone. Finally. This churchyard had to be one of the most beautiful she'd ever seen, yet here she was, all alone.

With her tea in one hand, phone in the other, and a sniffle tickling her nose, she found her crowd. A hodgepodge of people, some Regency clad and others wearing bonnets with T-shirts, all formed a circle around a tall gentleman in a beaver top hat, coattails, breeches, and—very familiar boots.

She meant to pocket her phone but now it buzzed and beeped with texts and a call, and in trying to shut it off she spilled her tea on her hand, and she sneezed, and yes, the familiar boots belonged to Julian.

He smiled at her, but whether he smiled in pity or as in *So great to see you again; you haven't changed a bit (except for the watery eyes and the red nose)* she couldn't tell.

Either way, she didn't want this to be her grand entrance! She'd fully expected to see him the day before in London with her hip little outfit and without her cold. Even though she wanted to see him today, she'd been lulled into thinking she wouldn't, and she hadn't even been thinking about him for some reason, and then, poof! He just appeared, looking just as good, or better, than ever.

The sight of his raised dark eyebrows brought back a torrent of feelings. She had to take a moment to blow her nose.

"Good morning, Vanessa," he said as he tipped his hat and offered a controlled Mr. Darcy smile. "Welcome to England."

Even though she knew he had to stay in character, his "welcome" seemed a little cold.

She had, after all, had sex with the guy! Couldn't he at least pull her aside and take a moment to speak privately with her?

Her mind flashed to them writhing and kissing and . . .

Meanwhile, everyone turned to look at her as if to ask *How does he know this American? We don't see anything special about her. Plus her nose is all red.*

She sneezed and then almost curtsied! "Oh, hi—Mr. Darcy. How's things? I didn't expect to see you here."

She said it as if she'd just dashed off to the corner store and bumped into him there. When in reality, she'd paid more than a thousand dollars for a last-minute airplane ticket, traveled more than four thousand miles to come to the Jane Austen Festival and his book promotion in Bath, and then proceeded to dash all over in his Dash for Darcy scavenger hunt.

There was nothing casual or accidental about this!

He eyed her phone as she tucked it into her bag.

"Things are very well, thank you," he said. "How are you faring? And your aunt?"

"Very well, thank you."

"Glad to hear it. I have just expressed my gratitude to the group for participating in this contest, and I should like to thank you as well, Vanessa."

"You're welcome," she said, channeling good duchess behavior.

One of the men in the crowd took out his monocle and looked at her through it, because intelligence marked the Jane Austen crowd and nothing escaped them. She could tell . . . that they could tell . . . that something had gone on between her and Julian. But what?

What, indeed.

She didn't want to define it as a one-night stand, but now that she stood in front of him like this, and he was treating her like a virtual stranger, the evidence stacked up.

Why, then, couldn't she just walk away? Just turn around and go get a Bath bun or something? Why did she want to talk with him, to laugh with him? Why did she want to be alone with him more than anything else in the world right now?

She reminded herself he had to act in this standoffish, Mr. Darcy way. So she had no choice but to win the damn promotional dinner with him, didn't she?

"I sincerely hope that one of *you* wins the dinner at my home. I am very much looking forward to the evening." He looked directly at Vanessa.

That split second reassured her.

He then addressed the group. "Right. Today you shall be putting together the puzzle of, and tracing the course of, Jane Austen's various lodgings here in Bath. It is of the utmost importance that you go in chronological order, as Jane herself experienced each abode."

A couple of the women in the crowd eyed each other, nodded, and smiled.

Vanessa knew nothing about Austen's life here in Bath except that she supposedly hated it. As the newest Janeite on the Crescent here, she felt at a distinct disadvantage.

"Whilst you're on your journey, it will be a battle of will to see if you can resist the pleasures that the festival, and Bath itself, offers en route to your destinations. Today will not be a test of endurance so much as a race against the clock. This will give you ample free time in the afternoon to attend festival lectures and events. Although, you will be expected to reflect upon Miss Austen's life here in Bath, and that may take a bit of time. Here are your instructions."

Vanessa had to forcibly look away from him, to stop thinking about the thick dark hair she had raked with her hands, the mouth she had kissed so fervently, the cheekbones she had brushed with her fingertips. She read the day's instruction sheet.

Fill In Jane Austen's Timeline in Bath, read the headline at the top of the page. When she looked up from the instruction sheet, where the letters had become a blur, replaced by thoughts of him, he smiled at her.

She suddenly wanted to ask him what his middle name was. Plus he seemed like he'd be good with puppies and children. How could she get a baby into his arms and see?

What the hell did she just think to herself?

She had no idea what he'd just instructed them to do, but the group began to disperse, and there, from behind Julian's back and across the churchyard, strode Chase.

Julian didn't see Chase coming, and for a moment they were alone. "Best of luck on today's hunt, my dear," Julian said. "It would be a joy if you won."

"Would it?"

"Oh, yes."

She sneezed and had to pull out the tissues.

Chase broke in with a smile, a kiss, and a squeeze on the ass for Vanessa.

She slapped his hand while it was still on her butt, and Julian was none the wiser.

"Hello, Julian," Chase said as he held out the very same hand that had just squeezed her, and they shook.

"Well, hello, Chase. I didn't know you were in England."

"I'm here on—business."

"Speaking of which, I have work to get done here," Vanessa said as she handed him the instruction sheet.

"I'll say you do," said Chase with a wink. "We'd best get going."

"Until our dinner then, Vanessa," Julian said.

"That's assuming I win."

"You'd best win!"

Chase led her away and then she thought better of it, deciding to ditch Chase and forgo the hunt to talk with Julian, but when she looked back at him, he was sitting on a bench with a dark-blond-haired woman with porcelain skin dressed in a blazer and skirt. In her lap sat a white puppy.

Who was this blond, puppy-toting woman? And why did Chase have to show exactly when he did?

To say Jane Austen saved Vanessa from losing her mind over the next hour and a half would be absolutely true.

Right from the get-go she needed to call in the scholarly reinforcements—her aunt. Since it happened to be the very early morning Central Time, Aunt Ella picked up the phone. She proved herself infinitely better than any audio tour or app out there, too.

Vanessa made her way to Number 1 the Paragon with long, quick strides and Chase by her side as her aunt spoke.

"She stayed at the Paragon, a part of town she didn't like, with an aunt she didn't particularly like, on her earliest visits to Bath and until they found their first lodgings. Mind you, after her father's retirement, Jane had been plucked from her lifelong home with just a few days' notice and forced to sell her family's entire household, including her father's library, before the move to Bath . . ."

The building stood on a busy street, among a row of similar town houses, without anything green in sight, and even Vanessa could relate to how a country girl who loved to walk must've been put off by the location, not to mention the unwelcome change.

Chase took a quick picture of her in front of the place. "We're so close to Walcot Street, the arty side of town," he said. "It's just one street over. Wouldn't you like to see the glassblowing at Bath Aqua Glass? There are some fantastic restaurants and galleries, too—"

But Vanessa was too focused to allow Chase to distract her. She cut across town along George Street toward Queen Square while Aunt Ella continued.

"On top of the surprise move, in 1799 Jane Austen's aunt, the one she stayed with in Bath, had supposedly shoplifted a card of lace from a Bath shopkeeper. But, you know, she vehemently denied she had stolen it, and in those days, it was merely the shopkeeper's word against hers. Anything stolen worth more than a shilling was punishable by hanging. She was put in jail for eight months and during her trial faced hanging or being deported to Australia for fourteen years."

"What?" Vanessa hurried past a gourmet deli, several boutiques, and a hair salon, all housed in gorgeous Georgian buildings. How could such beauty coexist with such brutality?

"The jury returned with a not-guilty verdict."

"Wow."

Jane Austen did not lead a quiet, uneventful life.

"Okay Auntie E, we're heading downhill now, on Gay Street, and can see Queen Square."

"We?"

"Chase came to Bath today." She eyed Chase, who smiled.

"I see . . . The only thing better than one man in a woman's life is—two."

Vanessa chose to change the subject.

"I've already seen the Queen Square town house. It's a great location."

"Queen Square was new and a very fashionable part of town when they stayed there in 1799," said Aunt Ella. "But just a few years later it fell out of favor to the newer crescents on higher ground. Austen even had one of the Musgrove girls in *Persuasion* say to her father, 'We must be in a good situation: none of your Queen Squares for us!' "

Aunt Ella gave her the rest of Austen's addresses and Vanessa scribbled them down, as well as some information required on the timeline, then she hung up, saying she'd call again. It felt good, really good, to be sharing in her aunt's enthusiasm for Austen. She'd missed out on a lifetime of it and had a lot of catching up to do.

She stood in front of the house and Chase diligently took her picture.

"Did it turn out?" Vanessa asked.

He checked the camera. "I need to see a little more leg. Could you hike up your skirt? Or maybe open a few more buttons on your blouse?"

Vanessa smirked as she descended the stairs to pinch his cheek, which happened to have that just-shaved feel that she loved on a man. She quickly pulled her hand away and looked at her notes from Aunt Ella.

"Off we go to Number 4 Sydney Place, where Jane stayed from 1801 to 1805." She took a sharp turn north, and, if she'd packed her running shoes, she would've run it. "I guess the house can be rented for short-term stays through Bath Boutique Stays," she told Chase in between breaths.

"Do they rent by the hour?" he asked with a smile.

Chase knew what he was doing. Thanks to that comment, she couldn't help it. The image of him on top of her on a four-poster bed in a Georgian town house popped into her head. She imagined herself tucking his hair behind his ears, running her hands down his bare chest—and why? He was her friend, come on!

"Is sex all you think about?" she joked. She knew he thought about lots of other things, and she enjoyed getting to know how his mind worked. She enjoyed both his playfulness and his intellect, and she might not have gotten to know him at all if she hadn't come to England.

"No, sex isn't the only thing I think about. I think about you, too. You. And sex. And a few other things."

Vanessa laughed. If only Julian could think that way!

"I'll prove to you I think of other things. Look at the cat up there." He pointed to a stone sculpture of a cat sitting outside a second-story window just above where SYDNEY PLACE had been etched in the stone building.

She looked at him suspiciously. "What man notices a cat?"

"This man does. I have three of them."

"You have three cats?" Maybe, just maybe, she could safely tell him about her work with the cat shelter. "I expected you to have a talking parrot."

"Oh, I have two talking parrots."

"Cats and birds?"

"It all works out."

Despite Chase continually trying to distract her with his talk of climbing to the top of Bath Abbey or visiting the Roman Baths or dashing off to Prior Park to see one of only four Palladian bridges of its kind, Vanessa stayed on task.

The house at Sydney Place stood advantageously across from Sydney Gardens, a large public pleasure garden that during Austen's time had swings and a labyrinth, her aunt had said.

Here lived Jane Austen 1801–1805, read the plaque above the number 4 on the house, and it struck her, jaded Vanessa, with certainty and importance. According to her aunt, Austen was happiest at this lodging in Bath and might have been happier than ever to return here on Tuesday, December 4, 1802.

Jane had accepted a marriage proposal from the wealthy Harris Bigg-Wither on December second, only to rescind it the very next day while staying at the Bigg-Wither home in her beloved Hampshire. Marrying him would've secured her future, as well as her sister's and her mother's, and it would've guaranteed a lifetime in her countryside home of Hampshire.

"She was engaged for one night?" Vanessa asked Aunt Ella while Chase looked on with a smile.

"I thought you knew that. See? You have more in common with her than you thought."

"She was engaged for one night, just like me," Vanessa repeated. "Wow."

"You were engaged?" Chase asked. "To whom?"

Vanessa shot him a smile. "Why did Jane change her mind?"

"We'll never know. But if she'd gotten married at twenty-three and had a succession of children, she might never have finished her novels. You and Jane Austen. Breaking men's hearts!" Aunt Ella said before they hung up.

The not-so-funny flip side of that remark: You and Jane Austen. Spinsters!

The house was gorgeous, attached at both sides to other town houses like all the buildings in Bath, with a garden in the back. It overlooked the entrance to the gardens and a stunning columned mansion made of Bath stone that now housed the Holburne Museum.

"No, we're not checking out Sydney Gardens," she told Chase as they crossed the street. "However, I do have to go to the ladies' room, and I'm hoping the museum here will oblige." Had she just said *oblige*?

"It's a fantastic art museum," Chase said. "And I don't dare go inside. You'll never get me out, so I'll stay here." He headed toward a table of used books and prints for sale on the grass and picked up a book and gently opened it. "I'll be waiting for you," he said.

First, the words stopped her. Then she took a mental snapshot she wouldn't soon forget. Him, the blue book with the tattered cover, the green English grass, Jane Austen's house in the background. Oh, and back to the "I'll be waiting for you."

Something every woman should hear at least once in her lifetime.

In the museum, she did feel the pull of the place, the paintings, and even the gift shop, but what grabbed her attention was a simple sentence etched across the width of two floor-to-ceiling windows in the new addition of the museum overlooking Sydney Gardens:

My dearest Cassandra, read the quote in frosted letters set against the greenery of the trees, *there is a public breakfast in Sydney Gardens every morning, so that we shall not be wholly starved.*

Jane Austen, May 1799

The windows led to the museum café, where wafts of coffee and toasted sandwiches floated about and the polite clinking of silverware could be heard. People sat with their families, their children, their lovers, their friends.

Vanessa, with the tip of her finger, traced the word "starved."

Starved for food? Starved for company? Companionship? Or all three? Staving off loneliness was a kind of starvation.

She wanted to know what the rest of that letter said.

"Vanessa." Chase walked right up to her and linked his arm in hers. Under his other arm he carried a very thick book. "It's starting to drizzle. Are you ready?"

"Yes—I'm ready." She looked back at the quote as they walked toward the open front doors and stopped for a moment under the portico while he popped open his umbrella for the two of them.

"Let's finish this up so I can treat you to lunch. I'm starved, aren't you?"

Funny, but she never felt hungry around him. Yet he kept offering her sustenance. "I could stand to eat something, sure. But right now I have to make my way to Green Park Buildings across town. Are you in?"

"Of course."

She steered them back across the Pulteney Bridge, where even she had trouble resisting the shops that lined the bridge on either side. They both lingered at the Antique Map Shop long enough to listen to the very friendly proprietor tell them that during Jane Austen's time certain expansions of Bath were planned, and the maps were drawn ahead of the construction, but not all the plans had come to fruition.

Vanessa had never known till now what it meant for plans never to come to fruition. She saw; she planned; she achieved. Why couldn't she land Julian?

"I bought you something," Chase said as they picked up the pace after crossing the River Avon.

"You did? You shouldn't have—"

Under the umbrella, in the steady drizzle, he showed her the powder blue cover of the book he had tucked under his arm: *Jane Austen's Letters* by Deirdre Le Faye.

"Thank you, Chase." She didn't know what else to say. Julian hadn't bought her—anything. Much less anything thoughtful.

She wasn't good at this kind of thing, at accepting gifts, compliments, or . . . affection. Why this hit her now she had no idea.

Here was a man, a very attractive man, who had rearranged his schedule and traveled to spend the day with her, and now he had bought her a gift.

Yet he knew she was here for Julian.

She pulled out her phone. Her phone would save her! And lo and behold, Aunt Ella answered again.

"I have looked everything up, Vanessa, and I'm surrounded by my books! Where are you now?"

Vanessa smiled at how happy this had made her aunt, and she beamed at Chase, who seemed to understand. "We're heading toward Number 3 Green Park Buildings East."

"Oooh! Remember," said Aunt Ella, "the house you'll be looking at is not the actual one she lived in. That was bombed during World War Two."

Vanessa felt the pang of such a loss.

"We're on James Street West—"

"Right now you're very close to what was considered to be a slum in Austen's time. The Lower Town happened to be rife with disease, crime, and prostitution, and evidently it reeked of dead animals and raw sewage from the river."

Vanessa found it hard to reconcile this with the upscale shops and restaurants all around her, many housed in Bath stone architecture. It occurred to her that cities could have complex histories just like people, and that places could go through tough times and great times, too.

"If it was so close to the slum, why did they move here, then?"

"Green Park Buildings were known to be affordable but respectable lodgings for the hard-up gentry. The house that she lived in was gorgeous, with iron balconies and fanlights above the doors, tall windows, and it was big."

Vanessa scribbled notes as best she could as she stood in front of the buildings.

Chase took the pictures.

"Jane's father died in Green Park Buildings in 1805. Once a retired man died, his retirement fund ended, so she, her mother, and Cassandra suddenly had no money and had to move."

"Again?"

"There are two more addresses on your list, Vanessa. The next one is 25 Gay Street, a much smaller home, on a noisy street."

They walked by the Jane Austen Centre on Gay Street, an entire house dedicated to . . . Jane Austen! The impoverished and mourning Jane Austen. Certainly she would appreciate the irony of a museum dedicated to her on Gay Street.

Chase took a photo of Vanessa in front of Jane's old house farther up the street, which happened to be a dentist's office, and from there they went just a few blocks south to Trim Street, the Austen ladies' last lodgings in Bath.

Even the name of the street suggested trimming the budget. The street seemed darker than most and hemmed in, without any greenery to be seen.

"We don't know which number house she lived in on Trim, but we do know that the street housed prostitutes and criminals. The Austens moved out of Bath in 1806, and I don't think it happened soon enough for Jane."

Vanessa hung up with her aunt, offering up quite a few "I love yous," suddenly feeling as if her aunt had really been with her.

Vanessa turned to Chase. "No wonder she didn't write much in Bath. Who could with all of these moves and her father's death?"

Chase smiled. "It sounds like you're a British-flag-waving member of the Jane Austen fan club now."

Vanessa laughed. "Hey, let's drop the book you bought me at my flat."

"I like that idea."

She laughed.

"The flat's just a street away from here."

"I wonder if your street is rife with the vices of prostitutes and pimps."

Once in the flat, he went to the kitchenette for a glass of water while she put the finishing touches on her timeline.

He sauntered out of the kitchen with his water in a wineglass and one of her lacy black bras dangling from his index finger.

"Is this a setup or are you just trying to torture me?"

Vanessa had forgotten about the underwear she'd hung all over the kitchen, but she had to admit Chase looked awfully hot holding her bra like that.

"Hawt," as Sherry would say.

Chapter 18

*B*ut that was nothing compared to seeing him in his swim trunks at the spa session he'd arranged for everyone at the end of the day. As the sun hovered seemingly right at the roof deck's level, Vanessa, Lexi, and David, whom Lexi still hadn't slept with, soaked in the heated mineral water pool on the roof deck of the Thermae Bath Spa, surrounded by the abbey spires, kelly green hills, and stately crescents. Sherry bobbed in the water across the pool with some festival friends she'd met.

Water from the original hot spring was pumped up here for modern-day spa goers to partake.

Lexi lounged in the water next to Vanessa. "The only thing that could make this spa experience better would be if we'd been carried here in sedan chairs by gorgeous footmen just like they did during the Regency era."

Vanessa could picture this in Lexi's case, but it took some doing to imagine herself being carried—anywhere. She rested the back of her head and elbows on the ledge of the pool and kicked her legs lazily in front of her, thrilled at the trifecta of warm water, a now sunny sky, and a day well spent, when Chase strolled through the glass doors in his sunglasses, looking very tan in his rented white fluffy bathrobe and slippers. A woman in a bikini followed him, trying to get his attention.

Chase spotted Vanessa and gave a big, goofy grin that prompted her to smile. His happy-go-lucky demeanor and playfulness were nothing short of infectious. Nobody, it seemed, had ever been so happy to see her—every time.

Her eyes followed him as he stepped out of his slippers, pulled off his sunglasses, slid out of his robe, and slung it on a chair.

"Will you look at the tight ass on that guy?" Lexi whispered. "You could easily get yourself a piece of that tonight."

Vanessa sighed—out of agreeing with Lexi on Chase's nice ass or in exasperation at Lexi always being on the make, she wasn't sure.

"Chase and I are just friends."

"Call it what you will. You know I don't think men and women are friends without an ulterior motive."

Vanessa steered her thoughts to Julian as she squinted into the sunlight. "Julian's got a great ass, too, you know." She closed her eyes.

"But does he have Chase's broad shoulders? That chest? Those abs? Jane Austen never got to see shit like this, you know, poor thing."

Vanessa laughed. "True."

She couldn't help herself. She opened her eyes and watched Chase as he stood on the side of the pool, steam rising appropriately in the air all around him. He breathed in and his chest, his admittedly chiseled and tanned chest, expanded just before he jumped in with a smile. Sun sparkled around him, and droplets of water glistened on his shoulders.

Vanessa tried to look away.

"You spent all day with that man? And nothing happened?"

"A lot happened. We had the hunt to finish off, for one thing."

"I'll tell you what you should've been hunting!"

"And after that we had Bath buns in the Jane Austen Room at Sally Lunn's."

"Sounds scintillating."

"Sally Lunn's happens to be one of the oldest houses in Bath, built in 1482. I mean—the 1400s, before Columbus discovered America? Sally Lunn invented the Bath bun, and I'm telling you it was as big as a plate, and fluffy! I had mine with butter and jam while he had his with bacon. The butter tastes so much better here. Why is that?"

"You resisted him *and* bacon?"

Vanessa laughed. "No, he gave me a forkful or two. Do you realize that at this very moment I have absolutely no idea what's going on in the world? I haven't watched the news in days. It feels good, actually. Maybe there is something to the healing powers of Bath."

"It's called 'vacation,' honey. Wait. He shared his food with you?"

"So what?"

"He's into you, all right. Men don't share their food. You've always been so clueless about the signals men give. I can't imagine the number of men you've glossed over just because you don't know how to read them."

"Come on." Vanessa leaned in to Lexi's ear. "Anyway, I think you're losing your mojo. Still haven't slept with Mr. Lancashire here?"

David seemed practically asleep with his head leaned back on the ledge and his eyes closed.

"We're taking it slow. Someday a guy will turn you all around, too."

Vanessa smiled. "Yeah. Julian already has."

"You just think he has. What else did you and Chase do today?"

"He gave me a tour of the Roman Baths, something he happens to know a lot about."

"Now, *that* is sexy, and we've always agreed that we just love a man we can learn a thing or two from, haven't we?"

"Yes," Vanessa acquiesced. "But Julian taught me a lot, too, you know. The Roman Baths make Sally Lunn's seem positively modern. Did you know the Romans called the city Aquae Sulis, meaning 'waters of Sulis,' the Celtic goddess of healing?"

Lexi bobbed underwater to get her hair wet. "Hydrotherapy. The only therapies that can beat it are massage therapy and sex therapy, of course."

Even as Vanessa laughed, she had to wonder if all of them—she, Lexi, Sherry, Chase, Julian, and maybe even Jane Austen herself— had been brought here to heal in some way. Granted, they didn't have gout or melancholia, but didn't they each have their own affliction to recover from? Didn't everyone?

"The baths were amazing," she continued. "But then he had to work, and I went to a Regency dance workshop. I think I'm ready for the ball with Julian!"

"It's just like you, Vanessa, to be ignoring something spectacular right in front of your face. Chase is not going to hang around waiting for you forever, you know. Look, there's someone after him already."

Chase smiled at the woman in the bikini, who had followed him into the pool, finished up the chat with her, held his breath, and dove underwater. The sunlight danced on the pool now and, combined with the steam, temporarily blinded Vanessa.

Someone grabbed at her ankles, and she knew in an instant it was Chase. He then raised her up out of the water and they stood face-to-face.

He pushed back his wet brown hair.

For some reason she thought, *So, this is what he looks like when he steps out of the shower.* Huh? She felt some kind of gravitational pull toward him; then again, it could've just been the energy lines that crisscrossed Bath, especially here, at the sacred, and some might say mystical, hot spring.

But she didn't believe in that crap, did she?

"Isn't this place fantastic?" he asked.

Droplets of water headed in one direction on his chest: south.

"Yes, it's amazing." She tried to step back, but she already was up against the pool wall. "Great recommendation. We can feel the healing power."

"Regardless of how you feel, you look great in a bathing suit." He eyed her dripping-wet chest. "As I knew you would. Of course, you'd look even better without it."

Flirt.

He beamed at Lexi and held out his hand to David. "I'm Chase. Are you Lexi's souvenir from England?"

"That I am." David shook hands.

Chase, in his signature way, stepped forward with slight deference, a smile, and a patting of his hand on David's arm as they shook.

"I'd like to treat everyone to a Bath bitter after this," Chase said. "How about it?"

"Hey, I'm paying for you tonight, Chase," Vanessa said. "You've been the best."

"The best what?"

She didn't quite know how to answer that. "Well, after traipsing all over London and Bath with me, I at least owe you a drink."

"Hmmm. Let me think of the ways you can return the favor."

He was flirting again, and he positioned himself next to Vanessa, their bodies brushing underwater, and rested his elbows on the pool ledge next to her, giving her an up-close-and-personal glimpse of his left bicep, brown and bulging with a small skull and crossbones tattoo on it.

Lexi had been right about Chase being a great guy. Vanessa could see them getting along very well as family and even joining forces on a project or two businesswise. The more she got to know him, the more confused about his role in her life she became.

"The water's perfect," he said. His nostrils flared slightly in the steam. "Ahhh."

For the next hour she chatted with Chase in the water while Sherry, Lexi, and David moved on to the scented steam rooms and lazy river. Something about the pool made Vanessa want to stay. It could've been the setting sun, the fact that getting out now would be cold, or maybe she liked having Chase so close, talking. And they had the pool all to themselves now.

"Vanessa?"

She wriggled away from Chase at the sound of the familiar British accent.

It was Julian in his little blue British swimsuit.

*V*anessa and Julian sat in the glass-enclosed eucalyptus mint steam room, sweat dripping from their bodies, Julian with his head in his hands. Apparently he'd found her at the spa by checking out one of her location networking sites! *He* had joined the site to find her, track her down, and tell her she hadn't won the competition after all. A woman from Sweden had come in just before her with all the right answers.

"Oh, well." She played it cool and shrugged her shoulders. "Without the hunt I never would've had the privilege of dragging a life-sized plastic Colin Firth all over England."

It didn't produce the smile she'd hoped for from him.

Through the glass walls she could see Lexi, David, Sherry, and Chase were in the lavender steam room nearby, with Chase sprawled on the cement bench.

"I have something important to say to you, Vanessa," Julian said.

She felt her temperature rising beyond the heat of the steam room. Her head began to spin, and even eucalyptus couldn't steady her. She hadn't eaten anything since the Sally Lunn bun, after all.

"I should have told you eons ago—"

A young woman stepped into the steam room with them and sat across from them.

"But this may not be the right place." He sighed and looked up at the dripping ceiling for a moment. "Perhaps I should invite you to see the house tomorrow. After all you've done to help my cause, I feel obligated—"

Vanessa put her hands on her hips and tried to breathe deep, tried to act like a duchess. But it was just an act, wasn't it? "Obligated?" She stood and paced while the young woman looked at her, aghast. "Don't feel obligated! I don't want to go anywhere with or *be* with anyone who feels *obligated!*"

This was why she didn't open up to men. This was why she never let them know her true feelings. It was just too painful.

"You know what?" She grabbed her towel, swung the glass door open, and shouted, "You don't have to feel obligated anymore!"

The young woman stared. Now everyone in the dimly lit, all-glass steam rooms turned their heads and stared at her as she bolted for the changing rooms, which were, unfortunately, co-ed.

She dried off as best she could and considered changing back into her clothes, but then she heard Chase calling for her.

"Vanessa? Vanessa? Are you in here? I'll be forced to look under changing-room doors if you don't answer me. Who knows what I'll be exposed to!"

So *he* came running after her and not Julian? That really pissed her off. She didn't want to see Chase. Not now. She stuffed her clothes into her bag, slipped on her flip-flops, and made a beeline for the stairs and the doors that led to Hot Bath Street.

The cold evening air hit her, and people on the street ignored her, in their polite British way, in her bikini. But something compelled her to look in on the Cross Bath across the paved square. It was housed in a Georgian stone oval-shaped building, complete with columns and an ornately sculpted portico, and the lure of a glowing light emanating through the glass door drew her closer.

She pressed her hands against the warm glass to see a couple drinking champagne and kissing in an oval-shaped blue pool with steam rising all around them. The Cross Bath could be rented out privately, and apparently, these two had done it. Her hands warmed on the glass as her body grew colder.

Would she always be on the outside looking in?

She sneezed, her nose began to run again after having been fine most of the afternoon, and she loped out of the little building, dashed toward her flat, but got turned around on Trim Street. The street seemed to close in on her, and her head ached with her cold. She couldn't remember which way on Trim she had to turn to get back to her flat.

All she could think of was Jane Austen, coming home late to this dark street, ducking the men looking for prostitutes and clutching her reticule so nobody would steal it.

Time to leave, Vanessa thought. Time to leave Bath.

Suddenly she felt a coat tossed around her shoulders, and it about gave her a heart attack. "What the—?"

"It's just me," said Chase. "I called your name, but you weren't listening."

He wrapped his sports jacket around her shoulders. "You're frozen. I'm taking you back to your flat."

She shivered. "I really had to give it a shot with him, Chase. I thought I had something with him."

"I know you felt you did. I saw that."

They stood out on her stoop, and he rummaged through her bag to find her key. He looked awfully cute digging through her purse, and it made her smile.

"But you know," he said, "love shouldn't be that hard."

He found the key, unlocked the door, and held it open for her. A slice of light came down on her from the hallway.

"What do you mean? Love is always hard."

"No, it isn't. It's easy. You shouldn't have to be playing games and hiding your feelings and guessing how he feels and trying not to text him until a certain amount of time has passed and all that."

They climbed the stairs and he opened the door to her flat.

She looked at him and she couldn't believe what he said. She'd been playing games with men her entire life. She prided herself on being one move ahead of them. She always left them first, before they could leave her. She had her own code, her own rules that she followed, and it worked.

Or maybe her code didn't work—*at all!*

"When a man really loves you, he shows you how he feels. He won't be running hot and cold. He won't be keeping you guessing. We're really quite simple creatures. When it comes from the heart, we're not able to play games. You'll know when a man truly loves you."

"And when he doesn't."

She followed Chase into the kitchen, where he removed three of her animal-print thongs from the stovetop to fill the kettle. He began opening the cabinets with her bras dangling from the knobs, looking for tea or something.

"It's usually very obvious when he doesn't."

He found a packet of hot chocolate and poured it into a mug.

"It's obvious to you, maybe. You're a man yourself."

He sighed. "You deserve better. Every woman deserves better than some guy who tosses her feelings around, plays games with her, sleeps with her, but doesn't want to date her or even text or call her."

He put it all so bluntly she felt compelled to defend Julian. It was not that he never dated her or that he never called or texted her!

Right? How could they date—living nearly five thousand miles apart? And, well, he never texted or called anyone.

She leaned against the doorjamb and pulled his jacket around her neck. "That's it. I'm going to die a spinster just like Jane Austen."

"You are not! Not you, my dear. You just need to find the right man." He stroked her chin. Then he took and folded her bras and thongs from various points in the kitchen. "Here." He handed her the tiny pile.

Maybe, she thought, *love happens in between loads of laundry and making hot chocolate together. Maybe it's not difficult and dramatic and cross-continental.*

Why couldn't Julian be more like Chase? Why hadn't *he* run after her when she left the steam rooms?

"Much as I love seeing you in your swimsuit, I think you should change into something warmer, and I'll treat you to dinner."

She reached out and hugged him, crushing her neatly folded underwear against his back. "I'm treating you to dinner tonight, Chase. Thank you. For everything."

As she changed in her room, she couldn't help but wonder what exactly Julian had come to tell her, anyway. Why did she assume it was something she wouldn't want to hear? A small, vulnerable part of her thought, *What if it was exactly what she wanted to hear?*

She knew what she had to do. She had to visit his estate and get some answers. If she only knew the questions.

Chapter 19

On her way to the train station the next morning she took the waters at the Pump Room, downing some cold meds with it. How did she come to a spa town completely healthy and manage to get sick?

Of course, running through Bath in a wet bathing suit on a September night probably didn't help matters.

Against Lexi's and Sherry's unsolicited advice, Vanessa took a train to Alton, where she had only about a mile to walk to get to Julian's estate. From there she would walk to Jane Austen's cottage at Chawton and meet up with a festival group tour, where she would take the "barouche" (a bus) back to Bath, all in plenty of time to get ready for the ball.

Chase had set himself up in his hotel to work for the day, and she didn't dare tell him about her plan anyway.

She figured rather than texting, e-mailing, or calling Julian, she would do things the old-fashioned way, the nineteenth-century way, and pay him a visit.

Lexi and Sherry, meanwhile, signed up for a festival tour of the

Assembly Rooms, where Jane Austen would attend dances, and the Orchard Theatre, which she frequented, then the Fashion Museum and high tea at the Pump Room.

A couple of weeks earlier, seeing Jane Austen's haunts wouldn't have tempted Vanessa in the least. But tempting as it now was, she couldn't imagine seeing Julian tonight at the ball without at least trying to figure things out. The visit seemed worth a shot. And something compelled her, before she left England, to see the estate that she had worked so hard for.

Sturdy walking shoes on, umbrella and raincoat in hand, once she'd walked the mile from the Alton station, she took her earbuds out as soon as she saw it in the distance. It proved impressive, made of hewn stone, and it stood tall, with three stories of windows, perfectly symmetrical with four columns and a pediment.

But iron scaffolding bookended it. It was a fixer-upper on the grandest of scales.

A blue Dumpster sat on one side of the curved driveway, filled to the brim with stone rubble. Construction truck tires had left tracks on the grass, gouged into the land. It seemed as if the construction crew had been there not too long ago, but abandoned it. A few of the windows on the second and third stories had been replaced with plywood. Cracks scissored through the front steps.

The scaffolding, the Dumpster, none of this had been in the pictures he'd shown her. She walked up the steps to the front door, where building permits had been plastered on the windows flanking the doorway. Above the permits hung a sign that read: ENGLISH HER-ITAGE SITE AT RISK.

She'd made the right decision in coming. When she looked back over her shoulder and saw the tombs of Julian's ancestors clustered on a nearby hilltop, they felt like long-lost family. It filled her with a great sense of purpose to know she'd had, and could still have, any part in saving this grand old home.

She almost forgot why she had come.

With a nervous hand she raised the brass knocker and knocked as loudly as she could, but nobody answered. The door was locked.

She decided to call him after all, but couldn't get a signal. No Wi-Fi, either.

Her instinct to take pictures kicked in, thinking she might be able to do something more to help the cause once she got home, no matter what her relationship, or lack of, with Julian. As she stood here at last, she felt for the home as if it were a living, breathing thing. She shot as much as she could, a little daunted by the amount of work that needed to be done, but able to visualize how fantastic the place could be with a lot of time, effort, and—money.

As much as it would take to whip everything back into shape, it seemed the alternative—allowing it to be condemned and torn down—would be a great loss.

Still trying to get a signal on her phone, she walked around the back, awed by the vast, overrun gardens marked by crumbling gateposts. On a backyard terrace a cloth tarp covered some furniture, and it flapped in the wind with foreboding.

Vanessa hadn't felt this cut off from civilization in a long time—if ever. It was so quiet she could hear herself think. She had forgotten how quiet the world was without her phone.

The house stood on acres of its own land, and the clouds in the sky parted, and sun and blue sky broke through, as if to mock her and her solitude.

Still no signal on her phone. It didn't seem as if he was here, though. But then she saw something white in the distance bouncing along the edge of the pond in front of an old gazebo surrounded by overgrown grass. She spotted someone from the back—Julian? He wore a Chintz robe and Turkish slippers, the ones he had spoken of in his show! As he stepped out of the gazebo, her heart leapt, and she ran toward him, slowly at first, then quicker, and then, she slowed again.

It wasn't Julian. It wasn't a man at all. It was a woman in an over-sized robe, picking up a white puppy. It was the same woman she'd seen in the Bath Abbey with Julian!

She couldn't think, but began to walk backward in the over-grown grass; her cold meds seemed to fail her as her head began to pound, her eyes began to water, and her throat ached with soreness. A cool breeze made her shudder and she all but dropped her bag and umbrella to put on her raincoat.

She turned up her collar, turned around, and went against the wind, toward Jane Austen's cottage, forgetting to put in her earbuds, not caring about getting a signal. According to her map, the cottage stood about a half-hour walk from here, and she couldn't get there fast enough.

For a while, she sat in a tearoom called Cassandra's Cup, across from Austen's adorable cottage. Convinced that both Jane and her sister Cassandra would be shocked by all this—the tearoom, the tour buses, the inevitable gift shop—Vanessa stirred her tea and honey, and ordered another scone and jam, even though, with her stuffed-up nose, she barely tasted it. She could feel the butter, though, that crazy-good British butter.

The tearoom really exuded that English quaintness, too, even though she wanted nothing more now than to hate England, or at least be indifferent to it, rather than falling a little more in love with it at every turn. China teacups of all sizes, colors, and patterns hung from the ceiling, and from her table at the window, downing some more cold meds with her tea, Vanessa looked out at the picture-perfect redbrick cottage that Jane had moved into in 1809. The story went that Jane felt settled again and happy here at Chawton, where she revised, wrote, and published her novels.

While Chawton had brought Jane Austen so much happiness, it brought nothing but despair to Vanessa. A woman wearing his robe *and* frolicking with a puppy on his grounds. Well, that explained it. He had a significant other of some kind after all.

The cottage couldn't be cuter, and this little intersection in Chawton, with the tearoom, the Greyfriar Pub next door, and even a thatched-roof cottage with flowers gushing from window boxes next to Austen's cottage, only added to the atmosphere.

A steady stream of tourists flowed in, out, and around the house and garden. Vanessa wondered if she was really up to going inside. But then again, she had to get her mind off Julian.

Could Jane Austen save her from herself?

She pulled out her phone and got a signal here, so she texted Lexi: *Went 2 his place—he wasn't there—was a woman on the grounds.* *#ampissed*

She felt numb even as she walked through Austen's lush garden and into, accidently, a portion of the cottage that housed the brick oven and where the Austen ladies' donkey cart had been put on display. The women couldn't afford a carriage, only a donkey cart, evidently. Donkeys. Asses. *He's an ass,* Vanessa kept hearing over and over in her head in Lexi's voice.

She didn't want to believe it.

She finally met up with the festival tour group in the cottage. She looked at, but didn't really see, and certainly didn't feel—anything— even as she stared at Austen's writing table at the very window that looked out on Cassandra's Cup. The table, small and worn, nothing but a pedestal table really, had atop it a quill pen standing in an empty glass inkwell. Austen evidently sat here, on a simple cane chair at the window, to write, facing the door.

Vanessa wanted to feel something, anything, other than anger, regret, and humiliation over this thing with Julian, whatever it was.

Here she stood at her newfound idol author's writing table, and she felt as empty as the glass inkwell before her.

She stared at the simple but elegant Wedgwood china set on the dining table, white plates encircled with a green oak leaf and brown acorn pattern, as if they would provide her with an answer. The acorn reminded her of the sculpted acorns that adorned so many buildings in Bath, especially those she had seen atop the houses in the Circus.

Two older women, also admiring the china, stood near Vanessa. "The acorn symbolizes strength and power in small things," one of the women said to both her friend and Vanessa in a lively Australian accent. "It can also mean growth and good luck. Fitting that Jane, Cassandra, and their mother would choose this pattern."

Vanessa could use some acorns. Then again, did they help Jane and Cassandra?

She went up to the bedroom where Jane Austen and her sister slept, but it wasn't the actual bed, so she stared at the worn quilt on the bed instead.

The whole tour seemed like some surreal, out-of-body experience. Why did she feel nothing?

Across from the four-poster bed, though, a blue and white chamber pot housed in a white wooden cabinet on a shelf below the washbowl in the bedroom seemed to mesmerize her. The rest of the tour had all moved on to the next room while she stood staring at the chamber pot.

That was where Jane Austen herself went to the bathroom, Vanessa thought to herself. And she smiled. There. She felt something. She felt that even Jane Austen might've laughed at the thought.

She found the tour group downstairs, gathered around a silhouette scene hung on the wall that Vanessa had walked right by on her way in.

She wedged her way into the group surrounding the silhouette to hear the tour guide. The guide looked suspiciously like a young Kate Beckinsale, who had played Emma in the 1990s, with gorgeous black hair, pale skin, and a slight smile that punctuated the end of every sentence.

"This silhouette, cut in 1783, illustrates Jane's brother Edward being presented to his wealthy distant relatives, the Knights," she said. "They adopted him and raised him as their own."

The scene, black on a faded tea-colored background, had a staged but all-too-familiar feel to it. Two Georgian ladies, both in tall wigs and gowns, sat at a game table while Mr. Austen in his powdered wig and buckle shoes presented Edward by easing him, with a gentle push on the boy's back, toward the adoptive parents, including Mr. Knight, who stood across the gaming table.

Edward was so young, so tiny in his breeches and tailcoat. His stockinged legs looked very thin.

Vanessa had to steady herself on a chair she shouldn't have been touching. "How old was he when he was adopted?" she asked without thinking.

"Twelve." Smile.

Twelve, a year younger than Vanessa was when her parents separated and before she moved in with Aunt Ella.

"The Knights weren't able to have children of their own, and as was common practice, they looked for and adopted an heir from the extended family. Edward left the Austens to live with the Knights, and in so doing, he became the richest of the seven Austen siblings. He inherited two massive properties, Godmersham in Kent and Chawton House, an Elizabethan manor just up the road from here."

Vanessa stepped in closer, to see little Edward reaching out with a hand toward his rich adoptive parents.

"To be chosen marked him as lucky. They raised him as a gentleman, and he even went on his own Grand Tour of the Continent, something none of the other Austen men had done."

"Lucky," Vanessa whispered to herself. She had always considered herself lucky to be taken in by Aunt Ella, but at the same time very unlucky to grow up away from her parents, flawed as they were. Seeing Edward in the same position, with two sets of parents, separated from his family, opened that hole in her heart.

"If Edward hadn't been adopted by the Knights, it's very possible his sister Jane would've never finished, much less published her novels."

A hush came over the crowd.

"I'll tell you about that as we walk over to what was Edward's inheritance, now called Chawton House Library and dedicated to early women writers. And a property very familiar to Jane."

The guide led them out of the cottage and north on a path alongside the road that had been labeled THE JANE AUSTEN TRAIL with a sign. Vanessa had been on a Jane Austen Trail, all right.

She walked next to the guide, wanting to hear more.

"After Mr. Austen's death in Bath in 1805, Jane, Cassandra, and their mother had no income. Women of their social status couldn't work, yet they barely managed to scrape by, moving frequently and staying with various relatives. Without her brother's offer of the cottage, Jane wouldn't have had the settled lifestyle she needed to write."

Vanessa felt for Jane and how dependent they had to be on men. Their life, their happiness, their everything—depended on a man. Imagine!

And there, at the end of the Jane Austen Trail, stood Julian in full Regency regalia.

*M*iss Roberts and friends, I presume," Julian said as he took off his hat and bowed to her. He wore a green coat this time. *No, no, the green one,* she remembered Darcy saying in the 1995 film version as he chose which coat to wear to meet Elizabeth.

"Pleasure to see you," Julian said.

As if there were no woman in his robe behind his house. As if there were no puppy frolicking on his grounds. As if there had been no steam-room incident.

If he happened to be giving this tour, she'd rather sit on the tour bus. She managed to speak. "Hello, Mr. Darcy."

Did he feel the ice in her delivery? She didn't like being passive-aggressive, but she couldn't quite get hold of her feelings, much less figure out how to express them. But something inside felt broken and tossed aside. Why had this all been so damn complicated?

Maybe Chase was right. Love wasn't hard. Which would mean this wasn't love or even the beginning of it.

Within moments, women (and men) from the tour group surrounded him, and it became clear that, as luck would have it, they wouldn't have a moment alone, thank goodness.

Ironically she had been seeking exactly that just an hour and a half earlier.

When she turned away from him and toward Chawton House, nothing could have prepared her for what she saw. A long, straight pea gravel road led uphill, past stone stables larger and more gorgeous than most American homes, and toward the largest Elizabethan manor she'd ever seen. It happened to be the only Elizabethan manor house she'd ever seen, but still. It looked straight out of one of her aunt's BBC costume dramas, with three gables, a three-story entrance porch made of flint, and a grand red roof, all surrounded by meticulously kept green lawns and sculpted shrubs.

All this for Edward Austen. All this now a library holding thousands of valued pieces of women's writing from the long-ago eighteenth century.

The crowd collectively gasped. Vanessa counted at least seven chimneys, and those were only the ones she could see. Trees framed the house and blocked quite a bit of the house itself from view.

"Any of you could have your wedding here," the tour guide said. "It's for hire."

Julian shot her a glance. "What a lovely thought."

She looked away. The nerve!

She stayed as far away from him as possible, sticking close to the tour guide but catching glimpses of him from a safe distance as they walked toward the house.

Was he a gentleman or—a rake? If only there were an app for figuring *that* out! Did he have a girlfriend, or—shudder—a wife?

Maybe he had a girlfriend *and* a wife.

Just because he didn't wear a wedding ring and never mentioned a significant other didn't mean anything.

The gravel crunched under her shoes until she found herself ushered through the entrance hall and inside a Tudor-era wood-paneled dining room bigger than her entire condo, looking straight at a larger-than-life oil portrait of Edward Austen Knight. He wore a powdered wig, breeches, cravat, and tailcoat, and looked very debonair leaning up against a tree so casually, with his walking stick.

He hadn't been born into money, but he looked the part.

Yet Vanessa harkened back to Cassandra's unfinished watercolor sketch of Jane on display at the National Portrait Gallery. It would hardly fill a corner of this painting.

She tried to concentrate on the Emma look-alike tour guide, but the stunning room, with the dining table set for twelve, the oriental carpet on the floor, the smaller but equally engaging oil paintings that hung about the room, and the ornate carvings above the fireplace dazzled her. What a contrast from Austen's simple cottage with sparse furnishings.

Across the room, Julian looked out one of the floor-to-ceiling windows.

Before she looked away he caught her staring at him.

"If I can draw your attention . . ." said the tour guide.

Vanessa instantly looked away from him.

"If you look at Edward's shoes in this portrait, you can clearly see the artist has painted in a horseshoe nail pointed toward Edward's feet."

Vanessa moved closer to the painting and sure enough, you could see a nail on the ground, pointing to Edward.

"This possibly symbolizes Edward's good luck at being adopted by the Knights."

The luck thing again. Vanessa thought of her aunt and all that she'd done for her, including bringing Jane Austen into her life.

But it was this trip, and Vanessa's own ragtag journey around England, that had brought Jane Austen *to* life. And now her brother Edward had sprung to life before her, too—the little boy grown into the man lucky enough to provide his impoverished mother and two sisters with a home and, for one of those sisters, the comfort needed to create her masterpieces.

Julian paced the floor across the room in front of the fireplace; she could see him out of the corner of her eye.

He seemed to hover, too, as they went up the north staircase and through the Tapestry Gallery, the Great Gallery, and the Map Room to a bibliophile's dream, the Reading Room, which housed the bulk of the library's collection; from there they went to the Oak Room, where Jane Austen herself would sit in the alcove window, reading.

She had come a long way from the prostitutes on Trim Street.

The group descended the great staircase into the old kitchen, where the worktable itself was about three hundred years old.

Julian leaned against the doorjamb. He hadn't said a thing during the entire tour. She had to wonder why he was there.

Once they were outside, for a quick tour of the grounds, he practically stalked her, standing behind her on the Arts and Crafts terraces, walking beside her on the serpentine gravel path to the upper terrace and fernery, and essentially blocking her at various turns in the walled kitchen garden between the tomatoes and the rosemary.

In the rose garden he somehow corralled her away from the group, and, near a bed of pink cabbage roses, their flowers heavy, browning at the edges of the petals, and drooping in the early fall air, he bent down to pick one and then stood in front of her, holding it.

"Vanessa, I would quite like to speak to you."

Just a few hours before, this gesture of his could've played out very differently.

"What is there to say? We slept together. That's all it was. Happens all the time, right?"

He held out the rose to her.

She didn't take it.

He twirled it in his fingers. "There's more to it than that, at least for me. It's complicated."

"Exactly. Too complicated."

"I should like to explain—" He leaned over and a small antique book fell from his frock coat pocket to the grass.

Before he could reach for it, Vanessa picked it up and opened the inside cover. In very ornate type it read:

Harris's List
of Covent Garden Ladies
or,
Man of Pleasure's
Kalender

He tried to gently nudge the book away from her, but she turned her back on him, flipped open to a page, and read:

Mrs. Griffin, Near Union Stairs, Wapping
This comely woman, about forty, and boasts she can give more plea-
sure than a dozen raw girls. Indeed she has acquired great experience—

He tried again to take the book away, but she hurried a few steps away from him and said, "What the hell is this, Julian?"

People from the tour group looked and then looked away again.

"*Harris's List*, from the 1700s. It's research for my next book—"

"It's a list of prostitutes!" She turned away again as he came closer. Prostitutes from the eighteenth century, yet it sullied his polite, gentlemanly reputation, didn't it?

Betsy Miles, Cabinet Maker's Old Street
Known in this quarter for her immense sized breasts . . . backwards
and forewards, are all equal to her, posteriors not excepted, nay in-
deed, by her own account, she has the most pleasure in the latter.
Entrance at the front door tolerably reasonable, but nothing less than
two pounds for the back way . . . (1773)

"Really?" She snapped the book shut and shoved it into his gut. "It's the great-grandfather of online porn!"

"I'm sure you meant to say it is the great-great-great-grandfather of—"

"Julian!"

"It's a very common book," he said. "Even that Jane Austen Books store in the States had a reproduction of it."

"Julian, it's kind of creepy to be carrying something like that around, don't you think? If it's research, it belongs on your desk. As your former PR agent, I would advise you to keep it at home. It won't score you any points with your target market."

Maybe she didn't know this man . . . at all. Maybe she had come all this way for nothing.

Her phone beeped with a text message and she dug in her bag to check it. Lexi had responded to her text saying *She could b his sister.* Vanessa laughed.

It never turned out to be a sister, or even a kissing cousin.

Then the tour guide raised her voice. "It's time to head to our 'barouche.' It's waiting for us at the end of the drive. Time to get back and get ready for the ball, everyone!"

Vanessa looked into Julian's eyes and he seemed sincere—about something—and opened his mouth to speak. But she didn't want to have this discussion in Edward Austen Knight's rose garden with the specter of Jane Austen lurking in one of the windows!

She headed toward the front lawn and looked back at him, in his green coat and boots, standing in front of the gatepost of the garden, with the avenue of lime trees just beyond him and the rose in his hand at his side.

Every girl should have her BBC costume drama moment, and this was hers.

But if you looked closely, the edges of the pink rose petals had gone brown. The little black book was exactly that—a little black book—from the 1700s, but still.

She could handle this like a duchess, or she could rant like only a thirty-five-year-old single American woman could.

Over her shoulder she said with a smile, "I have to go. My barouche awaits."

Chapter 20

*P*lastic Colin Firth had become a hat rack for a bonnet and several turbans and a coatrack for shawls and stoles. Necklaces dangled around his neck. He stood in the corner of the flat while Vanessa, Lexi, and Sherry vied for the limited resources of one bathroom and one well-lit mirror as they readied for the ball. Curling iron, hair dryer, and clothing iron cords created a spaghetti-like heap on the floor near the bathroom.

Lexi's bottle of cabernet had been emptied and now they were on to oversized cans of lager from the convenience store. British pop music blasted out of the clock radio in one of the bedrooms.

Lexi nudged Vanessa away from the mirror so she could put her lipstick on. Sherry fastened a simple, understated Regency-style topaz cross necklace on.

One thing they weren't willing to forgo for the costume ball was modern makeup.

"I wish I could meet a nice gentleman at the ball tonight." Sherry sighed as she tightened the ribbon under her bust.

"Be careful of what you wish for. You might meet someone who plays a gentleman onstage but carries around a catalog of prostitutes."

"What?" Lexi asked.

"I'm sure you've heard of *Harris's List*."

The corners of Lexi's lips curled up in a smile. "Mmm-hmm. But it's not as if any of the Covent Garden ladies are available to service him."

Sherry gave Vanessa a pained look. "That just sucks."

"In more ways than one," Vanessa said. "He claims it's 'research,' but I think it's just kind of creepy."

"Makes me curious what he's working on," Lexi said.

Vanessa rolled her eyes. "I'm beginning to think he's not what he seems to be."

Lexi puckered her lips in the mirror. "He's not what you've made him out to be. I keep telling you he's an ass. As for you, Sherry, I'm afraid Jane Austen events are the *last* place to meet eligible men. You will meet plenty of wonderful women and a lot of witty gay men, however. By the way, Vanessa, I invited Chase to the ball tonight— from all of us."

"Oh, thank you! I can't believe I forgot all about him."

"Come on. Since when am *I* nicer than you? I'll tell you why you forgot all about him: Julian. It's like you're on crack or something. Chase is here in Bath because of *you*. He is probably the best guy you'll ever *not* date. You're totally blowing it." Lexi poured herself and Sherry each another wineglass full of lager. "Beer's gone. You don't deserve any more, anyway, Vanessa."

"I just took another dose of cold meds, so I probably shouldn't drink."

Sherry looked at Vanessa's meds on the counter. "No, you shouldn't be drinking with this! Slow down, will you?"

Lexi took a sip of her beer. "Did you confront Julian about that other woman?"

"What other woman?" Sherry asked.

"There was a woman in Julian's robe with a puppy in his backyard today."

"Backyard." Vanessa laughed. "You should see his 'backyard.'"

"Ooooh," said Sherry. "A puppy . . ."

"Why does the puppy matter?" Vanessa paced the hall outside the bathroom.

"A guy. A girl. A robe. A puppy. Nothing good is coming out of that," Lexi said.

"I don't want to jump to paranoid conclusions. After all, the woman—"

"Could be his sister," they said in unison.

Lexi laughed so hard she almost sprayed her beer all over.

"I've left myself open to possibilities at the ball tonight."

Lexi sighed. "Well, if that's the case, then I certainly hope you're not wearing a thong under that gown, because Regency women didn't wear drawers. And you don't want your panty lines to show. Turn around, let me see." Lexi twirled her finger.

Vanessa acquiesced.

"Take 'em off."

"You can't see any panty lines!"

"Off."

"Sherry, are you wearing anything under your gown?"

"A lady never tells, does she?"

"Come on, Vanessa, we're going to party like it's 1799, okay?"

Vanessa laughed. "You're dating yourself in more ways than one with that line. And none of us are going to party like it's 1799, now that I've read the goings-on in *Harris's List*."

"You and Sherry should hit a pub after the ball. There are never eligible men at these Jane Austen things."

"Exactly. She'd certainly appreciate the irony that us modern women sign up and pay dearly for the kind of torture she had to endure in her social life. And you *won't* be going to the pub?"

"I have plans with David."

Vanessa was beginning to believe Lexi had changed.

Lexi stuck a two-foot-long white ostrich feather in her headdress, as if she didn't get enough attention everywhere she went.

"I'm up for the pub!" said Sherry.

Poor Sherry. She deserved to have some fun on her vacation, and not just by buying more Darcy paraphernalia.

Vanessa tossed her cold meds into her reticule. "They gave a lecture called 'What's in Your Reticule' yesterday. Well, I've packed my cold meds, my drink money, and my phone. And . . ."

She slipped off her leopard-print thong, twirled it around on her index finger, and flung it across the room, where it landed on Colin's head.

"Woot, woot!" Lexi shouted.

"Strumpet is in the house," said Sherry.

"I'm no strumpet. I'm a duchess."

"You're not fooling anyone," Lexi said. "You're no duchess. And we can tell you're *still* really hung up on him."

Vanessa managed a wobbly smile.

"You're going to need to attend my Break-It-Off boot camp, aren't you?"

"I'm remaining optimistic."

"Well, there's nothing to break off anyway," Lexi said.

"Enough!" Sherry said to Lexi as she handed Vanessa a masquerade eye mask done up in gold, white, and black.

"What's this?"

Sherry and Lexi had both already put on their masks.

"It's a masquerade ball," Sherry said.

Vanessa gaped at her mask. "What? How the hell am I going to find him in a room full of seven hundred masked people? How's he going to find me?"

"Relax," Lexi said. "It's a Jane Austen festival. Even in a mask he'll stand out."

*I*t wasn't easy navigating two-thousand-year-old pavers in ballet flats, a floor-length gown, and an ill-fitting mask, but Vanessa managed to get her glass of wine at the cocktail reception in the Roman Baths without incident.

Once again, she felt the crashing of eras as she gazed at the twelfth-century King's Bath, built on top of a Roman foundation, its water lit and glowing an intoxicating emerald green, surrounded by a golden building created in the eighteenth century, and here they were, time travelers from the twenty-first century, costumed in early-nineteenth-century clothes.

The mind boggled, even without cold meds and wine.

Both the formality of the venue and the clothing led to a certain raising of the bar among Vanessa, Sherry, Lexi, and David. David cleaned up nicely in his rented red British army uniform, and they all managed to behave as elegantly as they looked.

Revelers in Regency gowns and formal Regency coats, all of them in masks, filled the pavements surrounding the green pool, and the laughing and talking echoed between the ancient columns, while flashes from cameras reminded everyone that it was actually the twenty-first century.

Vanessa didn't see Julian anywhere, and the ratio of women to men did seem to be five to one.

"I hope Chase was able to get a costume," Lexi said.

It took Vanessa a moment to respond, she'd been so preoccupied looking for Julian. "Didn't he bring his pirate getup?"

"Well, he didn't think that would meet with the strict criteria here," said Lexi. "I'm going to text him and let him know where we are."

Vanessa looked beyond her small circle, craning her bejeweled neck to see if she could spot Julian. Without thinking, she finished her entire glass of wine.

"He's here," Lexi said, reading from her phone.

"He is?" Vanessa asked excitedly. "Where?"

"You know I'm talking about Chase, right? He says he's making his way toward the bar."

"Oh, right." Vanessa couldn't just stand here anymore, waiting for Julian to appear. "Sherry, shall we take a turn about the room?"

Sherry smiled and locked her arm in Vanessa's.

Oh, to be Sherry, open to the events of the evening and not overly invested in one enigma of a man.

Vanessa's phone vibrated in her reticule. Chase had sent her a text:

Save me? Cornered by a gaggle of German girls to the right of the bar.

Sure enough, once she and Sherry had crossed the length of the King's Bath and veered toward the bar, Vanessa could see the back of Chase's head, with his dark brown hair falling to just below the nape of his neck, and yes, he was surrounded by blond German women with angled faces, all angling for him.

She couldn't tell what Chase had on, though, because another, shorter woman stood right behind him adjusting the feather in her hair as she looked in her compact mirror.

"Chase, darling!" Vanessa waved her fan at him and deliberately overacted as she and Sherry approached. "Sweetheart!"

The shorter woman stepped aside, Chase turned around, and Vanessa seemed incapable of moving for a moment.

He wore a black eye mask and a shirt so snug it more than hinted at his muscular build, and he had a sword sheathed at his side, but what Vanessa wasn't anticipating was her visceral reaction to seeing him in a red and black Scottish—kilt.

Who knew a man could rock a kilt like that?

Of course, the inevitable question surfaced, within seconds: *was he wearing anything under that kilt?* Because traditionally, a Scotsman wouldn't.

Vanessa dropped Sherry's arm and cocked her hip. "Wow."

"Vanessa, my love," he said with that gleaming smile. "So fabulous to see you again, and looking so ravishing in that diaphanous gown."

With that he left the German posse in the dust, sauntered right up to her, and pressed one hand on the back of her head. He guided her hand to his kilted ass, tilted her head back ever so slightly, and kissed her, Frenched her, long and passionately.

She grabbed his hair and tried to pull him away until, finally, he did. He whispered "thank you" to her, then turned to Sherry and lifted her gloved hand to kiss it as he looked to see if the German women had dispersed. And they had.

"Sherry, a pleasure to see you."

Vanessa adjusted her gown, which only seemed to cling to her now. Had that been just a show to get rid of the German women? Because she'd never been kissed like that before! She'd kissed many a man in her time, too. What the hell! She'd been dating since she was, what, fourteen? She'd been missing *that* all her life?

She couldn't take her eyes off his lips, his mouth, and his tongue, as it moved. Oh, he was saying something.

"Vanessa, I asked you, can I buy you a drink?"

What did he say? She heard it, but she couldn't get past the fact that they were both wearing skirts, neither of them with anything underneath, and they were—just talking?

That tongue. That kiss. If it weren't for Julian, that kiss could have catapulted him out of the friend zone!

"I'll get you a glass of cabernet. I know you like your red. Sherry, you'd like a bitter, am I right?"

"Oooh, you're good," Sherry said. "Yes."

Vanessa finally found something to say. "Those German women were gorgeous—and young. Why would you want to get rid of them?"

Chase looked at her askance. "I've done a lot of traveling. Why would I waste my time with German girls when I know that there's nothing sexier than American women in general? Chicago women in particular, and PR women exclusively."

Now he was laying it on thick.

Out of nowhere, Julian appeared and strode right up to Chase.

He wore his Regency best and a silver mask.

"Typical Scotsman, ignoring all manner of British protocol."

Chase cracked a smile. "Hey, Julian. Can I buy you a drink? How's it going?"

"It's not *going* very well at the moment. You really must restrain yourself from such blatant displays of affection. Certainly that would never be tolerated in Regency times. An unmarried man and woman wouldn't even be allowed to touch except with gloved hands, at arm's length, on the dance floor. I must warn you the master of ceremonies and the dance caller are very strict here."

"You do realize, Julian, that we don't really live in the Regency era. Well, most of us don't, anyway." He laughed.

Julian sneered.

Vanessa had never seen him sneer.

He clenched his white-gloved fists. He had thrown down the gauntlet, but Chase didn't bother picking it up.

"How about I buy you an old-fashioned, Mr. Darcy?" Chase joked. Without waiting for a reply, he went to the bar.

Julian stared at Vanessa.

She had no idea what he could possibly be thinking, but maybe this was more about possession than anything.

"Julian's jealous," Sherry whispered in Vanessa's ear. "He was watching Chase kiss you and he stormed away from that group of people there as soon as he could."

Julian had shown some kind of emotion in public? Had the convergence of the energy lines here at the baths gotten to him?

So many possibilities rushed, like a torrent, through Vanessa's mind. Should she talk to him? Or, at this eleventh hour, should she do something more drastic? Once again, the course proved difficult to navigate. It confused her. She shouldn't have to make the next move here, should she?

"Ladies." Julian bowed to Vanessa and Sherry. "If you will excuse me."

Just like that he disappeared into the swelling crowd and she missed her chance. Would she ever find him again in this crowd of seven hundred? And she knew she shouldn't have had that lager, because now, of all times, she had to pee.

The crystal chandeliers dimmed in anticipation of the ball upstairs in the Pump Room. Vanessa's stomach went a little queasy. Each dance would be long, sometimes fifteen minutes. The evening would go quickly, neither Julian nor Chase had asked her to dance, and neither man was anywhere to be seen.

Sherry escorted Vanessa and Lexi toward the Pump Room fountain. "I'm treating us all to a drink of healing water! I'm slapping down my pound fifty."

Just as they raised and clinked their glasses and took a sip of the warm, mineral-rich water, a very nice gentleman in a blue tailcoat came over and very politely asked Sherry to dance, so Sherry set the rest of her water down on the wooden counter.

Vanessa's heart positively burst for her as Sherry raised her eyebrows and beamed.

David, too, asked Lexi to dance, and they did make an adorable couple. Lexi set her glass down.

Were the glasses half-empty or half-full? mused Vanessa as she stood alone. She drank her entire glass of mineral water, swallowed a few cold meds with it, and promptly sneezed.

Couples lined up across from each other on the dance floor, forming two long lines of dancers.

The dance caller spoke into the microphone. "Single ladies, don't be afraid to fill in for the men. Join in the dancing, everyone!"

From all angles of the room, women of all ages and sizes and equally varied costumes happily "filled in."

Vanessa went to the bar and asked the bartender for the strongest mixed drink he could concoct. She stood there staring down into it: Punch Royal, a deep red Regency mix of cognac, rum, and port, according to the bartender.

She went for her phone as the quartet began the very lively opening song. It wasn't easy to navigate the cracked screen with her gloves on, but there were no texts, no e-mails, nothing since she checked before she left the flat.

The ballroom glittered with shimmering chandelier light, dancers bounced lightly on their feet, music filled the room to the high ceilings, and Vanessa had never felt more alone. And abandoned by Julian.

But really, he hadn't abandoned her. She'd shared nothing of her heart with him. She hadn't opened herself up to him in any way. She'd given nothing, yet expected a return.

She read in the program—er, the "programme"—that a Regency libations lecture was going on in one of the other rooms, so she took her drink and made her way past the smiling lines of dancers to a bright room and took a seat in the back, sucking on her drink.

Before she knew it, her drink was gone, and the lecturer was speaking of small beer and orange wine and port, but nothing made any sense. She kept thinking about Julian and their time together, especially at the fairground.

The costumed crowd laughed frequently at what the lecturer said, and some nodded their coiffed heads in agreement, but once he appeared to turn blurry on her, Vanessa realized the harsh reality.

She was too drunk to be in a libations lecture.

*A*nd she needed to find Julian. She had to let him know how she really felt about him. She needed to take a chance. Maybe the booze had addled her brain, but her time had run out here in England.

She felt as if her time had run out at home, too, for that matter. How had she gotten to this point in her life—alone? Had she somehow forgotten to get married and have kids along the way? Had she been working too much or having too much fun or—her phone vibrated with an e-mail. It was from another eBelieve match.

Drinking all that mineral water and soaking in the magical spa waters of Bath had produced their cure, and Julian had been right! She had a virtual half life.

Right then and there in the lecture room, on her phone, she took down her eBelieve profile and deleted the in-box messages. Time to live! Time to love! Time to hoist up her gown, jump over stiles, and get her petticoats dirtied in six inches of mud! She could live in the nineteenth century and the twenty-first, but she wouldn't spend any more precious time living in the cyber world.

Standing now, she steadied herself with the chair in front of her and with as much finesse as a drunken duchess could muster, she turned to leave as quickly as possible, but somehow the hem of her gown must've gotten under the leg of the chair next to her, where a large older man sat dressed in his Regency best. With a great ripping sound, her ball gown tore.

These things happen when you grab your life by the—balls.

She didn't look back; she didn't look at the gown; she only aimed for the golden doorknob at the back of the room, turned it, and opened and quietly shut the door behind her, heaving a sigh that made her aware, once again, of just how exposed she felt in this gown.

There, across the hall, leaning against a doorjamb and checking his phone, stood Chase in his kilt.

"I've been looking for you."

Words that a woman would love to hear—from the man *she'd* been looking for. Especially someone she might have been looking for her entire life.

Chase happened to be a great kisser and a fabulous guy. But she was here to figure out what was in store for her and Julian. That was her plan. That was her mission.

"I see you've incorporated a slit into your gown," Chase said. "Very fetching."

Vanessa looked down, and shit! Her gown had torn all the way up the side seam, from the hem to about where she'd tied off her garter.

"Fucking hell!"

Chase smiled. "I'm not quite so sure you fit in with this genteel crowd."

"I can't go in the ballroom like this!"

"No. You can't. Let me take you back and we'll get that ruined gown off you."

He kept staring at her stockinged leg, completely visible now through the slit.

"I need to find some tape, some staples, something! I need to fix this gown right now!"

Chase moved closer and inspected the seam of the gown. "You know, you smell like a distillery, but that only makes you more alluring to me, a pirate at heart."

She laughed. "Seriously, I need to fix this." She needed to fix everything.

He opened the black leather Scottish bag attached to his belt and pulled something out and showed her.

"A sewing kit? You sew?"

"You don't?"

"No! What guy carries a sewing kit around?"

"A reenacting pirate does. Pirates know how to sew, cook, and clean. Oh, and we know how to tie all kinds of knots, too." He flashed that cocky grin.

Unsolicited, an image of Chase popped into her head, striking a pose in his pirate outfit, a rose between his teeth, a French maid feather duster in his hand, and ropes on his bedposts. She should never drink rum.

"Look, I happen to have white thread, too."

"I don't have time for this to be sewn up!"

"I could just tack it together with big, loose stitches. It won't take long."

Was he kidding?

"We just have to figure out where to go to get the job done."

One thing about Chase she'd always found attractive was his executive decision-making abilities. He had made the decision for her that yes, he would fix her gown.

"The men's room," he said. "Follow me."

And for once she followed someone else's lead.

*I*f it were Julian sewing up her gown, she might have thought it the sexiest sight she'd ever witnessed.

By the time Chase had finished tying off the thread at the hem, she'd sobered up some, and he'd, meanwhile, noticed her tattoo.

"A heart wrapped in barbed wire, interesting."

Vanessa didn't have time for this. "It's an old tattoo." She leaned her head back on the tile wall in exasperation and put her hand on his thick hair to tussle it, in hopes of changing the subject, offering a quick thanks, and getting the hell out of here and back into the ballroom. "Thank you, Chase. You're a man of many talents. I owe you!"

At that very moment, the door swung open, and it happened to be Julian, seeing Chase on his knees with Vanessa's gown hiked up and her hand in his hair. In the men's room.

As soon as Julian walked in, he walked out.

Vanessa lost her breath for a moment. "Damn!"

"Who was that?" Chase stood.

"Julian!" Vanessa ran after him. "Julian!"

She spotted him in the ballroom, where the music played. He stood with a crowd of impeccably dressed revelers with his back to her.

Vanessa strode right up to the crowd and broke into the small circle, just as any ill-mannered American would.

"Julian," she said with a smile, "can we talk?"

He returned the smile. "Of course."

"Julian?" One of the masked ladies passed judgment and sentencing with a single inflection.

"Oh. Vanessa, I would like you to meet someone very important to me." He made a flourish with his hand.

The woman stepped forward. She held her black mask on a stick and removed it to get a better look at Vanessa.

"Allison, this is my PR agent from Chicago, Vanessa. Vanessa, this is Allison, my fiancée."

This wasn't an act and not at all a part of his Mr. Darcy persona, was it? A sudden headache came on, a hangover jabbing into her brain, and her first thoughts, both shallow and swift, fired something like this: *Fiancée? Fiancée?!* Allison the fiancée didn't send off any cool or sexy vibes—at all. She stood there like a wilted flower with her plain-Jane face and nondescript gown.

In one-fifth of a second Vanessa judged and labeled Allison as a drag and nothing, nothing like her.

Next thought: Secret engagement? It was straight out of Austen's *Sense and Sensibility*!

Chase, who seemed to come out of nowhere, slid next to Vanessa with one hand on the handle of his sword while the other encircled her waist.

Could it be true? The engagement explained the hot and the cold, the sizzle and the ice, and the lukewarm to tepid.

Wait a minute. She'd slept with an engaged guy?

Allison limply held out her gloved hand, and Vanessa wanted to deliver a firm, confident handshake, and she did, by some miracle, manage to extend her hand even as, in her mind's eye, she saw nothing but her and Julian's naked bodies writhing together—until she pulled her hand back and propped it on her hip.

"Do you happen to have a white puppy?" Vanessa asked.

"Yes, yes, I do," the amazingly boring Allison said. "Did Julian tell you about her?"

Vanessa glared at Julian. "No. Julian didn't tell me a *thing* about her. I wish he had. He really should have! Right from the very beginning!"

Allison looked confused.

"I wanted to tell you about—the puppy. I tried to tell you—"

He looked sincere, he really did. Still.

Much like the water bubbling below the surface in Bath, she simmered.

"Oh, really? When did you try to tell me?"

The music had stopped, the dance ended, and hundreds of people, breathless, smiling, and sweaty, cleared the floor with their fans fluttering.

Her self-control reached the boiling point and her rage burst out in a torrent. "Was that before you slept with me or after?"

Her voice carried across the now-empty dance floor. Feathered heads turned. People set down their wineglasses to stare.

"Julian?" The amazingly boring Allison could speak with a modicum of passion, it seemed.

"Vanessa, let's not get all feisty and American over this," he said. "It was one night." He looked pained even as he said it, as if he were lying. Vanessa had only known him a short while, but she could read his face, his normally stoic face.

He looked at Allison. "It was a mistake."

No matter how he looked, and what his face said, his words stung. Blood rushed to Vanessa's head. Her hands shook. "A mistake?"

Some of the people in the circle laughed.

What? He wanted to incite her anger even more? That was another mistake.

Chase brandished his fake, blunt sword.

"Nobody's ever called me a mistake!" She yanked off her glove and slapped Julian across the face. It resounded across the dance floor.

He winced and squinted his dark brown eyes, his long lashes brushing against his high cheekbones. It hurt him more than physically, and Vanessa knew it.

A crowd gathered and some of them smiled, as if she, Julian, and Chase were actors and this were part of a rehearsed play or planned PR stunt. They had no clue this was for real. A man in the crowd handed Julian his replica sword in jest. Two TV cameras appeared out of nowhere and people in gowns and breeches began filming with their phones.

"You have insulted a lady's honor, Julian, and I challenge you to a duel," said Chase.

Julian laughed. "First of all, a challenge is never given at the time of the insult!"

"Well, I happen to be flying out tomorrow, so I'm skipping the usual hand-delivered note."

"And a gentleman can't duel with a clansman-pirate. We're not of the same class."

"Oh, you're in a different class, all right." Chase sheathed his sword. "How about fisticuffs?" He rolled up his sleeves and held up his fists.

"No, I choose swords. I accept the challenge. Name your second."

"Vanessa will be my second!"

"I will?"

They stood at the center of the dance floor now, with the entire room watching and entertained, the TV cameras bobbing and swaying for better angles.

"A woman as a second? Then Allison will be mine."

Allison couldn't take her eyes off Vanessa, and Vanessa realized this must be equally, if not more, of a shock to her.

A redcoat handed Vanessa his replica sword with a wink.

"I'm not going to need it," Vanessa said.

Within no time, and without any protocol, Chase and Julian began to spar, the room went abuzz, and Vanessa watched as the two incredibly agile and athletic men went at it with their fake swords, their arms bared and straining.

Half the room chanted "Dar-cy" while the other half chanted "clans-man," and just as Vanessa caught a glimpse of Chase's kilt flapping up above his muscular, tanned legs, a glint appeared out of the corner of her eye.

It was Allison, pointing a blunted sword in her direction. "You slept with my fiancé."

Allison had a very pale English complexion compared to Vanessa's dash of Italian. And now, rage had brought red splotches to Allison's face as she raised her sword toward Vanessa.

"Allison, you don't really want to fight, do you?" Vanessa put the tip of her sword on the ground and leaned on it, putting her emotions aside to appear cavalier. "I don't even know how to fight."

"You slept with him!"

"I didn't know he was engaged! How long have you two been engaged?"

"Almost a year." Allison spoke through bared teeth. As if this were Vanessa's fault! "He thought it would be best to keep the engagement secret to help book sales. To capture the female market."

"Well, he sure captured the female market, didn't he?"

Allison narrowed her hazel-brownish-greenish-whatever eyes. Vanessa didn't like her. Not at all.

"When's the wedding?"

"It's a Christmas wedding at Chawton House Library."

The very place, of course, where Julian had made eye contact with Vanessa about a wedding. The gorgeous, completely romantic estate once owned by Edward Austen Knight appeared in her brain, covered in a glistening blanket of snow.

Vanessa glared at Julian, who, she saw happily, seemed to be getting beaten pretty solidly by Chase. It was all Julian could do to defend himself against Chase's consistent and powerful attacks. A swelling, overpowering feeling of gratitude came over her. Never in her life had a man defended her in any way.

But Julian! Ugh. She looked away from him in disgust. How he could be engaged to this, this simpering woman and lure Vanessa into bed at the same time? Could two women be more different? Could the man be more of a jerk? "I wish I'd never even met the guy! Your fiancé's an ass."

With one fell swoop, Allison swung her sword, knocking away the sword Vanessa had been leaning on and sending her off-kilter.

"You're not going to take that, are you, Vanessa?" It was Lexi.

The crowd laughed and smiled, clasping their gloved hands together and fluttering their fans, still thinking all this had been staged. Vanessa noticed, however, that more men had taken up their own replica swords and were fighting their own fake duels in various corners of the dance floor. A fistfight had started in jest. Camera-phone flashes gave the room a strobe-light glare, and the old seventies song "The Ballroom Blitz" by the Sweet ran through her head. *Everyone attack and it turned into a ballroom blitz . . . ballroom blitz . . .* The entire room broke out in chaos and noise beneath the glittering chandeliers.

Festival organizers scrambled to regain order.

It was an event planner's nightmare but a PR person's dream. This would make the papers, the radio, the Bath TV news, if not the BBC itself. It could even go viral.

"Va-nessa, Va-nessa!" Sherry chanted and pumped her fist.

Allison stood ready, her sword in the attack stance.

Vanessa raised her sword in defense, and that was it: Allison went on the attack.

Allison proved to be a better, more animated fighter than Vanessa expected. Vanessa did her best to keep her form, adapting what she could from the choreography she learned with Chase during the swording workshop.

TV cameras were on them now, from what Vanessa could tell, and in a moment of inspired action, she went on the attack, practically knocking the sword out of Allison's hands. But she lunged a little too far forward, and the seam that Chase had sewn ripped, and then ripped a little more, revealing her garter and threatening to reveal more.

Various "gentlemen" in the crowd whooped with delight. Ladies pointed their white-gloved fingers at her.

Out of the corner of her eye, Vanessa saw the string quartet, with their expensive violins and cello, sneak out. The dance caller asked them all to "stop before someone gets hurt" but nobody listened.

Vanessa had to get out of here, but how? She went into defense mode and back-stepped, her sword crossing and intercepting Allison's at every turn until Allison clumsily swung at Vanessa's ankle with full force, throwing her anklebone into a fit of pain. Vanessa dropped her sword, clasped her ankle, and fell back onto the wooden counter at the fountain, sending half-full glasses of spa water crashing to the wooden floor.

She nearly fainted with the sound of shattered glass. Her ankle throbbed with pain. The room grew blurry. Allison seemed frozen, unable to move, her eyes buggier than usual.

Then, focus and calm overcame Vanessa. She sneered. "This little jousting game is over. You're fighting the wrong person. You need to kick his ass, not mine." She grabbed the ripped seam at her thigh and sauntered, as best as she could with a wobbly ankle, out the front door. TV cameras were on her; a reporter with a mike was asking her all kinds of questions.

She could bring Allison down on national TV, and Julian, too, for that matter. She was not afraid to speak to the press, into video cams—she had spent most of her adult life doing it. She could call him a fraud, a phony, an ass. But then she thought of that home of his, and of her aunt.

She pursed her lips and looked into the cameras. "No comment."

When she went through the front door of the Pump Room to the street, rain pelted down on her, and she hurried through the dark cobblestone streets of Bath, landing in puddles with her flats, hobbling every now and then on her ankle. At the door to the flat, as she turned the key in the lock, she saw that the rain had soaked through her entire gown and her stockings, and her gloves had gone translucent on her quivering hands.

She'd been to a ball in Bath but hadn't been asked to dance. Jane Austen may very well have been in the same situation. Austen, though, had never been in a sword fight in the Pump Room.

*W*hen Vanessa got up to the flat and caught a glimpse of plastic Colin Firth with her thong draped on his head, his once-friendly smile seemed smug to her now. She went straight to the bathroom, where she stripped off her torn gown, which did seem to be stained with six inches of dirt. She wrapped her shivering self in a towel and soaked her ankle under cold running water in the bath.

Allison had hit her on her tattoo and a purple bruise appeared right over the heart. She'd put herself out there and gotten hit—hard.

Had she mistaken proximity for intimacy? Sex for connection? Had she ever known this kind of humiliation? She'd been a fool for thinking there might have been a spark of something between her and Julian.

After her shower, Vanessa promised herself she wouldn't check the social networking sites, which she knew would be blowing up with amateur videos of the night. And she had a ton of texts that she didn't want to see, either. But when her phone rang and Paul's number appeared, she had to answer.

Had Aunt Ella gotten hold of the car keys? Vanessa's mind raced.

Paul spoke clearly, with authority and calm, but his words meant only one thing, and even as she spoke with him on the phone, she flung her suitcase to the bed and tossed her stuff in. She called a cab to take her to the train station, where her plan was to take the last train to London and get the first possible plane back home.

Aunt Ella had burned both hands on the electric stove, not remembering the burners were on. Her hands had been bandaged and she'd been released from the burn unit.

So that was it.

Vanessa was going home now. She wouldn't be attending Julian's

Undressing Mr. Darcy show the next day—well, she wouldn't have been doing that regardless. She left her torn, wet, and dirtied gown hanging in the shower and rushed out to the cab in the rain. On the way to the train station, the cab drove past George Bayntun's bookstore. She'd never even gone in.

This Side of the Pond (Again)

Chapter 21

There happened to be a Starbucks at Heathrow and, after a week of darting in and out of quaint and quirky English tearooms, she stood in line for the familiar, the predictable, the safe. Safe coffee, safe everything. It wasn't so much giving up as it was giving in.

Once in Chicago she didn't stop at her condo but went straight to visit Aunt Ella at Paul's.

Her aunt on the sofa covered in a blanket, reading another new scholarly tome about Jane Austen, looked thinner and more frail than when Vanessa had left her. The bandages on both her hands sent a shiver through Vanessa, but seeing her aunt's smiling face proved a comfort beyond compare.

Aunt Ella hugged her as she whispered in Vanessa's ear, "You are loved," she said.

"I know. I'm lucky. Just like Edward Austen Knight." She could see, in her mind's eye, a horseshoe nail pointing toward her peep-toed heels.

She pulled up a chair to Aunt Ella's side.

"Chase called and told us everything. Please don't be upset with him. He really has your best interests at heart."

"I know he does. It took me a while to see that. I'm a little slow on the uptake." Vanessa smiled.

And so did her aunt.

Vanessa had taken a chance, gone after Julian on a whim, based on something she had thought was there, but she had learned, now, to be more in touch and grounded. Eight hours on the plane without her electronics had given her time to think. Her plan now included being more a part of the human world and less susceptible to the distractions of the bright, shiny, and beeping cyber world.

"Here, my dear, I want you to have this."

In the palm of Ella's bandaged hand sat a reproduction of Jane Austen's turquoise ring, a bright blue stone with a gold band, the one Kelly Clarkson had bought.

"Oh, no, I can't—" Vanessa pulled up the blanket and tucked it around her aunt.

"I want you to have it."

"Thank you. I really just want to thank you—for everything." She kissed her aunt on the forehead, her soft, slightly wrinkled forehead.

"My pleasure. So I don't need to ask how it went, but how do you feel?"

"I'm fine."

"I'm so sorry I brought him into your life."

"I'm not. Not at all. The whole thing resulted in my *finally* appreciating Jane Austen—and that, as you know, is for life."

"There's a scene in *Pride and Prejudice* where Elizabeth sees Pemberley from a distance for the first time. Darcy's estate, you know, is very much like him. Symmetrical, balanced; the grounds are natural,

Elizabeth notices, without blatant artifice. Julian needs work. Just like his estate."

"I needed work, too," Vanessa said.

"Not anymore."

"You're right."

For the first time in a long while, she felt unbroken.

"I'm so thrilled you had an opportunity to really get to know Jane Austen, her work, and . . . yourself. It happened at the right time for you."

Vanessa smiled. "I'm a late bloomer."

"It's okay. Austen's Anne Elliot was a late bloomer, too. And in some ways Austen herself never had a chance to bloom."

"She died so young, too. Just a few years older than I am. What happened?"

"There are a few theories. She might have had Addison's disease, an autoimmune disorder, something we could easily cure today. Lindsay Ashford, author of *The Mysterious Death of Miss Austen*, has proposed she died of arsenic poisoning."

"Who would poison Jane Austen? I realize she wasn't the prim-and-proper type I'd assumed she was, but I'm sure she didn't say—or write—anything scathing enough to incite murder!"

"It's very likely the medicine she took for her illness contained arsenic, and over time, it poisoned her."

"Poor Jane!"

"Poor Cassandra. Sometimes, when two people are so close, what's worse is to be the one left behind."

Vanessa bit her bottom lip.

"Cassandra lived to be seventy-two. Did you see the letter she wrote to their niece Fanny after Jane's death? It's hung on the wall upstairs at their cottage in Chawton."

"I saw a lot of things, Auntie E, but I didn't see that, no."

Aunt Ella closed her eyes, and Vanessa braced herself for hearing a quote, but this time, she took it in, like nourishment.

"'I *have* lost a treasure,' Cassandra wrote. 'Such a Sister, such a friend as never can have been surpassed,—She was the sun of my life, the gilder of every pleasure, the soother of every sorrow, I had not a thought concealed from her, & it is as if I had lost a part of myself.'"

"They loved each other very much."

"They did."

Vanessa smoothed a lock of hair from her aunt's face. "I'm going to read all of Jane Austen's letters—Chase bought a volume of them for me when we were in Bath."

"Chase. Such a nice young—well, I'm done meddling. You'd think I'd have learned my lesson from Emma Woodhouse! You're on your own, my dear."

"We'll see how that goes!" Vanessa laughed.

"But you must be jet-lagged and tired."

Vanessa looked at her watch. It was ten at night in England. She rolled her watch back six hours to Chicago time.

"By the way, during my move, some of your books, including one of your old high school yearbooks, ended up in my library. They're on the table there. Don't forget to take them with you when you go."

"Of course. I'll be back tomorrow to tell you all about the trip!" Vanessa said.

"I look forward to it."

When she arrived at her condo, yearbook and suitcase in hand, she knew right away something was amiss because when she opened her door, the hall light was on.

Her desk drawers had been pulled out and dumped on the couch. Her jewelry armoire stood open and empty. Her flat-screen had been ripped from the wall and even her old DVD player was gone.

Julian had been right, damn it.

She'd been too cavalier about her whereabouts on social media, and she'd been robbed.

*W*hile the police took photos of the scene and dusted for fingerprints, Vanessa stared at her photo albums, which, happily, were not stolen and remained intact. It turned out the only things she really cared about were her memories. Memories of a happy childhood, both with her parents and with her aunt; a happy young adulthood with Lexi and a wide circle of friends; a happy several years with various boyfriends and later a fiancé, all of whom had left their own indelible fingerprints on her.

The jewelry didn't matter; the TV didn't matter; alerting all her credit cards to watch for potential suspicious activity and making a list of to-dos such as changing the locks and calling her bank to report possible stolen bank account numbers and checks—none of it mattered.

Above all, she still had her aunt.

After the cops questioned her, she absentmindedly picked up her high school yearbook from Aunt Ella's and flipped through the pages. It happened to be from her senior year, and once she hit the back cover, there were the signatures and well-wishes from tertiary friends, the ones who weren't so close, because they hadn't signed it first, on the opening pages.

Some people she still happened to be in touch with—often thanks to social media. Others not. Most had led full lives with marriages, kids, divorces, cancer, coming out of the closet, striking it rich, losing it all; one had even become a celebrated opera singer while another had landed in jail for embezzlement. Someone in the class had even committed suicide, and there was her name with a smiley face after her signature.

The very last thing she read was written in the bottom right

corner, and clearly, the person had been pressed for space and wrote
in a cramped, slanted hand.

Dear Vanessa,

*Will miss you now that you're graduating. Without you as president,
why go to student council meetings? Wish you much happiness &
success in college & life. I wrote you in as Sexiest Senior, but who
listens to juniors? I'll be looking for you in your bikini on the beach!
Wink wink . . .*

Love,
Chase (MacClane)

Wow.

Here was a seventeen-year-old boy reaching beyond the pages of
a yearbook, and across the decades, to make a thirty-five-year-old
woman who had just been robbed crack a smile.

Then she laughed at the thought of it. If he only knew.

"Are you sure you're okay?" asked one of the cops.

"Yes. Yes."

It was a simple formula, too. He praised her for brains and lusted
for her openly, but in a fun, teasing way. What more could a girl
want? Or, at least, a girl of eighteen?

So he had gone to her high school. She paged to the junior class,
and there he was, Chase MacClane, adorable as hell, but she still
didn't remember him.

A sad commentary on her lack of awareness.

Maybe she should answer the texts he kept sending her since
she'd left England.

* * *

*B*ut busyness set in and, after being tossed together for her aunt and Paul's wedding, she didn't text him back anything beyond a few polite answers to his questions and kind rejections to his offers to meet for dinner. Weeks later, Lexi roped Vanessa into going to a Halloween costume party hosted by a friend at some Scottish-themed place in the city.

Vanessa resisted at first. "I don't want to have women in halter tops, mini-kilts, and kneesocks serve me drinks."

But she'd already decided she would go, with the vague hope that Chase would be there in his kilt.

"Just promise me you'll wear a costume," said Lexi.

She decided to dress as a pirate girl and went to the party.

Lexi was soon going to be leaving the States and moving in with David. They'd set a date for their wedding already. But that was Lexi; she moved fast in every facet of her life. "Look, he's the One. It took one-fifth of a second for me to realize I wanted to sleep with him—because that's how long it takes to decide that, it's been documented—and about twenty-four hours for me to decide I not only wanted to sleep with him every night but wake up with him every morning. Why waste any more time?"

Indeed.

David the journalist had turned out to be quite the English gentleman, and Vanessa was really happy for Lexi.

"Visit us?"

"I will."

"Be my maid of honor?"

"Of course. You're not going to put me in a hideous dress, are you?"

"You wouldn't expect any less of me, would you? It's the bridesmaids' job to make their bride look good."

Lexi had even thought to bring home the torn gown that Vanessa had left in the shower stall in England, and now it hung in Vanessa's closet, dry-cleaned and repaired.

Vanessa had moved on from the whole Julian thing. Like a wave, it receded as quickly as it came in. What remained, like glistening gems on the shore, was nothing but fond memories of England and an interest in all things Austen.

Sherry, too, had just gotten a promotion and was now happily dating a local philanthropist. She had bought him a T-shirt that said, *I am Mr. Darcy*. It had been determined that she would inherit plastic Colin Firth, and all seemed right with the world once Colin had been installed in her apartment as the centerpiece of her shrine to Darcy.

Aunt Ella had a gorgeous little wedding, and she and Paul lived happily and quietly up north while he drove her around on little day trips and they made memories visiting and enjoying as many places as they could.

Julian's book had broken into the bestseller lists, and yes, they all had their fifteen minutes of fame when the BBC picked up the footage of the duel at the ball. Newspaper headlines read: DUEL AND FISTICUFFS MAKE FOR GREAT JANE AUSTEN FAYRE and THIS BALLROOM BELLE HAS . . . BALLS! and BALLROOM BABES BRANDISHING BLADES. The video went viral.

Kai had gotten his first screenplay optioned.

Vanessa had gone in for the third interview for an advertising account executive position, and it looked like she'd get it, too, at a great company, where she'd spend less time behind the computer and on social media and more time with people—and products like salad dressing—but hey.

Could their success have been attributed to the restorative waters in Bath?

Who knew?

But some guy dressed as Satan at this party wouldn't leave Vanessa alone. He gave a whole new meaning to "horny devil."

The sense of relief and the surge of joy she felt when she saw, across the room, Captain Jack Sparrow, she couldn't begin to measure. She went right up to him and put her arm around him. But it wasn't Chase of course, and with her heart sinking into the depths of disappointment, she found herself having to explain to the man—and his wife—that she thought he was someone else.

When the one you wish for isn't in the room, no matter how many other people are, you know it. You feel it. It can make a crowded room seem vacant. She missed him; she needed to see his goofy grin. That had to have been the moment she admitted, finally, that she felt more for Chase than she'd let on to even herself.

She'd felt it happen to her several times before, like when he had left her on the beach to go amuse the kids at the birthday party, or when he'd turned his back on her and walked away in Trafalgar Square and then again in front of the British Library. Something deflated and dissipated once he'd gone. Everything deflated and dissipated once he'd gone.

But it didn't have to be this way. She could be near him, and she could make it happen! She didn't have to be the one who left. She could choose to be the one who pursued—the one who . . . chased.

Something Jane Austen could never do, but any modern woman could.

And suddenly she couldn't wait a minute more. As Lexi would say, why wait? How much time had she lost? How much time did she have left?

Before the devil at the bar could track her down, she'd tracked down Chase, thanks to the locational social network. He was at a little amusement park just outside the city, called Haunted Hollow.

She stuffed her tricorn pirate hat in her messenger bag and, on her way to the parking lot, she walked right past a white Chase Bank sign all lit up in the night. A CHASE sign. Maybe she did believe in signs after all.

The amusement park happened to be packed, dark, and resounding with howling and screeching sound effects and machine-made blue fog. He could be anywhere—at the mini-golf course pulsing with bloodred water fountains, in the haunted house, on the go-cart track. She had no idea where in the park he could be, so she texted him.

wassup? what cha doin?

As she waited and hoped for his text back, she scoured the park looking for him for what seemed like forever, finding only zombies and Frankensteins and vampires and kids until, finally, a text from him pinged in:

great 2 finally hear from u! u won't believe it but i'm in line for bumper cars I'll call u when I'm home

No pirate girl had ever in her life run faster to a line for bumper cars. Tipping her hat down over her eyes, she climbed into one of the last available bumper cars in her little pirate skirt and buccaneer boots. She heard his voice across the way but couldn't see him; he must've been behind one of the support poles. He was joking around with some kids, from what she could hear. Another birthday party, possibly.

As soon as the bumper cars had been activated, she accelerated toward where she'd heard his voice. There had to have been at least fifty cars in the place, but at last she spotted him, and yes, he had his pirate costume on. This time, she made sure it was him, and then, as if out of nowhere, she floored it and rammed right into him head-on, with a smile.

"Vanessa!"

He was surprised. She could see it in his lopsided grin.

"So glad you bumped into me like this," he said.

He looked better than she remembered, even in heavy kohl eyeliner.

A few boys crashed into him, too, and he acted all goofy, trying to escape. Then an extremely gorgeous blonde, also dressed in a pirate outfit, crashed into him and Vanessa at the same time.

Then wham! Kid after kid bumped into Vanessa's car.

Of course. Why hadn't she thought of it? He could be here on a Halloween date. With a girlfriend—or fiancée. It was a Saturday night, after all.

"Vanessa," Chase laughed, "you have to meet Caitlin."

"Hi, Caitlin." Vanessa forced herself to lift a hand and wave. Someone bumped her car again.

Caitlin looked like fun. She had on a sexy pirate blouse very similar to Vanessa's, and she even had an eye patch. Her blond curls bounced as she laughed when the birthday party boys crashed into her. "Shove off, mateys! Or I'll make ye walk the plank," she said. In fact, she exuded playfulness and sexiness. Vanessa wouldn't expect Chase to date anyone less than the perfect combination of fun, sexy, and smart. She did seem a little young, though.

"Hi," Caitlin said to Vanessa. "How cool to finally meet you! Chase has told me so much about you."

"He has?" Vanessa accelerated but had no idea where to turn. She wished she hadn't come. It was so impulsive! This was what she got for forgoing the safety of a text! And why had he been telling his girlfriend about her?

Chase took the opportunity to really gun it, and he hit Vanessa's car on the side, spinning it around. "Caitlin's great fun, isn't she?" He smiled.

"Yeah." Vanessa flashed a smile.

"I'm so glad you two have finally met."

"Yeah. Me, too!" Vanessa put the emphasis on the exclamation point.

"Well, it's really nice of my baby sister to help me out with the kids. It's a party of twenty tonight!"

"Caitlin's your—your sister?"

He bumped her car again, softer this time. "Of course she is! What did you think? If she were my girlfriend, I don't think I'd be telling her about you!"

"You're not kidding about her being your sister, are you?"

"No!" He laughed. "Why would I?"

Vanessa couldn't believe her luck. She couldn't wait to tell Lexi. Then his sparkling brown eyes lasered right in on her cleavage. "You make a hot pirate, me beauty!"

He turned to bash into Caitlin's car, and she hadn't been expecting it. "Chase Henry MacClane! You're in for it!"

"Your middle name is . . . Henry?" Vanessa asked.

"Yes," Chase said quite seriously. "After my father."

It brought to mind Henry Tilney from Austen's *Northanger Abbey*, the Austen hero with the best sense of humor. Now she knew his middle name.

Several boys crashed into their cars. Bumper cars buzzed around; sparks flew from the contact points on the ceiling; kids laughed and screamed.

"Why did you show up here, Vanessa? Just to find out my middle name?"

She laughed. "Yes. And because I missed you, okay? That's all I'm going to say for now."

She felt exposed, revealed, *undressed*, even though she was fully clothed—or mostly clothed—in her pirate costume.

He bumped her car. "That's all you need to say. It's a start."

It was more than a start.

He smirked. "Do you want to do the go-carts? You can chase me all around the track. I really enjoy having you pursue me for once," he said as he sped off.

She accelerated and buzzed after him. "Haven't I chased you around enough?"

"It'll never be enough for me."

She laughed.

"I like to make you laugh," he said over his shoulder, with bumper cars all around them. "To make you happy."

She found all this hard to resist.

"You know what I like about us?" he asked as he turned his car around to face her. "We make each other better. We're better together than we are alone."

The birthday party kids found them and cajoled them into going on the go-carts after all, where yes, she chased him and realized she hadn't had this much fun in a long time.

Chapter 22

After weeks of dates: walking along the beach in the unusually warm month of November, evenings at the theater, the orchestra, and hot new restaurants, and even a night spent on a historic Chicago gangster ghost-hunting tour—and with a trip to San Francisco in the offing—Vanessa couldn't get enough of Chase and his lust for life.

These days, she had incorporated some new hobbies into her life and was now part of an acting troupe called Babes with Blades. And when she wasn't wielding swords or saving cats, she could often be found in the park, on a bench, reading Jane Austen.

Laughing and kissing, their hands all over each other, he hurried her onto his boat after the Swashbucklers' Ball.

Chase should've taken in the boat weeks before, but he'd gambled on the warm weather, and now he sailed her out onto the lake.

He'd just managed to raise ten thousand dollars for the third year in a row during the pirate ball for Chicago area—cat shelters.

Whether it was the cats or the man, Vanessa wasn't quite sure, but they'd been told by Chase's friends to "get a room."

One of his friends let it slip that Chase had already had her engagement ring made! He'd designed it himself.

Much as she liked his friends, she'd been looking forward to getting Chase all to herself. He'd be flying out the next day for some auctions in Prague, and this time she couldn't go with him—she had a presentation to give and clients to entertain for her new job.

As soon as he dropped the anchor, she kicked off her boots and he kicked off his.

She put her hands on his stubbled jawline, brought him in toward her for a hungry kiss, and took off his dreadlock wig. She loved his hair, she loved the way he kissed her, she loved the way his mind worked and how he played around with her. She loved the way he made and followed through on plans with her both now and into the far future. She loved—him.

He reluctantly pulled away to dot her neck with kisses and licks. He landed on the laces of her pirate vest, and with one end of the lace in his mouth, he untied the vest and relieved her of her blouse and skirt.

"Ah, you wore the corset." He smiled as he deftly freed her. "And nothing else. I guessed right." He grew harder against her back.

"I didn't want any panty lines showing." She arched an eyebrow at him. She felt good in her skin around him.

She unbuttoned his ruffled shirt, and with a flick of her wrist she removed his belt and unzipped him as quickly as she could.

He pulled a condom out of his pants pocket before he flung his pants over the boat's steering wheel. In one smooth motion he lifted her up and carried her to the starboard side padded deck bed. She was out on a boat on a November night with a man who loved cats and wore eyeliner, not to mention a fake beard with beads in it, which he now peeled off.

He sensed her momentary hesitation. "What?"

She smiled. "Well, this isn't very conventional, is it?"

"Conventional. Traditional. They're *not* your destiny. And it can get much wilder than this, trust me."

She did.

"I love you," he said.

"And *aye* love you."

He kissed her as if it were her first time ever being kissed, because that was how he kissed her *every* time, looking into her eyes and cradling her face before devouring her. He caressed her breasts with his warm hands and she pressed her entire body against him with desperate, raw need.

He'd grown hard and she wanted nothing more than to take him into her mouth, but he wouldn't let her—yet—he said.

"Pirate ladies first," he whispered in a husky voice. "X marks the spot." He went down on her and brought her to the brink while the city sparkled on the shoreline. Her back arched with an ache for more and she quivered watching him, intent upon her, so generous, so tantalizing with her legs wrapped around his neck and the entire skyline between her knees.

He coaxed out desires in her she never knew she had, making her writhe with want, and, after he slaked it all by finally entering her, with the sound of water lapping up against the boat, she decided that yes, this was what she wanted, now and forever.

Even if he did look better than she did in black eyeliner.

*L*ove appears when we least expect it, and often, when we're not able to recognize it. For some people it manifests in a flowing gown or formal tailcoat.

But sometimes it shows up in a pirate costume. Other times it makes its entrance in a kilt.

Keep an eye out.

Author's Note

If you are a Jane Austen fan or Anglophile, please consider donating to Chawton House Library (www.chawtonhouse.org), English Heritage at Risk (www.english-heritage.org.uk), or Jane Austen's House Museum (www.jane-austens-house-museum.org.uk).